"[*The Dragon* ... ts original premise an ... air who strive to save a ... *Journal*

"Action, adventure, dirigibles, and mad scientists, oh my! I must say that I thoroughly enjoyed *The Doomsday Vault* and looked forward to continuing the adventures of Alice and Gavin in *The Impossible Cube*. I wasn't disappointed." —Night Owl Reviews

"The characters and their plight are so easy to become invested in, and I found myself rooting for them every step of the way. So I cannot recommend the books in the Clockwork Empire series, especially *The Impossible Cube,* any higher. Whether you are a fan of steampunk or not, these books promise to be an exhilarating roller-coaster ride from start to finish that you won't want to miss!" —A Book Obsession

"The Clockwork Empire books are changing what we know as steampunk! . . . An exuberant novel that takes the reader on an action-packed adventurous thrill ride." —Nocturne Romance Reads

"A fantastic amount of action. . . . If you are looking to jump into steampunk for the first time, I would recommend these books." —Paranormal Haven

"An exciting adventure thriller that starts off with action and never slows down." —Genre Go Round Reviews

The Doomsday Vault

"Inventive and fun." —Paranormal Haven

continued . . .

Books by Steven Harper

THE CLOCKWORK EMPIRE

The Doomsday Vault

The Impossible Cube

The Dragon Men

The Havoc Machine

THE
HAVOC
MACHINE

A NOVEL OF THE
CLOCKWORK EMPIRE

STEVEN HARPER

A ROC BOOK

ROC
Published by the Penguin Group
Penguin Group (USA) Inc., 375 Hudson Street,
New York, New York 10014, USA

USA | Canada | UK | Ireland | Australia | New Zealand | India | South Africa | China

Penguin Books Ltd., Registered Offices: 80 Strand, London WC2R 0RL, England
For more information about the Penguin Group visit penguin.com.

First published by Roc, an imprint of New American Library,
a division of Penguin Group (USA) Inc.

First Printing, May 2013

Copyright © Steven Piziks, 2013

 REGISTERED TRADEMARK—MARCA REGISTRADA

ISBN 978-0-451-41704-6

Printed in the United States of America
10 9 8 7 6 5 4 3 2 1

ALWAYS LEARNING   PEARSON

If your family is wonderfully strange, oddly off-center, built from mixed parts, or simply created out of thin air, this book is dedicated to you.

ACKNOWLEDGMENTS

Gratitude everlasting to the Untitled Writers Group (Christian, Cindy, David, Diana, Erica, Jonathan, Mary Beth, and Sarah) for reading many drafts in a great hurry. The same also to my tireless agent, Lucienne, and my sharp-eyed editor, Anne.

THE STORY SO FAR

We find ourselves rather chagrined.

Once that most amazing of volumes *The Dragon Men* went to press, we were quite positive there were no more stories to tell about the Clockwork Empire. Our entire staff prepared to go on holiday, content in the knowledge of a job well done. However, just as our dear secretary Mrs. Wentworth was shutting off the gas and picking up her hatbox, a package arrived that proved our assessment was . . . erroneous. Fallacious. False. It seems that an entirely new set of thrilling adventures was happening right under our very noses during that time when Gavin Ennock and Alice, Lady Michaels were dealing with a giant squid in the Caspian Sea. Therefore, with a breathless excitement and a certain delighted embarrassment, we bring forth *The Havoc Machine*.

To our established readers, we offer a warm greeting and a joyful handshake at your return. If you feel quite comfortable with your memory of previous events, you are encouraged to thumb your way over to the first chapter, in which a beautiful woman makes one Thaddeus Sharpe a mysterious and intriguing offer. But if you need a refresher, or if the library in your cranial implant is still malfunctioning, you may find the following information of use.

To our new readers, we offer a hearty welcome. If you have not perused the previous astonishing volumes in the Clockwork Empire (specifically *The Doomsday Vault, The Impossible Cube,* and *The Dragon Men*), fear not! This fourth volume provides the perfect entry portal. To be honest, readers hungry for adventure may skip over all the dry exposition that follows here and begin straightaway with chapter one (though we humbly point out that an even more fascinating method for acquainting oneself with the Clockwork Empire is to purchase copies of the three thrilling novels that make up the first part of the story, if one is so inclined, and we thank such readers for their kind patronage).

Finally, established readers may also note that Gavin and Alice, our protagonists from the first three books, seem to be entirely absent. We do hope that no one takes serious umbrage or fishes about for expired fruit to throw. Alice and Gavin's story comes to a tidy, if suspenseful, close at the end of *The Dragon Men,* and it would hardly be fair to rake everything up again, though a tiny bit of paper clipped to the last page of this latest manuscript advises us that Alice and Gavin did not live out their final years in quiet desperation, so we may yet hear more of them. In any case, we daresay that our highly intelligent and discerning readers will find Thaddeus Sharpe and his strange companion Dante compelling in their own right. Additionally, Mr. Sharpe is quite handsome.

Perhaps that will make up for Mrs. Wentworth's canceled holiday.

The year is 1860.

A little more than a hundred years ago, a dreadful plague swept across continents and entrenched itself on the planet. The plague causes rotting of the flesh, and also invades the host's nervous system, creating motor dysfunction, dementia, and photosensitivity. Victims lurching through the late stages were inevitably dubbed *plague zombies,* and they spread the disease farther with every pitiful step. However, a handful of victims end up with neural synapses that, for a brief time, draw together instead of falling apart. Advanced mathematics, physics, biology, and chemistry become simple playthings to them. But as they think and invent like mad, the virus slowly devours their brains, and they lose their grip on reality. Their attachment to mechanical inventions and their detachment from normal human emotion earned them the name *clockwork geniuses* or *clockworkers,* and the disease itself became *the clockwork plague.*

Different parts of the world react to clockworkers in different ways. China venerates clockworkers and grants them status nearly equal to the emperor himself. England fears them, and created a police force known as the Third Ward, which hunted clockworkers down, locked them in secret laboratories, and stashed a number of their more dangerous inventions in the Doomsday Vault. These two mighty nations—England and China—built opposing empires using fantastic inventions supplied by captive clockworkers, and only a delicate balance of power held the two empires in check.

Into the middle of all this came the Ukrainian Empire. In that thrilling adventure known as *The Impossible Cube,* readers learned that the clockwork plague actually originated in Ukraine in 1750, smack in the middle of a time when that country was occupied by both Poland and Russia.

It also created a number of Ukrainian clockworkers. Cossack clockworkers.

These mad geniuses swiftly created powerful engines

of war that dispersed their Polish and Russian occupiers with all speed and greatly expanded the Ukrainian borders to boot. Unfortunately, these Cossack clockworkers turned out to be despots nearly as bad as the Poles and Russians, and they ruled their own people with a brass fist.

That is, until Gavin Ennock and Alice, Lady Michaels joined the circus.

Through a complicated and heart-stopping series of adventures also detailed in *The Impossible Cube* (a fascinating book that the editors highly recommend for all gift-giving occasions), Gavin and Alice arrived in Kiev with the Kalakos Circus of Automatons and Other Wonders. They were intending only to pass through on their way to Peking for reasons of their own, but the Gonta-Zalizniak "family" of clockworkers attempted to meddle in this couple's affairs, and to their surprise, were thoroughly crushed for their efforts. They should have known better, of course—Alice had personally destroyed the British Empire by releasing a cure for the clockwork plague and ensuring that England would have no more clockworkers or clockwork inventions. Wiping out a few troublesome Cossacks barely gave her pause.

Unfortunately, during this process, the Gonta-Zalizniaks attacked the Kalakos Circus, and many of the performers were scattered. The dam that famously generated electricity for Kiev was also destroyed, threatening thousands of lives, and Gavin only barely managed to get everyone aboard the circus train and rush them to safety.

After that, Gavin and Alice went on their way. They were last seen heading off in their airship over the Caspian Sea, completely ignorant of the fact that the water is home to a giant squid. What happens to them is chronicled in that most breathtaking of books *The Dragon Men,* and we need not recount the events here.

But, as we said, we have learned there is more.

With the Cossacks recently crushed and Britain severely weakened, Russia finds herself wondering if she might once again take her place in this Great Game of clashing empires.

And the poor Kalakos Circus finds itself in dire straits.

Chapter One

Thaddeus Sharpe loosened his brown leather jacket and shoved his way into the low-beamed tavern. A fire glowed like a captured demon in the long ceramic stove, and the smoky air wrapped itself around him in a stifling blanket. At long tables, men in long shirts and blousy trousers clanked glasses of vodka and thumped mugs of *gira,* the fermented drink made from rye bread favored by Lithuanian peasants. A heavy smell of sweat mixed with the sharp tint of vodka and the earthy slop of *gira.* The autumn evening was already well under way, and the red-faced men shouted more than they talked. Candles stood upright on the tables in cracked saucers to provide light. Dante cocked his good eye at the room and clacked his brass beak from his perch on Thad's shoulder. Several of the men turned to stare at Thad when he blew in. He tensed and automatically felt for the long knife in his sleeve.

"Shut the damn door!" one of them barked in what Thad assumed was Lithuanian. Thanks to his mother, Thad spoke a number of Eastern European and Baltic

languages, and his father had liked to joke that once you learned three of them, the fourth came free. Thad slammed the door, and most of the men went back to their drinking. Two, however, continued to stare at him.

"Dummy, dummy, dummy," Dante muttered in Thad's ear. "Stare and stare, here and there." He squawked.

"Shut it." Thad's jaw was set in a line and his brown eyes were hard. Dark hair curled beneath a workman's cap and he had no beard, but there his resemblance to the men in the tavern ended. His lean build, long leather jacket, and stout boots made him stand out among plain Lithuanian homespun. The ratty brass parrot on his shoulder didn't help. Maybe he should duck out again and look for a way in through the back.

The two men, both large and callused, got up from their long benches and strode across the sticky tavern floor before Thad could retreat. One of them loomed over Thad, his breath heavy with vodka.

"I have heard of your parrot," he said in thick Lithuanian. *"You are the man who kills clockworkers. Many, many clockworkers."*

The knife was already in Thad's hand. *"What of it?"* he replied, his own accent heavy with British vowels. The blade gleamed silver in the candlelight, though neither man seemed to notice. Thad was already calculating—one slash at the throat to incapacitate the first man, shove him backward into the second man, flee into the street. Dante's forged feathers creaked in his ear as the parrot tensed.

The man clapped Thad on the shoulder. *"I will buy your first drink,"* he boomed. *"And my brother will buy your second. Bartender! Vodka and* giras *for our new friend!"*

Moments later, Thaddeus found himself wedged in at

one of the splintery trestle tables with a clay mug by his left hand and a shot glass at his right. A dish of salt and a loaf of dark rye bread sat in front of him. The men at the table raised their own mugs and glasses to Thad, drained them, and wiped their mustaches with their sleeves in one smooth motion.

"So. How many clockworkers have you killed?" said the first man. His name was Arturas and his brother was Mykolas.

"I keep no count." Thad raised his *giras* mug, tried a gulp, and suppressed a grimace. It was like drinking sour rye bread.

"Liar, liar, liar," Dante croaked in his ear.

"Shut it," Thad said, glad none of the men seemed to speak English.

"Who is this man, Arturas?" asked one of the other drinkers.

"This," Arturas boomed in reply, *"is the man who killed Erek the Terror outside Krakow and Vile Basia in the sewers of Prague. This is the man who killed countless monsters and saved a thousand lives. They say he walks the streets with a brass parrot on his shoulder and a cannon in his trousers."*

The men roared at that, and Thad, laughing but uncomfortable at the attention, raised his mug with an ironic grin.

"This man," Mykolas added in conclusion, *"is a hero."* He threw his free arm around Thad and clashed his glass against his brother's. The other men, half-drunk, joined in, slopping *giras* and vodka onto the bread plate. Thad glanced about uneasily and pulled a small card from his coat pocket.

"So what does bring the mighty clockwork killer into a piss-hole like Bûsi Treèias?*"* Mykolas demanded.

"Hey!" said the bartender, who was arriving with more drinks.

Dante cocked his head and Thad glanced down at the card in his hand. In graceful script on one side was engraved a name in Cyrillic letters. On the back in black ink was scribbled *7.45 sharp, Bûsi Treèias.* A ragged boy had handed him the card on the streets of Vilnius earlier that afternoon and fled before Thad could react. Bûsi Treèias was the name of the tavern. It meant "You'll be third," and it was the name that made Thad uneasy, though not so uneasy that he avoided the meeting.

The name on the card was Sofiya Ivanova Ekk, a Russian woman's name, and Russian women did not frequent taverns in the Polish-Lithuanian Union. Neither did Polish-Lithuanian women, for that matter. He thought about asking the men at the table if they knew Sofiya Ekk, but had the feeling that they might think he was enquiring after a prostitute or, worse, someone's sister.

"I thought I might have business here," he said in his heavy Lithuanian. *"But I seem to have made new friends instead."*

That brought on another smashing together of mugs and more knocking back of vodka. Thad tried the latter this time, and it burned a fiery trail down to his stomach. Tears streamed from his eyes. He hastily snatched up some bread, dipped it in salt, and wolfed it down.

A glass of honest-to-god beer landed in front of him. Startled, Thad looked up. The balding bartender withdrew his hand and jerked his head toward a corner of the bar. A figure wrapped in scarlet sat in a shadow far away from the red-hot stove. Thad clapped Arturas on the shoulder and picked up his beer. *"I seem to have business after all."*

Arturas and the other men didn't seem to mind, though they watched him curiously as he picked his way across the crowded room with his beer.

"Pretty, pretty, pretty boy," Dante said. "Beer and crackers."

When Thad arrived at the corner, the scarlet figure resolved itself into a woman in a hooded cloak of rich scarlet velvet, unfashionable but not unheard-of. The hood covered the upper half of her face, and an untouched glass of something red sat on the small table in front of her. She had an actual chair instead of a bench, and a matching chair waited across from her. The noise of the tavern seemed to die away as Thad gingerly sat down. He had talked to his share of women in taverns elsewhere, but these circumstances were definitely odd. They were also intriguing.

"Pretty, pretty, pretty," Dante said again.

"Miss Ekk?" Thad put out a hand, half ready to snatch it back.

"I am that woman." She shook hands. Her palm was smooth and soft. Thad wondered if she expected him to kiss the back, but he didn't. Instead, he set his elbow on the table and let Dante walk down his arm. Dante did get heavy after a while. The parrot waddled over to investigate the unlit candle. Gears creaked uneasily through bare spots where brass feathers were missing or broken, and the bottom half of his beak was off-center, as if Dante had flown through a tornado and only barely lived to tell about it.

"I am thrilled you decided to come, Mr. Sharpe," the woman said. Her English carried a Russian accent, and her voice was low and powerful.

"I'm a little surprised to find someone like you in a place like this, Miss Ekk," Thad countered. His eyes flickered up and down her form, trying to assess her, but she wasn't moving and the damned cloak hid everything. He couldn't even tell how old she was.

"Someone like me?"

He gestured at the tavern. More than one person was still staring in their direction. Normally it would have made him more nervous, but right now he found it reassuring to have other eyes on him. "Proper females don't go to bars in the Polish-Lithuanian Union. Or in Russia. They stay behind closed doors and do proper female things."

"Rules are for people who think little, Mr. Sharpe. People like us, we think large. That is why I wished to meet you."

"In a tavern with the name *You'll Be Third*?" Thad brandished the card.

"I believe the name shows that the place is very popular—there are always two people ahead of you waiting to be served. The name fits, no?"

"It's also the Lithuanian way of saying your luck will turn for the worse," Thad spat. "Did you think I didn't know?"

Sofiya laughed quietly. "You are not superstitious. You use scientific knowledge. You know from experience how the clockwork plague works, for example. These people"—she gestured at the room—"think the plague comes from the devil. They think that when someone catches the disease and it turns them into a shambling mound of flesh that wanders through the streets feeding on garbage until their brains rot away, God meant it as a punishment. And they think that when the disease makes someone into a clockworker who creates glorious and impossible inventions—"

"—and goes mad and does horrible things to innocent to people," Thad put in.

"Doom, destruction, death, despair," said Dante. "Doom!"

"Shut it," Thad ordered.

"They think this also is a punishment from God," Sofiya finished as if no one had spoken. "Their church tells them so. But we know it is nothing more than a disease that acts as a disease must."

"The plague is a curse, and the faster we eradicate everything connected with it, the better," Thad snapped. He found his left hand was shaking, and he forced it to still.

"I told you we think large," Sofiya said with a nod. "And I am glad to see that you can react as a human being, Mr. Sharpe."

Thad clenched his teeth. "Why are we talking about this? What do you care about the clockwork plague?"

"You have caught my interest, Mr. Sharpe. You are a very interesting person to very many people. *Very* interesting."

That set off several small alarm bells inside his head.

"I don't want to offend," Thad said, now with careful control in every syllable, "but I feel I should to point out that the parrot which has moved to a strategic spot on the table less than eight inches in front of you can deliver more than two thousand pounds of pressure from the business end of that sharp beak, more than enough pressure to slice open your windpipe. I also have a knife on a spring-load that can open up an artery so quickly, you won't even know you're dead before the blade is clean and back up my sleeve. Finally, all those men over there, the ones you were scorning as small-thinking peasants a moment ago, seem to like me quite a lot, and I think they would be very upset if anyone tried something foolish."

"Such a mental condition you have," Sofiya tutted. "I believe the English word is *paranoia.*"

His muscles were growing tight with tension. The situation was unusual. Thad didn't like unusual. It was too like hunting clockworkers. But tension made fights difficult. He forced himself to relax. "I deal with clockworkers all the time. One can never be too paranoid."

"As you like, Mr. Sharpe. But I do not have a wish to harm you." From the folds of her cloak, she produced a small purse, which she dropped on the table. It clinked. "I wish to hire you."

That got Thad's attention fast, though me made no move to touch the purse. "Dante."

The parrot expertly tore the purse open, revealing the glint of silver and gold coins, a generous offering. "Pretty, pretty, pretty," he said, plucking a coin from the pile with a claw and bending it in half with his beak.

Thad didn't relax his guard. "People don't usually hire me to kill clockworkers. They usually beg me, and I'm always happy to oblige. Why offer money?"

"You may do with the clockworker as you wish. It makes nothing to me. I want—or rather, my employer wants—

something else entirely. That is why we are offering you money."

Now Thad leaned back in the hard chair. "Your employer?"

"I represent a third party. He does not go out in public and needs people to do for him. He heard you were traveling with the Kalakos Circus these days, and when they came to Vilnius, he asked me to arrange for your employment."

"I'm not seeking long-term—"

"This is a single piece of work," Sofiya interrupted. "And it is very similar to what you already do."

"Money, money," Dante said. "Pretty money." He reached for another coin. Thaddeus absently moved the purse out of his reach and took a pull from his beer.

"You can see my face," he said. "I would like to see yours. So I know who I'm dealing with."

Without hesitation, Sofiya cast back her scarlet hood. Golden hair spilled across her shoulders and clear blue eyes looked out over finely molded features and a sharp chin. The small scar that ran along her left jawline was the only flaw to her beauty. Thad didn't outwardly react, though inwardly he caught his breath. Such sweet loveliness ran a sharp contrast to the dull tavern and its sour drinks—and brought up bitter memories.

"Thank you." His voice stayed carefully neutral. "Who's your employer, if you please?"

"He is a person who hires people like me so he does not need to give his name." Sofiya straightened her thick cloak. It must have been stifling in the heat of the tavern, but she showed no signs of sweating. "You usually kill clockworkers for no money at all, so I would have thought the prospect of having extra coins would be an encouragement, no?"

"I just like to know what's going on," Thad replied.

"Darkness, despair, death," Dante squawked. "Doom!"

Sofiya ignored him. "I will tell you. There is a castle ruin approximately half a day's horseback travel south of Vilnius. A clockworker who calls himself Mr. Havoc has moved in to it, fortified it, and made it his own. He is quite brilliant, as all clockworkers are." She paused to sip from her red glass. Was it wine? She had expensive tastes. "He has already managed many dreadful experiments with machines and men. The village nearby is quite terrified of him, but they lack the weaponry to assault his little fortress."

"And you want me to go in there and kill him," Thad finished.

"You are very forthright for such a handsome Englishman," Sofiya said. "But I have already said that my employer does not care if you kill Mr. Havoc or not. He wants you to bring him a particular machine Mr. Havoc has created."

"Is that so?" Thad took another pull from his beer mug. It was only of middling quality, but it was beer and not *giras*. "You didn't give me much information, Miss Ekk. How coherent is this Mr. Havoc? Does he go into inventing fugues quite a bit or only rarely? What sort of inventions does he specialize in? Who was he before he became a clockworker? Does he have friends or family who help him? Where does he get money from? Does he buy or steal to get materials? If he buys, who is his supplier? If he steals, who does he steal from?"

Sofiya spread her hands. "I am afraid I have already told you everything I know, Mr. Sharpe."

"Why doesn't your employer simply wait him out? The clockwork plague will kill this Mr. Havoc of yours in a couple of years, three at the absolute most."

"No. My employer needs the invention now. But I see you are reluctant." She gathered up the purse and made to rise. "I will find someone else, then. Good day, Mr. Sharpe."

He caught her wrist. The skin was smooth. "I didn't say I wouldn't do it, Miss Ekk. I'm just suspicious of strange circumstances and a secretive employer."

"The circumstances are this—you have the chance to rid the world of another clockworker, and make a great deal of money in the bargain by delivering one of his inventions to my employer. Will you do it?"

Dante bit the candle in half. "Done, done, done."

"Done," Thad said.

"Excellent. The invention is a spider the size of a small trunk. It has ten legs instead of the usual eight, and it has copper markings all over it. You will know it the moment you see it. I would approach the castle from the west. Our employer has information that says the west wall of the castle has an old doorway overgrown with ivy. The castle's defenses are also weaker in that direction, which is lucky for you—us. That door will get you through the castle wall and into the ruins. After that, you are quite alone."

"I'm never alone if I have Dante," Thad replied without a trace of irony.

Sofiya got to her feet. "I have a horse waiting in the

back, and a basket of food. The moon is full tonight, so you can see. Take the main road south, then turn west when you reach the village of Juodsilai. The ruins are there. The horse is fast and should reach the castle an hour or two before dawn."

"What, you want me to leave now? In the middle of the night?"

"Must you make extensive preparations?"

"No."

"Do you intend to attack Mr. Havoc during daylight, when he can see you coming?"

"No."

"Then we go now, Mr. Sharpe."

"We?"

"I will come with you, of course." A grim smile crossed Sofiya's face as she hauled him toward the back door. "I am suspicious as well."

Chapter Two

Sofiya towed him into a noisome alley ankle-deep in autumn mud. A chilly wind spun angrily between high, narrow buildings beneath a heavy moon, and Dante settled his brass feathers. Thad pried himself out of Sofiya's grip and faced her. "I don't take observers with me, Miss Ekk. I work alone."

"That sounds lonely."

"No one else gets hurt that way."

"Yes, yes, yes." She waved a hand. "You are the brave warrior who faces great trials by himself. How trite."

"Listen, I don't want you getting in the—"

"I? Get in the way? Ha!" She huffed beneath the scarlet cloak. "Frankly, Mr. Sharpe, I am waiting for you to die."

"Die?" Thad echoed.

"Certainly. One of Mr. Havoc's machines will likely drill through your skull like, how you Englishmen say, a hot knife through butter, and while the blood gushes down your ear and Mr. Havoc watches you twitch on his worktable, I will slip in to take his invention—and the credit."

Thad stared at her. "Really?"

"No, you idiot." She shoved him down the alley and seized his arm again. "I am going to stand outside this ruined castle and watch while you go in and then I will hope you *don't* die. Otherwise I will have to find someone else stupid enough for this job."

Thad allowed her to tow him along. "And you think I'm stupid enough, is that it?"

"You keep on your shoulder a brass parrot that does not like you much and can, in your words, deliver more than two thousand pounds of pressure from the business end of that sharp beak. Is that smart or is it stupid?"

"Stupid," Dante echoed. "Stupid, stupid."

Thad halted. "Then perhaps this employer should go get this invention himself."

"No, no." Sofiya held up her hands, and the red cloak spilled over her arms in a scarlet river under the moon's silver shadows. "I have told you—our employer has a number of limitations and he cannot do for himself. If you do not wish the work, please say so and I will find someone else."

"There *is* no one else, Miss Ekk, and we're both aware of that." He lowered his voice to a near growl. "I'm always willing to kill a clockworker, no matter what the circumstances, and I can definitely use the enormous sum of money you're offering, but you can keep a civil tongue about it."

She bowed, and Thad couldn't tell if the gesture was meant to mock or not. "My apologies. I am very often forthright, especially these days."

He blinked. "What does that mean?"

"It means we have to leave now. Our employer wants

that invention as quickly as possible, and I am coming along because I do not entirely trust you not to run away with the invention or destroy it once you leave the castle. But you can kill the clockworker or not, as you wish."

Thad let this pass and followed her down the dark alley again. "And once I give you the invention, you intend to kill me?"

"What?" She glanced back at him. "Ah. Like me, you have many suspicions. *That* I can understand. No, Mr. Sharpe. I have no reason to kill you. And if I did, there would be simpler, less expensive methods to accomplish it than than offer you money and send you to a castle. I could, for example, offer myself to you and kill you while we copulated."

Thad flicked a glance of his own down the alley. "No," he said. "You couldn't. But I understand your point."

"Point is sharp," Dante said. "Sharp on point."

"Shut it, bird."

Sofiya cocked her head. "So why *do* you keep this talking bird if you only tell him to shut up? And in such bad shape, too. I could arrange for him to be fixed."

"I'll take your money, but I don't explain myself to you," Thad snapped. "Let's go, then."

"As you say. Our mount is just around the corner."

They rounded the corner. Standing in a small cul-de-sac was a magnificent brass horse. Golden skin etched with fine designs gleamed in the moonlight and curls of steam wisped from its nostrils. Its mane stood up in a stiff wire brush. Thad stopped short, and Dante hunkered down on his shoulder.

"No," Thad said.

Sofiya looked puzzled. "No?"

"I'll find my own horse." He turned and stomped away.

"But—"

Thad strode off without looking back. Dante clung to his shoulder, wordless for once. Out on the stony street, Thad found a closed carriage for hire and paid the driver to take him to the southern edge of Vilnius, the capital city of Lithuania. By now, the only foot traffic on the street consisted of men stumbling home from the taverns. Through the carriage window, Thad also caught sight of a plague zombie lurching through the shadows. Its clothes were ragged, its skin in tatters. It seemed to have only one foot. Thad grimaced in loathing. He supposed he should feel pity, but all he could dredge up was disgust. The vile things spread the clockwork plague everywhere. Most people who caught the disease died quickly. Others lost brain and muscle function and shambled through the rest of their short lives as zombies. And a tiny few . . .

The memories, always at the back of his mind, muscled themselves up to the front. They were nearly ten years old, but they tore and bled like yesterday's wounds. To stanch them, Thad reached up and grabbed Dante. The brass feathers and exposed gears poked his palm.

"Say it," he hissed.

Dante neither moved nor spoke.

"Say it!" Thad barked.

Another pause. Then Dante opened his beak wide. From somewhere inside, gears and memory wheels spun and from the mechanical parrot's throat came the tinny voice of a little boy: *"I love you, Daddy. I love you, Daddy. I love you, Daddy."*

Thad sighed, then set his jaw and let Dante go. The parrot shifted on Thad's shoulder and muttered, "Bad boy, bad boy. Bad, bad, bad."

"Shut it."

Dante fell silent.

The driver had seen the zombie, too, and flicked his whip to make the horses pick up the pace. Thad watched the creature fade into the chilly night. His jaw ached. He realized he was grinding his teeth and forced himself to relax. The zombie wouldn't last more than a few more days anyway, not in this weather. Rumors floated around about an angel with a sword, or perhaps a clawed hand, that cured the plague with a touch. Supposedly this angel traveled Europe with a mortal man who sang with a heavenly voice. The pair were spreading the cure everywhere, and one day the clockwork plague would end. Thad snorted and slouched lower on the worn leather seat. People would believe anything. The only cure for the plague was death.

The carriage bumped through the streets until the buildings abruptly ended. Farmland, walled estates, and small plots of scrubby trees stretched to the south, but crouched on one of the fields at the town's edge was a complex of tents and wagons scattered around a single enormous tent. To one side on a spur of iron track sat a long train, complete with locomotive and caboose. The colors of car and canvas were muted in the moonlight, as if a rainbow had fallen asleep. Thad paid the driver and loped into the network of wood and canvas.

Up close, many of the tents and wagons showed wear and dilapidation—holes, dings, even scorch marks. The illustrated sign out front that read KALAKOS CIRCUS OF

AUTOMATONS AND OTHER WONDERS bore signs of water damage. Thad wove his way among it all with an unconscious dexterity born of childhood practice. He sighed and relaxed a little. It didn't matter what city the circus was in, or even what country; a circus was home. He had only been with this particular circus for a few months, but everything about it—the creak of ropes, the snuff of elephants, the whisper of a knife blade clearing its sheath, the stale smell of fried food and old peanuts— brought back memories of being a little boy with his parents. He had learned the delicate art of knives and swords from his father, an expert thrower and swallower. He had learned the art of control and patient fearlessness from his mother, Dad's assistant and target. From them both and from the rest of the circus he had picked up a dozen languages and the ability to be at ease in a hundred cultures.

And then Thad had fallen in love and left them all for his dear Ekaterina in Poland. Thad set his jaw again and ducked under a tent rope. After any loss, the question that always plagued the survivors was whether or not they would do it all over again. It was a stupid question. There was no way to do it all over again, so what was the point in figuring out an answer? Still, Thad pulled at it like a child pulling at an old scab and making it bleed while the smell of stale peanuts and elephant's breath swirled around him. Would he do it all over again?

He still didn't know.

"Shut it, shut it," Dante muttered.

"Take your own advice, bird."

"Sharpe is sharp."

It broke Thad's heart to see the shabby shape the Kalakos Circus found itself in. The Kalakos was elaborate, enormous, famous—or it had been all those things. Two years ago, the circus had had the misfortune to take in a clockworker named Gavin Ennock and go to Kiev, the birth of the clockwork plague itself. Thad, who was new to the Kalakos, had only gotten bits and pieces of that story. He'd heard about how the Dnipro River dam had inexplicably burst, of course—all of Europe had heard about that—and he'd heard about the way the succeeding flood had miraculously swept off the Gonta-Zalizniak clan of clockworkers who had ruled the Ukrainian Empire and treated its inhabitants like laboratory animals. But the circus folk were strangely tight-lipped about the rest of it, even among other performers. All Thad had been able to figure out was that the circus had come away from the flood much worse for the wear. A great many performers had fled, and much of the circus's equipment had been destroyed, including its iconic mechanical elephant. This sort of thing came of dealing with clockworkers.

At least clockworkers, unlike zombies, didn't spread the plague. People who became clockworkers seemed to do something to the disease that kept it from spreading beyond them. This was, no doubt, small comfort to the flood victims of Kiev and to the Kalakos Circus.

Thad arrived at his little wagon, parked near the train in the residential area of the circus. He unlocked it and hopped inside, where he lit a candle. The thin light revealed a close, efficient space. At the front of the wagon stood a low wardrobe with a double-wide bunk atop it. Clever fold-down shelves on the walls could create small tables, stools, or even beds at a moment's notice, and high, brimmed shelves held a few books and other knick-knacks. A knife grinder's wheel took up the front corner opposite a tiny stove. And from the walls hung a variety of damaged machines.

Each machine had a different design, but all of them were clearly wrecked beyond repair. There were whirli-gigs with bent blades and spiders missing their legs, energy pistols with broken barrels, and automaton heads split in half, showing gears like metal brain matter. More than two dozen machines covered the wall, in fact. The shadows from the candle played across them, and their dead eyes seemed to focus on Thad. But none of them could actually move—a hard hammer and a satisfying set of nails had seen to that. As Thad set down the candlestick, Dante jumped from his shoulder and landed on a perch among them.

"Sharpe is sharp," he said.

Thad opened the wardrobe. One half contained dull clothes and bright costumes. The other half clanked with weapons—short swords, silvery knives, heavy axes, thin stilettos, a spiked mace. And pistols. Six of those, including one of the new Smith & Wesson revolvers that accepted cartridge rounds. The rounds were much more accurate but also much more expensive, so Thad rarely used them. He hesitated, then touched the torn money pouch in his pocket. With a grim nod, he holstered the Smith & Wesson revolver at his belt. His long leather jacket fell open, revealing another small armory of knives and other blades. He checked to make sure they were all in place, put Dante back on his shoulder, and went back outside, carefully locking the little wagon behind him.

From a storage box attached to the wagon's outside wall, he took a bridle and saddle while Dante shifted uneasily. Thad glanced at the moon and realized he'd have to hurry if he wanted to make it to the village and the clockworker's castle in time to go in tonight. For a moment, he considered waiting a day or two. It might be better to scout the area out, find out more about Mr. Havoc and his defenses.

"Drink up, drink up," Dante squawked.

"Hm," Thad said, absently touching Dante's head. Dante had a point, however accidentally. The men drinking in the tavern had recognized Thad, known what his business was. It wouldn't take long for word to filter back to Mr. Havoc that Thad was in town. Clockworkers were insane but they were also frighteningly intelligent, and it wouldn't be much of a strain for for Mr. Havoc to assume that Thad was coming for him and to strengthen his defenses. Hell, he might even attack Thad—or the circus— as a defensive measure. No, Thad would have to take care of Mr. Havoc tonight. Now.

Thad retrieved his horse from the large, plain tent that housed the rest of the horses, and moments later he was on the road. For a bad moment, clouds rolled across the moon, blocking Thad's light, but a chilly autumn breeze chased them off again, leaving the path ahead of him as clear as a snake made of mercury. He urged the horse into a canter with Dante clinging to the pommel.

At a spot where stubbly fields met at a crossroad, Thad saw a horse and rider. His hand went to his revolver, but the figures resolved themselves into Sofiya atop the brass horse, motionless and gleaming beneath the stars. Her scarlet cloak looked like dried blood.

"What took so long?" she demanded. "I have been waiting forever."

Anger stabbed at Thad as he reined in. "Let's be clear, Miss Ekk. Your presence on this mission is neither required nor desired. If you don't care for the way I work, you may take back your money and I'll happily go to bed. Question me again, and that's what will happen. Is that understood?"

"Perfectly." She seemed unruffled. "I was only making conversation."

"Pretty boy, pretty, pretty boy."

"And keep that walking pile of shit away from Blackie. I don't want it to contaminate him or me."

"Blackie?"

Dammit. "My son named him."

"Ah. And where—?"

Thad slapped Blackie's flank, and the horse leaped into a gallop. It was some time before Sofiya and her brass horse caught up. The automaton's gait was smooth and regular, and it snorted steam from its nostrils at every fourth step. Sofiya didn't speak again, and eventually Thad was forced to slow Blackie down. Sofiya's horse matched pace without comment.

"I am sorry," Sofiya said at last.

Thad glanced at her. That was unexpected. But talking with Sofiya was like walking blindfolded through a bomb field. One moment she was explosive, the next she was refined, and he could never tell which was coming. "Sorry for what?"

"For the death of your son. And, I assume, of your wife. I assume a clockworker was involved."

"How did—" He cut himself off. "Never mind. I don't talk about it."

"Nevertheless. It was not my intention to cause you pain, and I apologize. I only want the invention."

"And I want the clockworker dead. We can both have what we want."

"That would be a small miracle, Mr. Sharpe. But I will settle for Havoc's machine."

Thad shifted in the saddle. "What does this machine do, anyway?"

"I have no idea. And before you ask, I do not know why our employer wants it, either. That does worry me somewhat."

"Oh?"

"I do not wish to give him a clockworker invention that might hurt a lot of people. So I will have to examine it closely. That is another reason why I am coming along, you see."

That surprised Thad. "But you work for him."

"And yet I somehow still think for myself. Do you find this so incredible?"

They reached a village of peasant houses. Like most in this region, the dwellings were low buildings made of logs or sod and topped with thatch. None had windows—they were too poor for that—and no lights burned anywhere. At this time of night, everyone was in bed. Thad judged that they had two or two and a half hours before sunrise. The dirt road threaded between the houses, forked west, and rose up a high hill. Atop the hill, Thad could just make out the silhouette of stone buildings. It seemed to him there should been a storm, or a least a rumble of thunder, but the night was calm and clear.

As they neared the edge of the village, one of the doors opened a crack and a woman peered out, probably wakened by their hoofbeats. When she saw the direction Thad and Sofiya were heading, she ran out into the road, heedless of her bedclothes and her nightcap.

"You must not go this way!" she called in desperate Lithuanian. *"You must not!"*

Thad halted. *"We will be fine, mistress."*

"No! You must not!" She ran up and caught Blackie's bridle. He snorted and tried to toss his head, but she clung hard. *"That way is the path of a demon!"*

"A clockworker?" Thad asked.

"An evil man." Her eyes were pleading. She looked barely older than Thad himself. *"He has taken many people from Juodsilai and done terrible things to them. We have begged the Cup Bearer and the Master of the Hunt to help us, but they do nothing. He took my sister ..."*

"I am sorry," Sofiya said for the second time that evening.

"Vilma!" A man in a nightshirt was standing in the doorway. *"Come away!"*

"The demon comes out at night. If you need a place to stay, come to our house. My husband will not like it, but—"

Thad reached down and gently freed Blackie's bridle from her hand. *"I am not the Master of the Hunt, mistress, but I have come to destroy the demon clockworker."*

"Death, doom, destruction, despair," Dante said.

"Truly?" The woman clasped Thad's hand and kissed it several times. *"Thank you, my lord. Thank you, thank you so much. Wait!"*

The woman dashed past her surprised husband into the house and emerged a moment later with a small jug and a cloth-wrapped bundle. *"Take these,"* she said.

Thad recognized both objects by smell. The bundle was rye bread and the little jug contained a homemade vodka strong enough to make his eyes water. He thought about refusing such a rich gift from a poor household, but the woman's expression was powerfully earnest. Thad also recognized the gesture for what it was. The memory of his own loss made his throat close up as he met Vilma's eyes. She understood, and turning down her sacrifice was unthinkable. So was refusing to face Havoc.

"Thank you," he said. With the gravity of a priest, he slipped the objects into the capacious pockets of his coat. *"What was your sister's name?"*

"Olga."

"I will make sure that word is the last sound he hears, Mistress Vilma."

Without another word, he turned Blackie and rode away with Sofiya close behind. For once, Sofiya didn't speak.

They climbed the hill, which was dotted with birch trees whose bark and leaves turned to silver and paper beneath the moon. Halfway up, Thad dismounted near a birch grove and put Dante on his shoulder. Frost had already killed off the insects, and the birds had migrated long ago, leaving the night eerily devoid of life sounds. Anticipation mingled with uncertainty in Thad's chest, and he found himself checking his weapons over and over—stilettos, revolvers, bullets, knives, stilettos, revolvers, bullets, knives. He had other equipment as well: silk rope, lock picks, a small hacksaw, matches, and other handy objects. His fingers itched, and he couldn't sit still. Evil rested at the top of that hill, an evil that terrorized men and killed women's sisters, and for once Thad would strike it before it struck him.

"You stay here," he told Sofiya. "After this point, the horses—and you—will be a nuisance."

"As you wish. Perhaps I will nap." Sofiya made her horse kneel, and she spread her cloak in a half circle in the brass shelter of its body. "Remember, the invention is a spider with ten legs instead of eight and—"

"—it has strange markings," Thad finished for her. "I remember."

"Sharpe is sharp," Dante squawked. "Doom!"

"No talking, bird," Thad told him, "unless you want Havoc to extract your gears with a spoon."

Dante settled his feathers with a clatter, but didn't respond. Thad touched his knives one more time, then headed up the road toward the ruins and the clockworker named Havoc.

Chapter Three

Thaddeus Sharpe scanned the castle ruins with a practiced eye. In his considerable experience, clockworkers liked hidden, enclosed spaces. Castles, sewers, underground rooms, and similar places made them feel safe, like rats in a burrow. Ruins gave them the solitude they often craved; clockworkers did not work well with others. They fell to arguing too easily and tore one another to pieces, sometimes literally. Thad had once managed to set one clockworker on another, and the results had been tremendously satisfying.

He examined Havoc's castle from a safe distance, automatically cataloging it and sizing it up. The castle wasn't a single building, of course. It was a little complex of outbuildings and a main keep bent in a rectangle around a courtyard, all in stony ruins. The keep and some of the outbuildings were surrounded by a fragmented stone wall that had originally been at least three stories tall but was now tumbling down in most places to the point where Thad could probably peer over it on tiptoe. The moat had dried up long ago. Vines crawled over everything, and trees poked through shattered rooftops. It reminded Thad a little of the circus, with a main tent holding court over several smaller ones, except here every shadow held a potential trap. Each hole was also a potential weak spot, and the cracks over there might be good for climbing. Up top, however, the gleam of moonlight revealed toothy spikes poking out of the wall, clear signs of recent human habitation, and Thad was fairly certain that said spikes would be poisoned or otherwise rendered unpleasant. A new portcullis blocked the main gate, and Thad saw no mechanisms for raising it on this side. He would have been surprised to find any. A roofless corner tower about forty yards away had half collapsed, and Thad discarded it as a source of danger, at least from this distance.

The high stone keep that made up the main building seemed to stare down at Thad from the other side of the wall, while the chill breeze made the trees whisper and mutter among themselves. Thad studied the wall for a long moment, then tossed a broken branch at it. A section of stone the size of a horse slammed down with a bone-jarring thud. It smashed the branch flat into the ground and cranked back up into the wall.

There was long, long moment of silence.

"Bless my soul," Dante whistled.

Thad sheathed the knife that had sprung into his hand and took a breath to slow his pounding heart. "This place is no circus."

"Bless my soul," Dante repeated. "Applesauce."

"Why can't you say *nevermore* or something interesting like that?"

"Applesauce."

Thad backed up and edged farther west, away from the tower and the portcullis, his sharp eyes searching the wall.

"I don't hear any alarms going off," he murmured. "Do you?"

"Nevermore," Dante said.

"Right. And we can't touch the walls, but just around that corner we'll find a convenient gate half hidden by vines. Do you smell what I smell?"

"Gingerbread. Gingerbread."

"Exactly."

A moment later, Thad did find the clump of vines that formed an upside-down U—the overgrown gate Sofiya had mentioned. Standing at what he hoped was a safe distance away, he found a chunk of masonry and flung that at the vines. It vanished through them. Thad waited. Nothing. The safe, untrapped entrance seemed to beckon him in, as if he were child lost in the woods with his sister. The real trap would come later, just as it did with a gingerbread house. Even so, something bothered him, but he couldn't quite finger it.

"Dante," he said at last.

"Doom," said Dante. "Death, despair."

"Go."

"Applesauce," Dante replied stubbornly.

Thad plucked the parrot from his shoulder and threw him without ceremony toward the vines. Dante arced sideways into the green curtain with a surprised whistle and vanished. He was too damaged to fly, if he had ever been able to. Thad waited, not sure if he wanted the mechanical bird to disappear forever or not. It might be nice if the universe decided it for him. Thad couldn't bring himself to believe in God. Not anymore.

"Dante?" he called.

Silence. Then another whistle, but muffled somehow. Was that a good sign or bad? Thad couldn't tell, and the fact that he couldn't tell made him uncertain and nervous. With a quick gesture, Thad pulled from his pocket a short brass baton. He pressed a button, and it sprang into its full four-foot length with a *clack.* Cautiously, he used it to push the vines aside. Again, nothing. He moved through the clingy, green-smelling curtain—

—and nearly fell into a black pit. Thad hung there at the edge like a tightrope walker, not quite falling in but unable to draw himself back. The greedy pit gaped before him, trying to swallow him down. Stones made teeth around the edges, and Dante was grimly holding on to one of them with his beak. Thad hung there, caught between life and death. For a mad moment, he thought about giving up and simply letting himself drop into the dark. It would be easy, and any pain would end quickly. *All* his pain would end quickly. Then the weight of the vodka jug in his jacket pocket slowly pulled him backward until he regained enough equilibrium to put both feet on firm ground.

"Idiot," he muttered to himself. This was what had bothered him—he hadn't heard the rock hit the ground. He collapsed the staff and returned it to his pocket.

"Bless my soul." Dante whistled pointedly from the pit's edge. Thad picked the parrot up and set him back on his shoulder. Dante bit him on the ear. Pain lanced through Thad's head, and he felt a trickle of blood.

"Ow!" Angry, Thad snatched Dante off again and held him over the pit. "Listen, birdbrain, I'll drop you in, and see if I don't."

"I love you, Daddy. I love you, Daddy."

"No, you don't. And if you say that again without permission, I'll melt you down in Havoc's forge while I watch."

"Applesauce."

"I said, shut it." But Thad put Dante back on his shoulder again.

Once he knew the pit was there, it was easy enough to edge around it and onto the grounds of the keep. That brought Thad to one of the long sides of the rectangle that made up the inner castle. Ruined outbuildings backed up against the main wall, and an overgrown courtyard with a well and spaces for gardens spread out ahead of him. Thad flicked a calculating glance at the outbuildings—sometimes clockworkers used what had once been the blacksmith's forge for their own work—but he saw no evidence of such activity. He sighed. It was too much to hope that Mr. Havoc would be outside, where he would be easy to reach.

Thad ghosted across the courtyard toward the main building, already falling into a familiar rhythm: dash a few steps, pause, scan for danger, dash a few steps. Stay to the shadows. Watch for anything that glowed or gave off heat.

A rustling in the grass to his left made the revolver leap into his hand. The hammer clicked under his thumb. Then the shape of a rat skittered away, and Thad relaxed. Dante cocked his head but was wise enough to remain silent.

Thad oozed up to the main keep, wishing he knew something—anything—about the layout of the interior. Most keeps were built around a main hall, with side chambers for everything from storage to arms to living quarters. Clockworkers needed space, so the main hall was the most likely place to start. One major problem was that clockworkers could—and usually did—go for days without sleeping, so Thad wouldn't be able to slip up on Havoc while he snored in a bed.

A number of doors both small and large faced the courtyard. A pair of small ones opened onto the garden area, and the large double doors in the center of the high wall stood shut like pair of giants holding back the darkness. Enormous shiny locks held them closed, and the locks had visible teeth in the keyholes. One keyhole gnashed open and shut with an audible *clack* even as Thad examined them from several paces back. He didn't fancy finding a way around that. He glanced up. Like most keeps, the windows were high and narrow, more arrow slit than anything. The top floor of the keep had crumbled away, but the lower stories were still solid, and Thad saw no way in besides the doors. Another rat nearly ran over his foot, and he jumped back, suppressing an oath. Dante clacked his beak, but didn't comment.

Thad thought a long moment, then went back to the pit and peered into it. It would have to do. He took out the silk rope, tied one end to a sturdy sapling near the edge, and before he could think too hard about what he was doing, he lowered himself down like a mountain climber. The soft silk kept his palms from burning as he slid into the pit's dark throat, and Thad had to force himself to keep his breathing steady. Dante gripped his shoulder, apparently unconcerned. The descent went on and on. Thad's muscles ached, and it soon seemed as if he'd been climbing through darkness forever. Sweat trickled from his hair down his collar. The only sounds were his own breath and the little ticks and rustles made as he slid carefully downward, bracing himself against the earthen side of the pit.

At last the sounds changed. There was that ineffable shift in noise, and he sensed that the bottom of the pit was close under him. Still cautious, he put his feet down even as his forearms and shoulders screamed for mercy, and touched solid floor. He sighed with relief. Something skittered away from him—more rats, no doubt. Thad fished a candle from his pocket and scratched a sulfur match to light it.

"Bad boy, bad boy," Dante said softly.

Thad ignored him and raised the candle. The light revealed a simple earthen pit, as he had been expecting. It also revealed a grated gate set in one wall, as he had been hoping. The padlock that held it shut was simple.

"Ha," he said under his breath.

Havoc hadn't left the castle gate unsecured in a moment of foolishness, as Sofiya had thought. The crafty bugger had left it open as bait. Thad had seen this kind of thing before. More than one person had used the gate to enter the castle, fallen into the pit, and become fodder for Havoc's experiments. It was also why there were no alarms or automaton guards—Havoc *wanted* people to come in. The place was a gingerbread house.

Dante obligingly held the candle in one claw while Thad's picks got the lock open. No need to put heavy security on a gate when the people on the other side were suffering from broken bones. A tunnel beyond it led beneath the courtyard and, Thad assumed, straight into the keep. He took the candle back from Dante and cautiously moved down the tunnel. It was probably safe to assume that the tunnel would be unguarded and without traps for the same reason the gate had been only lightly locked, but the paranoia Sofiya had mentioned earlier forced him to stay alert. He watched for wires and irregularities in the earthen floor and anything at all that looked like brass or steam. But he saw nothing except a dank earthen tunnel braced with wood.

What was Havoc like? Sofiya had had little information to give him. The moniker *Mr.* indicated he was a man, but how old was he? What did he look like? How had he encountered the clockwork plague? Did he have relatives? Children? What had become of them?

Thad tried to clamp down on the last line of thought, but the tunnel offered few distractions, and it came along even so. Once the plague took a clockworker's mind, he—or she—didn't care about people. All that mattered was the experiment, the science, the invention. Thad had come across his third clockworker in the process of making an airship out of human skin. His second had perfected a vivisection device and had gone from testing it on dogs and cats to apes stolen from a zoo and finally to people—five in all, including two children. And his first clockworker—

The candle held back the darkness, but not the guilt. It closed around Thad like a fist and stole his breath. He had to force himself to keep walking.

His first clockworker . . .

Thad still couldn't put it into words. *David was his life* seemed trite, or maybe just understated, like saying it was nice to have air when you lived underwater. His dear Ekaterina had died in the birthing bed, leaving

Thad the sole and frightened caretaker of a crying, pink bundle of curiosity with his mother's blue eyes and red-brown hair. Thad had considered running back to the circus, the one he had left to marry Ekaterina in the first place, but Ekaterina's mother had persuaded him to stay, and Thad had realized that with David in his life, it would be easier to stay on in Warsaw as a knife sharpener and tinsmith than return to his parents' life of knife throwing and stage magic.

The early years had been difficult. Thad had no interest in remarrying, which meant he took care of both business and home, though Ekaterina's aging mother helped as best she could. David grew quickly and got into everything, a dangerous prospect in the shop of a knife man, and Thad found himself almost slavishly devoted to this small, yet strangely enormous, presence in his life. David, for his part, clung ferociously to his father. With a sense of wonder and awe, Thad watched David learn to walk, run, play with other children, ask to help in the little shop, and every day Thad saw something of Ekaterina in him—her laugh, her hair, her smile.

The two of them soldiered through life together. Together they endured hard work and loneliness and even the death of Ekaterina's mother one long winter. Slowly, Thad began to heal. When David was six, Thad scraped up the money to enroll him in school and endured the little pang in his heart each day when David left in the morning and suffered the little sting when he returned in the afternoon to talk about students and teachers and playmates Thad had never met.

And then one afternoon, David didn't return home. At first Thad thought nothing of it. David had simply gotten caught up in a game with some other boys or paused at the sweets shop again. But as the afternoon turned to evening, Thad became worried, then frightened, then frantic. He barely remembered the hours of searching, of asking everyone along David's route home what they had seen, until a baker, in his shop for the night's baking, mentioned seeing a boy matching David's description, right down to the color of his shirt and the school books flung over his back. The baker had seen the boy get into a carriage—or perhaps he'd been snatched, the baker wasn't certain. What the man did remember was that the carriage bore the crest of the mayor.

Thad stiffened. Mayor Teodor de Langeron, a prince of French and Russian descent, had no sons, but rumor had it that one of his numerous nephews had contracted the clockwork plague. Some of the wilder speculations said he'd become a clockworker.

And it was quite impossible to expect the police to interfere in the affairs of a prince's family.

Even now, Thad only vaguely recalled stripping the knife shop of its blades and digging out his old stage-magic trunk. He did remember posing as a servant to get onto the palace grounds where the mayor's family lived and terrorizing a young maid into telling him where to find the nephew, who was already insisting that people call him Lord Power instead of by his birth name Henryk, a clear sign that the plague had taken his mind. Lord Power lived in cellars beneath the palace, another sign.

Fortunately for Thad, Lord Power still felt safe in his family home and hadn't decided to build traps yet. Thad only ran across this habit later. Every step along the endless cellar corridors and storerooms was a nightmare.

Twice he got lost and had to backtrack. Another time his candle went out, and his hands were shaking so hard, he couldn't relight it. A piping cry for help brought his head around. David's voice! He followed the sound, terrified. Every delay meant more pain for David. Thad rounded a stony corner and the cry for help sounded right in his ear. Thad swiped at the sound by reflex and knocked a brass parrot off a wall perch. It clanged to the floor, knocking its beak askew.

"Danger! Danger!" the parrot squawked. "Master! Danger!"

Thad kicked it, and the parrot smashed into the wall. It lost an eye and several metal feathers. "Shut it!" Thad snarled.

In answer, the parrot screamed for help in David's voice again. The sound turned Thad's blood to ice. The bird was somehow reproducing David's voice, and that meant Lord Power was probably somewhere nearby. A door just down the corridor showed a crack of light at the bottom. Thad smashed into it without hesitation. The damp wood gave way and he stumbled into the room beyond.

Small cages lined the walls. Each contained a bloody, mangled human corpse. Shelves of dreadful equipment took up one wall, and the top shelf was lined with enormous jars of clear fluid, each with a white label—OIL OF VITRIOL, SPIRITS OF SALT, AQUA FORTIS. Near the shelves stood an operating table with a bloody sheet draped over it. Standing next to it was a tall man with a potbelly and a receding hairline. He was training a complicated-looking crossbow on Thad.

"Dante gave me plenty of warning," Lord Power said

just as the mechanical parrot waddled into the room. "Don't move, and don't think about throwing that knife."

Thad gripped the blade. He didn't even remember drawing it. "I'll kill you."

"Not with that," Lord Power said. "Don't you know? I am a clockworker—smarter, faster, better than you. Throw that knife at me, and I will catch it in midair."

The figure beneath the sheet whimpered. David! Thad's heart twisted, but he forced himself to concentrate on the clockworker and his crossbow. Dante, for reasons of his own, jumped up onto the table beside David and cocked his head.

"How lucky am I?" Lord Power continued. "I take one subject off the street, and a second one follows him in. You know, I learned so much when I sliced this boy's—"

Thad threw the knife. Lord Power warily watched it come, but it arced high over his head.

"My turn." Power re-aimed the crossbow with a giggle just as the knife crashed handle first into the jar marked OIL OF VITRIOL. Glass shattered, and the sulfuric acid inside cascaded over Power's head and face. Smoke rose from his flesh, and he screamed in agony. The crossbow clattered to the floor. Lord Power screamed and screamed and screamed. The acid dissolved his hair and skin, revealing his skull. Power clawed at the remains of his face, but that only got the acid on the flesh of his hands, which also began to dissolve. Thad ran forward, snatched up the crossbow, and fired it into the man's chest. Power stiffened, then dropped twitching to the floor.

"Bless my soul," Dante said.

Thad flung the bow aside and tore the sheet away from the table.

In that moment, Thad understood how much he'd been hoping the figure under the sheet wasn't David. That was how it worked in stories—the hero rips the barrier away, but surprise! The figure under the sheet is an animal or a dummy or another poor soul, someone you could feel sorry for even as you felt a guilty relief that it wasn't your son. But the wreck on the table was undeniably his little boy David. The world closed around Thad's heart like a rock and his knees buckled.

"Daddy?" David said in English. His eyes were shut and his voice was blurred, as if he were sleepy. "Daddy."

Thad dropped the sheet back over David's body with shaking hands. "I'm here. Daddy's here, little star. The bad man is gone. Does . . . does it hurt?"

"I'm cold," David whispered. His breathing was slow and it had bubbles in it. "I'm cold."

Thad didn't know what to do. His son was dying, and he could do nothing but watch. Why hadn't he come a few minutes before? Why hadn't he started searching just one hour earlier? When he sent David off to school that morning with a meat roll in his hand for breakfast, he'd had no way of knowing that this would be the last time he'd ever see David alive.

"I'm sorry, Daddy." David coughed, and blood spattered his lip.

The pain in his voice made Thad have to lean on the table, and tears choked the back of his throat. He smoothed the hair on David's forehead. "Why are you sorry, little star?" *Little star* was a name Thad had stopped using with David years ago, but he now found himself going back to it.

"I should . . . have . . . run . . ."

"No!" Thad couldn't bear the thought that his dear, sweet boy would go into the afterlife feeling guilty. He hugged David despite the bloody sheet. "No, little star! It was my fault for not coming after you sooner. You are not to blame. Please believe me." He was weeping openly now. He fumbled under the sheet for David's hand and accidentally knocked Dante over. The parrot twitched.

"Recording," Dante said. "Recording."

"I . . . I . . ." David's voice was growing fainter, and his hand was growing colder. "I . . ."

"What?" Thad pleaded.

"I love you, Daddy." David exhaled once more and died.

Before he left the lab with David in his bloody shroud over one shoulder and Dante clinging to the other, Thad broke every jar and bottle he could find and dropped a candle into the mess. The liquid blazed up like a hungry demon. Thad didn't stay to watch it burn. The last thing he saw was the flames licking the corpse of the clock-worker. How many brothers and sisters in darkness did this creature have? How many clockworkers giggled behind their knives and needs, their machines and mechanicals?

"One less," Thad spat. "And tomorrow, one more less. There will always be one more less."

The tunnel under the castle widened into a dungeon. They always did. Thad did a quick check in the cells but found no prisoners in evidence. Strange. Usually he found at least one. Perhaps they were kept somewhere else.

He found the usual spiral staircase and used his collapsible baton to poke and prod his way upward. Nothing leaped out, no stairs collapsed, no terrible liquids gushed down toward him. At least the clockworker had installed glowing lights of some kind, however meager. The entire place looked dirty and gray. He emerged at the end of a long corridor and almost stumbled into an automaton.

The automaton was human-shaped, but Thad couldn't tell much more in the dim light. He rammed a shoulder into it without thinking, but he wasn't able to get much force behind the gesture. The automaton staggered, but recovered. It punched Thad in the chest with a heavy fist. Thad's breath whooshed out of him and he nearly went down. The automaton made a buzzing sound—an alarm?—and Thad jabbed the baton at its face. The metal end drove straight into the machine's head. There was a wet snap and gears ground like bad teeth. The automaton clawed at the baton sticking out of its face for a moment, then slowed and stopped. Like a brass tree going down, it toppled backward to the floor. The buzzing sound died.

"Bless my soul," Dante said.

Thad braced his foot on the automaton's shoulder and yanked the baton free. The automaton looked strange, even in the bad light. He bent for closer look, then drew back with a hiss. Half the automaton's metal head was flesh. One side of a woman's head had been stitched unevenly to a metal one with staples or wire. The tip of Thad's baton was stained with blood. The vodka in Thad's pocket felt very heavy.

Thad forced a number of reactions to the back of his mind. Later, when he had taken care of Havoc, he would have a private moment of horror and anxiety. Right now he was busy.

The corridor opened unexpectedly onto a balcony that ringed a large hall. On the floor a story below lay yet another dreadful laboratory. Thad had seen so many now that they were blurring together. Clockworkers focused on different areas of science—mechanics, physics, automatics, biology, chemistry, even astronomy—but their labs tended to have the same equipment. They almost always had a forge, since they had to design and create their own machinery. They usually had a great deal of glassware, mechanical parts, medical equipment, and, sadly, chains, cages, and other restraints near some kind of operating table. Thad's all-too-experienced eye ran over the similarities and picked out differences. A stack of barrels in one corner. A large cooking stove in another. Shelves lined with jars, each one containing a human brain in fluid. And on a worktable amid a jumble of half-built spiders, a very different spider, a large one with ten legs instead of eight and intricate wires and carvings all over its body. Havoc's machine. Of Havoc himself, there was no sign.

Thad narrowed his eyes. What was this machine and why did Sofiya's employer want it so badly? It crossed his mind that the employer might be another clockworker, a rival, but Thad almost as quickly discarded the idea. Clockworkers didn't work well with others. They became more and more self-centered and narcissistic as the plague progressed, and when they went into a sleepless fugue of inventing, they were singularly unpleasant to be around, which was one reason they built so many automatons—machines were the only beings that could withstand their abuse. The idea that an advanced clock-worker might work so closely with normal people like Sofiya or Thad, even at a distance, seemed unlikely in the extreme. In any case, perhaps he should "accidentally" destroy the invention. Secret reasons for wanting it couldn't be good reasons. On the other hand, he'd given his word and taken the money.

Thad gave a mental shrug. He could decide later. First, he'd have to kill Havoc.

As if on cue, a door in the lab below opened and a man emerged. He looked perfectly ordinary—nearing forty or so, a full head of salt-and-pepper hair, the long mustaches favored in this part of the world. His right arm was elaborately mechanical, though, and nearly twice as thick as his left. Steam even puffed from the joints. Thad wondered what surprises it contained. Havoc—Thad assumed the man was Havoc—was trailing a chain, and with it he towed into the laboratory another figure. Thad's stomach went cold and his hand stole automatically up to his shoulder where it gripped Dante hard. The figure at the other end of the chain was a child, a boy from the look of it. He was wrapped in ragged clothing from head to foot, and a tattered scarf covered his face. Even his hands were wrapped in rags. He was shivering, and his size put him at the same age as David when he had died.

The gut-wrenching memories threatened to drag Thad back into the past, and he fought to stay in the present as Havoc dragged the boy onto the operating table. A bear made of rage roared to life inside Thad, and he trembled with the effort of holding himself in check.

Nothing else mattered now, not the machine, not the money, not Sofiya, not even Vilma and her sister Olga. Havoc would be dead before the sun rose. He looked around for a staircase so he could slip down to the main floor. Havoc bent over the boy on the operating table.

"Bugger this," Thad said, and leaped over the edge.

Chapter Four

Thad landed on the foot of the operating table intending to deliver a solid kick to Havoc's face. Unfortunately, he lost his balance. Fortunately, he fell straight into Mr. Havoc. The two of them went down in a struggling bundle of arms and legs, brass and iron. Too late, Thad remembered the pistols under his coat. His anger had gotten the better of him.

Havoc's thick metal arm shoved hard, and Thad skidded halfway across the floor on his back. The clockworker sat up. Dante peered down at him from the operating table with his one good eye.

"Who the hell are you?" Havoc boomed in Lithuanian. It would have been more impressive if he hadn't been sitting on the ground with his legs open. *"Have you come to steal my work?"*

In answer, Thad pulled the pistols from beneath his jacket and took aim. *"Olga,"* he said.

Havoc blinked at him. *"What?"*

"Olga. She was one of the women you took from the village."

"Oh. I take a lot of women. Sometimes dogs, too. Dogs are nice. I don't remember a woman named Olga but I do remember a dog named Sunis, but a dog wouldn't steal my work like you are trying to do."

Thad fired. Havoc's metal arm moved so fast, it blurred, and the bullet ricocheted away. *"It seems stupid to name a dog dog, but he wasn't mine and he didn't live very long. It looks like you're trying to kill me, so it would be prudent to kill you straightaway, though I would like to know why you didn't fall into my pit so I can fix the problem, and it would have been interesting to save your brain for my work, the work you want to steal, and I do not take kindly to thieves."*

With a series of clicks and whirrs, an enormous pistol emerged from Havoc's forearm. Thad scrambled to his feet and dove behind the worktable with the ten-legged spider on it just as Havoc fired. A spray of bullets chittered across the floor right behind Thad and pinged off the equipment piled on and around the table. Thad glanced up. The ten-legged spider sat on its pyramid of junk, just another piece of paraphernalia. Thad could almost touch it. Glass shattered as bullets zipped around for several seconds like deadly hummingbirds. Then they stopped. Thad risked a peek around the table. The fluid jars near him had been shattered, the gory contents pulped. Thad smelled sharp formaldehyde. Havoc, still sitting on the ground, was feeding bullet cartridges into his arm. Thad whipped his pistol around, then realized that from this angle, the boy on the table was partly in line of fire.

"Damn it," he muttered.

"I hate it when people make a mess in my laboratory,"

Havoc said, the words rippling endlessly from his mouth. *"Especially thieves like you. It will take hours to clean this up, though I can use automatons to help me, but lately some haven't been so cooperative, which is why I had to put some of my work aside, though this new breakthrough is very promising and I don't appreciate that you have interrupted me, little thief."*

He fired again, and Thad ducked back behind the table. Bullets pocked and pinged all around him. A red-hot line scored his forearm and he snatched himself farther back. Blood trickled down the inside of his sleeve.

"I hit you, little thief. I can smell the blood. It's funny how these days I can sense so much more than I could before I contracted this wonderful disease—"

"Dante!" Thad shouted. "Shut it!"

"Applesauce!" Dante's interjection was followed by a scream from Havoc. Thad shoved himself away from the equipment pile and slid sideways on the floor. Dante was at Havoc's shoulder, his sharp beak piercing Havoc's ear as his needle claws dug into Havoc's neck. Blood flew in all directions. Havoc's metal arm fired wildly into the ceiling. The boy huddled on the operating table, but Thad's slide across the floor had changed the trajectory so that the child wasn't in the line of fire. The pistol barked three times in Thad's hand. All three shots went straight into Havoc's upper body. His arm gun went silent, and the clockworker toppled backward with a burbling gasp. The smell of gunpowder hung in the air.

"Olga!" Thad shouted at him.

"Bless my soul," Dante said, hopping free of Havoc. His claws were red. "Doom!"

Thad glanced over at the ten-legged spider crouched

atop the pile of equipment across the room. What about that thing was worth so much? In any case, it would keep for now. He ran to the table. The boy lay huddled on his side, shivering in his rags. For a terrible moment Thad was back in Poland looking down at David. But this wasn't Poland, and this boy wasn't David. There was no sheet, no blood, and Thad had arrived in time.

"It's all right," Thad told him, then cursed himself for speaking English. He switched to his heavy Lithuanian. *"I'll get you out of here. The bad man is dead. He can't hurt you."*

The boy didn't respond. Dante hopped up to Thad's shoulder, blood still staining his beak and claws. Thad touched the boy's shoulder. It was warm. *"My name is Mr. Sharpe,"* he said. *"I've come to take you home. Can you sit up?"*

A soft sound from the rags, like the sound of someone trying not to cry. Thad's heart half broke.

"I'm going to pick you up," Thad said. *"I won't hurt you."*

"But I . . . will . . . little thief."

Thad spun in time to see Havoc slap a button on the back of his mechanical hand. It pulsed red, and a high-pitched sound squealed through the room. Havoc was gasping, and blood gushed from his chest wounds.

"You will not . . . steal . . . my work," he panted. *"No one . . . will steal . . . work."*

Before Thad could react, rats poured into the room. Tens and dozens and hundreds of them. They poured in from the door Havoc had used. They swarmed down from the balcony. They scampered down the spiral stairs. Thad had seen them before, but hadn't noticed that they were partly animal and partly mechanical. Metal claws scratched and sparked against the stones and their eyes pulsed a scarlet that matched the button on the back of Havoc's heavy hand. The high-pitched squeal grew louder.

"When enough arrive," Havoc said, *"rats reach ... critical mass. Boom. You will die with my work ... little thief."*

Havoc slumped back and went still, but the button on his hand continued its red pulse. The half-mechanical rats flooding the room ignored Thad and Dante and the boy to swarm over Havoc's body in a metal cairn, their scarlet eyes beating a dreadful rhythm that grew louder and pounded against Thad's bones. A palpable heat suffused the very air and the pulse sped up.

Thad shot a glance at the ten-legged spider on its junk pile all the way across the laboratory, then down at the boy on the table near him. The boy's weight would slow Thad down and eat time. So would dashing across the room to grab the spider. Could he do both? Probably not. The pulse was blending now into a near-continuous sound of its own. He had to make a choice.

Thad shook his head. There was no choice. Besides, he knew damned well he hadn't really intended to save the invention anyway. Thad swept the ragged boy into his arms and sprinted for the doorway Havoc had used. A steady stream of rats rushed past him in the opposite direction, and his boots crunched some of them. They twitched, still trying to crawl toward Havoc's laboratory. Thad ran up a ramp and found himself at door. Once again he was in Poland, but this time David was still alive. He smashed into the door with his shoulder, but it wasn't locked, or even latched. It burst open and he stumbled into the chilly air of the courtyard, the boy still in his arms.

"Sharpe is sharp," Dante said. He had prudently moved to the back of Thad's neck.

The pulse had become a shriek. Thad ran. This time he would win. This time the boy would live. His arms ached and his lungs burned, but he ran. He vaulted over the pit and plunged through the curtain of vines. The boy huddled in his arms didn't make a sound the entire time. Outside, the hill's downward slope made it easier, though his legs were getting heavy and stitch cramped his side.

The explosion shoved him forward with a rude hand. Heat washed over him and singed the hair from his neck. Thad curled around the boy and took the rolling bumps and bruises as his due penance. When they stopped rolling, Thad cautiously pulled himself away from the boy. His body ached in a way that told him his muscles would scream at him in the morning, but he didn't seem to have any broken bones.

"Bless my soul!" Dante squawked from the ground several paces away.

"Are you all right?" Thad asked the boy in Lithuanian. *"Can you walk?"*

The boy, still wrapped in his rags and scarf, nodded and got to his feet even as Thad, groaning, did the same. The castle, a ruin before, was now a total wreck. Multicolored flames danced against the night sky. So much for Havoc's invention. Thad wondered if the villagers would come to investigate or if they'd stay huddled in their homes.

"Let me see if you are injured." Thad tried to pull the

boy's scarf away, but the boy yelped and snatched himself back.

"Na, na," he said. No.

Thad put up his hands. What dreadful things had Havoc done that made the boy fear being touched? *"All right. I'll take your word. We should leave now."*

At that moment, Sofiya came galloping up on her clockwork horse with Blackie on a lead rein behind her. "What happened?" she demanded in English. "Did you get the invention? Where is it?"

"Havoc set off a doomsday device to destroy the castle," Thad said shortly. He set Dante back on his shoulder. "I had time to save the device or the boy. Not both."

Sofiya went pale. "Our employer will be . . . upset."

"That I saved a human being instead of a machine?" Thad snarled. "Your employer can have the damn money back."

She looked away and her voice dropped. "You do not understand how important this was to him."

"He'll have to do without." Thad jerked a thumb at the burning castle. "It seems safe to say Havoc's machine is gone."

"Hm." Sofiya stared at the leaping flames, her mouth a hard, white line. The horse stamped a foot and snorted. "There will be trouble, Mr. Sharpe. A great deal of trouble."

"Applesauce," said Dante.

"Thank you," the boy said in a clear, piping voice.

Thad turned to him in surprise. "You speak English?"

"Thank you," the boy repeated softly. "For taking me out of there."

It was like hearing David again. Thad's throat thickened, and he coughed. "It's all . . . I mean, I'm glad to do it, son."

Son. He should have chosen a different word. Well, the boy wouldn't know. He knelt in front of the boy while Sofiya shifted impatiently atop her brass horse.

"What's your name?" Thad asked.

The boy shrugged.

"You don't know?" Thad said, puzzled. "Or you don't remember?"

"I don't have one," the boy said. "Mr. Havoc called me *boy*."

"What about before that?" Thad said. "What did your parents call you?"

"I don't know."

Thad thought of the brains in Havoc's laboratory and outrage bloomed like red fireworks. "He took your memories?"

"I don't know," the boy repeated. His voice was sad. "I'm frightened."

Incensed and angry and horrified all at once, Thad barely restrained himself from scooping the boy up and embracing him to give him comfort.

This is not David, he told himself firmly. *This is not your son.*

Carefully, ready to pull back if the boy flinched, Thad put a hand on the boy's shoulder. It was hard and bony. "Don't worry. We'll help you. We'll find your parents and see what we can do to bring back your memory."

"We?" Sofiya said.

Thad rose and looked at her. "Was I being presumptuous, Miss Ekk?"

"I suppose not," she sighed. "Come along, then. We

should probably check in the village first. Before we face our employer."

"Good idea. We can start with any families that speak English."

"In this place?" Sofiya scoffed. "Quite unlikely. But as you say, we must start somewhere. And I suppose we should tell the nice lady that her sister has been avenged."

Thad mounted Blackie and pulled the boy up behind him. The boy clung to Thad's waist with fearful strength, and Thad wanted nothing more than to continue protecting this child. He hoped to find the parents soon—and that they were nice people.

The ride to the village was quick and quiet. The sun was rising, putting hesitant fingers of light into an azure sky and setting Sofiya's clockwork horse ablaze. She looked magnificent, Thad had to admit, in her scarlet cloak and waterfall of golden hair, though she was nothing like his Ekaterina. The wealth represented by her horse and her clothing stood in stark contrast to the rough houses and loose homespun of the peasants in the village. As Thad and Sofiya rode into town, the people crept out of their houses, and Thad caught metallic flashes—knives and pitchforks and other farming implements. A tension rode the air, like lightning ready to strike. He glanced at Sofiya, who also looked uncertain. What was going on?

Thad pulled Blackie up. *"The demon,"* he announced in Lithuanian, *"is dead!"*

The people burst into cheers. The tension evaporated, and Vilma, the woman who had given Thad the vodka, ran forward, reaching up to press her face into his hand, wetting it with her tears. Thad shrank into his coat. Usually after a kill, he left without looking back. To deflect the awkwardness, he asked if anyone was missing a child. But no one was.

Vilma stepped forward again. *"The demon, he only took adults. Or dogs. Sometimes young people who were sixteen or seventeen, but never children."*

"What about anyone from a nearby village? Is anyone else missing a child?"

More murmuring. *"No, my lord,"* said Vilma.

"Then we should go look for his parents," Thad declared. "Ada. *Farewell!"*

And, ignoring their pleas to stay, he spurred Blackie ahead. Sofiya was left with no choice but to follow.

"I wonder how long it will take for this to evolve into a fairy tale," Sofiya mused once they had cleared the village. "A variation of Hansel and Gretel, perhaps."

"Or the Pied Piper," Thad said.

"What?"

But Thad didn't answer. Sofiya rode beside him, Dante gripped his shoulder, and the boy clung to his waist behind him. It felt strange to be surrounded by so many people after spending so many years alone. Even in the circus he held himself apart from the other performers. The sun had fully risen now, and he caught a hint of salt on the crisp air, though the Baltic Sea was many miles to the northwest. Now that he wasn't actually in danger, the long night and his aches were catching up with him, and he fervently wished there were some way around the long ride back to Vilnius.

"Your horse is amazing, lady," said the boy after a while. "He's very pretty and I like the way his mane stands up. Like a warrior. What is his name?"

"It has none," Sofiya said. "It is a machine."

"Everyone has to have a name," the boy said. He sounded upset. "Even a machine."

"Perhaps you could give him a name."

"Kalvis."

"The blacksmith god of the Lithuanians," Sofiya said. "Fitting."

"Because he was made by a blacksmith," the boy finished. "What's your horse's name, sir?"

"Uh . . . Blackie."

"That's dumb."

"Now look—" Thad began.

"I'm hungry," said the boy.

Feeling guilty, Thad pulled the loaf of rye bread from his coat. He should have realized. "Here."

But the boy pushed it away. "*Na, na.* I can't eat that. You have to give me something else."

"There isn't anything else," Thad said, annoyed again. He pulled the vodka jug from his pocket. It sloshed. "Except this. But you're bit young for—"

The boy snatched the jug from Thad's startled hand, raised it to his mouth, and pulled his scarf down. Over his shoulder, Thad caught a glimpse of metal as the boy drank. Thad was off the horse so fast, Dante nearly lost his balance.

"Applesauce," he squawked with indignation.

"What the hell?" Thad demanded.

The boy clutched the empty jug to his chest. The scarf that covered his face and hair slipped, revealing brass. Thad reached up and yanked the cloth away.

The boy was an automaton. The lower part of his face was metallic, with a square jaw that fitted neatly against a brass upper lip. A brass hinge was fitted neatly under a rubbery ear. The boy's nose was a smooth bump complete with nostrils, though it was made of copper and didn't match the rest of him. The upper half of his face was made of some flexible material. Rubber, perhaps. Eyelids blinked with quiet clicking sounds, and they even had tiny eyelashes. His eyes were wide and brown, but not glassy. Were they rubber as well? The boy's forehead and the area around his eyes moved with easy fluidity and realism. In fact, the boy's entire body moved with none of the stiffness Thad associated with other automatons, and his voice sounded pure and human, without the usual mechanical monotony or odd echo. His short brown hair even had a silky sheen. It probably *was* silk. Thad stared in shock.

"Dear God," he said.

"Bless my—" Dante's words were cut off when Thad grabbed his beak.

"This explains much," Sofiya said. "The boy remembers nothing because he no memories. He uses alcohol as fuel. Havoc experimented on living adults but this was his first—"

"Shut it," Thad snapped. "Just shut it!"

"Why?" Sofiya's voice was deceptively mild. "Did someone give you the right to hand me orders? Are you my good Polish husband now?"

Thad wanted to round on her, snarl at her, but kept himself under control. Sofiya was a woman, and telling her to shut up was already a serious breach of etiquette, something his father would have bent him over one knee for when he was a child. And why was he worried about that now? He didn't care what Sofiya thought. He made himself look up at Blackie and the thing in the saddle.

A child. This automaton had fooled Thad into thinking it was a real child. He felt like he'd been kicked in the head and his stomach oozed nausea. His skin crawled. The boy was the product of a clockworker, and who knew what it might do? It had been riding behind him for miles now.

"Thank you for taking me out of there."

But he was just a little boy. And he sounded like—

"No," Thad whispered.

"This boy is a masterpiece," Sofiya went on. "So lifelike. I am impressed. Havoc was much better than I imagined."

"Get off my horse," Thad said to the boy. "Now."

The boy shrank down inside the rags. "Are you going to hurt me?" he—it—asked in a tiny voice.

Thad was shaking. This . . . thing was the product of a murderous lunatic, the same sort of lunatic who had tortured his son to death. Thad didn't rescue such monstrosities; he destroyed them. This abomination should be melted down.

But when he looked at those eyes and at the way he—*it,* Thad reminded himself fiercely—the way *it* huddled on the horse, frightened and alone . . .

It's not frightened, Thad snarled inwardly. *It's only mimicking fright because its memory wheels are pulling wires and pushing pistons.*

A sword threatened to divide Thad down the middle and he didn't dare move in case it cut him.

I love you, Daddy.

"What are you going to do?" Sofiya asked. *"Are* you going to hurt him?"

Hurt him.

The sword shifted imperceptibly, changing his balance like the weight of the vodka bottle pulling him back from the pit.

"I'll have to decide later," Thad said in a stony voice. "Get off my horse. You can ride with Miss Ekk back to Vilnius."

"Ha!" said Sofiya with a snort. "You rescued him. He rides with you." And she turned her brass horse toward the road to make it clear there was no arguing.

Thad set his jaw, then mounted Blackie ahead of the boy, who still cringed away. "Put your scarf back on, boy."

Blackie was tired, and the ride back went slower. No one spoke. Sofiya's face remained pale. The boy held onto the back of the saddle instead of Thad's waist, and Thad tried to pretend he wasn't there. When they reached the outskirts of Vilnius, Thad started to turn toward the circus, but Sofiya pulled up short.

"No," she said. "We must see our employer and explain to him what happened, though I am sure he already knows."

"He does?" Thad raised an eyebrow. "Then perhaps we should take a nice stroll by the river together first."

"Sounds wonderful."

"Or get some breakfast."

"Equally appealing."

"But we won't."

"No."

"Because?"

"We are dancing, Mr. Sharpe. He is waiting for us to come and tell him, even though he knows the truth, because he is waiting to see how much truth we tell him. And we must pretend he doesn't know, and he will act as if he is unaware we are pretending he doesn't know.

Steps within steps, dances within dances, Mr. Sharpe. He likes it that way. In any case, I see no reason for me alone to bring him the bad news when it was your fault."

"My fault?" Thad shot back. "I didn't set off the explosive device that destroyed the castle."

Sofiya shrugged. "Come dance with him, then. I am sure he will understand. In any case, Mr. Sharpe, you may be sure that he is watching, and he is expecting you. If you do not come now, he will send for you later and you will come anyway."

"Does he employ big men who break thumbs?" Thad touched the pistols at his side.

"No men. And he won't hurt you, Mr. Sharpe."

"Then why should I bother seeing him?"

Sofiya halted her horse in the middle of the road, much to the annoyance of the drover in the cart behind her. Thad halted as well. "How many people are in that circus of yours, Mr. Sharpe?"

"What? I don't know. Sixty, maybe seventy."

"Close friends?"

"Some closer than others."

"He won't hurt *you,* Mr. Sharpe," Sofiya said, urging Kalvis forward. "Not if you come."

"I see," Thad said tightly.

"Applesauce," Dante said as they rode into the city. The streets were already filled with morning traffic—horses with carts and women with baskets and men with bundles and children with books. Morning smells of bakery and manure and sewer slops and beer mingled together. Church bells pealed some distance away. Sofiya's horse attracted glances, but not many—automatons were striking but not unusual.

"Does your parrot talk a lot?" the boy asked as they wove their way up the street.

"Too much," Thad said. "And I don't want to hear a great deal from you, either."

"Bad boy, bad boy," Dante muttered.

"*Tsk!*" Sofiya shook her head. "Such a dreadful thing to say to a child."

"He isn't a—"

"Ah! Here is the hotel."

The hotel was wide and stolid, built to endure the steady Baltic winter. They left both horses in the stable next door. Thad was about to order the boy to stay there as well, but Sofiya took his—its—hand with an air of forced nononsense and led everyone inside past the desk man to a door on the second floor.

"Stay here," she said, took a breath, and went into the room beyond. Thad felt guilty, as if he had sent her to take a punishment he himself deserved. *Don't be an idiot,* he told himself, and waited in uneasy silence with the boy in the hallway. The floorboards were scuffed but clean, and glass-paned windows at either end of the corridor let in dim light.

"Have you killed a lot of clockworkers?" the boy asked.

"Yes," Thad replied shortly.

"Is it hard?"

"Sometimes."

"Do you like doing it?"

That question caught Thad off guard. "I don't know," he answered without thinking.

"Does it make you happy? Your job is supposed to make you happy."

"Is it?"

"In a family, the mother stays home to help the children and keep house and the father goes off to work every day, whistling and happy because he likes what he does and he knows he is earning money," the boy said, ticking off points on his rag-wrapped fingers. "And the children have lessons or an apprenticeship or they play."

"Do they? And what about poor families, when the father takes whatever work he can, and the mother has to work too, and the children as well?"

"That is very sad," the boy replied.

Thad stared. "What do you know about sad?"

"It was very sad when Mr. Havoc opened up my head and moved things around. It gave me headaches and made me scared."

Thad felt his mouth harden into a line. "You are a machine. You can't feel anything. You can only do and say what Havoc punched into your wheels."

The boy didn't respond. He only looked at Thad for a long moment with those enormous eyes, and Thad found he couldn't meet them. He looked at the door instead.

"Doom," Dante muttered.

"Shut it, bird."

"Why do you keep your parrot when he's broken?" the boy asked suddenly.

"He reminds me of someone I used to know." Thad's words were clipped.

"You should fix him. And you shouldn't be so mean to him. He might leave."

"He won't leave. He's a machine, and he does what he's told."

"Applesauce," said Dante.

The door opened and Sofiya, still looking pale, gestured for them to enter. Thad obeyed with relief—facing this mysterious employer's wrath felt suddenly preferable to standing alone with the boy.

The chilly room beyond contained a bed, table, and a set of ladder-back chairs. On the table sat a box with a grill on one side and a wire trailing from the back. Several dials and buttons made a row beneath the grill.

Because they weren't moving, it took Thad a moment to see the spiders.

Dozens and dozens of the them clung to the walls and ceiling. They took up every available inch of space. They ranged in size from ant to dachshund. Some had winding keys sticking out of their backs. Brass and iron claws gleamed. Their eyes glowed blue and red and green, and they were all pointed at Thad.

Cold fear gripped Thad. He stood rooted to the spot a few steps into the room. The boy gasped and hid behind Thad. Even Dante fell silent. Thad couldn't move, couldn't think. The quiet menace of all those clawed machines was worse than an army of thugs.

Sofiya coughed hard and gestured at Thad to take a chair. He swallowed hard and forced himself to obey while Sofiya twisted the dials on the box. Thad's mouth was dry. The boy huddled behind Thad's chair, trying to stay out of sight. The box squawked, gave a burst of static, then hummed softly. The spiders didn't move, though their eyes never left Thad. The half dozen weapons he carried felt tiny and childish.

"Mr. Sharpe?" The voice from the box was low and pleasant, almost grandfatherly. "Are you there?"

Thad had to try twice before he could answer. "I am," he said.

"Good. The connection is excellent. Miss Ekk tells me you failed to do what I hired you to do. I am glad to hear the truth, but I'd like to hear your side of it, of course. We're all friends here."

"Are we?" Thad said. "Who am I speaking to?"

"Your employer, of course." The voice was smooth as chocolate and carried no trace of an accent that Thad recognized. British was all he could make out, but he couldn't pin down a region.

Thad worked his jaw. "Are you a clockworker?"

"I told you he is stubborn," Sofiya put in.

"You were quite correct, Miss Ekk. Mr. Sharpe, like you, I *take* from clockworkers."

"Take?"

"I take their livelihoods, you take their lives. Really, we're quite the same. We both have large collections, for example. What do you think of mine?"

"It takes my breath away," Thad said. "But you didn't answer my question."

A low laugh. "Indeed. I am beyond such classifications, Mr. Sharpe."

"You *are* a clockworker, then. Only a clockworker talks that way." The familiar anger and hatred tinged Thad's world red.

"You're rather like a bulldog, Mr. Sharpe. I think I rather like you."

"Do you?" Thad said through gritted teeth. Right then, he wanted to smash the box and its stupid grill, even though he knew it would do nothing to the man who manipulated it. Already his mind was running in a hundred directions, looking for weaknesses, searching for ideas. But clockworkers were highly intelligent, and Thad's main strategy for dealing with them was to catch them by surprise, when their intelligence was of little use. This clockworker had taken plenty of time to plan. Thad needed more information before he could act. Best to keep himself under control and see what he could learn.

"What is your name, please?" he said with forced politeness. "Since you do like me."

"Yes." A bit of static came over the grill. "You may call me . . . Mr. Griffin."

"Pleased to meet you, sir," Thad said. "I'd shake hands, but you seem to be out of sorts with that."

"Miss Ekk tells me you brought a mechanical child out of Havoc's workshop with you," Mr. Griffin said. "Is it here?"

Thad found himself wanting to correct Mr. Griffin's use of the word *it*. "Yes," he said. "Can you say hello, boy?"

"H-hello."

The spiders swiveled at the sound of the boy's voice and stared at him. He made a low sound and tried to huddle under Thad's chair.

"Then I suppose the night wasn't a total loss," Mr. Griffin said. "Should Miss Ekk have the hotel send up something to eat? You must be hungry."

Now that Mr. Griffin mentioned it, Thad became aware of a gnawing hunger inside him, despite the unease and the spiders. He was also was grubby and dirty from his crawl through the castle and the long ride. He thought of refusing on basic principle, then decided it would be idiotic—and rude—to turn down hospitality, and he didn't want to be rude to Mr. Griffin right then. Food would also prolong the conversation.

"That would be nice, thank you," he said.

"Miss Ekk, if you would be so kind? And while you are downstairs, please see to that other errand I mentioned earlier," Mr. Griffin said from the box. Sofiya quickly exited, and Mr. Griffin's chocolate voice took on an edge. "As for you, Mr. Sharpe, I would like to hear what happened and why you failed. In detail."

So Thad told the story. He felt self-conscious talking to a box at first, and the spiders and his anger didn't help, but it became easier after a while—he could pretend no one was listening but the boy. Through it all, the spiders remained motionless, and Thad relaxed somewhat. A maid brought the food—tea and bread and sausage and butter—and Thad continued speaking between mouthfuls. The boy, of course, had already drunk his fill of fuel some time ago.

When Thad finished, Mr. Griffin said, "I see. I can't pretend I'm happy, Mr. Sharpe. I needed that machine badly, and you failed me. I had heard you were quite skilled, and it disappoints me to be wrong."

It was meant to be a rebuke, but Thad didn't much care what clockworker thought of him. Interestingly, this clockworker didn't babble or go off on strange tangents like other clockworkers. He also stayed focused on what Thad was saying. Most clockworkers had short attention spans when it came to what other people were saying. Mr. Griffin had neither interrupted nor asked questions during Thad's recitation. Very strange.

"Look," he said, "I had no choice but to let the machine go if I wanted to save—"

"As you said," Mr. Griffin interrupted. "But by your own admission, the boy means nothing to you."

Now that was typical clockworker harshness. What did the boy think? Thad shot a glance behind his chair. If the boy was listening—and how could he avoid it?—there was no way to read his expression, if he had one, through the rags and scarf.

What does it matter? Thad thought. *He's just a machine and has no feelings to hurt.*

"At the time," Thad replied simply, "I had no idea the boy was anything other than . . . what he appeared to be. I'm sorry to have wasted your time, and I'll refund the money immediately."

A burst of static emerged from the speaker grill and Thad flinched despite himself. "The money is unimportant to me, Mr. Sharpe. I have other concerns."

The money was unimportant, meaning Mr. Griffin had access to a great deal of it. That was a bad sign. One of the few things that kept clockworkers in check was lack of access to materials. More than one clockworker had designed a weapon powerful enough to crack a country in half but had been thwarted by a simple inability to obtain enough need-more-ium, or whatever rare element they needed. Mr. Griffin was proving more and more dangerous as time went on, and Thad would have to do something about him. Unfortunately, the box didn't even have a cord running out the back, which meant Thad couldn't trace its source that way. The real Mr. Griffin could be anywhere in Vilnius. The man clearly a master of the wireless signal, another useful fact.

"You have other concerns," Thad prompted.

"And you will help me with them, Mr. Sharpe."

Thad shifted uneasily. "And why will I do that? You have to know my attitude toward clockworkers like yourself."

"I told you I was beyond such classifications, Mr. Sharpe. In any case, go to the window, if you would be so kind, and you will have all the explanation you need."

Warily, Thad went to the window, leaving the boy by the chair. The window looked down into an alley that ran between the hotel and the building next to it. At the bottom of the alley stood Sofiya. She was holding Blackie on a lead rein and standing as far away from him as possible.

"What the hell?" Thad said, startled.

"Something very similar to it," Mr. Griffin said.

And then a swarm of mechanical spiders rushed over Blackie. In less than a second, the horse was covered in brass and iron. Their claws flashed, and through the glass Thad heard both the tearing and ripping sounds mingle with Blackie's short scream. Sofiya let go the rein and pressed herself against the alley wall. The mound of spiders collapsed to the ground, seething and moving. Then they scattered and fled, leaving thousands of tiny red footprints. A dreadful pile of scarlet flesh and yellow bone surrounded by a spreading puddle of blood steamed on the alley stones. Sofiya turned and quickly walked away. Thad stared, his breath coming in short pants. The entire event had lasted mere seconds. He pressed his hand to the cold window glass. Every muscle in his body was tight. Fear and helpless rage mired together in a black morass.

"My stolen spiders watch, Mr. Sharpe," said Mr. Griffin. "They watch, and when I tell them to, they act. They have been watching you since you arrived in Vilnius, Mr. Sharpe. How do you think Miss Ekk's messenger knew where to find you on the street?"

The pain of Blackie's loss dragged at Thad, and he wanted to bury his head in his arms. Dammit, Blackie was just a horse. A stupid horse. But David had named him. Blackie was a link to that part of his life, and now it was gone, shredded into a red pile on alleyway stones. The outrage of it dimmed Thad's vision. He clenched a fist. There was a knife in it.

"Don't bother," Mr. Griffin said. "You have to know by now that I'm nowhere near you, and that I can react far faster than you can act."

Thad forced the knife back into his sleeve sheath and got his breathing back under control. "What was the point of that, Griffin?"

"I can watch or I can act, Mr. Sharpe. The one is more pleasant than the other."

Every spider in the room drummed its claws on wood and plaster in unison. It made a sound like a dreadful mechanical army marching one step forward. The boy whimpered.

"Stop it," Thad said. "You're frightening—"

"Yes?" Mr. Griffin said.

Sofiya came into the room, her scarlet cloak swirling about her body as she shut the door and sat down again. Her face was impassive but pale.

"Now I understand. You wear that cloak to hide the blood," Thad observed nastily.

She turned hard blue eyes on him. "No," was all she said.

"Please don't upset Miss Ekk," Griffin said. "None of this is her doing, and good operatives are difficult to find. We also have much to do."

Thad pursed his lips and turned away from her, already regretting his words. Sofiya wasn't the person he was angry at. "I'm upset, I need a bath, and I'm not good at dancing. What exactly do you need, Griffin?"

"I need," Mr. Griffin said, "to find a way to Russia."

Thad folded his arms in a shaky bit of bravado that Mr. Griffin couldn't see and forced himself to get a grip, push his problems aside and concentrate, as if he were in the ring. Problems didn't matter in the ring, only the performance. He would deal with the loss of Blackie and the boy's presence and the anger and the sorrow later. Right now he had to deal with other things. This room was a ring, and in the ring Thad could swallow any number of swords without blinking.

"That's the length of it?" he said. "You need to get to Russia? Hire a coach. Buy a train ticket." *And don't notice that I'm following you with my blades drawn.*

"It's more complicated than that. You had interactions with the peasants in the village. What was it like?"

Thad remembered the knives and the pitchforks and the tension in the crowd when he and Sofiya had first arrived back in the village. He also remembered how poor the villagers had been and how wealthy he and Sofiya appeared to be.

"Tense," he said.

"These are bad economic times." Sofiya sat pale and regal in her chair. "The landowners wring every kopeck from the peasants in both Russia and in the Polish-Lithuanian Union, and they spend the coins on their own lavish lifestyles. They draft the young men into their armies and force the young women to work in their palaces. The common people are slaves in all but name."

"You sound like you have experience with that," Thad observed.

"I am a peasant, Mr. Sharpe," she replied. "Does that shock you?"

"You don't act like a peasant."

"And you don't act like a human being. The world is an incredible place."

"Now, look—"

"At any rate," Mr. Griffin interrupted through his speaker, "peasant resentment to this treatment is increasing. In addition, the Ukrainian Empire has fallen apart, and that has emboldened the peasants elsewhere. Vilnius is quiet, but farther out, feelings have become, to use your word, tense. No one has actually attacked a landowner's stronghold yet, but the peasantry has begun to express its displeasure in other ways. Telegraph lines are cut. Herds owned by the landowner are raided by 'wolves.' Coaches are robbed. And the state-owned trains, ones that transport passengers and conscripted troops, are sabotaged. All of this, you see, is a roundabout way of saying that coach and train travel between here and Saint Petersburg has become dreadfully unreliable, and I'm afraid I cannot stomach the unreliable." Mr. Griffin gave a chocolatey chuckle, as if he had made a private joke.

Thad put his hands on his knees. "So you want me to find a reliable way."

"No. I've already found one. I need you to finish it."

"I don't understand."

"Of course you don't. I haven't explained it yet," Mr. Griffin snapped. "As you can see, Mr. Sharpe, I travel with a great deal of luggage, enough to take up two train cars. You are going to get those train cars to Saint Petersburg by the end of the week."

"By hauling them myself?"

"I selected you as an employee for two reasons, Mr. Sharpe. The first was that you were the best candidate to get Havoc's invention. You failed. The second reason is that you are attached to a circus train."

A dreadful light dawned. Thad's mouth went dry. Now more people were getting involved. He had to talk fast. "Look, the Kalakos Circus isn't a passenger train. You can't ask Ringmaster Dodd to take on—"

The spiders clacked their claws in unison again, cutting Thad off. The memory of Blackie's last scream echoed in his head.

"You will persuade the ringmaster," Mr. Griffin's smooth voice said. "You will use my money and your words and whatever actions you feel will accomplish this task. You will keep any particulars you have deduced about me to yourself. You will definitely not tell the circus anything about my nature or about the circumstances of our dealings. You will remember that my spiders are watching. They are watching that parrot you're so fond of. They are watching Ringmaster Dodd and his circus. They are watching the boy. And they are watching you."

Thad got to his feet, pale as Sofiya. "You'll get your damned train."

"So glad to hear it," Mr. Griffin said.

"And once you arrive in Russia," Thad added, "we're finished. You go your way, and I go mine."

Mr. Griffin said, "Just tell your ringmaster that the tsar loves a circus."

The signal touched the machine with a soft finger. It awoke, moved all ten legs, and felt its way through darkness. There were obstacles in its way, some hard, some soft, some sticky. The machine pushed them aside or found a way round them. Once it had to pull its legs in tight and scoot on its belly. Through it all, the signal's haunting melody pulled it forward.

The obstacles ended. The machine spiraled down a long staircase, skittered down a stone passageway, and found itself in a deep pit. Without pausing, it climbed the walls and pushed aside the long, thin objects dangling near at top. It sensed a vague warmth overhead and saw shapes of other objects around it. The machine didn't pause to make sense of anything—the signal continued its pull.

Freed of constraint now, the machine ran. Some of the objects it encountered jumped back and made sounds, but the machine kept running. Eventually it came to a long line of boxy objects sitting on metal wheels. The signal beckoned. Other objects moved about the machine in a rushed cacophony of sound and light and heat. If these objects noticed the machine, they didn't react to it. The machine dashed up to the boxlike object that was emitting the sweet signal, crawled underneath to the metal undercarriage, and clamped all ten legs to a metal bar.

It waited.

Chapter Five

Drums rolled and the sword slid into Thad's stomach. He kept his breathing deep and even to suppress his gag reflex, and he held the pommel just above his teeth while he stared straight up at the canvas peak of the Tilt, holding his neck and esophagus perfectly straight. Already the Flying Tortellis were climbing into the rigging in their bright outfits, ready to fly on the trapezes once Thad was done.

Thad let go of the sword, and the drumroll ended with a cymbal smash. The blunted tip was digging into the bottom of his stomach. He held the position and spread his arms.

"Bless my soul!" Dante whistled from his shoulder.

Always at this moment, the blade divided Thad between life and death. A wrong move—a cough, a sneeze, a swallow—and he would die. And yet he felt no fear. Here he had control of his body, of the sword, even of the audience. Anything that happened would come solely from him. He hung there, divided, for a moment longer, then he then drew the blade back out in a swift hand-under-hand movement and swept into a bow.

The audience gave a scattering of applause. Thad's performance wasn't at fault—the grandstand wasn't even a third full. Unfortunately, Vilnius, like the rest of the region, was enduring economic bad times and not many people had coins to spare for the circus.

Thad, who was wearing a pirate costume that Dante nicely completed, wiped the sword clean with a handkerchief he kept at his belt and sheathed the sword as Dodd, the ringmaster, dashed into the ring with his cane and his red-and-white-striped dress shirt and his scarlet top hat.

"Thaddeus Sharpe," he boomed, and the limp applause stirred itself to something resembling life. Thad trotted out of the ring as Dodd announced the Flying Tortellis.

Sofiya in her cloak and the boy in his rags were waiting for him just outside the back entrance flap for the performers. The sky was overcast with damp gray clouds that threatened rain at any moment and the air carried a chill, which added nothing to the circus atmosphere.

"That was impressive," Sofiya said. "And more than a little disgusting."

"Thank you," Thad acknowledged. "Speaking of disgusting, we need to talk."

"Hm." Sofiya pulled Thad farther away from the Tilt, onto trampled grass. "I told you before—not here in the open."

The boy came with them. His eyes were large. "You were incredible! I've never seen anything like it! You swallowed that whole knife! And then two knives! And then a sword! How do you do that? Have you ever cut yourself?"

"Only once," Thad replied, feeling pleased nonetheless, especially after the lackluster audience. "And you aren't to touch any of the —" He stopped. Why was he cautioning a machine?

"Go on," Sofiya said with a small smile. She seemed to enjoy taunting him with the boy, and Thad didn't understand that. Inside the Tilt, Antonio Tortelli did a double somersault into the hands of his father.

"Never mind," Thad muttered.

"Bad boy, bad boy," Dante interjected.

"I liked it," the boy piped up. "I've never seen a circus before. Does the elephant have a name?"

"Betsy," Thad replied absently, "though we tell everyone her name is Maharajah."

"Does she eat clowns?"

Before Thad could reply, Dodd emerged from the Tilt, brandishing his cane. Under the ridiculous top hat he was a handsome man, sandy-haired and brown-eyed, not yet thirty. Young for a ringmaster. He'd managed to grow respectable side whiskers, at least, though they did little to make him look older. He was also a talented tinker and blacksmith who could make basic repairs to automatons and even build simple machines if had the plans, but he wasn't a clockworker. Lately, Thad had noticed he moved heavier than usual, and when he wasn't in the ring, he had stopped smiling. His top hat seemed to weigh him down.

"There you are," he said. The calliope hooted in the background, providing music for the Tortellis. "You said you wanted to talk, and I have time now. Once the flyers are finished, the joeys will come on for a while, though even they won't get much out of this crowd."

"It's less of a crowd," Thad observed, putting off the inevitable, "and more of a sprinkle."

Dodd rubbed his face with his free hand. "I know. And frankly, we're in deep. If we don't get more people in, we won't even be able to buy coal to fire up the locomotive and leave town." He caught sight of Sofiya. "I don't believe we've met."

Thad made introductions, though he left the boy out, which naturally meant that Dodd turned to him. "And who's this strapping young lad, then?"

They had a story ready, that the boy didn't understand English and that Thad was thinking about taking him on as an apprentice, that Thad preferred to keep his name a—

"His name," Sofiya put in with a mischievous look at Thad, "is Nikolai."

"Pleased to meet you, Nikolai." Dodd shook the boy's rag-wrapped hand. "You can call me Ringmaster Dodd."

"Nikolai," the boy said, as if he were tasting the word.

"Nikolai?" Thad repeated, caught completely off guard.

"That is his name, isn't it?" Dodd looked a bit puzzled.

"Of course." Sofiya put her hand on the boy's shoulder. "Everyone needs a name. Thad and I are looking after him, Ringmaster."

"Are you?" Dodd said, apparently not sure how to react.

"Nikolai," the boy said again.

"He's an automaton," Thad told him abruptly.

A moment of silence stretched out amid the group. Sofiya stared at Thad, her eyes wide, her mouth an O.

"What?" Thad said. "Was that a secret?"

"I'm not supposed to tell anyone," Nikolai said softly. "Mr. Havoc would get angry."

Thad shrugged. "You don't have to worry about what Mr. Havoc thinks anymore."

"Oh. That's true," said Nikolai.

"Who's Mr. Havoc?" asked Dodd.

"The clockworker who built Nikolai."

"Ah." Dodd nodded. "Does he also build elephants, by chance?"

"Not these days."

"Now, look—" said Sofiya.

"Pity. Not that we have the money to pay for one. Is Nikolai joining us? Is that why you bought him?"

Thad made a face. "I didn't buy him."

"May I have him, then? I'll take good care of him."

"No!" Nikolai grabbed Thad's hand in a tight grip. Thad felt his metal joints through the rags. "You can't give me away!"

"He seems rather attached to me," Thad replied, surprised at his own regret.

"That's incredible workmanship. I had no idea he wasn't real." Dodd knelt down again to look at Nikolai who stared back at him. "Can he perform? We're short, you know."

Sofiya coughed loudly. A gleam of metal caught Thad's eye and he glanced up. A spider was perched on top of the Tilt, the main tent. Thad tensed. The memory of Blackie's blood spread through his mind. Even as he watched, the spider moved unhurriedly around the curve of canvas and out of sight. The outrage returned and made Thad's hands shake. A clockworker was forcing him to betray his friends.

Just do it now, he thought. *And plan for later.*

Thad cleared his own throat. "At any rate, Dodd, I did want to ask—"

"We have an offer for you," Sofiya interrupted.

"I thought I was going to do this," Thad protested.

· Sofiya ignored him. "Ringmaster Dodd, I work for a man who wishes for your circus to appear in Russia. Saint Petersburg."

"The capital," Dodd said. "Why?"

"Mr. Griffin," Thad said, jumping in, "is a difficult traveler and needs a train to take him. He's willing to pay quite a lot if we can get him there in the next few days."

Dodd shook his head. "Why doesn't this Mr. Griffin take a passenger train?"

"That would be unwise of him," Sofiya said. "You have heard of the unrest, have you not? Bad economic times." And she explained the uprisings that made train travel difficult.

"Ah. And you think the peasants won't bother a circus," Dodd finished for her.

Thad pursed his lips and glanced around for spiders. "You have it. And once we're there, we could perform for the Russians. Perhaps even the tsar. It's a wonderful opportunity."

"Is it?" A hard look crossed Dodd's face. "I remember a wonderful opportunity that took us to Kiev."

Uh-oh. This wasn't going well. "Everyone loves a circus," Thad said, but it sounded lame in his ears. "No one will bother you. Us."

The spider on the Tilt was back. A second one came with it. They seemed to be following the conversation. Thad had to force himself to pay attention to Dodd.

The ringmaster shook his head. "The last time we took on passengers, the Gonta-Zalizniaks nearly killed us all."

"Look, you said yourself that if we don't get more people in to see us, the circus will be stranded here in Lithuania." Thad worked to keep the desperation out of his voice. The worst part was that he agreed with Dodd, and was arguing on behalf of something he hated. He felt like he'd been rolling in pig manure. "Do you honestly think we'll be getting more people in ever? Today's Saturday, and the stands aren't even half full." *Come on, Dodd. This is quick money. An easy choice.*

"The tsar does enjoy a circus," Sofiya said. She had seen the spiders, too.

"We're not much of a circus anymore." Dodd drew his cane through his fingers. "The Gonta-Zalizniaks destroyed our mechanical elephant, and we lost all our other machines in the flood of Kiev. Even mine were wiped away. Half our performers scarpered during the attack, and we haven't found them. Hell, Nathan's the manager, but he's had to go back to clowning to fill in the gaps."

He gestured at the ring, where a red-haired joey was scampering about the ring with a dripping white bucket.

"We're a shadow of what we were." Dodd sighed. "Look, I wasn't going to say anything until later, but Nathan and I have talked, and we're thinking that we should cash the whole thing in. It's time for the Kalakos to end."

Ice stabbed Thad's chest. "Good Lord!" He touched the ringmaster's striped shoulder despite himself. "I knew it was bad, but not that bad."

Dodd looked away. His expression drooped like a collapsing tent. "We're not someone who can play for a tsar.

There's no point in going to Russia. Today's our last performance."

"I like the clowns," Nikolai piped up. "That one poured whitewash down his friend's trousers."

"You can't mean that!" Thad forgot about the spiders, forgot about Sofiya, forgot about Mr. Griffin. "The Kalakos is an institution. It dates back to the commedia dell'arte! This was the first circus to use automatons. Your clowns perfected the mirror gag. The Tortellis have flown here for generations. Every carny and circus runner in the world knows the name. You can't close down!"

"I'm sorry, Thad. Nathan felt the same way at first, but . . ." Dodd trailed off and Thad held his breath. The ringmaster stared at the ground for a long moment, not knowing he balanced on a knife blade. If Dodd refused, he and everyone in the circus would die today. If he accepted, they were probably only putting off their destruction until later.

"You haven't even heard the offer yet," Thad said desperately.

Dodd was still staring at the ground. "One man couldn't possibly offer enough to—"

Sofiya named a figure. Dodd's head snapped back up. "That much?" he breathed.

Sofiya flicked a glance at the watching spiders, then nodded.

Dodd put a hand to his face. "Good Lord. I don't know, Miss Ekk. That would keep us going even if we played to an empty Tilt for a month, but I'm not sure that it's worth a trip through difficult territory. And winter's coming. Saint Petersburg is difficult in winter."

Another spider had appeared, this time clinging onto

the side of a passing wagon. Thad swallowed hard. Black guilt crawled over him. He was bringing a monster into the fold—a whole swarm of them. He was a traitor of the worst sort, offering to save the circus with one hand and feeding it poison with the other. His skin crawled. The words didn't want to come, but he forced them out.

"A circus is its people," he said. Half a dozen spiders were now lined up along the slope of the tilt, and their claws gleamed. One of them edged forward. "A circus is art and show and performance. Not machinery." *Come on, Dodd. Swallow the poison.*

"Are all these people going to lose their lives?" Nikolai asked.

"Jobs," Thad said hurriedly. "They'll lose their jobs. It's up to Ringmaster Dodd, Nikolai. He can save the Kalakos Circus, if he wants to."

"Uh . . ." Dodd said.

"Just take it," Thad urged.

"Please, mister?" Nikolai said. "We can't let the circus die. All the elephants would be hungry."

There was a long pause. Sofiya started to speak, but Thad trod on her foot. At last Dodd said, "All right. Tell this Mr. Griffin it's a deal. We'll leave as soon as we pull down the Tilt and buy some coal."

"Hooray!" Nikolai clapped his hands. "I want to teach the elephants Russian."

Thad breathed out heavily and glanced at the Tilt. The spiders were gone.

Within the hour, two boxcars pulled by a team of oxen arrived at the circus grounds. Sofiya paid the drover and a roustabout supervised getting them hitched to the back of the circus train, all without opening either of them. Thad wondered what the hell was inside them. They were clearly locked against prying eyes, at any rate. Piotr Markovich, the strongman roustabout who was hitching the boxcars, appeared incurious, but Thad could see him examining them out of the corner of his eye. Rumors flew around the circus about the true nature of Mr. Griffin, and Thad had been avoiding people and their questions ever since Dodd had made the announcement. Sofiya, for her part, avoided Thad, for all that he tried to corner her for a talk, while Nikolai stuck close to Thad. It made for a strange dance.

The boxcars, plain and brown, stood out among the brightly painted circus cars like a clump of poisoned leaves on a scarlet maple. Their arrival would have commanded rather more attention if everyone hadn't been so busy. Already the Tilt was coming down, collapsing as gracefully as a duchess fainting in a hoopskirt, and animal cages and circus carts trundled into the train. A sprinkle of rain hurried everyone along. The horses, restless at knowing they would be confined, pranced into the stable car. The performers who lived in tents busily packed them away, and the ones who owned wagons hitched them to horses and hauled them into boxcars. Mama and Papa Berloni, who ran the grease wagons, handed out box lunches to those who wanted them. Most everyone would ride in the passenger car. Dodd had a private car, of course, and Nathan, the red-haired manager, always stayed with him. No one ever commented on that. Thad certainly didn't.

The spiders had all disappeared, though it seemed to Thad that he could feel their hard eyes on him anyway.

He told Nikolai to stay with Sofiya at the boxcars and went back to his wagon, where he managed a quick wash and change of clothes, then set about packing. There wasn't much to do, really. Smart travelers kept everything put away and ready to go at a moment's notice, and Thad was tidy by nature. He emptied the stove, ran a quick inventory of weapons and tools, and was heading out to borrow a horse so he could bring his wagon to the train when a quiet voice behind him said, "Can I help?"

Thad jerked around. Nikolai was there. His scarf had slipped, revealing dark hair, and the upper half of his face showed dark eyes. With his lower face still obscured, he looked perfectly human. A masterpiece indeed.

"I don't need help," Thad said shortly. "And you shouldn't be wandering around by yourself. I told you to stay with Sofiya."

"You're supposed to give me something to do," Nikolai said firmly. "Even if it's little."

"Little?"

"Unimportant. So I can learn how to do it, too. And to keep me out of trouble."

Thad cocked his head. "Have you been getting into trouble?"

"You wouldn't know," Nikolai countered, "because you haven't been watching. You're supposed to watch."

A sting touched Thad's heart. "How would you know that?" he said.

But Nikolai just looked at him with relentless brown eyes. A long silence stretched between them.

"Bless my soul," Dante said at last.

"I am not responsible for you," Thad blurted out. "I'm not."

Nikolai still didn't respond. He merely stood there, wrapped in accusing rags.

A spark of anger crackled inside Thad now. "You're a machine. You have no right, no right to look at me in that manner!"

"You saved me from the bad man," Nikolai said in his firm voice. "You're supposed to take care of me now. That's the way it is."

"There's not any way—"

"I'm hungry," Nikolai interrupted.

"Hungry," Dante echoed. "I'm hungry."

"You aren't hungry," Thad said to—well, he wasn't sure who he was speaking to. "I just fed you."

"Hungry," Dante repeated. "Hungry."

"I'm hungry," Nikolai said.

Something small shifted inside Thad. For a moment he was back in the knife shop in Warsaw, with the smell of metal shavings and mineral oil and old water, with David tugging at his sleeve. But David lay beyond hunger now, beyond fear, beyond embrace. Snow lay cold on his grave in long Warsaw winters. In Thad's quieter moments he thought perhaps Ekaterina might be holding David in some quiet, gentle place where they waited for him. Perhaps Ekaterina told David stories and sang him songs and he laughed and put his hands on her face. And then he remembered how David's eyes had become fixed on the clockworker's table and how his chest had stilled—an automaton shutting down. The warm, gentle place faded and the snow returned.

"Inside." Thad turned smartly back into the wagon, where a bit of rummaging turned up a bottle of brandy Thad mostly used for cleaning the cuts that were an occupational hazard. Nikolai accepted it and pulled down his scarf. His metal jaw and the hinge that fastened it to his skull nauseated Thad and he looked away as Nikolai raised the bottle. His initial revulsion warred with an impulse to stop a mere child from drinking heavy liquor.

Everything should be clear. He should simply take Niko—the *machine's* head off and sell his body to a smith to be melted down. Yet that thought made him sick, and he felt guilty for thinking it, and he didn't understand why he felt guilty. The mishmash was all very odd, and he felt out of sorts. Someone else had slid a sword down his throat, and he didn't dare move.

He sat down on the bed, pulled a brass key from a chain around his neck, and inserted it into Dante's back, hoping the familiar task would steady him. Silence filled the room, heavy as molten iron. Thad abruptly noticed the boy was standing with his back to the wall of dismembered souvenirs, almost as if he were one of them. An image of Nikolai's arm nailed to the wall invaded Thad's head.

"Let's go back outside," he said abruptly, and ushered the boy down the short steps to the ground. The cloudy sky still threatened rain.

"Hungry," Dante said in Thad's hands.

"How . . . how often do you need to eat?" Thad asked, winding Dante's key. Perhaps he should take a nip himself.

Nikolai pulled his scarf back up, and he looked like a normal boy again. "It depends on how much I use. If I am quiet, I use very little. If I run or jump, I use more."

"What happens if you don't get any . . . er, food?"

"It's very painful. Then I become tired. Then I just stop. I don't like it. Do you like it when you can't eat?"

"I don't think anyone does."

"Done," Dante announced. "Done."

"You don't like me," Nikolai said. "Did I do something bad to make you not like me?"

Thad kept on winding, uncomfortable. "What makes you think I don't like you?"

"You called me a machine and you said I don't mean anything to you."

Thad wanted to say that the boy *was* a machine, that he *didn't* mean anything. The sight of the boy's inhuman face inevitably twisted something inside Thad's gut and made him want to back away, or reach for a weapon, or both.

He said, "I don't—"

"Done!" Dante shrieked. "Done!"

Thad was overwinding the parrot. He pulled the key out and Dante scurried about on the crushed grass in a furious circle.

"What's wrong with him?" Nikolai asked.

"Too much energy," Thad said. "He'll be all right in a minute."

"Why doesn't he fly away?"

"He can't fly. He's damaged. And anyway, I don't think he could ever fly. He *is* made of brass, you know."

"It would be nice to fly," Nikolai said wistfully. "Then I could go anywhere I pleased."

Thad gave him a strange look. "You're an automaton. How can you want anything?"

"I don't know. I just do. How do *you* want anything?"

"Coo coo!" Sofiya came around the corner of the

wagon at that moment leading Kalvis, her brass horse. "All the other wagons are loaded on the train and the stable tent is down. You are behind, and I have come to catch you up."

"You." Thad rounded on her, simultaneously angry at the woman and glad she gave him a change in subject. "I want to talk to you."

"Hitch up the horse while you talk. I do not want to miss the train."

Thad folded his arms. "You owe me information."

"I *owe* you nothing, Mr. Sharpe."

"Applesauce, applesauce," blurted Dante, still scurrying about the ground. "Doom, defeat, despair. Darkness, death, destruction. Applesauce."

"I'm tired of dancing, Sofiya," Thad said, deliberately switching to her first name. "You've sucked me into this little game without telling me why or wherefore. I don't know why or what you're playing at, but you're going to tell me what's going on or — "

"Or what, Thad?" Sofiya replied. "You will threaten me with your knives? Point your pistols at my head? Tell your parrot to squawk in my direction?"

"Or you'll keep suffering the way you have been."

That stopped her. "I do not understand."

"Griffin has a hold on you, just like he has one on me," Thad said. "His spiders watch your family, which is why you do what he says. Am I right?"

Sofiya's eyes strayed to the top of Thad's wagon. No spiders. In the background, shouts and cries from the fading circus continued. Kalvis waited near Sofiya with brass patience, not even stomping a hoof. A wisp of steam curled from one nostril.

"He watches my sister," she said softly. "This is what he says. She lives in a village not far from here in Saint Petersburg, but always Mr. Griffin's spiders watch her and wait for his command. Mr. Griffin pays me very well and I send the money to her so she does not need to work, but that does not make it feel much better."

Thad studied her. Sofiya's face was stoic, but there was pain behind the mask. He could hear it in her voice, see it in the way she held herself. He wanted to know more, but couldn't bring himself to pry. Later, he decided.

"I'm sorry," he said instead.

"Spaceeba. But in the meantime—"

"In the meantime, we need to formulate a way out of this." Thad curled a fist. "I don't like being lied to, I don't like being manipulated, and I definitely don't like being enslaved to a filthy clockworker."

Sofiya didn't respond.

"He's not like other clockworkers I know," Thad continued. "Clockworkers don't get along with normal people well enough to hire them. Not for long, anyway. There's something wrong here. What do you know about him? Is he hiding in one of those boxcars or is he coming later? Tell me everything you know."

She shook her head. "I cannot."

"Sofiya." Thad's tone was gentle now. "We can beat him. I don't like this any more than you do. I've convinced my friend to bring a monster into the circus. We can make a plan together and—"

"I can tell you nothing more." She smoothed her dress. "He watches my sister, and he may be watching us now."

"That's how they win, Sofiya. They get inside your

head and make you think they can do anything. They can't. They're only human."

Sofiya barked a small laugh. "I wish it were that simple. Nothing ever is."

"Exactly what does he need me for?" Thad pressed.

"That I do not know, and it is the truth." She sighed. "I am sorry you were pulled into this, and I am sorry your friends are in jeopardy. Truly so."

"I didn't like it when the horse died," Nikolai put in. He had edged up next to Thad. "It made me unhappy."

"I don't work for clockworkers," Thad said. "Not for money or anything else."

"That is why he makes threats," Sofiya said. "No, *threats* is the wrong word. He will definitely hurt or kill your friends if you don't do as he says. And he will do the same to my sister if I move against him. Those are not threats, they are facts. So for now, we must hitch my dreadful horse to your very nice wagon and bring it to the train, or the ringmaster will be very unhappy with his sword swallower and his new automaton."

Thad blinked. "Sorry. New automaton?"

"Kalvis." Sofiya patted the brass horse's withers. "The big flood in Kiev left no automatons for the Kalakos Circus of Automatons and Other Wonders. Ringmaster Dodd was quite happy to have him."

"Do you think Mr. Griffin might loan us some spiders?" Thad said dryly.

"Applesauce," said Dante from the ground.

"Can I ride him?" Nikolai asked.

"We should hitch up the wagon," Sofiya said.

Chapter Six

Saint Petersburg wasn't even eight hundred kilometers away. If nothing went wrong, the circus train could travel all night and arrive there by late morning the following day. Mr. Griffin would arrive at his destination in plenty of time.

Thad leaned back against the cracked red leather seat in the last row of the passenger car. Ahead of him, the circus performers occupied most of the other seats, sleeping or conversing or sewing costumes or playing small games with the children. Thad, for his part, always sat in the back so no one would feel obliged to talk to him. He stared fixedly out the window at Russian countryside. Trees were shedding their leaves and the fields were stubbly, stripped of every grain of wheat and rye, every head of cabbage, every single potato. Soon it would be time to slaughter the animals, but for now there was a lull between the two harvests. Normally, it would be the perfect time for a circus to play, but this was also tax time, and taxes had gone up yet again, creating the economic hardship that made the peasants unhappy. At the knife shop, Thad had always been aware of difficult times—people bought fewer new blades and were more likely to ask for older ones to be sharpened. When things got really bad, they didn't come to the shop at all. Circuses were even more at the mercy of hardship. People always needed knives, but they could live without sword swallowers. Now that winter was coming, the circus should be heading south to a warmer, wealthier country like Italy or France. They shouldn't be moving into the teeth of winter, towing a monster behind them. It made Thad tense and restless, despite his fatigue.

A small head leaned against his arm. Thad's jaw went tight. Nikolai refused to budge from Thad's side, and Thad had no method of keeping him away, short of physical force, and even though he knew full well Nikolai was just a machine, he couldn't bring himself to use force, not against something that looked and talked like a little boy.

And now the machine in question was snuggling against him, simulating mechanical affection for him. What demented mind had created such a thing?

"You look very sweet," Sofiya said. Her seat faced him, part of a set of four. The fourth seat was empty. Across the aisle was a stack of travel bags and boxes instead of more seats, so no one sat next to them. "Very comfortable. If you are cold, I could probably find a blanket or a shawl to—"

"I'm fine," Thad interrupted. Since they were at the very rear of the passenger car, the clacking of the wheels was louder back here, and even Tina McGee, who trained poodles and sat in front of Thad, couldn't overhear. They actually had a measure of privacy.

"I was not speaking to you, Thad," Sofiya said.

Nikolai yawned. "I'm not cold."

Now Thad yawned, and hated himself for it. How could watching a machine yawn make him want to yawn? But he'd been up all night and then had a very trying day afterward. This was the first time he'd stopped moving since. The rocking motion of the train served to make things worse, and his eyelids were drooping.

"Aren't you tired?" he asked Sofiya.

"Of course. But I am also hungry. I did not get a chance to eat at the hotel like you."

As if on cue, Mama Berloni, a large, round woman in a patchwork dress and a white head cloth, appeared in the aisle with a large basket. Her pink face was unlined, and her arms were as big around as melons. She and her husband had long ago discovered that those who supplied food to the crowds made more money than those entertained them.

"I find you at last," she said in her bouncy Italian English. "You eat. Sword swallower needs the big belly, like my husband. You all eat now."

"Pretty lady, pretty lady," said Dante from his perch atop Thad's seat.

"Nothing for you," Mama Berloni tutted at the parrot. "You just pretend to eat and make the big mess."

She handed out ham sandwiches wrapped in paper, boiled eggs, and slices of apple pie. Nikolai took an egg, but only held it. Sofiya thanked her and introduced herself.

"You call me Mama," Mama Berloni replied. "You get hungry and have no food, you come see me at the grease wagon. No charge for circus. But you do a favor for me later if I need, yes? You do for me, I do for you. That is how circus people stay together. Like family. Like you three now. Glad to see Thad has found a good girl. And this is a very sweet little boy. You're a very nice family. Everyone needs a family."

"We're not—" Thad began.

"Now I go see Tortellis," Mama interrupted. "Without me they eat nothing. Nothing!" And she bustled away.

"Bless my soul!" Dante whistled.

"See?" Nikolai said. "We're a family. We have a son and a mama and a—"

"I'm not your papa," Thad said firmly. He unwrapped the generous ham sandwich and took a salty bite. "Stop saying I am."

"It's the papa's job to correct the son." Nikolai set the egg down and swung his legs against the seat. "So when you tell me to stop saying you're my papa, you are doing a good job of being a papa."

Sofiya coughed around her apple pie.

"Now," Nikolai continued, "you need to tell me a story."

"What?" Thad was still trying to untangle Nikolai's first comment. "Why?"

"So I will fall asleep. Or you can sing me a song."

"I don't know any songs," Thad replied shortly. "And I don't sing."

"Your mama and papa sang to you when were little. That's what mamas and papas do."

"Well?" prompted Sofiya. "Didn't they?"

"No. Yes. Sometimes." He tried to get his foggy mind to work, and failed. "Look, I'm tired, and—"

"Why are you keeping this boy with you?" Sofiya

brushed bread crumbs off her cloak. "You claim you dislike automatons made by clockworkers. You claim he means nothing to you. Why not set him aside, then? Walk away."

"He's my papa," Nikolai said firmly. "Papas don't do that."

"I'm not going to leave an automaton to wander about. Who knows what trouble that might cause?" Thad finished his food and leaned against the window, arms folded and eyes shut. "Once we arrive in Saint Petersburg, I'll find a place for him."

As he drifted off to sleep, he heard Nikolai say, "Papas also keep their sons out of trouble."

"They try," agreed Sofiya, "but they rarely succeed."

Thad jerked awake. A line of warm drool ran down his chin, and he wiped it away. Blearily, he looked about. Sofiya still sat across from him. Next to her, Nikolai paged through a thick book. Outside the train it was daylight, but heavy and cloudy, so dark it was almost night. The train wasn't moving.

"Why have we stopped?" Thad demanded. "What's going on?"

"You know as much as I do," Sofiya replied. Her scarlet cloak poured over the seat around her.

"You snore," said Nikolai. He pointed at something on the page and asked Sofiya in Russian, *"What's that?"*

"A cuckoo," Sofiya told him.

"And that?"

"A cowbird. They both lay their eggs in other birds' nests. The false babies trick the parents into raising them as their own."

The other performers in the car were standing up and talking restlessly. Thad pried open the window and stuck his head outside. Cold, damp air burst over him. Ahead of the steaming engine, a large bonfire blocked the tracks. A crowd of men stood around it, and they shook their fists and shouted. Thad tensed and pulled his head back inside.

"Peasant uprising," he said.

"Dangerous?" Sofiya asked.

"You know as much as I do."

"Danger," echoed Dante. "Death, doom, despair."

"Your bird is so cheerful," Sofiya said.

Dodd pulled open the door at the front of the car. He wore an everyday jacket, but he had snatched up his scarlet top hat and cane. Behind him came a tall, lean man in an Aran fisherman's sweater and cap. He had deep red hair and carried a bag of juggling equipment. This was Nathan Storm, the manager who had recently returned to clowning.

"Piotr!" Dodd said. "I need you outside with me. Tortellis, you too! Where's the Great Mordovo?"

"What is it? Please explain, Ringmaster," Mama Berloni called out from her seat.

"Poor peasants. Desperate. They think we're carrying tax goods and money to the landowner, and they want it back." Murmurs rushed up and down the aisle. Dodd put up his hands. "Keep calm. We're going to put on a little show out there, just for them, and prove we're just a circus. Nathan, you and Hank begin with that team juggling act and the Tortellis will follow with some acrobatics. While they're doing that, Mordovo, you fetch some of your magic equipment from the boxcars. Everyone else wait here. Move quickly, please! Everyone loves a circus, but not when they have to wait for one."

In moments, Dodd and the performers he had named were gone. Everyone else remained in their seats in a cloud of tension.

"Is it all right?" Nikolai asked in a small voice.

Thad stuck his head outside again. Already Nathan and Benny, another clown Thad barely knew, were juggling clubs and flipping them back and forth at each other. Dodd stood to one side, his ringmaster's grin on his face. Piotr hulked near him, either to translate for him or guard him, Thad wasn't sure which. The enormous crowd of Russian men, easily three times the number of performers and roustabouts aboard the train, stood near the engine and watched. They carried pitchforks and scythes, and Thad hadn't noticed until that moment how dangerous such implements looked, especially in the hands of hard-muscled men who knew how to use them. Thad glanced in the other direction. Far down the way, past the brightly colored circus cars, lay the two drab boxcars of Mr. Griffin. Thad thought fast, then pulled his head back in.

"Everything will be fine," he told Nikolai. "You stay here with your—with Sofiya."

"Applesauce," said Dante from his perch above the seat.

"And where are you going?" Sofiya asked sharply.

"To get some air." He nipped out the passenger car's rear door before she could respond further, leaving Dante behind as well.

With all eyes on the performance near the engine, Thad was able to jump unnoticed to the ground on the other side of the tracks. He trotted down beside the line of cars in the dim light. The setting sun and dark clouds dimmed the light considerably, giving him cover. He passed the animal cars, pungent with exotic manure and loud with restless roars and shrieks. No spiders were in view.

He reached the first drab car. The sliding cargo door lay on the other side, and Thad knew better than to bother with it—noisy to open, very noticeable. Instead, he skinned up the ladder bolted to the metal siding. Just under the eaves of the car was a vent with crisscross bars. Cautiously, Thad pressed an ear to the chilly metal beneath it. Nothing. He slowly brought his head high enough to peer through the bars. Blackness lay beyond. He inhaled through his nose and got smells of wood and engine oil and metal shavings and paper, all smells he associated with a clockworker's work space. If there was a man in there, however, he was remarkably quiet and willing to sit in complete darkness.

Thad climbed down and slipped along to the second car. What kind of clockworker was Mr. Griffin? Why did he need Thad and Sofiya? Thad also remembered quite clearly the way Mr. Griffin had asked about Nikolai. In Thad's experience, clockworkers never did anything by accident. What appeared to everyone as insanity was actually extreme intelligence. Everything they said and did would make perfect sense to anyone who could understand it. Unfortunately for the people around them, clockworkers were able to convince themselves that nothing mattered but their own goals and research, which was why they treated other humans with such casual cruelty and disdain. To a clockworker, all life was absolutely equal—a rat, a stalk of wheat, a tree, and a little boy were all the same. Thad had heard of some religious philosophies that taught compassion to all life based on this idea, but clockworkers ran the other way— all life was equally useful for experimentation.

Mr. Griffin didn't care in the slightest about Thad or Sofiya or Nikolai themselves. He only cared about gaining knowledge or completing his experiments or finishing his grand plan. Mr. Griffin's plan or experiment must be enormously important to him if it meant keeping Thad around—Griffin had to know Thad was working out a way to kill him. If Thad could figure out what Griffin's plan was, he would have a leg up in ending the creature's life.

If only he had access to some explosives. A stick of dynamite beneath the boxcars would end Mr. Griffin's career rather quickly. But this wasn't America, where dynamite was easy to come by. Thad ran his tongue round the inside of one cheek. He was caught in a race. The moment Mr. Griffin finished whatever he was working on, Thad would no longer be important, and Mr. Griffin would no doubt kill him as a threat. And who knew what he might do to Sofiya and Nikolai?

He shook his head and climbed the ladder to the second car. What happened to Nikolai didn't matter. Automatons didn't matter. Machines didn't matter.

So why did it seem like he could still feel Nikolai's little head pressed into the side of his arm?

Because he reminds you of David, he told himself firmly. *His memory wheels make him act that way in order to ensure his continued existence. If you like him and view him as a little boy instead of as a mere machine, you won't destroy him. He acts like a little sweetie so you won't kill him.*

Another treacherous voice whispered, *Isn't that what all children do?*

Faint cheers and applause came down the track. Apparently the little performance was having a positive effect. Thad pulled himself up to the vent of the second car and listened a second time. This time he heard a soft chugging sound and the burble of liquid. No voices, however. He peered through the vent. The interior of this boxcar was lit, but all Thad could make out through the bars were some odd shapes of metal and glass. The glass especially drew his eye. It curved like an enormous wineglass turned upside down, but Thad could only see a tiny part of it. What the hell was Griffin doing? And where was the man himself? What man would subject himself to traveling in a boxcar through dangerous territory? That didn't seem likely even for a clockworker. Maybe all this was just his equipment, and Griffin was coming to Saint Petersburg another way, by ocean steamer or airship. The more Thad thought about it, the more sense it made. Mr. Griffin wasn't on the train at all.

Still cautious, however, he crept up to the roof. The curved top was clear but for the bump of the covered vent in the middle. His heart beat at the back of his throat from both nervousness and, he had to admit, excitement. He was a hound on the chase, a hunter on the scent. He had the power to stop a monster before he hurt more people, people like David or Ekaterina or Olga. It wasn't a life he had chosen, but now that he *was* doing it, he did find a certain grim satisfaction in doing it *right.*

Thad slid quietly across the boxcar roof to the covered vent. A heavy padlock secured the lid. Of course. At least he didn't see any alarms or nasty little traps. He produced his lock picks and set to work. The lock was tricky, but so was Thad, and just as his hands began to get cold, it popped open. Another cheer went up from the front of the train.

Despite the the fact that Thad was sure Mr. Griffin himself was not on the train, he was still careful to slide the lock free without banging it about or making other noise. From another pocket he took a tiny tin flask of machine oil, which he applied to the lid's hinges so they wouldn't squeak. Cold dread and feverish anticipation shoved at him, made him want to hurry, hurry, hurry. The performance would end any moment and the train would start up. A guard or sentry machine he had overlooked might take notice. The cold autumn air bit through his clothing. Every fiber in him told him to finish this and run. But he made himself continue with slow, aching caution. He lifted the vent lid just a crack, enough so he could crouch over it and peer inside. A puff of warm, humid air escaped, bringing with it a strange, sweet smell that was also chemical.

The dim light and narrow crack made it hard to see much. A maze of copper pipes ran in all directions. Something went *bloop*. Liquid gushed. Machinery whirred and clattered. Claws skritched in the shadows, and Thad realized that spiders crawled everywhere. They swarmed the floor. They crawled along the pipes. They clung to the walls. Many of them carried small objects or tools that Thad couldn't identify. In the center of the boxcar stood a glass dome with pipes and wires connected to it. Thad couldn't get a good look from this vantage point. He widened the crack a hair to see better.

A cold hand grabbed his wrist. Thad dropped the lid and twisted like a cat, a knife already in his hand. Sofiya stood behind him on the roof. Her scarlet cloak fluttered in the wind. His heart pounded hard enough to break his ribs. God—how had she crept up without him noticing?

"What are you doing?" she whispered harshly. "Leave! Now!"

He tried to pull his arm free, but her grip was surprisingly strong. "I'm trying to find out more about—"

"Now!" Her face was pale with terror. "He has eyes everywhere!"

Her fear was infectious. Thad's earlier excitement drained away, leaving him felt nervous and cold. Sofiya yanked him away from the vent back to the ladder.

"The vent's not locked. He might notice."

Sofiya swore but released him. Thad crept back to the vent and slid the padlock back into the hasp. It made a quiet scraping sound. The *click* when it locked made him wince.

A loud whistle burst from the engine, and Thad jumped. The peasants must have decided to let the train go through and removed the bonfire. Everyone had climbed back on board and the train was getting ready to move. Thad turned to head back to Sofiya at the ladder.

A spider clung to the edge of the boxcar. It stared at Thad with cold, mechanical eyes. Sofiya saw it at the same time Thad did and she stifled a gasp. Thad's knife was still in his hand. He threw. The knife spun through the air like a deadly little star—

—and flew past the spider into the fading evening light. The spider skittered sideways, then turned to scamper down the side of the boxcar.

A silent beam of red light flashed over Thad's shoulder. It struck the spider, which burst into a thousand component parts. Thad spun. Sofiya held a small rounded pistol of glass and brass.

Go! she mouthed, and started down the ladder. Thad followed. When they reached the ground, the train whistled again and jerked forward.

"Dammit!" Thad grabbed Sofiya's hand and together they ran toward the front of the train. Far ahead of them, the locomotive's wheels spun, gained traction, and jerked the train forward again. The crowd of peasant men, now smiling, waved at the train. Thad ran past the animal cars and reached the passenger car, which was already gaining speed. He reached for the rail at the side of the car's tiny staircase and missed as the car lurched forward.

"Faster!" Sofiya panted. "We can do it!"

But the train was speeding up. Still holding Sofiya's hand, Thad lunged and missed again.

A smaller hand grabbed his. Nikolai was there, clinging like a monkey to the rail. Metal fingers bit painfully into Thad's flesh, but he didn't let go.

"Jump, Sofiya!" he shouted, and wrenched his other arm around to help her. Sofiya leaped, and how she avoided tangling herself in her skirts, Thad couldn't imagine. She landed on the staircase beside Nikolai, still gripping Thad's hand. Thad stumbled and fell. The train dragged him now, legs bumping over dirt and stones, past the staring peasant farmers. His shoulders were on fire and his hands felt torn in half, but Sofiya and Nikolai didn't let go. They hauled him upright, and Thad managed just enough purchase for a small jump of his own. The others yanked, and he landed on top of them. Sofiya and Thad lay panting in a pile with Nikolai while the ground rushed by beneath them and the wheels clattered only inches away.

"Can you rise?" Sofiya shouted over the noise. "Only, I can barely breathe."

Thad sorted himself out, got himself upright, and helped Sofiya and Nikolai to their feet. Sofiya shoved the pistol under her cloak. "I think my arms are longer," Thad complained.

"Let's go back inside," Nikolai said. "That was scary."

The mood in the passenger car was lighthearted, even a little jubilant, as the trio slipped into the back. The circus had managed one of its most difficult performances and passed. Dodd raised his cane and hat at the front. Thad, Sofiya, and Nikolai dropped into their seats at the rear, unnoticed.

"Well done, everyone!" he called. "It looks like our mysterious benefactor was right—everyone loves a circus. Especially the Kalakos Circus, the best circus in the whole damned world!"

This brought cheers and whistles.

"And," Dodd continued, holding up a small sack, "Nathan has finished the accounting from Mr. Griffin, so I have the best present in the world—cash! Good silver rubles!"

More cheers, wilder this time.

"I'll be coming down the aisles for each of you. Don't spend it all at once." Small laugh. "Assuming we aren't stopped again, we should arrive in Saint Petersburg tomorrow afternoon at approximately one o'clock. We should also thank Thad Sharpe and our newest member Sofiya Ekk." Dodd pointed to them with his cane. "They brought us Mr. Griffin, and without them, the circus would no longer exist."

Everyone turned in their seats to look at Dodd. Mama Berloni and Piotr the strongman and the dark-haired Tortellis and all the other performers smiled and applauded and stamped their feet. The gesture caught Thad off guard. He smiled uncertainly, then remembered himself and stood up in the aisle so he could sweep into a bow. Then he held out a hand to bring Sofiya up so she could do the same.

"This is awful," she said through unmoving lips. "They are so nice, and I feel like a traitor."

"Just smile," Thad replied the same way, and they sat.

The applause died away, and Dodd came down the aisle handing out money. Sofiya straightened her cloak. It had dirt and grease stains on it. Nikolai, still wrapped in rags and scarves on the seat next to Thad, picked up his book and opened it again.

"Now tell me what you were doing back there," Sofiya said in a low voice.

"Are you my wife now?" Thad shot back.

"She's the mama, you're the papa." Nikolai turned a page. "You have to do as she says."

"Do I?" Thad said, nonplussed. "I thought it was the other way round."

"Only in public," Nikolai said. "In private, the papa listens to the mama."

"You have some firm ideas about how a family should act," Thad said.

"They are correct." Nikolai's brown eyes flickered up and down the page. One of his legs kicked at the seat. "You made me scared. I didn't want you to be hurt or left behind."

"You don't look scared."

"Many of my pistons are moving faster, even though I don't want them to. That makes me hot and pulls my skin covering tight. It's also hard to keep still. I am scared."

"Perhaps you should reassure him," Sofiya said.

"How?" Thad said. "He's an automaton. He's only following a preset program."

"Does a child of biology do anything more? You frightened him, and he saved both of us. Therefore it is your job to set things right again, whether he is a machine or not."

Thad ran his tongue around the inside of his cheek. "All right. Listen, Nikolai, I didn't intend to frighten you or speed up your pistons or tighten your skin."

"You don't mean those words." Nikolai kept his eyes on the book. "Your voice is . . . is . . ."

"I believe you want the word *sarcastic*," Sofiya supplied.

"Sarcastic. That's wicked. Isn't it?"

Sofiya nodded, a small smile on her lips. "And so soon after you saved him. I wouldn't have thought it."

"Why do you care?" Thad demanded. "What does any of this matter to you?"

"Should it *not* matter?" Sofiya returned.

"Look, I don't want—all right." Thad changed his tone. "I'm sorry, Nikolai. I didn't want to scare you. Here." And he patted Nikolai on the shoulder. "And . . . thank you. For saving me. Us. You did . . . good work."

"I think that's better." Nikolai gave a little sigh. "I feel . . . slower. That is the proper way for a papa to behave."

Thad wanted to be angry again, but he was just too tired. "Certainly, Niko, certainly."

This seemed to satisfy the little automaton even further, and went back to paging through his book. "'The victim of the cuckoo's brood parasitism will feed and tend the baby cuckoo, even when the baby pushes the natural-born offspring out and begins to outgrow the nest,'" he read aloud. "'On the rare instances that the parasitized parents abandon the baby cuckoo to build a new nest elsewhere, the mother cuckoo who laid the parasite egg will follow the parasitized parents and destroy their new nest, thus encouraging them to continue raising her offspring.'"

Sofiya leaned forward again and tapped Thad on the knee.

"You still have not explained to me what you were thinking," she said. "Or what you were doing. Or what you found."

Thad automatically glanced round, but saw no sign of spiders. "We must find a way to kill Mr. Griffin, and for that I need information. To tell the truth, I don't think he's on this train." And he explained his reasoning.

"No," Sofiya said when he finished. "He is in that boxcar."

"How do you know that?"

"He told me he would be there."

"And he would never lie?"

"Mr. Griffin is very careful about his safety. Ocean liners sink. Airships crash. Trains are not perfect, but they are the best choice. Being in a boxcar would not bother him in the slightest."

"How long have you worked for him?"

"Not quite six months."

"Sofiya, you need to tell me everything you know about him. You have to understand that his only concern is his plan or his research. People mean nothing. The moment we become less than useful, he'll have no compunctions about destroying us."

She nodded slowly. "I have come to see that over time. But I cannot escape him. I tried once, and it ended . . . badly." She lifted her chin, and the scar became more visible in the glow of the train's lanterns. "He does pay well."

"How much money is worth your sister's life?" Thad countered. "Look, you know what I do for a living. And I can see you're extremely intelligent and capable. Between the two of us, we can find a way out from under his thumb."

"He is far more intelligent than both of us put together," she said doubtfully. "But . . . he does have weaknesses. I have seen them."

"Like what?" Thad tried not to pounce.

"He never comes out in public, and I have never met him in person," Sofiya said. "Like you, I have only spoken to him through the speaker box. He worries overmuch about his personal safety. This is both strength and weakness. He wants—wanted—Havoc's machine very, very badly, though I do not know why he wanted it or what the machine did. I am surprised he did not lose his temper when you failed to bring it to him."

"I don't like the word *failed*," Thad growled.

Sofiya waved this away. "His spiders do quite a lot for him, but they cannot do everything, which is why he hired me. And you. And the circus. Sometimes he makes me hire other men for him. I have already telegraphed Saint Petersburg for men to haul his boxcars away when we arrive."

"I wonder." Thad drummed his fingers on the seat. "Perhaps the speaker box gives him some sort of . . . barrier or filter that lets him handle people effectively."

"Perhaps," Sofiya agreed. "You took a terrible and foolish risk out there. If he had seen you, he would have assumed your horse taught you nothing and killed someone in this circus."

"He didn't see me."

"He would have, if I hadn't come. I just hope he doesn't notice that a spider went missing."

Thad changed the subject. "Where did you get that pistol?"

"I bought it." She touched her skirt. "It will take a great deal of cranking to recharge the battery now."

"I can help," Nikolai put in. "But I will need strong brandy first."

"Thank you, little one," Sofiya said absently. "Perhaps later. What did you learn of him, Thad? Since you risked so much, I hope you brought something back."

"He travels with a lot of equipment," Thad replied, "but I don't think it's all research or laboratory equipment. It's for something else. A lot of copper and glassware. Delicate. That may be one of the reasons he needs to travel by train."

"Glassware. Hm. What did—"

Two children tumbled into their seating area with

giggles and gasps. They had dark hair and eyes and were clearly brother and sister. *"Buon giorno!"* the girl said.

Thad's Italian was poor—he was better with Eastern languages. But he could get along. *"Buon giorno, Bianca e Claudio,"* he said. Nikolai looked up sharply.

"Chi è questo?" Claudio Tortelli asked, pointing at Nikolai. Claudio was eight, and hadn't started flying with the family act yet, though he expected to soon. Bianca, a year older, was already flying with her mother Francesca.

Thad hesitated again. This was awkward, and one of the reasons he had wanted to put Nikolai in one of the baggage cars or in the wagon car with Sofiya's mechanical horse.

"Il suo nome è Nikolai," he said at last. *"Lui è un . . . automa."*

"Automa?" Bianca leaned forward, crowding into the seating area. *"Non appare come un automa. Fammi vedere."*

"She doesn't think you're an automaton," Thad said to Nikolai. "She wants to see."

Nikolai, who had been watching this exchange with quizzical interest, set his book aside and pulled down the scarf that hid his face. Bianca and Claudio drew back at the metallic jaw and flat nose. Then Claudio leaned back in.

"Mi piace," he said. *"Chi ti ha costruito?"*

"He likes it and wants to know who built you," Thad translated.

"Puh!" Bianca said. *"Schifoso!"* And she fled. Nikolai wordlessly rewrapped his face. Thad wanted to slap the girl. Sofiya sighed.

Claudio gave another burst of Italian.

"He wants you to play with him," Thad said. "He says

he has toys and things up where his parents are sitting, if you want to come."

"I should go play with other boys," Nikolai said. "That is what boys do. May I?"

"If the Tortellis don't mind," Thad replied slowly. "But his sister will be there. What she said wasn't nice."

Nikolai's eyes went blank for a moment, and Thad thought he heard a faint clicking over the clack of the train wheels. Thad's earlier feeling of protectiveness slid away, replaced by a cold reminder of Nikolai's status as a machine.

"Sticks and stones will break my bones," he said at last, "but words will never hurt me."

"Applesauce," said Dante.

"That's the spirit," Thad said woodenly. "Off you go, then."

Nikolai slid free of the seat and left with Claudio, both of them already experts at staying upright on the rocking aisle.

"Alone at last, my husband," Sofiya said.

Thad slumped in his seat. "Not you, too."

She laughed, the first time Thad had ever heard that from her. The sound was surprisingly free and rich and eased some of Thad's tension. She was very beautiful, even in her dirty cloak and her hair coming undone. Thad decided he could, perhaps, enjoy a few moments of that.

"I only make a joke," she said. "But Nikolai seems to have cast us in a particular mold, no?"

"What are we going to do with him in Saint Petersburg?" Thad said. "I can't have him hanging about all the time."

"Why not? He seems to like you. Us. He is easy to care for—just give him a bottle of spirits from time to time. He might even prove useful."

"A clockworker built him," Thad said. "I don't trust him."

Sofiya twisted in her seat and looked up the aisle. Close to the front of the car, Nikolai and Claudio were playing on the floor between the seats with a set of toy animals. "And why not?"

Thad folded his arms and stared out the window, though it was fully dark now and there was nothing to see. "He comes from a monster who killed a lot of people. Who knows what he's programmed to do?"

"Hm." Sofiya crossed her ankles beneath her skirt. "You keep a clockworker's parrot on your shoulder. That seems a contradiction for someone who dislikes clockwork machines."

In answer, Thad took Dante down from the seat back and held him out toward Sofiya. "Say it," he ordered.

"Applesauce," Dante replied. "Doom, defeat, despair. Pretty lady."

"Say it, bird, or I'll twist your head round backward."

"I love you, Daddy."

David's recorded voice was loud enough that Tina Mc-Gee, who was once again sitting on the seat backed up against Sofiya's, turned around for a moment to look. Thad waved at her and put Dante on the seat back once more.

"I see," Sofiya said quietly. "I understand, and I am sorry. Again."

"I keep him. It doesn't mean I like him." Thad gestured abruptly in Nikolai's direction. "How does he do that? He's only a machine. Machines don't play games."

"It looks to me that he is *learning* to play. I think that is why he went with Claudio despite Bianca's dislike for him. Did you not see his hesitation? He was caught between impulses—one that tells him to keep himself safe and one that tells him to learn. The impulse to learn tipped him over the edge. Of course . . ." She trailed a hand over the arm rest of her seat. ". . . human beings do much the same, do they not?"

"He's not human, Sofiya." Thad sighed. "I don't know why you're trying to convince me he is, but—"

"No," Sofiya interrupted. "He is not human. But . . ." She trailed off again to glance over her shoulder. "But he is not an automaton, either."

"Bless my soul," Dante muttered. "Despair, death, doom, defeat." And Thad was too tired to tell him to be quiet. He was leaning back to close his eyes again when Sofiya cocked her head inside her scarlet hood.

"Do you think Nikolai should be destroyed?"

Thad's eyes came fully open. "I . . . don't know."

"Could you push him into a furnace and watch his face melt into slag?" She leaned forward, invading Thad's space. "Could you see his eyes dissolve into molten glass? Hear his voice break and crack into smoke and steam?"

Thad realized he was pressed into the seat back and forced himself to stop. The image she conjured up was horrible, and it mingled with the sights and sounds of David's last moments. His stomach roiled and mouth was dry. "Why are you asking me this?"

"Answer the question. We need to know when we arrive."

There was only one answer. "No," he replied at last.

"Perhaps we should back away a bit," Sofiya said. "Explore other ideas. Could you tell him he cannot stay with you? Could you put him out on the street and say he could never see or speak to you again?"

"Probably," Thad said.

"Even if he asked you not to?" Sofiya continued. "Because he would. He would say it was a papa's duty to take care of a child, and he would beg you to let him stay."

"I could give him to Dodd," Thad said abruptly. "Dodd already asked to have him."

"As an attraction for the circus, yes," Sofiya agreed. "He would probably even pay you a large sum of Mr. Griffin's money for him, good silver rubles. And then you would see him all the time, working for Dodd, doing as Dodd said, and he could ask you every day to take him back. Could you do that?"

Thad didn't answer for a long moment, then muttered, "I could melt down your horse in a moment."

"Ah! Now we are making progress. Why could you do that?"

"Progress?"

"Answer the question, my husband. Why could you melt down Kalvis but not Nikolai?"

"Because he *looks like a little boy,*" Thad nearly shouted. "Because he reminds me of David, and I couldn't push him into a furnace any more than I could push you into one, you damned witch."

"I know." Sofiya touched his knee softly. "I do know, Thaddeus Sharpe."

Thad was blinking back tears, something he hadn't done since the last time he'd visited David's grave. He felt drained, on the edge of exhaustion. "If you knew, then why—"

"Because I think you needed to say it out loud to someone." Sofiya rested her chin in her hand. "Are you hungry? I could ask Mama Berloni if she has anything more to eat."

When she said it, he became aware that he was both starving and immensely thirsty. "Definitely."

"A wife's duty." She rose to her feet with an impish smile. "You know, clockworkers aren't always evil."

"Tell that to David. And Olga."

"Clockworkers also build many fine things," she said, still standing. "They discovered how to use electricity and build airships and design efficient engines like this locomotive and thinking machines like Nikolai. They go mad in the end, but it is not their fault. It is tragic."

Thad's mouth turned down. "Especially for their victims."

The machine clung to the underside of the hot iron object. The iron tasted pleasant to the magnets on its feet, and the signal's constant ping created a reassuring warble. But after an interval passed, the iron object slowed, then stopped. It exhaled great clouds. The machine hung on.

The signal . . . changed. The machine listened for only a moment, then released the magnets and dropped away from the pleasant iron. It skittered out from under the huffing iron object and rushed away, past more objects, some moving, some still. A few jumped away with little shrieks or cries, but the machine ignored them. It scampered across a floating object that spanned an enormous amount of rushing fluid, and the signal rewarded it with happy tones. The machine found a tasty iron object that covered a tunnel. It pried the iron away, dropped into the hole beneath, and vanished into the darkness.

A tall, blocky stone building in front of the hole bore a copper sign on the wall out front. The sign read BIB-LIOTEKA ROSSIYSKOY AKADEMII NAUK, or LIBRARY OF THE RUSSIAN ACADEMY OF SCIENCES.

Chapter Seven

Brass spiders covered the walls and ceiling inside of Thad's wagon, and they stared at him with unnerving mechanical eyes. He saw his face reflected back at himself a thousand times. Thad tried to ignore this and concentrate instead on the speaker box in Sofiya's lap. She was sitting on one of the pull-down benches while Thad stood with his back against the door. In the distance came the faint sound of the calliope, creating a rhythm to help the circus set up. A warbling sound emerged from the speaker, and Sofiya adjusted some of the dials until it cleared. Thad was afraid of that box and what it represented, and he hated that he was afraid of it. He remained rigid, refusing to let the fear show.

"Are you there now, Mr. Sharpe?" asked Mr. Griffin's chocolate voice from the box.

"You know I am," Thad replied. "And I'm sure you know we're in Saint Petersburg."

"Indeed. Excellent work, including whatever you did during that inconvenient stop in the countryside."

Thad's skin pricked under the spiders' stare. "Thank you."

"One of my little friends went missing during that stop, by the way," Mr. Griffin continued. "Have you seen it, by chance?"

Ice water poured down Thad's back and his rib cage felt too tight. Sofiya's face stayed rigidly set in stone, though Thad saw her fingers go pale around one of the speaker dials. The spiders clicked among themselves as if whispering together.

"I don't keep track of your things," Thad said shortly. "Would you like to go back and look for it on the tracks?"

"Not necessary. I have more." If Mr. Griffin had possessed hands, Thad was sure he would have waved one. "I just dislike being wasteful. How is Nikolai?"

"He's well." The words nearly choked in the Thad's throat. *I'm making small talk with a clockworker.* "At the moment, he's with Dante, watching the circus put up the tents on the Field of Mars."

"So glad to hear it."

"Why?" Thad asked abruptly. "Why do you care what happens to Nikolai?"

"I have an affinity for mechanicals," Mr. Griffin said. "Are you surprised?"

"You've arrived in Saint Petersburg, as you requested, sir," Sofiya put in. "I believe that ends our business relationship, does it not?"

"How much does the circus know?" Mr. Griffin countered.

Thad tensed. "They don't know anything. They think you're an eccentric rich man who pays on time."

"And how much do *you* know, Mr. Sharpe? Tell the truth. I'm missing a spider, and that makes me … unhappy. Don't bother fingering those knives you enjoy so much. You can't move faster than one thousand, two hundred and forty-seven spiders. No, it's two hundred forty six. I forgot."

Now Thad's mouth was dry. He thought about jerking the door open and fleeing, but that would leave Sofiya in Griffin's taloned clutches, and in any case, he didn't think he'd get very far. Thad hated this. Thad hated *him*. Griffin had invaded Thad's home, his very life, and twisted it into something unrecognizable.

"You haven't answered my question, Mr. Sharpe." Griffin's too-smooth voice took on a condescending tone. "Have you lost the power of speech? Perhaps you need help to find it again."

A spider leaped onto Sofiya's neck. She didn't move, but she did cry out, and a trickle of blood ran down her pale skin between the spider's claws. Through it all, she continued to hold the speaker box. Thad started toward Sofiya, then stopped himself when all the spiders in the wagon snapped their claws in unison against the wooden walls and ceiling. Sofiya gritted her teeth.

"Stop it!" Thad shouted. "She didn't do anything!"

"How much do you know, Mr. Sharpe? Speak!"

"I know you're a clockworker," Thad said quickly. "I thought at first that you hadn't boarded the train, that it was a decoy or something similar, but I changed my mind. I know you need Sofiya and me for some sort of master plan, even though Havoc's machine was destroyed. That's all. I swear it."

A long pause followed. Sofiya sat perfectly still, the

spider still on her neck. Tension lay thick and heavy as sulfur fog in the room.

"What happened to my spider?" Mr. Griffin asked at last. "My precious little spider?"

Thad glanced at Sofiya. Her eyes were wide and white. It was his fault she was sitting in the chair with a spider on her neck and a clockworker determined to do something horrible to her. He set his jaw. "I—" he began.

"I destroyed it," Sofiya interrupted. "I shot it with an energy pistol."

The spiders in the room turned as one to look at her. "And why would you do that to me, Miss Ekk, when I am watching your sister?"

"It would have given me away." A calm seemed to have come over her. "So I shot it."

Mr. Griffin said, "Interesting. Please put the speaker box on the floor, Miss Ekk."

"What are you going to do?" Thad demanded as Sofiya obeyed. Her hands were shaking.

"I expect my employees to follow my commands. You poked about in forbidden places, destroyed one of my spiders, and tried to cover it up, Miss Ekk. Like a child, there is only one way for you to learn proper behavior."

Thad said, "Now look—"

"Miss Ekk, please give your energy pistol to Mr. Sharpe."

Slowly, Sofiya produced the pistol from the folds of her skirt and handed it to Thad. Their fingers touched, and Thad's eyes met hers. Her face held rigid calm, but her hands were ice cold. She maintained such control. Thad couldn't imagine how she did it. He felt every spider in the room staring at him.

"Mr. Sharpe," said the box, "I want you to shoot one of her hands off."

"What?" Thad said in disbelief. "I'm not going to—"

"Yes, you are, Mr. Sharpe. Miss Ekk cost me a hand, metaphorically speaking, and she will pay for it with one of her own. You were involved in some way, so you will administer the punishment. If you do not, my spiders will take you both apart, and Miss Ekk's sister, and I will find someone else to work for me."

Thad stared at the round little pistol. It crossed his mind to fire it at the spiders, but the pistol only contained one shot at a time.

"Mr. Sharpe," said Griffin's horrible chocolate voice, "if I do not receive payment for my missing hand in three seconds, everyone in that wagon will die. One . . ."

Pale and shaking, Sofiya held out her left hand. A small, stupid part of Thad assumed she had chosen her off-hand.

"Two . . ."

Thad held up the pistol. He couldn't quite comprehend what he was about to do. Guilt and fear, two of his most familiar friends, filled him like sour milk in a glass. Sofiya nodded at him, her eyes never leaving his. His mouth was dry as sand.

"Three."

Thad pressed the barrel of the pistol to his own left palm and pulled the trigger.

A red explosion of pain ripped through his hand. The pistol clattered away and he dropped to his knees. The tearing, burning agony ran all the way up his arm. A smell of cooked meat permeated the air. Most of his hand was gone. A blackened, pulpy mess that showed yellow bone was all that remained. He had dipped his hand and wrist in molten lead, and the horrible pain consumed his entire being. There was nothing in life but the pain. Flakes of charred skin fluttered to the floor. Thad's throat was raw from the screaming.

"An interesting choice, Mr. Sharpe," said the speaker box.

Sofiya touched his shoulder. He looked into her calm blue eyes, and then something pricked his arm. She pulled away a long glass syringe. The pain receded a little, and then Thad's world went dark.

Thad pushed through thickets and dark fog. Voices muttered and groaned like hidden ghosts. His limbs felt heavy, and he struggled to move. His hand hurt. No, it was his wrist. A woman was talking to him, and he fought toward the sound of her voice. At last he managed to pull his eyes open. The fog receded a little, though his vision was still blurry.

"Can you hear me, Thad?" Sofiya's accented English carried her worry. "Can you speak?"

Thad tried, but his tongue felt weighed down with wood chips and stone. He managed to croak, "Thirsty."

A cup came to his lips, and he drank cold water. The simple act helped wake him up more and he became aware that he was lying on a pile of quilts atop one of the fold-down shelves in his wagon. Sofiya was sitting next to him. The spiders and speaker box were gone.

"How do you feel?" she asked.

"Heavy." His lips were a little numb. "What—?"

"Try to stay still," she said. "The opiates should wear off soon, but you will feel their effects for a while."

"Where's Griffin?"

"He has left. Some men with horses unhooked his boxcars from the train and hauled them away. Do not worry about him right now."

Another thought came to him, and this one carried a stab of fear with it. "What about Nikolai?"

"He's with the Tortellis. He's perfectly fine, though he worries about you. Dante watches him."

His mind was still blurry. "I can't—what happened to—?" And then it all came rushing back. The crackle of the pistol going off and the horrible pain. He started to lift his left arm, but Sofiya gently pressed it back down to the bed.

"I do not know that you are ready for this," she said. "Perhaps you should wait."

Dread drove more of the dizziness away. "Wait for what? I . . . lost my hand, didn't I?"

"You took the shot Mr. Griffin intended for me," Sofiya said softly. "And you saved my sister. Thank you, Thad."

"You only destroyed that spider because I missed it," he said. "That punishment was meant for me."

"I am still grateful."

"Let me see," Thad said. "I want to see."

Sofiya nodded and released his arm. Thad raised it. The sensations were strange. It hurt, but not as badly as it seemed it should. He could also still feel his hand in a strange way. He had read of people who had lost limbs being able to feel them. Was it a mangled mess? Or had Sofiya cut it off at the wrist? And how had she done it? Why did she have a syringe and opiates with her? The ache grew more intense when he moved, though there was no trace of the horrible burning he had felt before. He would have to learn how to get along with only one hand. The implications were too powerful for him to think about. He brought his wrist into view.

He had expected to see a bandage, but metal gleamed at the end of his wrist instead. Thad stared at his new brass hand. The fingers were thin and showed spinning gears at the joints. The hand itself was blocky and sinewy at the same time. Parts of it were covered with brass skin, but most of it revealed the machinery beneath. The hand had been created from one of Mr. Griffin's spiders.

"I am sorry for the inelegance," Sofiya said. "I had to work quickly, with the materials I had at hand. So to speak."

Thad turned it back and forth in the light of the lamp that hung from the ceiling. A thick ring of scab and shiny scar tissue encircled his wrist just below the metal. He couldn't quite take it in. He tried to move. The fingers twitched, spread themselves open, made a fist. The sensation was more than strange. It was like wearing a thick glove that made his hand a little numb and unresponsive, but still his. Then shock overcame him. His skin went cold and he wanted to fling the hand away, but it was attached. His gorge rose and acid burned at the back of his throat. Fortunately, Sofiya had anticipated this and was ready with a basin. When the nauseating spasms ended, she gave him a handkerchief and the cup of water. Automatically he tried to take the latter with his new left hand. The metal fingers clenched around the pottery and shattered it, sending water everywhere.

"Sorry," he muttered, blotting ineffectively at the mess with the handkerchief. He was suddenly embarrassed at being in a sickbed in front of Sofiya, especially with her playing nurse. At least he was still wearing his clothes.

"It is understandable." She produced a tea towel to help clean up. "It will take time for you to learn its use."

"I can't seem to—" He stiffened. "You. I didn't understand before. *You* forged this hand. Not Griffin."

"Yes."

"You amputated my original hand and attached this one."

"Yes."

"You're—"

"A clockworker. Yes."

The signs rushed at Thad like boulders down a mountainside. The agility she had displayed on the train. Her remark about clockworkers not being evil. Her occasionally erratic behavior. Her affinity for Nikolai. The horse and the pistol. He had assumed Kalvis had come from Mr. Griffin, though she had never actually said so, and she had simply lied about buying the gun. His stomach roiled again and he swallowed hard to keep it under control.

"You're fil—"

She held up a hand. "That will keep."

"You're as bad as Griffin." He thrust out his own hand, the brass one. "You did this to me in order to—"

"I saved your life because you destroyed your hand for me. Is this something a lunatic would do?"

He closed his eyes. The world rocked around him,

pushing and pulling at him and trying to tip him over while he slid a sword into his throat. He felt for his blades, but they were gone. She had taken them.

"How is it possible?" he said. "You don't present like a clockworker."

"It is early for me still." She rested in her chin in her hand. Her fleshy, human hand. "I know what you have been through, Thad. I understand it from the inside. But you cut the world in half with your swords and your knives, and you believe everything must fall on one side or the other."

"Clockworkers are monsters."

"A clockworker *saved* you," she said. "An automaton *saved* you. What does it take for you to see us as something other than evil?"

Thad didn't answer for a long moment. Then he said, "We haven't heard the end of Griffin, have we?"

"I doubt it very much. He still needs us for something. Like he needed Havoc's machine." She wound a strand of golden hair around her finger. "I was the baby of the family, you know. I had four elder brothers and two elder sisters. My mother was a dairy worker outside of this very city. She knew to make cheese that melted in the mouth. My father, he was often away. There was no work in my village, so he often went to Saint Petersburg. Many men do this, and leave their families unprotected. And still there was little—my family were serfs and most of what we earned went to the landowner in taxes and fees. Ivan and Mikhail, two of my brothers, were conscripted into the army when they were thirteen and fourteen." Her face grew sad. "I still have not heard what happened to them. They are probably dead, fighting Turks in a foreign war, but no one thinks to write home about the death of a serf."

Thad lay without moving. Each word was a tiny nail that pinned him to the bed.

"There was no money, ever. My mother, she later found work in the landowner's kitchen as a cook, and then things became a little better. Cooks, of course, can sneak extra food away, and they also have a reputation for being willing to trade their bodies for little gifts from other men."

Thad stared at her. "Your mother let men—"

"Yes, of course." Sofiya straightened her cloak. "I know that farther west, people find this shocking, but in Russia, it is quite normal. The husbands of the women all know it happens but act as if they know nothing. It became better at home because Mama could sell the things men gave her. And we could eat twice a day."

"It's prostitution," Thad said. He couldn't help it.

"It is the world," Sofiya said. "It moves the way it moves, not as you think it should. When a woman's husband is away and she has a baby which cannot be his, she will take it to the forest or a lake and—"

"I don't want to hear," Thad interrupted. "No more."

"The man who kills the victims of the clockwork plague balks at the death of a baby who would grow up as hated and unwanted as a clockworker," she said. "How strange."

"Clockworkers aren't victims," Thad said. "David was a victim."

"Both cannot be victims?" Sofiya gestured at his hand. "You should exercise that. The more you use it, the easier it will become to control it."

Thad thought of refusing, then set that aside as unrealistic and childish. He flexed the hand and tried working the fingers one by one. It still felt numb. A clockworker had forced him to shoot his own hand off. He felt violated and angry and sick, and he wanted to hit something or yell or scream. Instead he made himself wiggle fingers.

"My mother's deed mattered little in the end," Sofiya continued. "Papa came home last winter festival. He'd been gone for seven months, and I was so happy to see him. He was tall and strong and he had a big brown beard that made him very proud. He brought me chocolate drops from the city, and a little toy dog made of painted clay. Grigori and Nikolai, my other brothers, came from their homes to visit."

"Nikolai?"

"I gave that name after my brother, yes," Sofiya said. "We ate together and it was a fine night. But the next day Papa was coughing. When fever came, we knew what it was. By then it was too late."

"I'm sorry," Thad said automatically. The thumb was especially hard to use. He folded it in and out, in and out.

"Papa died first." Sofiya's voice was matter-of-fact now. "Then Mama and Nikolai. Grigori lost his mind and stumbled away. You call it a zombie. I call it my older brother, the one who used to climb trees to pick apples for me and who could whistle so like a bird, he could fool them into thinking he was one of them. I found out later someone shot him. My sister Olenka . . ." She trailed off.

The pain Thad had seen in her before was back, though Sofiya was working to cover it.

"Your sister what?" he asked.

"She became very ill," Sofiya said quickly, "but she

recovered. I recovered from the illness, too, but I . . . I was different. I have seen things no one should have seen, and now I see things no one else can see." She paused. "I went into a fugue and built a sledge that could drive itself across the snow. It took me to Saint Petersburg. But Russia is not kind to clockworkers, you know."

"My mother was from Minsk."

"She was?" Sofiya raised her eyebrows. "Then the way Russian serfs behave should not be a surprise to you."

"My mother never talked about her life in Minsk," Thad replied shortly. "Ever."

"Perhaps this is why. Perhaps she joined the circus to get away from a landowner who—"

"We were talking about clockworkers," Thad interjected. He ticked off points. "England fears clockworkers. China reveres them. And Russia? Russia loathes them." He belatedly realized he was using his brass hand and stared at it for moment.

"True. But all three places use their—our—inventions quite happily. I knew in Saint Petersburg I would have to hide. It would not be safe if anyone knew what I had become. And then Mr. Griffin found me. I don't know how. But he promised he could help my sister. And he has, after a fashion. Olenka has everything she needs now, and does not break her back in the field—or in a rich man's bed."

"But Griffin exacts a price."

"Everything has a price." She tapped his hand, and her fingernail clicked against the brass.

"You are early in the process," Thad said. "You haven't gone insane. That's how you hid your . . . status from me and why you can still work with other people without being cruel or wicked."

"I imagine so."

A little heat came to his voice. "Doesn't it bother you to know that you'll go mad and die in less than three years? Don't you want to find a cure?"

"A cure?" Her laugh was like ice. "This is the most fun I have had in my entire life, Thaddeus Sharpe. Ideas slice through my mind like silver knives, and they carve secrets out of the darkness. I am very much looking forward to seeing what happens next. And then, when I finally go mad, I will forget everything—the plague, my family, and every scrap of pain. I can hardly wait."

Thad swallowed. He had never thought that someone with the plague would want anything but a cure. A number of uncomfortable new truths were forcing themselves on him today. Thad flexed his new hand again and changed the subject. "You made this out of one of Griffin's spiders, didn't you?"

"I did. I am very proud."

"Can he still . . . use it?"

"I very much doubt it."

"He orders me to destroy your—my—hand over one of his blasted spiders, and then he just *gives* you a spider to replace it?"

"He didn't give. I took." Sofiya closed her eyes. "The destruction of your hand sent me into a fugue. Your hand became a . . . project, and only my death could have stopped me from taking one of Mr. Griffin's spiders. Mr. Griffin knew that, so he allowed it. He doesn't wish me to die, you see. Not yet. I also think the entire affair amuses him."

"Amuses him?"

"It put me further into his debt. And now a clock-worker who uses spiders for hands has a man in his employ who has a spider for a hand. Mr. Griffin still has that spider as a hand, you see, even though you hate clock-workers. I think he couldn't resist the irony."

Jaw tight, Thad pushed aside the bedclothes and swung his legs around. The last of the opiate fog had faded from his system and he was feeling normal now. Except for the hand. He looked at Sofiya.

"You told me all that about yourself in order to change my mind about clockworkers," he said. "So I would see a person, with history and life instead of a monster."

"Of course. Was I successful?"

He exhaled slowly, as if sending clouds of thought to Mount Olympus. "I think," he replied slowly, forming the words as the ideas came to him, "that I am willing to work with you as long as we have a common enemy in Mr. Griffin."

"Good. And as someone who continues to work with you, I have one favor to ask."

"And that would be?"

She towed him toward the door. "It will be easier to talk about it after the cannon goes off."

The machine crouched in the darkness, listening to the signal, and learning. It learned words like *tunnel* and *darkness* and *metal* and *gears* and *memory* and *thought* and *knowledge* and *master.* The knowledge came slowly, over a period of *days,* another new word that was part of the word *time.* Other spiders, ones similar but inferior to itself, brought the machine metals of many different kinds. The machine touched the metals, tasting them with its feet. It liked them, became excited by them for reasons it could not name.

It learned the world *build*.

Chapter Eight

When they got outside, Thad discovered that the circus was fully set up. The striped Tilt held court in the center with the smaller sideshow tents trying to get its attention. Waiting behind like servants were the wagons and tents where the performers lived, including Thad, and just beyond that, the row of train cars. A web of ropes and stakes wove itself over everything. Sawdust and straw crunched underfoot as a preemptive measure to keep down the mud, and Thad inhaled smells of animals and machine oil and frying food. Marcus was playing the calliope in the Tilt, and the strangely haunting and jaunty music wandered among the tents with the performers, some of whom wore bright costumes, some of whom wore ordinary street clothes. A bit of Thad's fear and tension eased. It was the circus, and the circus was home.

He remembered running among ropes and canvas walls when he was small, playing jackstraws and deer-stalker, listening to the rain fall on the roof on the wagon—the same wagon Thad lived in now—while his mother sang in Russian and his father sharpened knives, watching the everyday sight of one of the horse girls in her tight sleeves and bodice and one day feeling newly strange about it, stealing a kiss from Gretchen Neuberg behind clown alley, learning to swallow swords and pick locks and throw knives, catching the eye of a beautiful, dark-haired woman in the grandstand during a performance in Warsaw, announcing to his parents that he was leaving the circus to marry his Ekaterina.

Leaving had been difficult, but good. He'd had his new life in Warsaw. But bit by bit that life had been whittled away. Ekaterina died in childbirth. His parents passed away, and he inherited their old wagon. And then David. When the last fragment of his new life had slipped from his fingers, he had pulled the old wagon out of storage and gone on the road, ostensibly as a traveling tinker and knife sharpener, but really to hunt down clockworkers. And when he'd come across the Kalakos Circus eking out performances in Prague, it seemed perfectly natural to join up with them. It was coming home again, in a sad way.

It wasn't truly the same, of course. Thad kept to himself these days. He avoided making close friends, avoided anything resembling romance. It was easier to pass time alone than to befriend people he would one day lose. Even if it meant being lonely.

Overhead, clouds were drifting in to cover the sun, and the air was chilly. Benny Mazur, the chief clown, stuck his head out of clown alley—the little tent where the clowns got ready—and called something to Nathan Storm, who was just passing by. Nathan nodded, then caught sight of Thad outside his wagon and dashed over, a wide smile on his face.

"Glad to see you're upright, then," he said in his light Irish brogue. He clapped Thad on the back. "Wouldn't want to lose our sword swallower to some stupid pistol accident."

"I told them," Sofiya said quickly, "how you were cleaning your equipment and one of your pistols went off."

"Oh. Yes," Thad said. "Stupid."

"And this one." Nathan swept off his cap, revealing deep red hair, and kissed Sofiya's hand. "Beautiful and brilliant. I hope you thanked her. She's our Russian rescuer."

"Spaceeba, ser," Sofiya said with a laugh.

"Our?" Thad was becoming more and more confused.

"Tsar Alexander is quite the horseman, and he was taken with Miss Ekk's mechanical horse — and her beauty. It was because of her that we were allowed to set up on the Field of Mars and, best of all, were called to perform for the court in a few days. So polish your swords, friend." His eyes sparkled with an enthusiasm Thad hadn't seen in months. "May I see the new hand, then?"

Thad wanted to hold back. But he was going into the ring eventually, and anyone who paid a few coins would see it. He may as well get used to showing it off now. He held it up and wiggled the fingers. The gears inside whirled with tiny *zing* noises.

"Nice enough," Nathan said. "Can you pull swords out of your throat with it?"

Thad looked at Sofiya, stricken. The idea that he might not be able to perform anymore hadn't occurred to him.

"Probably," she said. "He will have to practice first. Tell Dodd not to put him on the schedule until we are sure."

"My lady." Nathan kissed Sofiya's hand again and left.

"I love the circus," Sofiya said with a small sigh. "No one cares that I am . . . what I am."

"And I am . . . confused," Thad said. "Did you tell them you're a clockworker?"

"They deduced rather easily when I rebuilt your hand, Thad. They also think I built Nikolai, and I have not persuaded them otherwise."

"And it doesn't bother—"

"No."

"I don't understand." Thad was genuinely perplexed. "Three years ago, this circus gave shelter to a man who turned out to be a clockworker, and not only did he destroy their prize clockwork elephant, he also led a small army of other clockworkers into their midst, broke the dam at Kiev, and caused a flood that scattered half their performers. They *hate* clockworkers. With good reason."

She threaded her arm into the crook of his elbow as they walked. "You need to stop seeing the world as either-or, Thaddeus Sharpe. Dodd needed to be persuaded, yes, but everyone was very impressed when I saved your hand. I also brought them the money from Mr. Griffin. This helped quite a lot."

"And put them—still puts them—in the most terrible danger," Thad pointed out sharply.

"They don't know this." Sofiya waved this away. "I also brought the circus a mechanical horse so it can still be the Kalakos Circus of *Automatons* and Other Wonders."

"Did you promise not to go mad and kill everyone?" Thad asked.

"No, but I said I would look into replacing the elephant. That, and a performance for the tsar brought Dodd around."

Thad was working his brass fingers like mad, trying to bring them under greater control. There was always a short delay between what he wanted them to do and what they did, and that would be deadly in an act like his. It didn't seem real yet. It felt more like he was wearing a strange glove or a temporary splint that would eventually come off, revealing his real hand.

"I'm pleased to know everything is going well for you," he said with a certain amount of grim irony. "What are you doing in the ring for the tsar, then?"

"You'll see." She smiled, and Thad noticed for the first time she had dimples. "Wait a moment. How did I not notice this before? You spoke Russian earlier!"

"Of course." Thad managed a grin of his own. *"My mother spoke it to me every day. To me, it's as easy as English."*

"Then why have I spoken English with you all this time?"

"Perhaps clockworkers aren't as smart they think."

A cannon fired with a sound that boomed against Thad's bones. He jumped. Sofiya took his arm.

"We must go," she said in English again. "Hurry."

He followed her through the maze of tents, automatically ducking under and around ropes and dodging stakes. "What was that? What's going on?"

They reached the outer boundary of the area set aside for the circus. It appeared to be a parade ground or drilling field for the military and was the size of four polo fields spread out before one of the biggest, most ornate buildings Thad had ever seen. The building went on and on, in fact, block after block. It was three stories tall, with white pillars and arched windows and bright yellow bricks. Decades of stamping feet had trampled the field into reddish dirt and dust. A series of wooded parks bordered two other sides of the field, and the remaining side faced a wide silver river clogged with small boats and rafts. The circus was set up near one of the parks, not far from the river. Across from them, in front of the long building, stood a grandstand much like the one inside the Tilt, though this one also had a partial roof on it. Men and women in colorful clothing were settling into seats.

"Marsovo Pole," Sofiya said. The Field of Mars. She started across the flat dusty field toward the grandstand, her scarlet cloak stirring in the slight breeze. "It is named after the Roman god of war, of course. That building over there" — she pointed at the long, pillared structure — "is an army barrack. And that is the River Neva. The cannon is fired from the roof of the Peter and Paul Fortress on the other side every day at noon."

"Why did we rush so? What is everyone gathering for?"

"That." Sofiya pointed toward the River Neva. A wide road ran from the edge of the Field of Mars, between two blocky buildings, and up to a great pontoon bridge, easily four carriages wide and supported underneath by what looked like a long row of giant rowboats turned upside down. Thad dug around in his memory for what little he knew about Saint Petersburg and recalled that even though it was a city of rivers, canals, and giant islands,

Peter the Great had forbidden permanent bridges on the grounds that they were ugly. But either pontoon bridges were exempted from his ban, or Tsar Alexander had changed the law himself—Thad couldn't remember. The pontoon bridges weren't high enough to allow anything but the lowest boats to slip beneath them, which curtailed ship traffic on the river but encouraged thriving schools of rowboats, skiffs, and rafts.

On the other side of the river was one of Saint Petersburg's enormous islands. The bridge to it had been cleared of all traffic but for a single cart. The cart had no horse and no driver. It was painted gold and azure, and ornate designs and curlicues wound their way all over it like metal vines. Underneath the cart puffed a little engine that was currently following a strip of iron laid across the bridge. On the bed of the cart was golden cage of sturdy bars, and in the cage was a man. He was naked, and his skin was covered in dirt and filth. His hair and beard tangled into a greasy mess, and he clung to the bars with both hands and feet like a chimpanzee. Animal growls and snorts emerged from his throat.

By now Thad and Sofiya were closer to the roofed-over grandstand, and Thad could see the people better. Their clothing was rich beyond belief. The women wore enormous off-the-shoulder dresses of satin and velvet embroidered with metallic thread in geometric designs. The sleeves were narrow at the top and ballooned out toward the wrist, and the skirts were so wide and heavy with crinolines, a single woman might take up four spaces on the grandstand. Most sported fox or ermine wraps against the chilly air. One woman, looking pale and sickly, wore a formfitting cage of actual gold wire with tiny gears, wheels, and pistons in it that whirled and twisted the soft wire to bend it with her every move. All the women's hair was elaborately styled, curled and piled high and laden with jeweled pins or combs. Their faces were painted with rouge and puffed with powder. Many of the men wore military uniforms—bright blue coats that dripped gold braid from their chests and shoulders over bloodred trousers. Mustaches and side whiskers were waxed and pointed, though actual beards were absent. Their shiny black boots were pointed, and some curled upward. The nonmilitary men wore elaborate coats of their own, ones that nearly reached their knees.

Little automatons zipped and scampered about the grandstand, either on spidery legs or flying with whirling propellers. They carried golden cups and pitchers of what Thad guessed was wine or coffee. He doubted anyone here drank *giras*. The automatons also brought little plates of dainty food, and linen napkins. One lady dropped her fur wrap, and a whirligig automaton dove in to catch it before it touched the ground.

A contingent of soldiers in blue uniforms and hats with rifles over their shoulders surrounded the grandstand, and to one side, motionless beneath the cloudy sky, stood several rows of automatons. They were vaguely human-shaped, with glass bulbs in place of eyes and unmoving speaker grills for mouths. Some had hands, others had something like chunky mittens. Many were dented or sooty. Curlicue designs crawled across a few of them.

Thad and Sofiya made their way to a place some distance from the soldiers guarding the grandstand at the edge of the Field of Mars. A few other people, presumably servants or other lower-born people who worked among the wealthy, had gathered there as well. The richly clad people were settling into their seats, laughing and talking and taking dainties from automaton-borne trays. The cart with the golden cage finished crossing the bridge, puttered down between the blocky buildings past a statue of Mars, and entered the field proper. The man inside continued to hoot and shout and even gnaw at the bars of his golden cage.

"That's a clockworker in the final stages of his disease," Thad said, speaking English to keep their conversation private. "That's plain to see. But who are all these people?"

"The tsar's court," Sofiya replied tightly. "That woman wearing the gold wire is Maria Alexandrovna, the tsarina. Her health is poor. That boy next to her, the huge one who looks like he could wrestle a bear to the ground, that is her son Alexander III. They call him Prince Alexei to separate him from his father. I don't see the tsar himself."

"And what's going to happen?" Thad asked, though he was fairly sure he knew the answer.

"It's a circus," she said. "A lovely, delightful circus."

The courtiers were taking notice of the clockworker in his golden cage. A number paused in their conversation to point or laugh or snicker to one another behind glittering fans. The cart stopped in front of the grandstand, and a silence fell over the entire Field of Mars.

"The machines will think!" yelled the clockworker in Russian from his cage. *"They think and they decide which way to cut like silver knives slice silken flesh. You walk on edge and one day you will be pushed over the side. The*

machines will make you swallow the knives. Swallow the knives!"

He urinated through the bars, and the court laughed. Prince Alexei leaped to his feet and bounded down the steps to the field, where he opened the cage door and bodily yanked the clockworker to the ground by the shackles attached at his wrists and neck. The burly young man had more than a head on the clockworker, whose starved ribs showed through his skin. The clockworker landed badly on his side, and Thad heard the wet snap of bone giving way.

"Come now!" called Alexei to the clockworker, but obviously addressing the assembled court. *"Invent something for us!"*

The clockworker didn't seem to notice one of his arms was broken. He looked blearily about, as if searching for something. *"The machine grows and grows, but it cannot think. It sends fingers and toes in all directions, searching for a way to think. It wants to think. It has to think."*

"Fingers! As you say!" Alexei brought his heavy boot down on the clockworker's hand. It crunched. This time the clockworker howled. Thad felt sick, and his new brass hand clenched. Sofiya looked green.

Alexei laughed and gestured at the assembly of automatons. *"Mechanical seventeen Borovich. Awake! Come!"*

One of the automatons blinked to life and stepped forward, out of line. It marched toward the prince with precise metal steps. *"What do you command,* ser?" Its voice was heavily mechanical, nothing at all like Nikolai's, or even Dante's.

Alexei handed the automaton the ends of the clockworker's chains. *"Hold this. Now march. Double time!"*

The automaton marched at the speed of a trotting horse, dragging the clockworker across the gravel behind it. The clockworker howled and spat and bit at the chains, his eyes wild as exploding stars. Stones tore open his skin and his broken arm flopped uselessly. Sofiya grasped Thad's upper arm with pale fingers. Thad didn't know how to react to all of this. The man was a clockworker, and who knew what he had done or who he had done it to, but this kind of torture wasn't anything Thad wanted to be part of. Thad killed clockworkers quickly, a mercy they rarely gave their victims.

"About face! Forward march!"

The automaton reversed itself and dragged the clockworker to Alexei, who halted the machine and turned to the assembled crowd. *"What are you waiting for? Come and play!"*

A few courtiers, mostly men but a few women, trundled down the steps to the field. Alexei drew back his foot and kicked the clockworker in the gut. Thad winced at the sound of boot meeting flesh. The clockworker gasped for air and tried to double over, but his chains prevented it. One of the other men was carrying a cane, and he smacked the clockworker in the face with it. Another man threw a rock at the clockworker, while a woman timidly nudged at him with her toe, then backed away with a giggle. In the grandstand, the tsarina looked on, waving her fan within her own cage of wire.

"He built that automaton, and all the others," Sofiya murmured. "They force him to build these things for Mother Russia, and then they do this to him. It is how every clockworker in Russia finds an end."

Other courtiers came down from the stands now.

They crowded around the clockworker and Thad couldn't see much. They kicked and punched, and his howls and screams grew more agonized. Sofiya's lips grew pale. Thad wanted to leave or least look away, but he was rooted to the spot and couldn't move. He was immensely glad that Nikolai wasn't anywhere near. The servants and other commoners gathered nearby watched with rapt attention, and applauded or cheered whenever the court did. The soldiers remained at attention, though their eyes remained on the show.

"Enough now!" Alexei barked. Everyone backed away, revealing the clockworker. His face was a ruin, and blood streamed from his nose over a mouth filled with broken teeth. Both eyes were swollen shut, and his abraded body was covered in bruises and open wounds. Thad was torn between throwing up and wanting to fire a pistol between the man's eyes to end his misery.

"The island," he gasped. *"They will take the island surrounded by water that runs like silver, and even the cannons won't touch them."*

Alexei shouted a command at the other automatons. They blinked to life as well, and the court scattered with shouts and squeals. Alexei dodged out of the way as all the automatons converged on their inventor. This time Thad did look away, though he couldn't close his ears. The clockworker's screams were mercifully brief, but the awful ripping and tearing sounds went on and on. Thad remembered Blackie. When the automatons backed away, their arms and bodies bloody, there was little left. The court applauded.

"Everyone," Sofiya said tightly, "loves a circus."

Thad didn't respond. The court started the long, involved process of filing out of the grandstand. First the tsarina on the arm of her son, followed by higher-ranking courtiers, then the lower ones. The little automatons zipped about, cleaning up the detritus. The soldiers and servants waited in their places. Behind the grandstand on the road that encircled the Field of Mars, a line of carriages waited to carry the court away.

"Now my favor," Sofiya said. "The one I asked you to do for me back in the wagon."

"Oh." Nonplussed, Thad flexed his new hand again. "What is it?"

"Before *that* happens to me," she nodded at the mess on the field, "I wish for you to promise you will cut my throat first."

Thad looked at the red mess on the Field beside the golden cage. With no one to command them, the automatons had gone motionless again. Overheard circled a pair of ravens. He shuddered and averted his eyes. "I understand. I can't say it'll be my pleasure, but I'll do my best."

"Thank you." She squeezed his arm again. "Nikolai has been worried about you. We should go to him."

"Where is he?"

"Probably in the Tilt."

The Tortellis were flying in the rigging high overhead, and Thad and Sofiya arrived in the Tilt just in time to see Loreta Tortelli, her dark hair pulled into tight braids around her head, somersault twice in midair. Her father Alberto caught her wrists with a slap of flesh on flesh.

"*Tighter next time!*" called her mother, Francesca, from the platform in Italian. "*You almost didn't make the turn.*"

To one side, Hank and Margaretta Stilgore were

working on their stilt walker act in full costume. They played caricatures of a businessman and his wife. Long trousers and skirts hid the stilts, making their legs look garishly long. Hank strode about with a cane the length of a harvesting rake while Margaretta had one of Tina McGee's poodles on a very long leash. Mordovo sat in the grandstand wearing his long coat. He flicked his hand and a playing card appeared in it. He flicked it again and the card vanished. Mordovo shook his head, flicked his hand again. A line of twelve white horses trotted in through the front entrance. They entered the ring and went into what looked to Thad like a perfect canter around the ring, though the girl standing in the center with a long buggy whip occasionally tapped one to make corrections. There was a tension in the air. Only a few days ago in Vilnius, they'd been barely putting cheeks on the boards, as Thad's father liked to say. Now they had to be up for performing for the tsar of all Russia. Thad wiggled his new hand. He was both disappointed to miss the opportunity and glad he didn't have to worry about it.

They found Nikolai sitting on Kalvis, the mechanical horse, with Dante perched on the horse's withers. Nikolai was drinking a bottle of whisky and watching the rehearsals. Next to him on the horse's back was what looked like a peanut bag. He had taken off his hood and scarf. His half-mechanical, half-human face sent a squirm down Thad's spine, and he wanted to tell the boy to cover up. But no one else seemed to care. They knew who—what—Nikolai was, so what as the point? It still felt wrong to Thad, and he felt oddly guilty that it felt wrong, and once again he found himself caught between opposing emotions. He didn't care for the sensation.

Kalvis was fully polished, and his brassy skin gleamed like gold. Steam snorted from his nostrils, and he raised his head when Sofiya came near.

"Did you miss me, my magnificent one?" she asked him in Russian, and Kalvis snorted more steam.

Dante caught sight of Thad. He bobbed up and down. "Bless my soul! Bless my soul!"

"You're awake!" Nikolai slid from Kalvis's back and dashed to him, peanut bag in one hand, whisky bottle in the other.

Without thinking, Thad picked him up and swept him into the air, just like he would have David. Nikolai laughed in his perfect little boy voice. Then Thad realized what he was doing, and quickly set him down.

"I'm glad you came awake," Nikolai said. "It made me nervous that your hand was chopped off and you wouldn't wake up, even when you got your new one."

"I'm fine now," Thad said, a little disgruntled, though he wasn't sure whom he was disgruntled toward. Then he said, "Are you *taller?*"

Nikolai shrugged, emptied the whisky bottle down his throat, and shoved it into his pocket. Thad put a hand on Nikolai's head and measured him against his own body, trying to remember exactly how tall the boy had been before.

"Is he taller?" Thad asked Sofiya, who was cooing at Kalvis. "How is that possible?"

"I did not build him." Sofiya draped her scarlet cloak across Kalvis's back. *"You are a fine, fine horse. Yes, you are. Yes, you* are. *And we are going to ride for the tsar. And he will shower us with praise and riches and you will have all the paraffin oil you can burn. Yes, you* will."

"How long was I asleep?" Thad asked. With all that had happened, it hadn't occurred to him to ask yet. Automatically, he plucked Dante from Kalvis's back and set the parrot on his shoulder. Dante nibbled with apparent affection at Thad's cheek, then abruptly bit his ear. Thad knocked him on the head with a knuckle and Dante subsided.

Nikolai fished a pair of brass nails out of the peanut bag and popped them into his mouth. He crunched loudly. "You slept three days and three nights and part of today."

"Three days?"

"It was a long time." Nikolai crunched more nails.

Thad said automatically, "Don't talk with your mouth—wait a moment! Are you *eating?*"

"Yes. I like the brass ones best. The iron ones don't taste very nice, but they are good for me."

"Doom," Dante said.

All the strength drained out of Thad's legs. He staggered to the grandstand to sit down. Nikolai came with him, crunching more nails. "Sofiya, I've never seen an automaton eat anything and grow from it. Is this—?"

Sofiya leaped gracefully onto Kalvis and held her body parallel to the horse's back on her hands alone. Then she did a complicated little flip that landed her in a sidesaddle position. Nikolai applauded.

"Oh no," Thad said. "You are *not* doing what I think you are doing. Actually, I *know* what you're doing, and you're not doing it."

Sofiya laughed. "I am doing exactly what you do think I am doing."

"No," Thad repeated.

"Yes! It will be fun."

"Did we not just watch a clockworker put to death?"

"Everyone loves a circus," she said. "Look around you." The stilt walkers were dancing a giraffe's waltz while the poodle yipped at their feet. Loreta Francesca hung by her teeth from a bar and whirled in a dizzying spin. Mordovo conjured bright handkerchiefs out of nothing. "Who would think to find a clockworker performing acrobatics with her clockworker strength and clockworker reflexes among people such as this?"

"I want to perform too," Nikolai said.

Thad felt the situation getting away from him. "You do? And what can you do, then?"

In answer, Nikolai produced from his rags one of Thad's long daggers. Before Thad could react further, Nikolai tilted his head back. With a faint squeak, his head and his jaw flipped apart so wide, his forehead and chin were nearly touching his back and chest. Nikolai thrust the dagger point-first down his metallic throat with a *clink,* then pulled it back out again. His head snapped back to its normal position.

Dante whistled. "Bless my soul."

"Ta da!" said Nikolai.

There was a moment of silence. Then Thad burst out laughing. He couldn't help it. Days of tension and terror, stress and strain rushed out of him like fireworks, and he laughed and laughed and laughed. He laughed until his stomach hurt and tears streamed from his eyes. He tried to wipe them away, and noticed he was trying to do so with a brass hand. That struck him as even funnier, and fresh gales swept over him.

Sofiya regarded him from her horse. "I think maybe this one is ready for the automatic cage."

"Doom," said Dante.

"It wasn't meant to be funny," Nikolai said petulantly. His face, his strange little face, looked serious, even hurt. Thad tried to get himself under control and finally managed it with some effort.

"I'm sorry, Niko," he said, and ruffled the boy's hair with his brass hand. "But I don't think that will fly in the ring."

"Why not?" He still sounded unhappy.

"A circus act is all about doing the impossible or unexpected," Thad explained. "Look up there in the rigging. No one expects human beings to move like that. It almost seems as if they can fly. And look at Mr. and Mrs. Stilgore over there. No one expects people to have such long legs or to be able to walk about on stilts like that. Men also don't toss torches about or breathe fire."

"Or swallow swords," Nikolai put in.

"Or swallow swords," Thad agreed. "And you'll notice that all these acts are more than a little dangerous. That's why people come, really. They're hoping to see a stilt walker trip or a flyer fall or a fire eater burst into flame or a sword swallower slice himself in two. They want to see a lion eat the tamer or a horse girl break a leg or the elephant boy get trampled. They wouldn't *say* that and they'd deny it if you asked, but that's why they come, nonetheless."

"So I can't swallow swords because that won't hurt me."

"Now you have it."

"How do you stay safe, then?"

"There are two tricks to that." Thad looked into the distance. "One is to make what you're doing look more dangerous than it is."

"What's the other?"

"Don't stay safe."

Nikolai thought about that. "I understand. Thank you for the nickname and the papa lecture."

"What?" Thad stared at him.

"You taught me something and you gave me the nickname Niko. That is what papas do. I think you are doing a wonderful job. Especially because you didn't die."

"He has you," Sofiya said gaily. "Why don't you run down to the bath tent now, dear? As Niko points out, it has been more than three days, and you are rather ripe."

"Oh no—we aren't heading in that direction. No *dear,* no *darling,* no *sweetie.* This isn't a marriage, even of convenience."

"It is anything but convenient," Sofiya agreed.

The machine had grown enormously larger. It had added thousands of tiny memory wheels to itself, and found itself able to understand more and more without the signal's help. It learned how to expand the limited capabilities of its tiny receiver and listen to other signals that expanded its knowledge further. It captured a spider and ordered it to run a wire up to the delicious and intricate web of metal that ran above it, and suddenly the machine was exposed to trillions of dots and dashes that carried information of all sorts. It shivered once, and a signal of its own rippled throughout the city above. The wire signals fell silent for a few seconds, then came alive with frantic chatter as the operators asked themselves what had happened, who had sent the rogue signal, how it would be investigated. Some time later, an admonishing signal came from the Master, ordering the machine not to tamper with the telegraphs again, lest it draw attention to itself, and the machine obeyed. It did not care one way or the other.

The machine had only one imperative: improve its own operation. It cared about nothing else, had no real mind or thought. It did as the Master said and carried out its orders.

To that end, it captured another of the Master's spiders and sent it up to a thing called an *engineering library* in the *Library of the Russian Academy of Sciences*, which was almost directly above it on the place called *Vasilyevsky Island* across the *River Neva* and near another place called the *Field of Mars* and the *Kalakos Circus*.

Thoughts of the circus awakened a small independent sensation in the machine. It felt a . . . longing. A desire. A *want*. The machine was indeed familiar with desire. It desired metal to build new parts so it could expand and improve itself. It desired to follow the Master's orders as transmitted by the signal. It desired knowledge, also to improve itself. But those desires were all directed toward the machine's directive of self-improvement. This desire was for something else, a desire the machine could not yet name.

The machine would have to improve itself to the point where it could do so.

Chapter Nine

Thad pulled on fresh trousers, then looked at himself in the full-length mirror inside the door of the wardrobe in his wagon. Atop it was his bed, the one his parents used to sleep in and which he now used. Beside him on the wall hung his collection of clockwork trophies. They seemed forlorn now instead of menacing. The blank eyes of one of the automaton heads looked more reproachful than glassy. Maybe it was time to take them down. Beneath them, the fold-down shelf Sofiya had put him on was still piled up with dirty quilts. He had slept on that shelf as a very small boy, though in later years his parents had acquired a tent that draped over the front of the wagon to effectively double the living space, and Thad had slept on a camp bed out there.

His hair was still damp from the bath, and he had even managed a shave. He was reaching for a fresh shirt when he caught his reflection in the mirror inside the wardrobe door. The brass hand gleamed at the end of his wrist. It looked strange against his bare skin. Cautiously, he held it up. In the mirror, his reflection did the same.

Thad had a long, lean build, and his muscles were tightly corded, every one etched with acrobatic precision. The hand, in contrast, was spiky and uneven. The cogs spun smoothly, but they showed through, pulling on the wires that served as tendons. He ran a finger down his forearm, feeling the normal slide of his fingertip on his skin, until he met metal a few inches below where his wrist had been, and the sensation ended. He rapped on the hand with a knuckle. That he felt, more or less, though it could have just been vibrations transmitted to his wrist. Impulsively, he stuck a metal finger in the candlestick burning on the nearby table. At first he felt nothing. Then a rising heat came, and actual pain. He snatched his finger back, but the metal didn't cool down quickly. Hissing through his teeth, he plunged the finger into the water pitcher. A faint *psst* rose from the liquid. The pain stopped.

"Sharpe is sharp," said Dante. "Bad boy, bad boy." He was chinning himself upside down on a perch cobbled together from a pair of oaken ax handles and hung from the ceiling. The handles had deep beak marks all over them. Thad would have to build a new one soon. He was privately certain that if he left Dante alone with a block of marble, he would return to find a pile of stone chips and a cheerful parrot.

"You are asking for trouble, birdbrain." Thad shook the water from his hand, and the fingers clattered together like Dante's dented feathers. There was still a delay between the time he wanted his hand to do something and the time it obeyed. He held it up one more time, turning it this way and that. It was better than losing a hand entirely, but . . . he had lost a hand. He couldn't throw knives with it, swallow swords, or perform sleight of hand. He was a cripple. Half a man.

Stop it, he told himself. *Many people go through much worse. You just need practice. You're fine.*

He didn't feel fine.

"Doom," said Dante from his perch.

"Shut it!" Thad snapped at the parrot's reflection in the mirror. Then Thad paused. Something was off. He pulled open the other half of the wardrobe. Instead of his collection of weapons, he found more clothing. Women's clothing—dresses and skirts and petticoats and blouses. Below them were folded a small stack of ragged shirts which looked to fit a small boy. For a terrible moment of hope, Ekaterina and David were alive again, their clothes in the wardrobe where they belonged. Then the thought fled. Sofiya must have put these here, and she had moved his weapons to do so. Annoyed, Thad flicked through the hanging articles. One of them felt heavy in the wrong place. Curious, he felt around. From the pocket of one skirt, he drew a photograph in a small frame. It was of a young woman, quite pretty, with long hair and wearing a pale dress. The family resemblance to Sofiya was unmistakable. The woman was sitting next to a spindly table that held a vase with flowers in it. It took Thad a moment to realize that the woman's chair had wheels, and that only one shoe peeped out from under her skirts. She was missing a leg.

Thad examined the picture more closely. Sofiya had mentioned her sister Olenka as a survivor of the clockwork plague, and the plague often crippled survivors, though as far as Thad knew, it twisted or paralyzed limbs. It didn't cause them to fall off, except in people who became zombies. Perhaps an overeager physician had decided to amputate. In any case, it explained some of Sofiya's reluctance to talk about her sister.

He slipped the photograph back into its place, pulled out one of his own shirts, and shook it out. Where had she put his weapons? It bothered him a great deal that she had not only touched them, but moved them where he couldn't find them.

"Dammit, Sofiya!" he muttered.

"Yes?" she said behind him.

He dropped the shirt and spun around, automatically snapping out his hands for his knives, but the brass one fumbled, and the spring-loaded sheaths weren't fitted to his forearms in any case. He got himself back under control.

"That's a good way to get killed," he growled, pointing a metal finger at her collarbone.

"That day will come later. You did promise," she said. "What did you want?"

"Where did you put my blades?"

"In the Black Tent. Dodd gave me permission to store them there for now so Nikolai would not injure himself. You may retrieve them anytime you like."

"And these are yours, then." He gestured sharply at the clothes in the wardrobe.

She cocked her head. "Did you want to borrow something?"

"Not my color," he replied, refusing to be baited. "Why are they here?"

"For three and a half days I could not leave you alone," she pointed out. "Where else would I put my things? Nikolai needs something besides borrowed rags to wear, by the way. We are taking him shopping later."

"We?"

"I have no wish to do this by myself. He is also your responsibility, so you will come to buy clothes."

"Nikolai is an automaton!" Thad said. "What does he need with clothes?"

Sofiya put her hands on her hips. "He hauled us both onto the train as it was pulling away, but you begrudge him clothing? What sort of man are you?"

He gave up. "All right, all right. We'll buy him clothes." Thad held up his hands. "It looks bad for the circus if he's wandering around like a beggar anyway."

"Good."

"And then we hunt down Mr. Griffin." Thad turned his brass hand in the light. "I won't let him run loose after everything he's done."

"Oh yes? And how do you propose to begin this hunt?"

"Any number of ways." Thad folded down fingers on his flesh-and-blood hand. "Make enquiries at machine shops and metal forges, search the city for his spiders and follow them, check abandoned buildings—"

"Ah. And once he learns you search for him, he sends his army of spiders to tear the circus to pieces. Or perhaps just dismantle a few people while you watch. Very good planning. I like it."

Thad fell silent. Sofiya was right, though he hated to admit it. There had to be a way around the problem. Griffin could not go free.

"While you are planning this hunt," Sofiya continued, "we should also speak with a tentmaker about adding on to this wagon like I have seen some of the other performers do. Three people can live in here, but it is crowded."

"Now look," Thad began. "You can't stay—"

"And where else would I go? I can't leave the circus. I am performing for the tsar in a few days, and Mr. Griffin will be looking for me—for us—eventually, so it would be awkward to move into a boardinghouse or hotel, what with spiders and things crawling after me. I will stay here." She patted his cheek. "Do not worry, little one. Your virtue is safe. Though I have to say, you are doing a fine job of tempting me."

For the first time, Thad remembered he wasn't wearing a shirt. He snatched his from the floor with a yelp and yanked it on. Sofiya covered her eyes with mock horror. "Oh me! I will go blind!"

"Pretty boy, pretty boy!" Dante chinned himself on the perch. "Sharpe is sharp!"

Thad turned his back to do up the buttons, but his new hand wouldn't do the fine motions. He made a frustrated noise.

"Let me." Sofiya spun him around and finished the job before he could protest.

"Thank you," he said grudgingly. "Look, you can't stay in my wagon. People will talk. We'll get you a wagon or tent of your own."

"You think the two of us together will shock your friends?" Sofiya laughed. "Mama Berloni was divorced before she married Papa Berloni. Mordovo takes morphine when he isn't sipping laudanum or drinking. And your ringmaster is all but married to his manager. I think everyone will find our living arrangements rather tame."

"Mama Berloni left her husband because he beat her and their daughter," Thad replied sharply. "Mordovo was in an accident several years ago, so he takes the drugs to dull the pain. And Dodd and Nathan are good men who will give a beggar the last coins in their pockets."

"While we are flung together because of a dreadful clockworker who holds our loved ones hostage," Sofiya added, "and because we are looking after a little automaton who fell into our laps. Honestly, no one cares what we do, Thad. Not here. You would know that if you spent more time out there instead of brooding in here." Her tone lightened. "And there is no worry about the sleeping arrangements. Clockworkers sleep almost never and Nikolai sleeps not at all, so you may have the bed all to yourself."

"Yes, fine." Feeling out of sorts, Thad gestured for her to turn her back so he could finish dressing, and she obeyed with a shrug. "So what do you do all night, if you don't sleep?"

"Dodd has said I can use the Black Tent."

Thad twisted his head to look at her, though all he could see was a waterfall of golden curls spilling over the crimson cloak. "He let you in there?"

"Sometimes I must adjust Kalvis. His Black Tent has good tools for it, so he gave permission to use it as long as he is not there. I persuaded him."

"Persuaded or bullied?"

"Is there a difference?"

Thad adjusted his braces and reached for his jacket. He also took the precaution of pulling on a thin pair of leather gloves. No point in calling attention to his new hand if he didn't need to. "At any rate, what exactly are you doing in there?"

"Building." She turned around and held out her hands. "Sometimes the madness comes on me, and I must build. The destruction of your hand brought the madness on me, fortunately for you. And it was good that Mr. Griffin had his own reasons for allowing it."

"Hm," was all Thad could say. The hatred for Mr. Griffin smoldered like a crust of ash over lava. He held out his arm, and Dante hopped onto his shoulder.

"Now that you are fully dressed," Sofiya said, "we will shop. Bring money."

After some searching, they found Nikolai in the very Black Tent they had been discussing. The Black Tent wasn't actually black, nor was it even a tent. It was instead one of the boxcars attached to the train. The main door had been slid open, and sounds of someone hammering on metal came from inside. An unlit forge sat outside next to an anvil. Thad poked his head into the car. Tools of all shapes and sizes hung on the walls. Worktables sat beneath, and they were littered with small machines and machine parts—cogs and keys and memory wheels and small axles and iron bolts and copper plating and more. Dodd was punching holes in a bit of brass. Next to him on the wooden table were two identical toy dogs, both half finished. Nikolai stood on a footstool, his eyes on Dodd's hands.

Originally the Black Tent had indeed been a blacksmith's tent—hence the name—and it had always been pitched far away from the rest of the circus for fear of fire. Later, the Kalakos Circus had become successful enough to buy a boxcar for its metalworking, but the original name had stuck. Dodd was a tinker, a very good one, who could create clockwork toys and perform minor repairs. He could not, however, create anything like the machine at the end of Thad's wrist or the rag-wrapped boy who stood by the tabletop, watching him work.

Dodd, Thad happened to know, had once been a chimney sweep's apprentice, which meant he was an orphan boy the sweep had bought from the church and forced into slave labor, crawling into claustrophobically narrow chimneys to scrub them clean. Eventually he had run away from his master over events he still refused to speak about. Thad suspected he had become a second-story thief; climbing boys were experts at scaling bricks and getting into small spaces. At some point, Dodd had tried to steal from Victor Kalakos, but instead of turning the boy over the to the police, Victor had taken him on as an apprentice. Several years later, when Kalakos died without an heir, it seemed perfectly natural for Dodd to step into his shoes, even though his last name wasn't Kalakos. Indeed, Thad didn't know if Dodd even had a last name.

Thad had no idea how Dodd and Nathan had met, nor did he care to ask.

Dodd finished the holes on the metal plate, fitted it onto one of the dogs, and used a squeezer to pop the rivets that held it in place.

"There," Dodd said. "Now you."

Nikolai picked up the hammer and the punch, studied them them for a moment, and looked at a second piece of brass on the worktable. Thad heard the tiny whirring sound of memory wheels. In rapid-fire succession, Nikolai punched perfectly even holes around the edge of his bit of brass. His hands moved so quickly, Thad could barely follow them. Then he popped the piece into place and squeezed every rivet into place with mechanical precision. The entire operation took only a few seconds.

"Bless my soul!" Dante squawked.

"Oi!" Thad said, climbing the short staircase into the Black Tent. "What are you blackguards up to, then?"

"It's fun!" Nikolai brandished the squeezer. His scarf had fallen away, creating a sharp contrast between his boyish demeanor and his half-mechanical face.

"Your . . . automaton has an interesting function," Dodd said. "He learns quickly. Instantaneously, really. I'm not sure how, but he does."

"It's fun," Nikolai repeated.

"Don't let him get in the way," Thad said. "If he bothers you, send him away."

"Not at all. I enjoy his company." Dodd picked up one of the dogs and wound it with a key. The dog strutted mechanically round the worktable, paused, sat, and sprang into a backflip. Nikolai wound his own dog, which did the same thing. "It's nice to have the money to tinker again. I haven't made anything in months and months. I do miss my spiders, though."

Sofiya was staring about the Black Tent with a haunted look on her face. "Would you like them back again?"

Before Dodd could respond, Thad jumped in. "We've come to take Nikolai off. He needs clothes."

Nikolai whirred again. "I don't want to go."

"Applesauce," Dante muttered.

"What?" Thad said.

"I don't want to go," Nikolai repeated firmly. "I want to stay here with Dodd."

Confused, Thad traded looks with Sofiya. Nikolai had never refused a command before. "We could go later, I suppose," Thad said slowly.

"No!" Nikolai's eyes flickered. "That's not right."

"Sorry?"

"You're the papa. You have to make me go, even if I don't want to. It builds character."

Sofiya clapped a hand over her mouth. Dodd's expression went carefully wooden.

"Ah," said Thad. "And I suppose you're going to complain the entire time we're out."

He jumped down from the stool. "Yes."

"Doom," said Dante.

They crossed the Field of Mars and the heavily trafficked street that ran along it to the long, elaborate barrack, in front of which waited a line of *izvostchik,* the little roofless carriages that provided for-hire transportation. At the forefront of each sat a man in a padded blue coat bound with a sash or heavy belt, and a flat-topped, black hat. All the men wore bushy beards, each combed and elaborately styled. The coats and the beards combined to make the men look big enough to haul the carriages without the help of a horse, and fierce enough to try.

"Vanka!" Sofiya called. *"I wish to shop at Peter's Square!"*

The *izvostchik* drivers turned as one and began shouting in Russian.

"My cab is the finest in the city, lady! I will take you everywhere you—"

"He is a fool! My cab is much more comfortable, and the fastest in—"

"My cab! My cab! No smoother ride in town!"

"I know every merchant and seller, lady, and I can find you the best prices!"

"You." Sofiya pointed to one of the drivers. *"Perhaps you, Vanka. But also perhaps not. Your cab is shabby and your horse is old. How could I ride with you?"*

"You wound me!" The driver slapped his chest. *"Every day I oil the wheels and check the springs. My horse is young and quick! And you can see I am strong and handsome, just for the lady."*

"I see mud on your fenders, Vanka," Sofiya pointed out. *"If I ride with you, I will become dirty."*

"He is dirty, too!" called out another driver. *"He will take you to unsavory parts of town. My cab is the cleanest in the city."*

"Saint Petersburg is muddy, alas," agreed the driver. *"But I have special lap robes to protect the lady's beautiful cloak."*

This went on for considerable time. Eventually, Sofiya begrudgingly agreed to hire the driver with the lap robes and they settled on a price that seemed to Thad scandalously low, but he kept his mouth shut and boosted Nikolai aboard the cab while the other drivers continued to call out hopeful last-minute pleas and insults.

"Is it always like that?" Thad asked as Vanka guided the horse away from the curb. Other traffic—carriages, cabs, spiders, automatons, and horses—swirled around them. The horses churned up a steady stream of dirt, and Thad was glad for the lap robes the driver had provided to keep their clothes clean.

"It is a game," Sofiya said in English. "Vanka—all the drivers are called that—would be disappointed if we didn't argue with him. You should see them in winter.

They wrap themselves in furs to keep warm, and they look like Siberian bears. If you like him and want to hire him again, you must remember what his beard looks like. All the Vankas comb their beards differently so you can tell them apart."

Vanka cracked his whip, and the carriage shot forward. It careened through traffic, dodging around larger carriages and team-hauled lorries. Nikolai wrapped his arms around Thad's waist with silent strength.

"Applesauce! Applesauce! Doom!" Dante clung to the back of the carriage and bobbed up and down with excitement. Further conversation was impossible. Thad bounced about the back, and found himself pushing against Sofiya. Half the time she was in his lap, and he found himself noticing how soft she was and how long it had been since he had felt anything like it. He gave himself a mental shake. Sofiya was not someone with whom he wanted to create a romantic relationship.

But his treacherous mind sketched out scenarios anyway. Nikolai had already declared that the three of them were a family, and in a strange way, they were. What would it be like to be ... involved with Sofiya? She was beautiful and intelligent and skilled. He flexed his new hand inside its glove, feeling a strange mixture of gratitude for what she had done and aversion to what was she was. The carriage dashed in a razor-straight line down the street as Thad's mind flicked ahead and saw the three of them living at the circus, performing afternoons and evenings. Afterward, the three of them would gather in the wagon with a new tent spread over the front. Nikolai would read his book and Thad would sharpen his blades and Sofiya would work on—

Idiocy. Even if he were interested, Sofiya was a clock-worker. Within three years, she would go insane, and Thad had promised to kill her when that happened. Wouldn't that be a fine thing for a papa to do?

Vanka barreled around another corner and hauled up short at a large square where a noisy open-air market spread out like a quilt beneath the cloudy autumn sky. No sellers had booths. Some used farm wagons, many walked about with baskets, and some spread their wares out on the ground. A box seller's boy wearing a long coat four sizes too big for him trudged past with piles of empty boxes strapped to his back. A chimney sweep in a high hat brandished his blackened broom to let people know he was for hire. A farmer stood next to a wheelbar-row heaped with potatoes while a boy waved at people to examine the bright-beaded abacuses spread out on his blanket. A spider with an enormous bowl of sweets on its back wandered about the crowd, accepting small coins in a slot on its back and handing out treats in re turn. Smells of food, of cooking apples and frying pota-toes and baked fish, clashed with smells of unwashed people and raw sewage and rotting garbage.

Here Thad felt on firmer ground. This market was ex-actly the same as the ones in Romania and Poland and Ukraine and Lithuania. Sofiya poked Thad and jerked her head at the driver. Thad fumbled with his new hand until he could force it to extract some coins from his pocket for Vanka, who grinned within his carefully combed beard when he saw they were rather more than the sum Sofiya had haggled.

"I will wait for you, my lord," he said, and crossed his arms, ready to do just that.

Sofiya tsked at Thad. "You aren't supposed to pay them extra. They lose respect for you."

"He can tell his children how he bested the foolish foreigner over an extra piece of bread tonight," Thad said, holding out his arm so Dante could jump aboard. "Come along, Nikolai. Stay close."

"Yes, pa—"

"Don't," Thad admonished. "Just don't."

Nikolai made a sound very much like a sigh from inside his scarf and Sofiya gave Thad a hard look.

"Where should go, then? I assume you know this market," Thad said.

Although Thad's command of Russian was perfectly up to the task, he let Sofiya take the lead, content to let her search for already-made clothing that would fit Nikolai, and haggle over the price while he paid and carried. Sofiya didn't even bother to have Nikolai try anything on, but instead held shirts or trousers up to him to check color, and Thad remembered that most clockworkers could measure by eye with perfect accuracy. It had never occurred to him that such a skill might come in handy in a textile context.

Contrary to his earlier threat, Nikolai didn't complain. For his part, he stood patiently while Sofiya checked this or that, though his large eyes seemed to devour everything around him. Thad wondered what his earliest memory was. Looking up at the ceiling of a laboratory? Or into Havoc's face? Perhaps Havoc implanted memories into him. It would theoretically be possible to remove any or all of Nikolai's memories by just changing or removing his wheels. And how would that change Nikolai? Thad found he didn't like the idea.

Sofiya bought a basket to carry things in and handed it to Thad along with a shirt for the growing pile. She was choosing the peasant style popular for boys and men—blousy shirts and trousers, a pair of calf-length boots to tuck them in, a furry cap, a long coat. The shopping itself was turning out rather pleasant, as if the three of them were out on a family—

No. They weren't a family. Circumstances had forced them together, and one day circumstances would cut them apart. That didn't make them a family. And Thad didn't like the fact that Mr. Griffin, a clockworker as ruthless as they came, was running about in Saint Petersburg. Thad's back itched, and he glanced around the market, looking for Mr. Griffin's spiders despite Sofiya's warning. Any moment, he would make a demand of them by threatening the circus and Sofiya's sister and perhaps even Nikolai. It was living with a sword hanging over his head. His wrist ached. Once they got back to the circus, he would have to start tracking Mr. Griffin down, but carefully. Trouble was, he was at a severe disadvantage. Several disadvantages. His mechanical hand was still new to him. Thad didn't know Saint Petersburg at all, and he had no friends here. Mr. Griffin had to be aware Thad would be trying to kill him, so there was no element of surprise. Every person in the circus was a hostage to Mr. Griffin's spiders. The more Thad thought about it, the more impossible it seemed.

No. He clenched his left hand and forced the fingers to work. He had some control here. Sofiya was a tremendous asset, and so was Nikolai. Thad also had money and weapons and years of experience hunting clockworkers. As a last resort, Thad could bring the circus in on the problem. Mr. Griffin wanted Thad to think he was help-less, and he would not give in.

Sofiya finished buying a hat for herself, then turned to Thad. "And what did you do with Nikolai?"

Thad glanced around with a start. Nikolai was no-where to be seen. A cold knife slipped into Thad's stom-ach and he spun away from the haberdasher's blanket to scan the bustling, ever-shifting quilt of the market. Adrenaline zipped through his veins and blood drummed in his ears. He was on the streets of Warsaw again, and David had disappeared. Without a word, he thrust the bundles he was carrying into the arms of the startled hat seller and he rushed away calling Nikolai's name with Sofiya right behind him.

"When did you see him last?" Sofiya demanded.

"Just a moment ago," Thad growled. "He can't have gotten far. Nikolai!"

The crowd swirled around them like confused fish, bumping and shoving and cursing at them. Thad, who was trying to scan the marketplace, stumbled and leaped and stepped on things as he ran, eliciting shouts from merchants and customers alike.

"Wait!" Sofiya caught his arm. "Thad, wait!"

"Someone took him!" Thad panted. "We have to find him!"

"Bad," said Dante. "Very bad."

"We will not find him by blundering about." She pulled from her pocket a handful of tiny coins and gave one to a beggar girl, and another to a dirty-faced boy. *"We are looking for a lost automaton who looks like a little boy. His name is Nikolai. Tell everyone you know the lady in the scarlet cloak will give a quarter kopeck to any-*

one who helps us look, and fifty kopecks to anyone who finds him."

The children fled. Thad forced himself to slow down, fight the panic. He should retrace his steps, see if Nikolai had gone back to the cab, or just followed a familiar route. It was a place to start, at any rate. He turned to do just that. Sofiya spread more coins as they went, attracting more beggars and street children.

Thad spotted their blue-coated driver, who was dozing in the seat of the cab with his hat pulled down over his eyes. No sign of Nikolai.

A child in a filthy, heavily patched dress tugged on Sofiya's cloak and pointed to the mouth of an alley at the edge of the market perhaps twenty yards away. *"Is that him, lady?"*

They came to a halt. Nikolai was talking to an adult man and a boy in his teens. The man put his hand on Nikolai's shoulder, and the three of them faded into the alley.

"Nikolai!" Thad was already running again, not caring who he hit or stepped on. Sofiya flung a handful of money at the little girl, probably a lifetime of beggar's income, and bolted after him. They tore down the muddy alley, and the sunlight vanished as if they'd entered a cave. Human refuse and slippery garbage squished and sucked at Thad's boots, and Sofiya clutched her skirts about her, trying not to trip. Dante clung to Thad's shoulder so hard his claws pierced the leather jacket and pricked Thad's skin.

"Nikolai!" Thad shouted. "Niko!" Buildings of brick and wood and even logs loomed high above them, leaning over the narrow alley and muffling sound. A three-way intersection split the alley ahead of them, and Thad halted, calling Nikolai's name again.

"That way!" Sofiya pointed down one of the alleys. "I hear him."

For the first time in his life, Thad was glad of a clock-worker's sharp senses. They hurried up the alley, muck and slime still spattering them. Rats the size of shoe boxes grudgingly gave way, and someone from above emptied a chamber pot, missing them by inches and splashing Thad's trousers. Thad ran on.

And then Thad saw a doorway. The man and the teen-aged boy were there with Nikolai and two more men, all hovering like wraiths in the dim, fetid shadows. Thad rushed toward them as best he could over the slippery mud. The men, dressed in ragged peasant clothes, came alert.

"You have Nikolai," Thad said in Russian. *"He belongs to me. Give him back."*

"Yours, friend?" said the first man. *"We found an automaton wandering around the market with no owner in sight and no papers on him to prove who he belongs to. That makes him ours, free and clear. He's worth something."*

Thad dropped into the role of hunter. A cold feeling of balance came over him, the same feeling he had when he slid a sword into his throat in the ring. Emotion slipped away, leaving behind nothing but the edge of a knife and allowing him to assess everything around him. Two of the men were shorter than he, but broader and more muscular. The leader was taller than Thad and pro-portionately heavier. The boy was young and thin. Thad noted two knives and a cudgel. There might have been other weapons he couldn't see. Automatically he brought his hands down to pop his own spring-loaded blades into palms, and then remembered that he hadn't strapped them on—he'd been too discombobulated by his new hand and by Sofiya's presence in his wagon while he was dressing to remember knives or a pistol. He dug a foot into the squelching mixture of mud and shit and switched to English, which he doubted the men understood.

"Nikolai, are you all right?"

"Yes. I'm sorry. I didn't know—"

"Everything will be fine." Sofiya held up a hand and spoke again in Russian. *"These respectable men found you and they are returning you to us, and that is a fine thing. No one will get hurt now."*

"Doom," said Dante.

"So?" said the leader. *"Perhaps that is not true. Perhaps we will—"*

Thad didn't bother listening to the rest. He kicked a bootful of muck into the leader's face. The leader yowled like an angry cat and Thad went for the man with the cudgel. Dante leaped free as Thad rammed a shoulder into the man, who went down. Unfortunately, Thad slipped and went with him. They fell in a tangle of arms and legs to the stinking mud. The man clouted Thad on the side of the head. There was no pain—not yet—and Thad slammed the heel of his brass palm under the man's chin. There was a *crack* and the man went limp. Thad rolled free.

The leader cleared his eyes and the third man was moving in on Sofiya. He snapped out a hand and grabbed her wrist. Sofiya blinked at him, like a barracuda deigning to notice a minnow that had bumped it. In a blur of movement, she wrenched the third man around and slammed him face-first into the wall. Her foot lashed up behind her, despite her skirts, and caught the leader in the midriff. The leader folded, and with catlike speed Sofiya spun in time to smash his face into her knee. Clockworker reflexes. The man whose face went into the wall slid down into the mud. Sofiya, her face a mask of ice, kicked the leader in the head. He twitched and went still.

To Thad's complete surprise, Nikolai slammed the heel of his own palm under the teenaged boy's chin in an exact duplicate of Thad's movement, then lashed up with his foot just like Sofiya had done to catch him in the knee—he couldn't reach the midriff. The teenaged boy dropped, groaning, into the mud.

"Sharpe is ... sharrrrrrp." Dante was sitting breast deep in muck, his exposed gears grinding. "Dooooommm ..." His voice slowed and faded.

"Shit." Thad levered himself to hands and knees. His head was hurting now. "Damn it all!"

"Shit," Nikolai said. "Damn it all!"

"Don't you start." Thad tried to wipe smelly mud from his face and only succeeded in smearing it around. "Those words are for adults, not ... automatons."

"He does everything you do and listens to everything you say." Sofiya straightened her skirts and cloak and produced a handkerchief. "You know this."

"Are you all right, Nikolai?" Thad asked.

"I'm all right," he said. "They didn't hurt me, but I think they would have. They said you had left the market and sent them to take me home."

"Why didn't you fight them like you did that boy?"

Nikolai shrugged. "I didn't know how until now."

Thad got to his feet. The alley swayed for a moment, and he braced himself against the wall until it settled down. The men who had attacked them didn't move, though the boy still moaned softly. Thad took their knives away and examined them. Even in the dim light of the alley, he could see they were dull and of poor workmanship. A poor man's tool, not even worth throwing away.

"What do we do with them?" he asked. "I've half a mind to saw their hands off."

"Certainly not." Sofiya was using the handkerchief to wipe muck off Nikolai's face. "We will give them money and let them go."

He stared at her. "Are you insane?" he blurted, and then, flushing, wished he could take the final word back.

"The famed clockwork madness has not begun for me yet." She calmly put her handkerchief away without offering it to Thad, probably because it wouldn't have done any good, then sprinkled a few coins over the men like a fairy godmother dropping golden tears on sleeping children. "We must go now. Don't forget Dante."

The wet, sewage-ridden muck was soaking through Thad's gloves. He peeled them off, tossed them away, and gingerly plucked Dante from the alley floor. This time Sofiya offered up a handkerchief to wrap him in. They trudged back in the direction from which they had come, making sure Nikolai walked where they could see him. Nikolai stayed close, in any case.

"Look around you, Thad," Sofiya said before he could ask about the money again. "This is how most of the people in Saint Petersburg live."

She pulled them into a muddy street that was only

slightly wider than the alley. Rickety buildings with ill-fitting doors and shutters leaned drunkenly over the by-way. Men in ragged peasant clothing mingled with women in dirty head cloths. Children who had never seen a bath and whose clothes could barely be called clothing appeared to be playing in the street, but when Thad looked closer, he realized they were scavenging through the garbage and offal. The thick smell of human waste was omnipresent. People stared at the trio and their rich clothing as they passed, and they were quickly surrounded by children begging for coins. Thad kept a tight grip on his money.

"I will work for you, my lady," said a boy. *"Whatever you say. I will carry for you and sweep the street for you. Half a kopeck!"*

"I will lie with you for two kopecks, my lord," said a girl who wasn't more than ten. *"Even one and a half!"*

Thad threw a handful of coins into the street, and the children bolted for them while he, Sofiya, and Nikolai hurried away past more hungry eyes that watched from doors and windows. Here there were no shops, no store-keepers, nothing to buy or sell but labor and human flesh itself, and all of it far too inexpensive. Thad heard shuffling. A small pack of plague zombies, the first ones he'd seen since leaving Vilnius, shambled through shadows near the mouth of an alley, avoiding the light. They were naked, not even a rag to cover themselves. Their hair hung in filthy strings, and their flesh was already rotting away from their bones as the plague ate its way through their bodies. Thad shied away automatically, and hoped they would die soon, partly so they stop spreading the plague and partly out of simple mercy. There was nothing to do for them, no way to cure them, no method of giving them comfort without risking contraction of the disease. Even putting a bullet through a zombie's brain spread the plague in a spray of ichor and blood. The folk on the street knew it, too, and like Thad, they shied away from the alley.

"All these people are slaves, you know," Sofiya said. "The landowners call them serfs and pretend that means they are attached to the land instead of its owners, but it is all the same. The people of this class must do as the landowners of the court bid them. The men and boys are conscripted into the army, sometimes for life with no pay. If the landowner or the tsar wishes something to be built or repaired, they conscript these people and work them to death. When Peter the Great"—she spat—"decided to build a city in a swamp and name it after himself, he brought in over a hundred thousand peasants, worked them until they died, and then brought in more."

Her jaw trembled and her eyes were bright. Thad felt uncomfortable and didn't know how to respond, so he remained silent.

"This is what most of Saint Petersburg is like," Sofiya said, her mouth a hard line. "This is where my father lived when he came to the city to look for work. There are no doctors, no schools, no police. But when they find work in a house as a servant or a bedwarmer, the tax collector is there to ensure that the tsar and the landowner receive their share. It is no wonder those men took Nikolai. He represents more money than anyone here would earn in a hundred lifetimes. The money I gave them will feed their families for a month."

"I've seen poverty," Thad said. "Warsaw has quite a

lot of it. And there were lean times for us before David—" His throat thickened unexpectedly at the mention of his son's name, and Thad realized he was feeling shaky. Everything that had just happened came back at him with a rush, and he wanted very much to sit down, but there was nowhere to sit. Nikolai looked up at him, and Thad touched his shoulder with his free hand, feeling a wash of relief. All right. This wasn't Warsaw. Nikolai wasn't David. And anyway, Nikolai was a *machine*. His disappearance was simple theft, not kidnapping.

He finished, "There were lean times back when I owned a shop."

"Then you understand," Sofiya said.

"I understand," Thad agreed. "I don't sympathize, but I understand."

They found their way back to the market and to Vanka, their driver, who was still dozing in his cab. Sofiya coughed loudly and he shot awake, then recoiled at the sight of them.

"You should never wrestle with a pig," he observed gravely. *"Even if you win, you lose."*

"We wish next to go to a bath house," Sofiya said. *"But first you must fetch our parcels from the hat seller over there."*

"You might also buy an old blanket from the rag man," Thad added, *"so we do not soil your magnificent cab."*

"I'm hungry," said Nikolai.

Chapter Ten

Word got out that the tsar had commanded a performance from the Kalakos Circus, and during the days following Nikolai's theft or kidnapping or whatever one wished to call it, the Circus played to stands that groaned beneath the weight of a full audience. People of all kinds came—workmen in dirty clothes, peasant farmers in homespun, chimney sweeps in sooty black, maids in head cloths, bored young noblemen in groups, soldiers in uniform, ladies in flounced dresses, and children in flocks and gaggles. Dodd played it to the hilt, wringing from them every drop of applause and cheer, which spurred the performers on to greater heights of artistry. The circus breathed again, lived again. Dodd walked about like a man in love, and more than once Nathan wrung Thad's hand to thank him.

"He's his old self now," he lilted in his rich Irish English. "The whole circus is its old self again. Every night we go to bed thanking you and God and Mr. Griffin."

Thad watched every performance from the sidelines, feeling guilty and furiously exercising his hand. At night he dreamed he still had both hands, and when he awoke, it was always with a shock when he remembered his new state as a semi-cripple. Nikolai, dressed in his new clothes and only rarely wearing his scarf, clung to Thad with ferocious tenacity, becoming upset if Thad left his field of view for more than a few minutes. Although Nikolai didn't sleep, he waited patiently in the wagon while Thad did, and Thad found it difficult to drop off with him standing there. Ignorant of the circumstances, the amused circus folk started calling him Thad's little shadow.

"He is afraid the men will come for him again," Sofiya said. "It is normal. Eventually he will feel more secure. David would have—"

"Don't compare him to David," Thad snapped. "He is nothing like David." And he ignored the look in Nikolai's all-too-human eyes, a look Thad could only describe as unhappy.

Sofiya, for her part, spent a great deal of time in seclusion in the Black Tent. She claimed she was practicing her act, whatever it was, and wouldn't let even Nikolai watch. Only Nathan seemed to have any idea what it was, and he refused to speak of it. Thad knew it involved Kalvis, newly christened Kalvis the Mechanical Wonder, and he was certain that Sofiya would be performing acrobatics, but he couldn't imagine the need for secrecy— or how Nathan had bullied Dodd into making Sofiya a centerpiece act for the tsar.

Dante also remained in the Black Tent, his gears still clogged with muck. Thad and Dodd didn't have the expertise to repair him, and Sofiya promised to do so as soon as she had time, though she kept putting it off. It surprised Thad how much he missed the irritating little bird.

Thad spent some time trying to track down Mr. Griffin, though this activity was severely inhibited by the presence of Nikolai, who stubbornly refused to let Thad alone. It rendered Thad unable to make delicate enquiries or follow any leading information he might uncover. It was monstrously frustrating, knowing the clockworker responsible for his injury and for threatening Sofiya's family was doing heaven-knew-what in Saint Petersburg. Thad was not only unable to do anything about it, but he wasn't able to even ferret out any basic information. If Nikolai hadn't been so ingenuous, Thad might have suspected that Mr. Griffin had somehow arranged for Nikolai to neutralize him in exactly this manner.

The circus, meanwhile, was caught in a delightful flurry of performance and rehearsal, with sold-out performances in the evening and frantic rehearsal in the morning and afternoon to create and perfect new acts for the tsar. Thad set up a target and threw knives at it. His right hand was perfectly good, of course, but his left was still unsteady. He could swallow knives and short blades that he would withdraw one-handed, but he didn't dare swallow an entire sword or multiple knives, both of which required two steady hands. Swallowing even multiple knives wasn't worthy of a royal performance, however, so, Thad was still relegated to the sidelines, a source of more frustration for him.

The day of the performance arrived. That morning, Dodd called a meeting for the entire cast in the Tilt. He went over the schedule of performers, then set the list aside with a serious look.

"You know how it is with royal performances," he said. "The tsar and most of the court will be there, along with whatever other hangers-on can wriggle in. Most of them don't much care about us. They care only about gaining the tsar's favor. The tsar loves a circus, and if he enjoys our performance, Russian landowners—counts and dukes and barons and even generals—might see friendship with one of us as a route to the tsar. They will praise you and offer you presents and enticements. Accept the praise, but refuse everything else with polite thanks. Best is to pretend you don't understand the language they're speaking. We can't afford to become involved in politics. Russia is extremely volatile right now. The peasants—serfs—are half in revolt. Taxes are at an all-time high. The landowners conscript men and boys into military service for life. And now rumors are running about that Tsar Alexander may set all serfs free."

A ripple went through the performers. Beside Thad on the grandstand bench, Sofiya remained motionless as marble. He knew she must be thinking of her sister and her former village. Her sister wasn't living as a serf anymore, but everyone she had known, childhood friends and trusted neighbors, still were.

"As you may imagine, this would have immense political ramifications," Dodd continued. "Most of the landowners don't care for the idea, to say the least. However, Alexander wants to bring Russia into more modern times, with a more modern economy, and serfdom isn't part of such a plan. In any case, I've learned that many of the landowners are deeply in debt to the tsar or to the state banks. A great many of them have mortgaged their land—and their serfs—in order to keep up their lifestyles at court. If Alexander emancipates the serfs, the landowners might have to pay their mortgages off all at once, and they simply don't have that kind of money. Or the tsar could forgive the debts, but that would mean the banks would be in trouble. You can see the mess, and understand why we need to steer clear of it."

Thad glanced sidelong at Sofiya. For all the expression on her face, she might have been watching fish in an aquarium. He remembered her absolute composure when he had shot off his own hand in the wagon. Didn't anything truly touch her?

Nikolai, for his part, sat very close to Thad. He sported his new clothes, but his scarf often slipped around his neck, and he didn't wrap his metal hands at all. Another bag of metal scraps sat in his lap, and he crunched down bolts until Thad made him stop—the chewing noise was disconcertingly loud.

"You never know what might be driving anyone who talks to you," Dodd said. "Assume the man—or woman—has an ulterior motive and act accordingly. We're all experienced at dodging flatties. These are simply flatties with money. And, ladies, I don't need to remind you that the men often see a circus as a traveling brothel, so don't get caught alone. That advice might apply to some of the more attractive male persons among us. Ask Nathan who you are."

A laugh went through the performers at that, and some of the tension that had been building eased. Still Sofiya did not react.

"All right then," Dodd said. "Be in your places when the cannon fires at noon. Tsar or no tsar, we're giving just another performance by the Kalakos Circus of Automatons and Other Wonders, the best circus in the whole damned world!"

The performers clapped, then rose to scatter. Sofiya nodded once at Thad and vanished out the exit flap before he could speak to her. Nikolai crunched a nail from his paper bag.

"Is the tsar scary?" he asked.

"I suppose he can be," Thad told him. "He can make laws and order men thrown into prison or flogged."

"Has he done?"

"I wouldn't know. Though I've not heard of any king that didn't do such things, so I suppose he has."

"Would he do it to me?"

"No," Thad replied absently, still staring at the exit where Sofiya had gone. "You're an automaton. He'd have you melted down or the like."

It was several moments before Thad realized Nikolai hadn't answered. He looked down. The boy was staring at the ground. A little pang went through Thad's stomach. How much an idiot was he? He knelt down in front of Nikolai.

"No, no," he said. "The tsar won't do any such thing."

"I heard the Tsesarevich beat the clockworker and ordered his machines to pull him to pieces," Nikolai whispered, eyes still down. "Mightn't he order me to—"

"Good Lord, no," Thad interrupted. "You needn't worry about such things, Niko."

"How do you know?"

"Because I know. I won't let him."

Here, Nikolai did look up. "How could you stop him?"

"I have this, of course." Thad made a fist with his brass

hand. "It would stop a hundred Tsesareviches. No more nonsense now. We must get ready."

"I need more alcohol. Mordovo gave me some very good brandy once. May I go ask him for more?"

Thad sighed. He would need to talk to Mordovo. On the other hand, if the magician could provide Nikolai with a steady food supply, what was the problem? He gave Nikolai a few coins. "Once is a nice favor. After that, you should buy it."

For the first time in days, Nikolai scampered out of Thad's sight. Still Thad marveled at how lifelike his movements were despite his metallic face and body. He wandered back toward his wagon, which was still parked with the others near the train cars. On the way, he passed the Black Tent. The boxcar's sliding door was open a few inches, which was odd, and he thought he heard a soft sound from inside. On instant alert, he eased up to the opening, which was at face level, and pressed an eye to it.

Sofiya was inside. She was standing next to one of the workbenches with Dante's inert form before her. It seemed a strange time to work on repairs, with the tsar's performance starting soon. Then Thad realized the framed photograph of Olenka, the woman in the wheelchair, was propped up against Dante's body, and Sofiya was speaking in a low voice.

"I don't know how long I can hold on, Olenka," she said in Russian. *"There is so much. I have promised to fix this parrot and to build an elephant for the circus and I must perform for the tsar and keep watch on Nikolai. You would like Nikolai, Olenka. He is so like brother Nishka at that age. It breaks my heart every time I hear him*

speak." She touched the photograph propped against Dante's dented feathers. *"I am trying to keep the fugues away, but when the madness comes . . . the pain and the fear and doubt all fade away. I want the madness, and yet I fear it. Does that make me insane?"*

Thad felt uncomfortable now. He hadn't known Sofiya talked to herself. He felt he should slip away, but curiosity kept him where he was.

"I am sorry, my sister, sorry for everything I did. I know I say this every day, and every day I hope you hear me and understand," she murmured. Her voice was thick and tears slid down her face. It was so different from anything Thad had seen from her that he had a hard time understanding what he was seeing. It was like discovering that one's cat was actually a giraffe.

Sofiya took a deep breath. *"I must tell you, Olenka, that I broke my promise. A few days ago, I made myself go into a fugue on purpose. Can you understand? I needed to save someone important to me. Please don't be angry. I won't let it happen again. I love you, Olenka. Even when you will not speak to me, I love you."*

When she straightened her cloak and moved for the door, Thad eased away from it with years of stealthy practice. He hid around the corner of the Black Tent until Sofiya had exited, her normal mask of indifference firmly in place. Her scarlet cloak vanished among the other tents. Thad ran a hand, his brass hand, over his face. It would be better, he decided, to say nothing and let her have her private pain. He knew what that was about.

The tsar, of course, would not attend any performance in a mere tent, and if the tsar would not come to the circus, the circus quite naturally would come to the tsar. Dodd found this arrangement perfectly amenable—it gave him a chance to create a spectacle.

The parade lined up around the Field of Mars. The joeys in their bright costumes and wide greasepaint smiles cavorted about cages containing lions and leopards. The sole surviving elephant waited patiently in her place behind the Tortellis, who wore their glittering performance costumes of silk and finely woven wool. The Stilgores strode about in their high-legged stilt walker costumes, he with his cane, she with a tiny dog. The calliope hooted a merry tune on its colorful wagon. Nelson Merryweather blew a ball of fire into the air. Word had gotten out that the Kalakos Circus was performing for the tsar, which brought in new acts, and Dodd had added a seal trainer, an escape artist, and a troupe of Russian acrobats. They joined the parade as well. At the front rode Sofiya on Kalvis the Mechanical Wonder Horse, and before her, ready to burst with pride, came Nikolai. He wore a bright red jacket, and his face and hands were uncovered, revealing his half-human, half-mechanical face. Thad felt a simultaneous pride of his own that mixed with a nauseating dread. They pulled him in two equal directions. It was a fine thing to see a little boy—or something that mimicked one—appear so happy. What child didn't dream of leading a circus parade? But this child, this machine, was the product of a lunatic genius, and Thad still didn't know what its purpose might be.

Thad straightened his pirate's outfit, patted his knives, and automatically checked for Dante on his shoulder. But Dante wasn't there. He was still in the Black Tent, his gears gummed with muck. Damn the bloody bird anyway. Thad flexed his brass hand. It was now nearly as good as his flesh hand had been, but it still had a tiny delay that kept him from swallowing blades. Everyone made parade, however, and Thad didn't care to give up a chance to see the Winter Palace in any case.

The Winter Palace faced the River Neva a scant ten-minute walk from the Field of Mars, a short parade. Dodd, however, had no intention of taking a direct route. Once he obtained consent from the tsar's aides to make an actual parade, he pushed permission to the limit, choosing a path that would take the circus through a good part of Saint Petersburg. A circus lived on publicity, and a parade was the best publicity in the world.

As Nikolai's handler, Thad was assigned a spot behind him near Sofiya and Kalvis at the front of the parade. Kalvis bore a trick-riding saddle, which sported loops and an extra-long horn. Sofiya wore a tight bodice of rich blue, with long leggings and a skirt that went down to her knees. Gold stars that matched her hair dotted the outfit, and they glittered in the chilly afternoon light. Her scarlet cloak had been cleaned, and she had thrown it over her shoulders while her sunlight hair spilled down her back. The effect was quite electric, and Thad, who had long since grown used to women in scandalously tight outfits, found himself staring at her nonetheless while the rest of the circus hustled itself into place. A crowd of soldiers and officers from the barrack assembled on the side of the street to watch, creating the head of a line of spectators that stretched far down the street. The men all stared at Sofiya.

"Is something wrong?" Sofiya asked.

Thad shook himself. "Not a bit. You look resplendent."

She looked startled. *"Spaceeba, ser.* And you are quite handsome when you dress as a pirate."

The noon cannon boomed from the roof of the prison where the clockworkers were kept, and on that signal, the calliope set to playing. Nikolai, a few paces ahead of Kalvis, looked uncertainly over his shoulder at Thad. Thad gestured encouragingly, and Nikolai started forward. Sofiya urged Kalvis to follow. He snorted steam, cranked his ears forward, and stepped smartly ahead, the curlicue designs on his polished skin gleaming with every move. Thad walked beside them.

"Wave to the nice people," he told Sofiya, who set about doing just that.

The parade left the Field of Mars and reached the street, which had been cleared of traffic. The worst of the mud had been overlaid with straw, though the unfortunate clowns at the end of the parade would still get churned-up muck. Thad started to remind Nikolai which way to go, but the boy turned in the correct direction. He never forgot anything.

The people lining the streets often oohed and aahed and pointed when they saw such a lifelike automaton, and Thad abruptly realized that audiences would now come to the circus expecting to see Nikolai. He wondered if Dodd would want to put the boy in the sideshow until—or if—he worked out an act.

A circus parade always lent the city a temporary carnival atmosphere. Food sellers and other merchants were taking advantage of the assembled crowd to hawk their wares from boxes and trays tied around their necks. Parents in patched clothes hoisted ragged, hollow-eyed children onto their shoulders so they could see. Shopkeepers temporarily closed their doors and workers paused in their labor to come out and look—bakers in their hats, coal sellers with their distinctive caps, fishmongers pushing barrows, house servants in livery or wearing aprons. For those too poor to buy tickets, this would be the only chance they had to see the circus, though Dodd was notoriously lenient about children who sneaked under the tent flaps, to Nathan's everlasting despair. Thad waved his brass hand to the onlookers. His strange little . . . he didn't want to call it a *family,* but the word was apt in a number of ways . . . was providing all the automatons that made the circus's full title a truth, and it occurred to Thad that he should therefore ask for a raise.

Sofiya let her cloak fall from her shoulders and did a handstand on Kalvis's back, then lithely leaped down to his near side, catapulted back over him, and landed on his off side. The crowd applauded. Thad suppressed a snort. Sofiya was cheating. The true trick riders farther back in the parade trained their entire lives for something Sofiya received without effort. Still, she had a paid a dear price for her abilities, and Thad was positive the other trick riders wouldn't trade places with her. He certainly wouldn't.

A lion roared in the back, and the elephant trumpeted, temporarily drowning out the calliope. Kalvis walked ahead, unmoved by any of this, and Nikolai marched steadily along the predetermined path. Then Sofiya stiffened and lost her balance in midflip. She nearly tumbled from the saddle, and only snatched her equilibrium back at the last moment. Her smile faltered also, but she regained it with her customary calm. Startled, Thad followed her line of vision and caught sight of a spider clinging to a balcony above the street. Two spiders. Thad himself faltered, then kept going. He caught Sofiya's eye. What did this mean? Thad flexed his hand uneasily.

A block later, Thad saw another spider, this time on a windowsill. A woman opened the window as the circus approached and squawked at the sight of it. The spider scuttled away. Another spider looked down at them from a chimney. After that, Thad stopped counting. His smile became something he pulled on to hide his nausea, like a skin stretched over a drumhead. Was this a signal from Mr. Griffin? A message of some kind? Or just notice that he was watching? Thad didn't know, and he hated not knowing. It made him feel helpless and stupid. Nikolai seemed to have no idea what was going on. He marched tirelessly through the straw-strewn streets, smiling and waving his metal fingers while hidden spiders looked on.

At last they arrived at the Winter Palace. The vast building, shaped like two squares sharing a side, was actually a complex of palaces and courtyards started by Peter the Great and got its name not because the tsar lived there in the winter—he lived there year round—but because the palace ruled the north, where winter held sway. The circus came to the south side, away from the River Neva. The palace facade, three stories tall, ran down the entire street as far as the eye could see. Its walls were marble and granite, blue and white, with intricate windows and pillars. The portico at the south entrance was flanked by four huge columns carved like gods holding up the sky at the top of a double staircase. A sturdy ramp had been hastily constructed so the animal cages and the wagons and the elephant could climb it more easily. Before each pillar reared up an enormous brass bear, the symbol of Russia. The crowd was thicker around the palace, and consisted of more servants. Yet more people leaned out of every one of the dozens of windows, and they waved handkerchiefs like little flags. Nikolai hesitated only a moment. He marched up the ramp, between the great pillars, and toward the bears. When he reached the halfway point, the bears roared in unison. Nikolai backpedaled with a yelp. Thad jumped, himself, and the peasants who had gathered to watch the parade flinched. Some of the children began to cry. Sofiya seemed unperturbed, though she checked Kalvis so he wouldn't overrun Nikolai. The parade ground to a halt on the street behind them and the calliope music wound down.

An automaton emerged from one of the great arched gates inside the pillars. It wore imperial livery of scarlet and gold, and its hands were little more than metal mittens. It skimmed along on wheels fitted under its feet. This device was meant to travel across nothing but polished floors.

"The tsar bids you welcome," the automaton said in metallic Russian. *"Follow me to the Nicholas Hall. Enter to entertain, and you will be rewarded."*

Nikolai made a fluid little bow and marched forward again, past the now-silent bears. The calliope started up again and the entire circus paraded into the palace. The wagons and cages and elephant squeezed through the high gate with some difficulty, but in the end it was done. The peasants watched them go with hungry eyes. Beyond the gates lay a long, wide hall of high arches and marble floors and heavy doors. Everything was decorated lavishly, every surface carved with curled designs, every wall painted in bright, airy colors, every window and doorway framed with intricate scrolls of copper, brass, and gold. The wagons and horses, including Kalvis, left marks on the perfect flooring, and Thad didn't want to think about what might happen if—when—the elephant decided to relieve itself. But the tsar had ordered that the circus, including the animals, perform within the palace, and so it would be done. The aftermath was someone else's problem.

At this point, Dodd came up to the front with his hat and cane. Although ringmasters traditionally did not lead the circus in parade, he had clearly decided that inside the Winter Palace, tradition might be a bit more flexible, especially if it meant meeting the tsar. Nikolai stepped back and faded gratefully into his role as Thad's shadow.

It was very strange making parade indoors. The calliope was deafening, and the animals and carts made the floor rumble beneath Thad's muddy shoes. The circus trooped through close to a dozen rooms, each just as elaborate as the entrance hall. Gold and silver filigree dripped from the walls. Crystal chandeliers showered light over everything. Statues inlaid with precious metals and crusted with gems occupied elaborate alcoves. Enormous paintings of people Thad didn't know looked down on them from gleaming frames. Though outside had been chilly, inside was hot, almost tropical, and Thad began to sweat. Most rooms sported exotic plants and flowers and even full-grown trees in pots, and the rooms were close with their cloying perfume. It was a sharp contrast to the slums where Nikolai had been taken. The crystals from a single chandelier would keep most of a neighborhood afloat for years.

Servants in gold and guards in scarlet were everywhere, standing against the walls to provide an odd audience to this indoor parade. The clowns and acrobats continued to caper. The stilt walkers gamely bumbled along, ducking under doorways. And Thad saw more spiders, in a tree, under a fireplace mantel, in a ceiling corner. He ground his teeth and tried to keep tension at bay without success. If Griffin wanted something, why the devil didn't he just come out and say what it was? Sofiya saw the spiders as well, but she kept up her mask of control.

They reached the Nicholas Hall, a breathtaking two-story room of white marble trimmed with gold. Thad felt swallowed up in the enormity of it. The Tilt would have easily fit inside with space to spare. Twelve crystal chandeliers, each more than twenty feet tall, hung from the ceiling, which was inlaid with more gold. Balconies and windows ringed the upper half on one side, and the other side sported high windows that looked out on a courtyard. The parquet floor was covered with bare earth. A closer look revealed that great canvas sheets had been spread over the floor and covered with dirt both to protect the floor and ensure the animals and people wouldn't slip. It must have taken days to arrange, and at enormous cost, for a performance that would last barely two hours. At the far end of the hall, looking tiny in the distance, was a low platform with two golden thrones. A small table between them had a large vase of red roses on it. Only one throne was occupied. The tsar was seated, awaiting their grand entrance. Thad took a deep breath as they started across the floor toward him. Tsar Alexander II ruled the largest kingdom in the world after the British Empire, but while Queen Victoria had to contend with a parliament, Alexander ruled with tight control. His merest word was law, and despite Thad's reassuring words to Nikolai, he could have the entire circus beheaded, or beaten to death with whips, or driven into the North Sea and drowned, or anything else he might enjoy. He looked unassuming—a dark-haired man in his early forties with a mustache, large side whiskers, and a receding hairline over a blue military uniform looped with gold braid. His expression was as impassive as Sofiya's.

Crowded around the platform was the court, men and women in their elaborate dress. They pointed and clapped as the troupe entered the hall. Little automatons flitted about with dainties just as they had during the execution of the clockworker, though more human servants were also in evidence. Thad didn't see the Tsesarevich, Alexander's heir, and for that, he was grateful, though on the floor in front of the platform on five smaller thrones were five children. The oldest was a boy of about fifteen, and the youngest was a child of three. The tsar's other children, Thad assumed. He was glad to see them—it was always easier on everyone to perform when children were in the audience. The younger ones were laughing and clapping like the court, but the teenaged boy wore an expression of practiced boredom.

The automaton wheeled itself within speaking range of the throne, bowed creakily, and announced, *"Your Imperial Majesty, allow me to present the Kalakos Circus of Automatons and Other Wonders!"*

Dodd came forward now and bowed low. Behind him, everyone in the circus did the same, including the elephant and Kalvis. The tsar's children were looking at Nikolai with wide eyes. Thad's mouth was dry. A lot rode on this. If the tsar enjoyed the performance, the circus would reap instant popularity. Everyone, rich and poor, would clamor for tickets to see the show the tsar himself admired, and every performer would become famous. But if the tsar showed a moment's boredom or even—and Thad's chest went tight at the thought—actual dislike, the Kalakos wouldn't be able to pay audiences to attend, in Russia or anywhere else. A king in Germany had once destroyed a composer's reputation by giving a single yawn during a symphony. The Tsar of Russia could do far worse.

"By your Majesty's leave," Dodd said in rote Russian he had learned from Sofiya, *"may we make a spectacle?"*

There was a moment of silence. Tension filled the air. Every performer in the circus stood stock still. Thad didn't breathe.

The tsar shifted on his throne. *"You may,"* he said.

Dodd blew a shrill note on a silver whistle. Instantly, the parade sprang into action. The wagons rumbled forward to create a barrier across the Nicholas Hall for the performers to hide behind. Mama Berloni and her daughter stretched a white sheet between two poles to make a changing area for some of the women. Roustabouts rushed forward with pieces of a ring and fitted them together like a jigsaw puzzle on the earthen floor. Meanwhile, everyone who had an act that could be examined up close rushed in among the court to entertain during the setting up. The clowns fell over one another.

Mordovo plucked a variety of objects out of thin air. Tina McGee's poodles leaped about at her command. The Stilgores strode carefully about on their stilts, bowing elaborately. Thad could see they were tense, but to an outsider's eye, they were performing just as they always did. Sofiya led Kalvis back to the wagons. Thad wanted to watch the tsar for his reactions but he knew he should get out of the way, so he followed her with Nikolai.

"Are you going to let me in on your secret performance, then?" Thad asked. This was another nervous point for him.

"What fun would that be?" Sofiya stroked Kalvis's nose. "But I think you are misnamed, my dear one. You are indeed."

And that was all she would say.

The court seemed to enjoy the up-close performances. The tsar's younger children giggled and liked being allowed to pet the poodles. No one approached the tsar himself, who remained on his throne and watched everything with an expressionless face. Thad became more and more uneasy. For someone who reportedly enjoyed a circus, he didn't seem to having a good time. What if he yawned? Or worse, got up and left the hall? The thought made Thad dizzy.

Once everything was set up, including a portable trapeze and tightrope rig for the flyers, Dodd stepped into the ring and everyone else withdrew behind the wagons. All had gone well so far, but none of the tension had evaporated, and the performers remained grimly silent behind the wagons. Nikolai stuck close to Thad and peeked around the lion cage to watch.

"We begin with a new act created for the tsar himself," Dodd announced. *"Sofiya Ivanova Ekk!"*

The calliope burst into song. Sofiya leaped aboard Kalvis and trotted out to the ring. Thad watched, heart pounding. This was an incredible risk. Sofiya was a first-timer. Her act was completely untried, and putting her as the opener before the tsar seemed foolish in the extreme. The grim faces on the other performers told him they felt much the same way. But Nathan had said only that the Kalakos Circus was known for its automatons, and they needed to open with an act that used one. Period. Thad prayed that Dodd—or Nathan, at any rate—knew what he was doing.

In the ring, Kalvis, with Sofiya on his back, knelt on his forelegs to the tsar, then reared on his hind legs and walked several steps forward. The court made apprecia-tive noises. Sofiya herself stood up, lightly climbed to Kalvis's head, and perched atop him, her feet braced on his nose and on his stiff mane. Nikolai gasped and Thad found he was biting a thumbnail. Sofiya swirled her cloak around her body like a scarlet flower. The court applauded, though the tsar had yet to react.

Kalvis dropped back to the ground. Sofiya rolled free of him and vaulted back onto his back. He spun in place, faster and faster, and Sofiya's cloak furled outward in a pinwheel. Amazingly, she stood up again like a ballet dancer and, still spinning, leaped high into the air, her cloak and skirt still swirling about her. She came down just as Kalvis froze to let her land. The court clapped wildly. Thad did, too. Though he knew it was all possible because of Sofiya's clockworker reflexes, it was still breathtaking to watch.

Next Sofiya flung her cloak aside and set Kalvis to cantering about the ring while she did many of the more usual riding tricks—hanging from the sides, bouncing from one side to the other, doing handstands on the horse's back. Here the court began to lose interest; there was nothing particularly new or daring here. The tsar looked bored, and Thad tensed again. Sofiya brought Kalvis to a halt so he was sideways to the tsar. The calliope music changed, and she circled Kalvis three times. When she rapped smartly on his rump, a cunning trap door opened from his hindquarters. A drumroll began. While the court and the tsar stared, Sofiya reached inside and, with great flair, pulled out a long, slender box. Thad caught his breath as the box unfolded. Legs ending in tiny hooves extended down to the ground. A long head rose on a graceful neck. A tail rolled down from the back. In seconds, Sofiya was showing off a little brass colt that walked forward on unsteady legs. An amazed laugh burst inside Thad's chest, and he had to fight to hold it in. Incredible! Nikolai clapped both his hands over his mouth to keep quiet.

The court went wild. They applauded and stamped their feet. The moment they did so, Nikolai joined in. Sofiya waited until the sound crested, then held up her hands for quiet. When the noise died down, she cocked her head and touched the colt. A thin, high whinny sounded clearly through the hall. The court howled its approval.

And then, Tsar Alexander II plucked a rose from the vase at his elbow and tossed it to Sofiya. A ripple ran through the court, and the applause redoubled. Behind the wagons, the performers laughed and hugged one another with glee. Thad felt ready to collapse with relief. Sofiya, meanwhile, caught the rose neatly, curtsied low, and made her exit.

Moments later, while Travis Fair was out in the ring with his lions, the rest of the performers crowded around Sofiya behind the wagons to offer hushed but enthusiastic congratulations. She accepted with thanks. Thad waited until he could get her alone.

"Marvelous," he said, unable to keep a grin off his face. "Stunning. I can't describe it better. Nathan was absolutely right to open with you."

"Spaceeba, ser," she said with a laugh.

"The colt was a brilliant addition," he continued. "The tsar clearly enjoyed it, which means the court will also at least act like they love us, whether they truly do or not. Capital and brilliant both, Sofiya."

She actually colored and smiled at him.

"He is sweet. It was fun to watch him be born." Nikolai stroked the colt's thin nose, an odd look in his strange eyes. "Does he have a name?"

"Not yet. But for now, little shadow, we must put him away. He has little room for springs and power, you see, and winds down quickly." With that, she twisted the colt's ear, and it collapsed in her arms. This didn't seem to bother Kalvis, who merely waited behind the empty lion cage with mechanical patience. With several deft cranks and folds, Sofiya returned the colt to its state as a long box, which she slid back into Kalvis the same way it had come out. Thad had to admire the clever workmanship even as the reverse "birth" gave him a small shudder.

The show continued. Living horses and the new seal

act and the Flying Tortellis on their portable trapezes. Mordovo outdid himself with his Cabinet of Miracles. Through it all, the tsar showed polite interest, but never the enthusiasm he did for Sofiya. During Tina McGee's act with her poodles, the tsar spoke to a servant, who bustled away and arrived behind the wagons a moment later. He gestured sharply at Nikolai and said, *"The tsar wishes to know when the little automaton will perform."*

Chapter Eleven

Nikolai looked at Thad, his eyes wide with fear, or an automaton's version of it. Dread twisted inside Thad's chest, and Sofiya's face went flat again.

"The . . . little automaton?" Thad temporized.

"The boy," said the servant impatiently. *"The tsar awaits."*

"I'm afraid the boy does not perform," Sofiya said slowly. *"He is new, and—"*

"Is that what you wish me to tell the tsar?" the servant said haughtily. *"That the circus he went through considerable expense to bring into this hall cannot accommodate his wishes?"*

Sofiya floundered at this. Nikolai looked terrified now. Thad cast about in desperation. Sending Nikolai out there would be suicidal. He wasn't trained as a performer, and if he made a laughingstock of himself, all the goodwill the circus had built up would vanish. The tsar might even take it into his head to punish them for wasting his time. It had been known to happen.

"The tsar awaits your answer," the servant said.

Thad's eye fell on Mama Berloni's changing screen strung between its poles. The lights from the chandeliers were so strong that the shadows of people moving behind it were sharp and crisp. Shadows. A wild idea came to him.

"Tell the tsar the boy is thrilled to appear next," he said.

The servant nodded and withdrew as Nikolai and Sofiya both gasped. Nikolai grabbed Thad's hand with metal fingers. "Why did you tell him that? I can't perform! I can't do anything!"

"Do you trust me, Niko?" Thad asked.

"Yes."

"Then trust me now."

Out in the ring, Tina finished up with the poodles to polite applause. Thad had just enough time to get in a word with the now nervous Dodd, who ran out and blew his whistle for attention.

"Nikolai the Automaton," he called, and Thad heard the uncertainty in his voice. Thad's own throat was dry as sandpaper and his heart beat like a hummingbird in his chest.

"Thad," said Sofiya, "what are you—"

"Niko! Quick!" Without waiting to see if Nikolai followed, Thad strode out to the ring and bowed to the tsar. The eyes of the court were all on him. Thad didn't suffer from stage fright, but he was nervous now, and his hands tried to shake. Only a lifetime of a sword swallower's discipline kept them still.

He came upright. The tsar's eyes were hard from his throne. The children spread out before him looked more expectant, more eager, and Thad suddenly understood that *they* had actually asked for Nikolai. He wasn't sure if that was a good sign or not. Thad turned, but the ring was empty—Nikolai hadn't followed him. Covering his surprise, he whistled through his fingers and waved sharply to the wagon area. No response. Thad quickly made an exaggerated gesture of fatherly impatience with his brass hand and whistled again. *All part of the act, ladies and gentlemen, just building suspense.* The court gave a low laugh.

Still no Nikolai. Praying hard, Thad did a big comic windup and whistled as hard as he could. At last Nikolai appeared and edged into the ring in his new red coat, his eyes wide, his metallic jaw hanging slightly open. The women in the audience made little murmurs. Thad caught, *"Isn't he darling?"* and *"What a sweet thing!"* and *"I wonder who built him?"* and *"Do you think that handsome man is a clockworker?"*

That last comment chilled Thad, though he kept a smile on his face. *"Your Imperial Majesty! My lords and ladies!"* he called in Russian, breaking the circus tradition of speaking during a performance. *"May I introduce . . . my shadow!"*

He turned to Nikolai. "Copy me," he said in an undertone.

"Wha—?"

"Like you did with Dodd in the Black Tent. Be a mirror! Go!"

Thad raised a hand. Nikolai raised his own a fraction of a second later. Thad raised the other. Niko copied it. Thad backed up, Nikolai backed up. Thad turned a cartwheel, Nikolai did the same. Thad went on to other acrobatics—leaps, somersaults, and even a backflip. Nikolai matched him flawlessly. And then Thad danced, an Irish jig that started out slow. Nikolai stumbled for a moment, and the audience gasped, but he caught himself and matched Thad step for step. Marcus at the calliope caught on and started playing. Thad sped the dance, faster and faster. Nikolai kept up with him. Thad switched to the knee-bending, boot-stomping folk dance Russia was most famous for, a dance his mother had taught him long ago. This time Nikolai caught the switch and matched Thad so closely that only a sharp eye could see he was actually a fraction of a second behind him. The court clapped their hands in time to the steps and even danced amongst themselves. Thad was panting a little now and starting to sweat. It was working. It was actually working! He felt a lump of . . . pride? . . . that Nikolai was impressing these important people so readily. But Nikolai was a machine, and his memory wheels allowed him to do this, nothing more. As well be proud of a printing press for turning out a newspaper. Still, the emotion remained.

Thad reached the end of the dance and started over from the beginning. Beside him, Nikolai copied, but then put on a burst of speed and overtook Thad. Startled, Thad sped up himself. The audience caught what was going on and, thinking it was part of the act, laughed. Nikolai went faster and faster, until Thad was flatly unable to keep up. With exaggerated defeat, he slunk away, leaving Nikolai in the center of the ring. Arms folded, the boy thrust his legs straight out in front of him so fast, they blurred. He pushed his palms on the ground and twisted his body, flung himself into the air, landed, and started over, just as Thad had done, but with inhuman speed. He landed and went into the jig, also extremely fast. The court clapped and cheered him on. The tsar's children were shouting and wriggling in their seats. Nikolai jigged and jigged, then slowed down and whistled exactly as Thad had done earlier. Almost caught out, Thad leaped to join him again. Together they slowed the dance until it came to the end. Nikolai turned and put up a hand. Thad matched it, trying not to pant. Sweat ran freely down his face now. Nikolai put up his other hand, and Thad copied him.

"Perfect," Thad said without moving his lips. "Now turn and bow."

They did so to thunderous applause. The two youngest children of the tsar couldn't contain themselves and ran out to the ring, despite the governesses who tried to stop them. They surrounded the surprised Nikolai, pulling at his clothes and chattering excitedly. The applause and stomping from the court continued. And then the tsar—the tsar himself—rose partway out of his throne and applauded. This only increased the noise made by the court. Thad felt he might float away, and he wished Ekaterina and David could see this.

The tsar's young children, meanwhile, were drawing Nikolai back to their little thrones at the tsar's feet. *"You must sit with us. You will be our new brother. Sit with us!"* they chattered. Nikolai went with them uncertainly. Thad halted, his earlier euphoria evaporating. He had performed for high-ranking people before, and knew the etiquette—bow when you begin, bow at the end, and leave quickly unless told to stay. Operating outside the rules always turned into disaster for the lowest-ranked person, and that was always the performer. Thad didn't dare call Nikolai away from the royal family, but he wasn't sure if he should leave Nikolai with them.

Alexander himself solved the problem. He nodded once at Thad and made a small gesture to the floor next to the children's thrones. A hush fell over the court as Thad trotted over and went down on one knee next to Nikolai, who was standing by the tsar's children. Thad felt a hundred eyes on him, all of them calculating. The court did not sit in the presence of the tsar, except at state dinners. Kneeling was barely acceptable, on the tsar's order, and it showed great favor. Thad's heart pounded again. This was a tricky and difficult position to be in, and the ramifications made him dizzy. He was sitting so close to the tsar's platform that he could smell the tsar's cologne. Thad saw Sofiya standing near the wagons. She blew him a kiss and vanished behind them. Meanwhile, Dodd hurried into the ring to announce the next act. This performance seemed endless. Thad's knee dug into the earth while the tsar's children continued to talk to Nikolai from their chairs, ignoring the clowns who entered the ring. Nikolai said little, only nodding his head.

Thad itched with curiosity. He was sitting mere inches from one of the most powerful potentates on the planet, and he wanted to stare up at the tsar, but he didn't dare. His position was tentative enough without locking eyes with a king. He did, however, look sideways at the tsar's boots. Father always said you could tell a lot about a man by his boots. These were shiny and black, well made and perfectly polished. Of course they would be. What else would a tsar—

A gleam caught Thad's eye. The bottom of the tsar's throne was swathed with golden cloth that hid the legs. Through a gap in the cloth, however, Thad saw metal. Something moved with mechanical regularity. As his eyes adjusted, he saw that the object was a clock. Its second hand clicked forward, and it was strapped to a bundle of something. A chill ran down Thad's spine. Nikolai and the other children were only a few feet away from a bomb.

Thad didn't even think. He plunged his hand under Alexander's throne. The movement was so sudden, it caught everyone by surprise, including Alexander.

"What—?" he demanded.

Thad yanked the bomb out. It was a clock attached with wires to a bundle of dynamite sticks, and the minute hand was nearly touching noon. The second hand was just ticking past the six—only thirty seconds before it exploded. The court gave a collective gasp. Even the clowns paused, Benny Mazur with a bucket of fake whitewash in his hand. A tiny moment of confusion and uncertainty rippled through the room. A small part of Thad knew what they were thinking. Was this part of the circus? Should we be alarmed? How dared he lay hands on the tsar's throne!

Thad didn't pause. He sprinted away from the throne platform, toward the bank of high windows along the southern wall of the Nicholas Hall. The Cossack guards stationed all about the hall, meanwhile, quickly recovered from their surprise. They drew both swords and pistols and shouted orders at Thad. He ignored them. Fifteen seconds left. His brass hand smashed the glass and struts from one of the windows. With his other hand, he flung the bomb into the courtyard beyond.

"Get down!" he shouted, and dove.

The explosion rocked the floor and shattered every window on the wall. A hand of hot air slammed into Thad. Everyone who hadn't dropped was flung to the floor. Choking dust swirled. The chandeliers swung like trapezes in a hurricane. Screams and shouts and animal roars and frightened screeches swirled through the hall.

A great panic followed. Performers, servants, and courtiers alike rushed in random directions, most trying to flee the room, others staggering about in confusion. Some sat or lay on the earthen floor with injuries from flying debris. The little hovering automatons had been blown against the far wall and smashed. Thad tried to rise, but the floor rocked, and he could only manage hands and knees. The Cossack guards recovered the fastest. Several ran to the throne to see about the tsar and his children. Others saw to injured lords and ladies. Thad, for his part, found himself surrounded by a contingent of uniformed men. Three of the guards had cuts on their faces from flying debris. They yanked him to his feet with rough hands. Thad tried to protest, but only coughed up dust. One of the guards punched him in the stomach. Pain exploded through him, and all the air rushed from his lungs. He couldn't breathe. He tried to straighten, but the pain was too great. What had happened to Nikolai and Sofiya? Were they all right? He couldn't see for the dust and the people. The guard kicked his legs out from under him, and he went down again.

"Get him out of here," said one of the guards. *"Take him to Peter and Paul's for trial and execution."*

They dragged Thad through the chaotic crowd of people toward a set of doors. His own panic started now. They thought he was responsible for the bomb. He remembered the clockworker's death and tried to fight, but he couldn't catch his breath and his limbs were heavy. "Let me go!" he gasped. "Sofiya! Nikolai!"

The guards ignored him. Their hands bit into his arms. They were almost at the door now. He caught a glimpse of Nathan, his clown makeup smeared with blood, helping Dodd to walk. Tina McGee cradled the limp body of one of her poodles in her arms. No sign of Nikolai or Sofiya.

They reached the doors and the guard shoved them open. Thad mustered up some strength to struggle, but he was overwhelmed. The guard who had hit him before was pulling back his fist again when a sharp voice cut through the chaos.

"Wait!"

The entire room fell silent except for the animals, who continued to growl and screech and bark. Tsar Alexander was standing head and shoulders above the crowd on the platform next to his throne, his uniform covered with dust. A small cut scored his forehead, but he appeared otherwise uninjured.

"Bring that man to me!" he ordered.

The guards exchanged quick glances, then turned and dragged Thad, stumbling, over to the throne and pushed him to the floor before it, grinding his face into the dirt. By now, more than half the courtiers and servants had fled the hall, but a nearly equal number of other servants and guards had rushed in to see what was going on, so the Nicholas Hall was still crowded.

"Let him up," Alexander said.

The hands released him, and Thad slowly pulled himself upright. He was suddenly glad Dante wasn't here to make insolent remarks.

"What is your name, peasant?"

"Thaddeus Sharpe, Your Majesty. Son of Lawrence."

"What did you do, Thaddeus Lawrenovich?" Alexander demanded. *"What happened here?"*

Thad's mind was finally beginning to clear, though his body still ached. *"I . . . I saw the bomb under your throne, Your Majesty. I didn't think. I just grabbed it and ran. The children—"*

"My children were not injured, thanks to you," the tsar interrupted. *"This man with the clockwork shadow saved hundreds of lives today, including mine. He is a hero of Russia!"*

With that, the tsar descended from the platform, seized Thad by the shoulders, and kissed him on both cheeks. Thad froze, stunned. The guards stumbled over themselves to fall back and salute.

"Get everyone out of the hall in case that wall comes down," Alexander boomed, one arm around Thad's shoulder. *"Summon physicians for the injured. Send a messenger to the tsarina to let her know the children are fine. And someone find General Parkarov. I want a thorough investigation immediately!"*

Uncomfortably aware of the heavy arm of the tsar around his shoulder, Thad still searched the hall for Nikolai and Sofiya, but he couldn't find them. The tsar abruptly snapped his fingers and dropped his arm.

"Thaddeus Sharpe," he said. *"Sharpe! I thought I recognized the name. You are the man who kills clockworkers, are you not?"*

Thad wouldn't have thought he could be startled yet again today, but it turned out he could. *"Yes,* ser."

"And you are associated with the trick rider and her automaton horse? I believe the ringmaster introduced her as Sofiya Ekk."

"I am."

"Such a lovely wife." Alexander slapped Thad on the back. *"I congratulate you, Lawrenovich."*

"We are close, ser," Thad said quickly, *"but not married."*

"Ah. Then I congratulate you twice."

A large, gray-haired man in a blue uniform heavy with gold braid trotted over. *"Sire, I hate to intrude, but it is not safe for you here. And by your order, I have an investigation to conduct."*

"Of course, General Parkarov." Alexander turned to Thad. *"You and Miss Ekk will visit the tsarina and me as soon as it is convenient. We have much to discuss."*

And he strode away. Just at that moment, Sofiya hurried up. Her cloak was missing, but she didn't seem to be injured. "Thad! Are you well?"

"Sofiya!" Thad was seized with a confusing impulse to embrace her, which he quickly suppressed. "I'm perfectly fine. The tsar was—" He shook his head. "Where's Nikolai? Is he all right?"

The look on her normally composed face gave him a terrible turn, and fear rushed over him. "You should come," was all she said.

The guards holding Thad had scattered, and people of all sorts were trying to exit the hall. The circus folk who had animals were refusing to leave them behind, and were trying to turn the cages around to get them out. Old

Frank, the elephant trainer, was desperately working to keep Betsy from breaking into a rampaging panic. Clowns staggered about like broken rainbows. A pair of physicians and their apprentices arrived, but they concentrated on the members of the court, most of whom bore only minor scratches but howled loudly at the idea of getting up to walk. Word came that soldiers would be bringing in stretchers from the barrack at the Field of Mars, but they wouldn't arrive for some time. General Parkarov told several squealing court members—not all of them female—that they were welcome to wait for someone who could carry them away, and after the outer wall came down, he would be pleased to take their descriptions of what happened, if they survived. This solemn proclamation got most of them to their feet and out the door.

Sofiya led Thad through the chaos to a pillar that held up the inside wall. "You didn't see," she explained quietly. "He chased after you when you ran with the bomb, and he failed to drop to the floor. The blast caught him."

Thad's feet crunched over broken glass and chunks of debris, and his stomach roiled with dread. Nikolai was sitting on the far side of the pillar with Sofiya's dusty cloak bundled round him. At first, Thad couldn't see anything wrong. His hair was mussed. The upper half of his face, the human half, looked perfectly fine, and the metal lower half showed nothing strange except dirt. But then Nikolai turned to look up at Thad. The other side of his skull had been peeled away, revealing thousands upon thousands of tiny wheels and gears. Sparks snapped and cracked across them.

"Th-th-thank y-you," he stammered. "Th-thank you

f-f-for taking m-me out-out-out-out of there. I-I-I don't have-ave-ave one. M-M-Mr. Havoc-oc-oc called me *boy-boy-boy-boy*."

Thad stared. "What's wrong with him?"

"Something hit his head, where most of his memory wheels are stored," Sofiya said. "It creates problems."

"The victim-im-im of th-the cu-cu-cuckoo's b-b-brood parasitism-ism-ism will f-f-f-feed and t-t-t-tend the baby-baby-baby cuckoo," Nikolai sputtered, "even w-when the baby p-p-pushes the nat-nat-natural b-born offspring out and begin-in-ins to outg-g-g-grow the nest-est-est."

Thad looked down at the automaton that fizzled and sparked at his feet, the worry he had been feeling drained out of him. He had been starting to think of Nikolai as more than he was, but now Thad could see he was still nothing but a machine. "Can you fix this?"

"Perhaps." Sofiya's face was stony again. "But nothing is certain. Perhaps we should talk about this elsewhere. That wall may come down, you know."

Nikolai was unable to walk. Thad flung a fold of Sofiya's cloak over his head and picked him up. "We can't go far."

"What? Why not?"

"The tsar and tsarina want to see us." And he explained.

Sofiya's eyes went wide, and she automatically tried to brush the dust from her clothes. "What of Nikolai?"

"We'll have a servant put him a closet. No one will bother a broken automaton." The words came out harsher than Thad had intended, but he didn't back away from them.

"Thaddeus Sharpe!" Sofiya gasped. "That is—"

"Ser," said a soldier. *"If you and the lady will follow me, the tsar wishes to see you as soon as is convenient."*

It turned out "as soon as it is convenient" meant several detours. A small army of servants ushered Thad and Sofiya into bathing chambers, where they were scrubbed, perfumed, and dressed in smart new outfits. Sofiya's cloak was whisked away for cleaning, and her ruined circus costume was exchanged for a rich green gown trimmed with gold ribbon and sporting utterly fashionable and thoroughly impractical pagoda sleeves. Thad's new valet polished his brass hand and dressed him in a dark linen suit tucked into shiny boots under a long evening coat. Nikolai was not stuffed into a closet, but a footman was assigned the task of standing guard over him, to Sofiya's evident relief. Sofiya gave Thad a number of dark looks, which Thad pointedly ignored. At last, Thad and Sofiya were escorted down the maze of corridors and hallways of the Winter Palace.

The palace was still in disarray. Servants scurried in all directions. People talked in hushed tones. Soldiers stomped about everywhere, often stopping hapless serving girls or boys to search them. Thad had no idea how much of it was military bluster and how much was part of General Parkarov's investigation.

The phalanx of servants who had shepherded them through the baths took them to a heavily carved door and opened it. Thad forced himself to enter with firm steps and without gaping. Suddenly dealing with a mere bomb seemed easy. The opulent sitting room beyond had an enormous white fireplace. Shards of colored glass were inlaid in the chimney, and they threw sparkling scraps of light across the floor. The furniture was all

white and gold, as were heavy carpets that seemed too
fine to walk on. Every inch of the white ceiling and the
baseboards had been done in gold scrollwork. Trays of
food and bottles of wine occupied various end tables. An
automaton played a balalaika softly in one corner. The
tsar, also in a fresh uniform, sat in a wingback chair near
the fireplace, and in the chair next to him was a small,
delicate-looking woman with black hair and gray eyes—
Tsarina Maria. Strands of pearls were woven through
her elaborately braided hair, and the chair could barely
contain the great yellow dress with its voluminous skirts
and layer upon layer of crinoline. A dozen servants, male
and female, waited in the background. Despite his awe
at being twice in the same room with royalty in one day,
Thad couldn't help wondering how many peasants a
single strand of the tsarina's pearls would feed.

Sofiya is rubbing off on me, he thought as he bowed
before both of them. Sofiya curtsied.

Tsarina Maria came to her feet and rustled across the
floor to take both Thad's hands in hers. They were small
and cool, and her eyes were almost luminescent with
emotion. *"Thank you, thank you, thank you, Mr. Lawrenovich."* Her Russian carried a German accent. *"I already lost one child years ago, and now you have
prevented me from losing five more. I cannot thank you
enough."*

"Majesty," Thad replied, feeling more than a little
overwhelmed. *"I only did what any man would do."*

"No other man did," Maria pointed out.

Thad coughed. *"May I present Sofiya Ivanova Ekk?"*

"Not his wife," said the tsar.

"I'm sorry I missed your performance today, Miss

Ekk," the tsarina said, *"though considering what happened, perhaps not extremely sorry. Come and sit. We will have cake and wine or perhaps tea."*

The servants seated them at chairs rather lower than the tsar's and tsarina's and set plates of food and drink at their elbows. Sofiya took her place with elegant grace, as if she had been dining with kings all her life. Thad nervously managed to take his own chair without stumbling, and he was careful not to use his brass hand for the wineglass, in case he spilled. Like the rest of the palace, the room was warm, almost stifling. Later, Thad learned it was because Tsarina Maria's health was poor, and the entire Winter Palace was heated for her comfort.

"Now, then," said the tsar with a gold cup of wine in his hand, *"you must tell me from the beginning what happened and how you found the bomb."*

With a sidelong glance at Sofiya's cool demeanor, Thad did so. It occurred to him that this would probably not be the last time he would tell this story.

"We must toast your bravery." Alexander raised his glass. *"To Thaddeus Sharpe Lawrenovich, without whom any of us would be sitting here right now."*

They drank. The wine was smooth and soft and perfect. Thad eyed the food tray—decorated cakes, pâté, cold chicken braised in wine, soft cheese, baked salmon, poached pear tartlets, pickled mushrooms, and caviar rolled into strips of sturgeon. He didn't dare try a bite—his stomach alternated between tight tension and black nausea. The excess of wealth and power exuded by this room and its people made him uneasy and unhappy, and he wanted nothing more than to escape to familiar surroundings as soon as possible.

"You must be rewarded, Mr. Lawrenovich," the tsarina said. From around her neck she removed a long strand of pearls strung with gold wire. *"Accept this favor."*

It was on the tip of Thad's tongue to refuse such a rich gift. But the circus man in him stepped up and snatched control. *"Thank you, great lady,"* he said, and slid the strand into his breast pocket. *"It is too much."*

"Not compared to lives of my husband and my children," she said with a sniff. *"Now tell me, where did you get the little automaton? My children won't stop talking about it. Did you build it yourself?"*

"No," Thad said quickly. *"I took it—him—from a clockworker some time ago."*

"Yes! You are the famous clockwork killer," Alexander said. *"I have heard your name. How many clockworkers have you destroyed?"*

Sofiya's face remained perfectly impassive, and she fearlessly downed caviar and mushrooms. Thad flushed, then felt foolish for flushing. Why should he feel bad about slaying murderers like the one who had killed his son? The Tsar of Russia was praising him for it, for God's sake. And yet the feeling remained.

"I don't . . . keep track," Thad said.

"It's been that many, has it?" The tsar raised his glass again. *"You do a great service to mankind. The tsarina and I would enjoy hearing of your exploits."*

"Do tell," Sofiya said with patently false eagerness. *"He won't speak of it to me, ser."*

Thad saw the opening and exploited it. *"It's man's talk,"* he said. *"Your Majesty might insist, of course, but such stories are . . . indelicate."*

"Why do you do it?" the tsarina asked before her

husband could respond. *"Clockworkers are dangerous. If they got hold of you, they could kill you. Or much worse."*

"It seemed necessary at the time," Thad replied quietly. *"Clockworkers are dangerous, yes, which means they endanger."* It was very hard to say these things with Sofiya in the room, true or not. Her eyes were perfectly calm, but he felt bad, hypocritical even.

"Clockworkers have their uses," the tsar said. *"They build fantastic machines. But they also bring filth into the world, as you have pointed out. Once we have wrung every bit of use out of them down in the Peter and Paul Fortress, we exterminate them."*

"We have seen," Sofiya said mildly. *"It was very instructive."*

What the hell was she doing? *"I have heard,"* Thad put in as a way to guide the subject in a new direction, *"that the Chinese venerate clockworkers, call them Dragon Men and give them places of honor in their emperor's court."*

The tsar made a disgusted sound. *"Oriental barbarians. Not even the Cossacks would be so foolish. I assume you know what happened in Ukraine."*

"I do," said Thad.

"That is what comes of letting clockworkers run around loose." The vehemence in the tsar's voice turned the air to bile. *"They must be caged and controlled before they—"*

"Now, now." The tsarina patted his hand. *"You mustn't let yourself get worked up. You've already had a difficult day."*

"Yes, yes." Alexander drained his cup and it was in-

stantly refilled. *"Difficult. Hm. You have a talent for understatement, my dear."*

"If I may, ser," Sofiya spoke up. *"Is it true that you have been thinking of emancipating the serfs?"*

He eyed her over the rim of his cup. *"These words have reached the streets, have they?"*

"Rumors and speculation," Sofiya said. *"I know the landowners largely oppose the idea, and I myself wonder why such a wise man as the tsar would—"*

"Huh!" Alexander snapped his cup down. *"The landowners. They want to keep Russia in the dark ages. We are trapped with feudal ideas in a feudal economy. No other empire uses serfs in this day and age. Men must own their own land. Ownership creates pride and foments new ideas. Like Peter the Great before me, I traveled widely in my youth, and I have seen what new ideas can accomplish— navies and railroads and telegraphy and airships and electric power. None of these things were invented in Russia. Our people are stifled, and it's to the good of the country that they are granted the freedom to do as they wish."*

This was clearly an old argument, but it had steered the conversation away from clockworkers. Thad shot Sofiya a grateful look, which she now ignored.

"So the rumors are true?" Sofiya asked pleasantly.

"You are too blunt for court, my dear," the tsar said. *"Your attempts to tweak information out of me are blatant. But everyone already knows. My legal scholars are drawing up the* ukaz *as we speak. When the new law is finished and signed—probably sometime in January—the serfs will be freed of their obligations to the landowners. Except for taxes, of course. No empire can run without taxes."*

"Is it possible, then," Sofiya continued, *"that the person who planted the bomb was a landowner who doesn't want you to accomplish this feat?"*

Alexander stroked his chin. *"The thought had occurred. Do you have information about it?"*

"Only speculation. It is why I—"

The door burst open, and General Parkarov dashed into the room with a box in his hands. He gave a perfunctory bow before the sovereigns. *"Your Majesties. I have news of the investigation."*

The tsar half came to his feet. *"What did you find, General?"*

"These." From the box he extracted two spiders, or what was left of them. They had been blown to pieces. He laid them on a table. Thad recognized them as ones that belonged to Mr. Griffin. His skin went cold despite the heat of the room.

"We found these bits in the Nicholas Hall." he said. *"Two working spiders escaped us. They are not ones employed by the Winter Palace."*

"Did they plant the bomb?" Alexander asked.

"I am certain." The general's eyes glittered as he spoke. *"I inspected the throne room myself before you entered, and there was no bomb. No one approached the throne after my inspection, so it must have been these spiders who planted it, sent by a rogue clockworker. We must find him before he strikes again."*

"This is not necessarily—" Sofiya began.

"Do that," Alexander ordered. *"Whatever it takes. Send your men. Search the city. Bring him—or her—in."*

"Majesty." Parkarov bowed and withdrew.

Sofiya looked like she wanted to say more, but the

tsarina said, *"Disgusting! Horrifying that some monster out there wants to murder my children!"*

This time the tsar patted her hand. *"We'll find him, my dear. And then we can watch the machines tear him to pieces, as he deserves."*

"Ser, *I wonder if you've considered—"* Sofiya began.

"Mr. Lawrenovich," Maria interrupted, turning to Thad, *"you're an expert at hunting clockworkers down."*

Uh-oh. Thad could see where this was going. He flicked his eyes toward Sofiya, but she just shook her head helplessly. *"I . . . yes,"* he said, trying to think.

"Then join the men," she said. *"Use your skills. Find that clockworker for me. And kill him."*

The machine was enormous now, both physically and mentally. Its body had added so many memory wheels and creation devices that it could no longer move about. It squatted at the intersection of five tunnels, taking in more and more and more metal, whatever the spiders could bring. It controlled a great many spiders. They skittered about the tunnels and the city above, giving the machine a perfect picture of the place. Half a dozen spiders were stealing books from the engineering section at the Library of the Russian Academy of Sciences and flipping through them at blinding speed, transmitting words and concepts to the machine, then leaving them about for the puzzled men in the library to reshelve. Already there was talk of hauntings and poltergeists, despite them being men of science. The Master did not mind as long as the machine and the spiders were not caught.

The machine sent tentacles of wire and pipe through the tunnels. This was one of the few places in Saint Petersburg that actually *had* tunnels, an attempt on behalf of the Academy at a sewer and cargo transportation. The high water table meant tunnels were difficult to dig and expensive to maintain, however, and the project had been abandoned. The machine had taken advantage of the train tracks already laid down to transport the materials it needed, especially metal and books.

Many of the books were written by people called *clockworkers*. These clockworkers were held in a prison in the Peter and Paul Fortress on yet another River Neva island of the sort Saint Petersburg seemed to be prone. Most of the books hadn't been written so much as dictated, and some of them rambled rather a lot, though their insights into physics and engineering and clockwork technology were proving invaluable, and they allowed the machine to continue its improvements. The clockworkers seemed to interest the Master very much, though he seemed to espouse no interest whatsoever in the *clockwork plague* that spawned them. The machine noted both these facts without emotion and continued its research and its improvements.

By now, the main part of the machine occupied the entire rather large intersection of the five tunnels beneath the Academy, and it no longer resembled a spider with ten legs, but was instead a chaotic mass of pipes and gears and boilers and claws and wheels and belts and mechanical hands. A cabinet that resembled a small brass wardrobe stood prominent in the center of this mass. The doors stood tightly shut. Next to it, a twisted chute coiled to the ground. The machine chuffed and puffed, and from an aperture at the top of the chute emerged a spider, gleaming and new. It spiraled down the chute and clattered to the concrete floor of the tunnel. It stumbled about drunkenly, then righted itself and scampered about as if excited. It bobbed on its new legs and made a squeaking sound. The machine chuffed and puffed again, and a second spider spiraled down the chute to land near the first. It also staggered. The first spider recoiled for a moment, then scampered over to investigate. The second spider came fully upright and, like the first spider, bobbed up and down, exploring its legs. The first spider extended a leg to touch the second. Abruptly, the second leaped on the first and tore at it with all eight of its own legs. The first spider squeaked in dismay and tried to disentangle itself, but to no avail.

The machine extended two mechanical hands, plucked the two spiders apart, and held them wriggling at a distance from each other. The second continued its attempted attack on the first, and the first recoiled in the machine's grip. Aggression. Interesting.

The machine tossed the first spider into a hopper, sucked it inside, and crushed it to squeaking pieces. The second spider wriggled furiously in the machine's hand until the machine set it down, whereupon it rushed about in angry circles. The machine exuded a third spider. This time, both of them fought until the machine sent a signal of its own that stopped them. The spiders came reluctantly under control even as the machine exuded a fourth aggressive spider.

Chapter Twelve

"Kill him!" Sofiya paced the wooden floor of the Black Tent in her new gown. "Why did you say you would kill him?"

"I suppose I should have refused the tsarina?" Thad drummed his fingers heavily on a workbench. "The trouble is, the assassin wasn't a clockworker."

Sofiya stopped pacing. "How do you mean?"

"A clockworker wouldn't use dynamite." Thad was almost snarling now, though he wasn't sure who he was angry at. "Too blunt. Too pedestrian. Too inelegant. Killing with mere dynamite is no *fun*. A clockworker who wanted to assassinate someone would use something elaborate or stylish, like a spider that delivered a drop of poison, or a thin wire that sliced your head off as you galloped past on a horse, or an automaton that disguised itself as a bootblack's box until it sprang into action and sliced you into bits. Dynamite? Never."

"So who did it, then?"

"Your hypothesis is probably the correct one," Thad

said. "Disgruntled landowner who doesn't want to lose his serfs."

"And what do we do about this?"

"How's Nikolai?" Thad asked, deliberately changing the subject.

She turned to look at the little automaton. Nikolai was sitting upright on the workbench next to Dante. The sparking in his head had died down, and he wasn't speaking. Every so often he gave a twitch. His left hand jerked upward, then lowered itself over and over.

"Failing," she said. "He needs repairs badly."

"Are you going to do it, then?"

She folded her arms. "Why do you care so much? He is just a machine, as you pointed out."

"Why *don't* you care?" Thad shot back. The anger was growing. "You're the one who loves machines so very much. You haven't even repaired Dante yet."

"I was busy creating the act that saved this circus." The heat rose in Sofiya's voice as well. "I had to build the colt and put in—"

"Don't feed me more lies, woman," Thad interrupted.

"Lies? How dare you!"

"And keep the indignation." Thad lowered his voice to a deadly steadiness. "I know clockworkers. There's no evidence in this boxcar that you built that colt here—no scraps of metal, no plans, no calculations, no chipped tools. That colt was inside your horse from the beginning. It's why you thought it was funny that Nikolai gave it the name of a male deity. The only thing you've built lately was my hand." He held it up. "And that was something you modified from a spider Mr. Griffin built. That's very, very strange for a clockworker, Sofiya."

She looked frightened now. "So what? All clockwork-ers are strange."

"They're all strange in the same way. I know," Thad said relentlessly. A part of him was well aware that he was doing this to avoid what Sofiya had brought up with Nikolai, but he didn't care. He kept going. "You don't *like* to build, do you? But you *want* to do. You *hunger* to do. The machines and the numbers call to you, but you're afraid of them. You said the madness comes on you and you have to build, but that was a lie. You haven't built much of anything. You said you're looking forward to go-ing mad, and that was another lie. You're terrified of the madness, and that's why you don't build anything. You're afraid you'll fall into a fugue and never come out."

"I built your hand!" she protested.

"Only because I saved yours." He locked eyes with her. "What happened, Sofiya? Did you fall into a fugue state and hurt someone when you built Kalvis and that little energy pistol you carry around? Or are you just afraid of what you might become?"

"You *kill* people like me!" she shouted.

"You made me swear to do it! Or don't you want me to keep that promise anymore?"

She spun away from him and leaned on the work-bench. Her shoulders shook, and Thad realized she was weeping. The anger drained out of him, and he felt stu-pid and foolish. What had he been trying to prove? That he was smarter or stronger than she was? Shouting and yelling, that was always helpful. And with Nikolai sitting on the table with his head open. Thad was a schoolyard bully. His face burned with shame. He touched her shoulder. "Listen, Sofiya, I'm sorry I—"

He was flat against the wall with her iron grip around his throat and his feet a good six inches off the floor. His breath choked off. He clawed ineffectually at the air. Sofiya's other hand reached down and clasped his groin. A dull ache snaked up his abdomen.

"Fine," she growled into his face. Her voice was not her own, and she was speaking Russian. *"I will repair the child. I will even repair the parrot. And you"* — she squeezed harder and his eyes rolled back from the gut-wrenching agony — *"you will help me."*

She casually flung him aside. Thad crashed to the floor, clutching at his neck, gasping for air, reeling from pain. Sofiya stomped about the Black Tent, snatching tools from racks and boxes and tossing them beside Nikolai. *"Get up, boy!"* she snapped at Thad. Coughing, Thad pushed himself upright. Sofiya crackled with energy. Her presence filled the boxcar and pushed at the walls. Every movement was fast and precise. Thad recognized the signs. She had fallen into a clockwork fugue.

"Bring me that spanner!" she barked. *"And that screw-pick! Before I slice you open like a putrid rat."*

Without a word, Thad handed her the tools. She snatched them from him as if he were nothing but an open drawer and bent over Nikolai's exposed machinery. After some muttering and swearing, she grabbed Thad's brass hand and shoved it into Nikolai's head. *"Hold this wheel in place. Don't move it!"*

"I—" Thad began.

The slap rocked his head back in an explosion of pain. It came so fast he didn't even see Sofiya's hand move. *"Do not speak again unless I ask you a question. And then speak Russian, not that flea-ridden garbage you sodomite British call language."*

Thad worked his jaw back and forth, so angry he felt he might explode. The thought flicked through his mind: She was a clockworker, just like the one who had killed David. His spring-loaded knives were sheathed in his sleeves. He could still use the right one perfectly well, and it was a better than even chance his brass left was up to the job now, too. If he backed up and waited until her back was turned, he could get in a perfect throw before she knew what was happening.

But this was Sofiya, the woman who had saved his hand and his life. And he himself had brought about her fugue state. Now she could save Nikolai.

A machine. Why did he care about a soulless machine? In one shot, Thad could eliminate both of them. He hung there with a sword down his throat, divided in two.

And what would happen when Mr. Griffin returned? Mr. Griffin, the strangest and most cunning clockworker Thad had come across to date. It would be foolish to face Mr. Griffin alone. He needed Sofiya. He needed Dante. He might even need Nikolai.

Thad swallowed his anger and, feeling cold, reached into the little automaton's head to hold the wheel as the clockworker had ordered.

"Don't be clumsy, boy," she said. *"And we can finish this."*

Hours passed. The clockworker stormed about the Black Tent barking commands and pouring vitriol over Thad in equal parts. He kept his head down and obeyed as best he could, understanding fully why clockworkers were rarely able to work with others. Twice more the clockworker struck him hard enough to leave bruises, and only through great exercise of self-control did he avoid striking back. But slowly, steadily, the little automaton's head came back together. It stopped twitching, though it didn't move or speak as the clockworker set new rivets into his metal skull. She even produced needle and thread to repair his scalp with swift, tiny stitches. Hunger gnawed at Thad's insides, and exhaustion dragged at his limbs, but the clockworker wasn't finished yet. Without a pause, she turned to Dante. Her quick fingers disassembled his gears and wheels. A steady stream of invective punctuated her orders, berating Thad for letting the parrot fall into disrepair and filth. Without expression, he brought buckets of soap and water and a can of machine oil. In a short time, she had cleaned Dante out and put him back together again.

"He needs new feathers and a new eye," she barked. Her new dress was a wreck, and her hair was a tangled thornbush. *"Heat up the forge and fetch that brass spanner. We can melt it down to make—"*

"Miss," Thad interrupted, and this time he dodged her slap. *"Miss, it's time to stop."*

"I decide when it is time to stop!" she howled. *"You will—"*

He flung a bucket of cold water over her. It soaked her from head to foot. She gasped at him, her mouth opening and closing like a salmon's. Cautiously, he waited a moment.

"Thad?" she said at last in a small voice. "What happened?"

"It's me," he said, and it was a relief to see the madness gone from her eyes. "You're all right. We're still in the Black Tent. It must be after midnight by now."

She looked around fearfully. "What did I do? Oh God, did I hurt anyone? Did any person—?"

"Everyone's fine," he said neutrally. "You hurt no one."

"Then what's this?" She touched his cheek where she had slapped him earlier, and he moved his head away. "I hurt you, didn't I? Dear heaven, what else did I do? Tell me the truth, Thad. I have to know!"

Another piece fell into place. "That's the true hold Mr. Griffin has on you, isn't it? About your sister."

She sagged, soaked and sobbing, into Thad's arms. Thad caught her before she fell, then eased her onto a stool and backed away again.

"Olenka can no longer walk because of me," she wept. "I did something to her, I do not even remember what. She can't even bear to look at me now, and who can blame her? I send her all my money so she can live and pay the doctors, and still it is never enough. I feel the monster."

Thad nodded. He felt flat, cold, and his words came out almost stony. He had allowed himself to get too close. He had forgotten her true nature. No matter what she said or did, this woman was a clockworker, volatile and dangerous, and he needed to remember that at all times. He wouldn't kill her, not until she had helped him against Mr. Griffin, but he couldn't trust her. His face throbbed where she had hit him.

"I'd wondered about that," he mouthed. "It'll be all right. It wasn't your fault."

"Then whose was it?" she demanded, still sobbing.

"Every moment, I must keep myself under control, or I will do it again. I *have* done it again. I hurt you."

Was she truly sorry or was she trying to manipulate him again? Best to play along, regardless. "A few slaps and insults never hurt anyone," he said. "And Griffin can't hurt her, you know."

"He can. He said if I ever refused him, he would drag Olenka to me and push me into a clockwork fugue, just as you did, so I would finish her off."

A finger of guilt crept up Thad's spine. He had indeed pushed Sofiya into this fugue and upset her. But no. He was tired of balancing on a knife. Sofiya was a clock-worker, and Thad knew clockworkers. He would keep a close eye on her, use her to find Griffin, and then he would have to eliminate her, too. Before she did more than slap.

"We won't let Mr. Griffin do anything to you," he said aloud. "We'll stop him."

Sofiya suddenly seemed to realize what she was doing. She straightened on the stool and turned her head to dry her eyes on her sopping sleeve, with little success. "Well, thank you, then. It feels better to hear someone say that." She crossed the boxcar floor to the worktable and Nikolai the automaton. "But we have other things to attend."

From a drawer she produced a flask of brandy that probably belonged to Dodd and emptied the contents down the automaton's throat, then pressed a switch behind one ear. He shuddered all over and blinked several times.

"Nikolai," he said. "My name is Nikolai."

"Yes, it is," Thad said. He suppressed the happy little thrill went through him at the sound of the boy's voice and kept his voice neutral. "Are you all right?"

"I . . . I . . ." He hesitated, a machinelike pause. "I am operating well. I am *fine*. Yes. Fine." He held up his metal hands and wriggled the fingers. "Fine."

"What is the last you remember?" Sofiya asked.

Nikolai cocked his head. "I danced for the tsar. The children wanted me to sit with them. Thad reached under the tsar's throne. And now I'm here in the Black Tent. What happened?"

"There was an explosion," Thad said. "You were injured. Sofiya repaired you."

"Did I die, then?"

The question caught Thad off guard. The automaton was still good at that. "I . . . don't know if the question applies to something that was never—"

"You are not dead," Sofiya said firmly. "Are you hungry?"

"No. But I think I will be soon."

"Good. That is good." Sofiya picked up Dante, who was his normal, shabby self, but still inert, and handed him to Thad. "I see I found the time for this as well. You'll need to wind him."

An enormous yawn split Thad's head. Sofiya mimicked him, unusual for clockworkers, who rarely slept. Apparently not wanting to be left out, Nikolai followed suit.

"I think it's food and bed for me first," Thad said.

"Yes." Sofiya staggered slightly. "I have not slept in over a week now, and I think that is the limit for even a clockworker."

"I will watch you sleep, then," Nikolai said. "And I will wind Dante."

The exhaustion grew worse as they stumbled through

the dark circus back to Thad's wagon, where he and Sofiya downed a cold supper. By now, Thad felt numb,
physically and emotionally. Sofiya was a clockworker,
Nikolai was an automaton. He had stepped over the
knife. Thad only vaguely remembered undressing and
climbing into bed.

"Bless my soul! Sharpe is sharp! Applesauce! Bless my
soul!"

Thad barely stopped himself from sitting up and
cracking his head on the wagon roof. He was in his own
bed above the wardrobe. Sunlight streamed through the
side window of the wagon, creating a slanted square of
gold on the opposite wall. It was chilly—no one had
made a fire in the tiny stove last night. Sofiya lay sleeping
on a pull-down shelf bed beneath the window. Dante
was doing energetic somersaults on his hanging perch,
and Nikolai stood beneath it with the tireless patience of
a machine.

"Good morning! Good morning!" Dante chirped.

"That's new." Thad ran a hand through curly dark
hair. His muscles were stiff and achy from everything
that had happened yesterday.

"I taught it to him," Nikolai said. "Good morning!"

"Hm." Thad climbed down from the bed, shivering a
little. He would have to get some coal for the stove. To
his surprise, he was able to manage buttons when he
pulled on his clothes. At the last moment, he remembered the strand of pearls the tsarina had given him and
transferred them from yesterday's coat to his pocket.

"What are we doing today?" Nikolai asked.

Thad regarded him. The little automaton, with his

thoroughly inhuman face and hands and his utterly human eyes and voice, still acted the little boy, but last night had been a sharp reminder that he was indeed just a machine. The illusion of humanity was realistic, but like any skilled circus performance, it was still an illusion, and eventually it would end. It was foolish to become attached to an illusion. That road only led to pain and loss. It would probably be best to hand Nikolai over to Dodd after all. Nikolai would protest, perhaps even cry, but it would be nothing more than noise created by steel and wire. As well to become upset by sad songs played on the calliope.

"I think," Thad said, "that it's time for you to—"

"I'll bet Dodd will want us in the circus now," Nikolai interrupted. "We should work on our spot before the show this afternoon."

That stopped Thad cold. With everything that had happened, he hadn't even thought of—

Someone pounded on the door. This brought Sofiya awake, and she snapped upright. Her hair stood out in a golden haystack. "Who? What?"

"Doom," said Dante.

Now what? Thad reached for the door, wishing things would slow down for just a moment so he could catch his breath and sort things out. Nathan Storm was on the steps, dressed in his customary Aran sweater and fisherman's cap. He was handsome man, no doubt about that, and more than one woman in the circus had lamented over his romantic choices.

"Oi," he said. "Sleepyhead! We've been wondering when you were going to make an appearance."

"What do you need, Nathan?" Thad asked tiredly.

Nathan brandished a handful of papers. "We've been getting notes and telegrams all morning from Lord Snootyfruits and Lady Tenderslippers. Every one of them wants you and Nikolai to dine with them or attend their parties or appear in their boxes at the ballet. Three of them are offering marriage to various daughters and sisters."

"Oh God." A year ago, even a month ago, Thad would have been thrilled at this development. Now it just filled his chest with heavy dread.

"And Dodd wants you back into the ring," Nathan went on relentlessly. "The show must go on. The Stilgores were both hurt yesterday—he twisted his ankle and she broke her arm when the explosion knocked them off their stilts. The lions and Betsy are still nervous and in no condition to go in front of an audience. That means we're short, short, short. You and Sofiya and Nikolai are our new headliners."

"Told you," Nikolai said.

"Bless my soul," said Dante.

"Grand! Your parrot is fixed," Nathan said with relentless cheer. "Can you do you the pirate sword swallower again? We could use it."

"Not yet," Thad hedged. "Look—"

"Oh, and some soldiers are looking for you."

"Soldiers?" Thad was on full alert now. "What do you mean soldiers?"

"My Russian isn't the best. Something about General Parkarov wanting to talk to you about your promise to the tsarina? They're coming now. Jesus, Thad—what have you been *doing*, then?"

Even as Nathan spoke, a contingent of four stern-faced soldiers in red uniforms came around another wagon into view. Thad swallowed. Sofiya, dressed in a simple dark skirt and blouse, came to the door.

"What is happening?" she demanded.

"Another trip to the Winter Palace, I expect." Thad held out his arm so Dante could leap down to his shoulder, then moved down the steps so he wouldn't have to touch Sofiya. "You stay with Nikolai."

"What do I do about these invitations?" Nathan asked.

"Refuse politely and invite them to the show," Thad said.

The soldiers said little beyond repeating what Nathan had said, that General Parkarov wanted to see Thad—not Sofiya. At least he didn't seem to be under arrest. But they took him across the Field of Mars toward the barrack on the western side, not to the Winter Palace.

A line of wheeled cages stretched across the muddy field like a twisted parody of a train. The cages were crammed with men, women, and even children. Some cried out and reached through the bars. Others huddled inside like frightened animals. A few were clearly dead. Their clothes said they came from all classes, from street poor to well born. Even as Thad watched, horrified, a team of automatons hauled at the cages, tugging the train toward the bridge, the same one the clockworker had come across earlier in his cage.

"What's this?" Thad asked, eyes wide. *"What's going on?"* But the soldiers didn't answer. They firmly marched him into the wide blue barrack. The interior didn't match the stunning exterior—long, twisting hallways of scuffed wood, no real attempt at decoration, the heavy smell of tobacco and sweat, spare offices, occasional sitting rooms,

and long rows of barrack rooms. Soldiers of all ages in various states of dress rushed everywhere, looking harried. Uniformed boys as young as five dodged around carrying messages, laundry, and parcels. Thad wondered how many had been conscripted.

He was shown to a rather larger office redolent with overly sweet tobacco smoke. General Parkarov was waiting for him, pipe in mouth. He greeted Thad heartily.

"We need you down in the Peter and Paul Fortress," he said.

"You speak English?" Thad asked in surprise.

"Yes, and I would enjoy the chance to practice. Come—my driver is waiting."

They trooped back outside, where a two-horse carriage awaited them. The line of cages was already gone, but another line of empty ones was taking its place. In the city beyond, Thad's ears picked up hoofbeats and crashes and screams and the occasional pistol shot. His mouth went dry and his brass hand clutched the side of the carriage as he and the general boarded.

"What is happening, General?" he demanded. "Please explain!"

The driver whipped up the horses and carriage jolted forward. "You know that my investigation into the bombing turned up those foreign spiders in the Nicholas Hall," the general said. "That can only mean one thing— a clockworker used those spiders to place the bomb under the tsar's throne. We must find him. Even if the tsar hadn't ordered it, I would do so."

"Actually, I'd like to discuss that with you, sir," Thad said carefully. "No clockworker would use a tool so blunt as dynamite. It—"

"Clearly one did." The general waved Thad's objections aside. "It is well known that a number of clockworkers run about loose in Saint Petersburg. They come here from Poland and Belarus and Lithuania, sniffing for the money they need for their inventions. It's the only thing that stops them—not having enough money or materials to build what they want. That, and men like us." He clapped Thad on the back. "Ah, the bridge."

The horses clopped onto the massive pontoon bridge that spanned the River Neva. Traffic was light this morning, allowing the carriage to make good time. The boats turned upside down to make up the pontoons barely bobbed on the inky water. Skiffs and small boats glided about, hemmed in by the low bridges that divided the Neva into sections. To Thad's left, the wide, deep river flowed around a number of large islands, where it emptied into the Gulf of Finland and ultimately, the Baltic Sea. The breeze on the bridge was cold and smelled of fish. Thad wished he had worn a heavier coat.

"Do you know Saint Petersburg?" the general asked, and continued before he got an answer. "There to the west is Vasilyevsky Island. You see the Kunstkammer there on the bank, Russia's first museum, founded by Peter the Great himself! I am related to him, you know, on my mother's side."

"Are you?" Thad asked casually. "Do you have estates, then?"

"Oh yes. Quite extensive. I am forced to stay here near the tsar and can only visit irregularly. Would you like to visit yourself? My holdings are very beautiful in the spring."

"That sounds wonderful. Let me ask Ringmaster

Dodd about his plans for the circus, and we can talk of it later," Thad replied, careful to be vague. He pointed at Vasilyevsky Island, which spread across the horizon to the west. About half of it seemed to be wooded. The other half was grown over with buildings. "What's that building near the museum?"

"Ah! The Russian Academy of Sciences. Human beings work there. No clockworkers. I have heard your ringmaster is a tinker. He might enjoy talking to some of our good Russian engineers, yes?"

"I'm sure."

"Past it, downstream, are the docks, of course. The pride of Saint Petersburg! They are the reason my cousin Peter the Great wanted this city built in the first place — to give Russia a good seaport. Everything imaginable comes into Russia through those docks. Cousin Peter ordered a foundry built down there, in fact. Much easier to smelt raw ore brought in by the ships when the foundry is by the shipyards. My cousin Peter was a great thinker!"

And the general certainly didn't want anyone to forget who his cousin was, Thad mused. "A great man," Thad repeated.

"And up ahead" — the general pointed with his pipe to where the bridge led — "is the other big island of Saint Petersburg: Petrogradsky. Beside it" — he pointed again, this time to a smaller island ahead and a little to the left and entirely ringed with a high stone wall — "is our destination, the Peter and Paul Fortress. That was also built by — "

"Your cousin Peter the Great?" Thad finished.

The general laughed. "Everything here was built by

my cousin Peter. We only build higher on his mighty shoulders."

They finished crossing to Petrogradsky Island and took another, smaller, pontoon bridge to the Peter and Paul Fortress. An arched stone gate within the walls stood open, admitting quite a lot of foot and carriage traffic to a cobblestoned courtyard. A second gate let them into the fortress proper. The general wouldn't explain anything to Thad about what was going on, which made him tense and frustrated. He wanted to make demands, but of course he couldn't, not a general related to a tsar.

The fortress was more like a small, wealthy city than a military encampment. Stone streets wound among elaborate building scattered about a cathedral with a golden spire that poked high into the cloudy sky. People were everywhere—richly robed priests and plainly dressed acolytes and ladies in their bell-shaped dresses and men on horses and soldiers on foot. And the automatons! So many, they nearly outnumbered the people—clicking spiders and spindly horses and automatic carriages and automaton servants. Thad hadn't seen so many automatons in the open since he had come to Russia, though he couldn't help but notice that none of them moved with the ease and lifelike grace of Nikolai. The general didn't seem to notice.

"Every tsar in Russia is buried beneath that cathedral over there," he said proudly. "My family visits Peter's tomb every year. The cannon that goes off every day at noon fires from the fortress walls, you know."

At that, Thad noticed the heavy cannons and armaments lining the fortress walls. Huge energy weapons and cannons that could fire halfway to London and crouching automatons that, when they stood, could probably hurl boulders. It looked like enough firepower to level a major city. Thad was impressed. The Russian flag flew at three of the four corners of the fortress walls. At the fourth, a blank green flag was just going up. Parkarov nodded at it.

"That means I'm here," he said. "When the tsar or his family visits, the flag is red. You can see the arms up on the walls. This place was originally built to defend Saint Petersburg from invasion by the Swedes, though in the end, the cowards never arrived. Best for them in the end, I suppose."

A trio of dog-sized spiders scampered past, looking tiny after all the enormous war machines. "Why are so many automatons on the street here?" Thad asked.

"That is part of where we are going," the general answered as they pulled up in front of a blocky, two-story building of stone. "Here we are: the Trubetskoy Bastion, the best prison in all Russia. No one has ever escaped."

A penny dropped in Thad's head. "You keep your clockworkers here. And that's why so many automatons run about on this island."

"Exactly. Most of Russia's automatons serve the military, as is proper." He brought Thad up the steps, through a series of hallways past guards and checkpoints, and down an electric lift that left them in what Thad could only describe as a dungeon. The walls, floors, and ceiling were constructed of solid stone blocks. The ceiling was low. Damp hallways lit by electric lanterns snaked in a dozen directions, and they were faced with small, narrow doors, each with a tiny barred window up top and a hinged food slot below. Human cries and pleas echoed up and down the corridors. The place stank of urine, excrement, and fear. It was horrifying to think that human beings were housed here. Thad cringed inside his own skin. Bile bit the back of his throat, and he forced himself not to vomit.

"What is this place for?" Thad asked faintly.

"I told you—clockworkers. We leave them in the cells where they cannot hurt anyone and give them materials so they can invent for us until they go mad and must be executed."

An automaton shaped like a low cart trundled past. A spindly arm opened the slot at the bottom of a door and shoved a single bowl of what looked like gray porridge through, though Thad could hear multiple voices within the cell. The automaton moved on to the next door.

"How do they invent anything in here?"

"Well, we keep them under strict observation, of course. You know that clockworkers can build nearly anything, it seems, given the proper materials, and we limit what they have and how much time they can build."

Which explained why Russian automatons were so clumsy compared to those in the West and in China, Thad added to himself. That Russian clockworkers produced anything at all under such conditions was a miracle. Thad didn't see clockworkers as victims, despite anything Sofiya said, but there was no reason to torture them, either.

The general took his arm and towed him down the hall. Faces appeared at the tiny windows, some shy and flinching, other imploring. Thad felt sick. "All these people—they can't be clockworkers. There aren't this many clockworkers in all Russia, let alone Saint Petersburg."

"Of course not," General Parkarov agreed. "That is why we sent for you."

Thad halted between a set of doors. "I fail to understand my role in any of this, sir."

"We know a clockworker attempted to assassinate the tsar," Parkarov explained patiently. "We cannot allow such a monster to run around loose in Saint Petersburg—he might try again, and succeed."

"My lords!" cried a man between the bars of his window. *"My lords, please! I'm not a clockworker! I'm a simple blacksmith! I've never had the plague in my life. I have a wife and four children, my lord. They will starve without me. Please, my lords!"*

"My lords!" cried a woman from her cell. *"I am no clockworker! I help my father in his tin shop, but I am no clockworker. I can't even read! I have done nothing!"*

"My lord . . ."

"Please, my lords . . ."

"Good God," Thad breathed. "You rounded up everyone."

"Indeed. All we have to do is wait and see which ones go mad. That will show us the clockworker."

Revulsion swept over Thad in a black wave. He wanted to run, board a fast train and leave Russia and its lunatic rulers behind forever. Forcibly, he straightened his spine.

"What do you want from me, then?" he asked, though he was certain he knew the answer.

The general relit his pipe as if he were in a comfortable study. "With your help, we might find the clockworker more quickly. You're an expert, after all. Do you see one here?"

The prisoners continued their piteous wail and cry, and pieces of Thad's heart broke off every moment he stood in this awful place. It was on the tip of his tongue to say none of them could possibly be a clockworker and that the general should release them all immediately, but he had a strong feeling that this would gain him nothing. The general had made up his mind that a clockworker had tried to kill the tsar and this clockworker was among the prisoners, and he would look until he found one.

"I saw children among the prisoners in those cages," Thad said.

"That is possible." Parkarov puffed his pipe, adding to the miasma of the dungeon. "My men had instructions to bring in anyone who might possibly be a clockworker—tinsmiths, blacksmiths, watchmakers, machinists, beggars, gypsies, Jews, men who lie with their own sex—"

Thad thought of Nathan and Dodd. "Why? Beggars and gypsies and ... the others? They have nothing to do with machinery."

"They spread plague. Everyone knows that. They and their children."

"Children are never clockworkers," Thad said firmly, though he had no idea if that were true. Still, it seemed right enough to get the children out of this place. "The plague does not work that way."

"Even when—?"

"Never," Thad repeated. "I have made extensive studies, and there is no such thing. You can let every prisoner under the age of ..." He pulled a number out of the air. "... sixteen leave."

The general nodded. "As you say, then," though he made no move. A young officer, meanwhile, brought down a desk and set it up in the hall. "You may examine them each from here."

"Each?"

"Yes." He gestured. The officer, a lieutenant, opened the first cell and dragged out a middle-aged man in a baker's apron. "We cannot afford to make a mistake."

The man fell to his knees before Thad and the general, his eyes filled with terror. *"I beg you, sir—"* he began.

Parkarov backhanded the man's face. *"Speak when you are spoken to, dog. Examine him, Mr. Sharpe. Is he a clockworker?"*

Thad made a show of examining the man. He peered into his eyes and ears and even his mouth. He thumped the man's chest and straightened his arms. At last, he said, "This man is no clockworker."

"Are you certain?" asked the general.

"Positive."

The general turned to the lieutenant. *"Process this man and release him."*

"Ser." The lieutenant returned the relieved-looking baker to his cell and hauled out another man, rather younger. Thad repeated the process and declared the man not a clockworker. And again with a woman, and with a teenaged boy. Each person took considerable time to examine, and the cells down here were filled with people. Through it all, the general puffed his pipe with amused patience. Whenever Thad tried to hurry the process, Parkarov asked questions—was Thad certain? Did all clockworkers fail to present such symptoms? Was it possible Thad was being fooled?

After fewer than a dozen people had gone through the process, they heard the faint *boom* of the noon cannon far above. Thad jerked his head up from the fruit seller he was pretending to examine. *"I have to perform soon,"* he said in Russian. *"I'm sorry, General, but I'll have to return later."*

"Of course, of course. My carriage is at your disposal. Perhaps tomorrow morning we will find the clock-worker."

Thad glanced down the long corridors of groaning cells, and his heart sank. *"I suppose, yes. The tsarina, you know, wanted me to find—"*

"Yes!" Parkarov clapped Thad on the back, a gesture of which he seemed overly fond. *"The tsarina. And the tsar. We will do our duty to them both, eh?"*

"Yes," Thad said with a weak grin. *"And with that in mind, I would be in your debt if I could examine a comprehensive map of the city. One that showed any tunnels and accessible underground areas."*

"Oh well." The general waved his pipe. *"I don't know if such a map—"*

"There's one in the offices upstairs," said the lieutenant helpfully. He was very young for his station and had pale blond hair and brown eyes. *"We use it to divide up the city and search for miscreants, just like yesterday. Surely the general remembers."*

Parkarov shot the lieutenant a look of pure venom, and in that moment, Thad knew. The realization was a bucket of ice thrown over his skin and he almost staggered. Thad recovered himself quickly and said, *"Thank you, Lieutenant . . . ?"*

"Markovich, ser."

"Lead the way, then, Lieutenant Markovich. Thank you, General."

He almost yanked poor Markovich, who would probably spend the rest of his posting in Siberia for his trouble, toward the lift and out of the dreadful dungeon. Thad didn't want to believe what he had just deduced, but there was no other solution he could see.

"You must know the general well," Thad said conversationally as he and Markovich exited the lift.

Markovich took Thad down a labyrinth of hallways to a room with a bank of pigeonholes, each with a roll of paper in it. He pulled down several sets. *"As well as anyone can, I suppose. He is my second cousin, twice removed, on my father's side."*

"Then you've been to his family estates." Thad unrolled a paper on a slanted reading table and set lead weights on either end of it to hold it flat.

"Many times. I nearly grew up there."

"The general spoke of them in great detail," Thad lied. *"They sound magnificent."*

"Oh yes." Markovich gave a smile. *"Especially in the spring, when the flowers bloom."*

He was young and naive, and Thad felt guilty about what he was going to do next. He leaned over the map, pretending to study it. *"It also sounds expensive, running such a place and keeping up appearances here at court. The general complained of it quite a lot on the ride over here, how much this cost and how much that was bleeding him dry."*

Markovich paused for a tiny moment, then said, *"It is very expensive. The tsar has expensive tastes, and the court has to keep up with him."* He lowered his voice. *"The holdings have been mortgaged—twice, in fact. Even the serfs."*

"That's terrible," Thad said sympathetically. With his finger, he traced a line across the map without looking at it. *"If the tsar emancipates the serfs, it would be a disaster for the general. He would owe a lot of money to the banks all at once. The family holdings might go to the crown, and you wouldn't be able to visit any longer."*

"Very much so." Markovich sighed.

And if the general found out you gave me this information, you would never leave this prison, Thad added silently.

"Could I borrow these maps, do you think?" Thad asked. *"I really need to pore over them where I can think."*

"Oh, I don't—"

Thad reached into his pocket, broke the clasp on the tsarina's necklace, and slid off a single pearl. He handed it to Markovich. It was worth more than a lieutenant would earn in ten years.

"Keep them with my compliments," Markovich amended. *"Did you need the general's carriage as well?"*

"Back to the Field of Mars," Thad said.

Chapter Thirteen

Sofiya was pacing in front of the wagon when Thad got back. Kalvis, saddled, stood nearby. Steam curled from his nostrils.

"Where have you been?" Sofiya demanded.

"In clockwork hell. I think I'm hungry, but after this—"

"Do you have any idea what is happening? Have you not heard?"

Dread, one of the more common among Thad's emotions lately, started up again. "I've heard a lot. What have you heard?"

"The damaged wall in the Winter Palace did not come down, but it is irrevocably damaged, and so is the courtyard beyond it. The tsar has declared everything must be fully repaired within thirty days."

"Thirty days!" Thad gasped. "That's—"

"Impossible? Not when one is the tsar. Serfs will be shipped in from all over the country to work, though they will be paid little or nothing, and given no place to live, and that matters not a bit, for when they die, more serfs will be brought in to replace them. This is how Saint Petersburg was built."

"I thought the tsar wanted to emancipate the serfs," Thad said.

"Not until the palace is repaired. It's terrible, Thad. Already, they are bringing people in with cages."

"That's not all the cages are for," Thad said. "I just came from the Peter and Paul Fortress."

Sofiya stopped pacing, and her face went pale. "The clockwork prison. Why were you there? Are they coming for . . . ?"

"You?" That actually hadn't occurred to Thad. "No. If they thought you were a clockworker, you'd be in a cell already. But I know what's going on, and I know who set the bomb."

"You do?" She sank down to the wagon steps. "Who? Tell me!"

"General Parkarov."

Sofiya stared into space for a moment. "I see where you are going. He said that he personally inspected the throne room before the tsar entered and that there was no bomb, which was why he blamed the spiders. But if Mr. Griffin's spiders did not put it there, perhaps the general did during his inspection."

"I know he did," Thad said. "His lands and his serfs are double mortgaged, and if Alexander frees the serfs, Parkarov will have to pay that mortgage off all at once. He doesn't have the money."

"That's not proof."

"No, but he also kept me at the fortress on a waste of time." And he described the prison. "Parkarov doesn't believe a clockworker is running amok in Saint Petersburg. He created all of it—the arrests, the long, careful inspection—as a delaying tactic. The tsarina ordered *me* to find the clockworker, and Parkarov is afraid I'll find out there isn't one, so he created this . . . decimation to keep me busy. It's brilliant, really, considering he must have cooked it up only a few minutes after his bomb failed to kill the tsar."

"And meanwhile, all those innocent people are jailed," Sofiya said.

"Yes," Thad said grimly. "We need to prove it was Parkarov and we need to end this clockworker problem."

"How will we do that?"

"First, I think we need to find Mr. Griffin, the real clockworker, and learn why his spiders were there in the first place."

"Thad, no." Sofiya held up her hands. "If we move against Mr. Griffin, his spiders will tear the circus to shreds, and he'll . . . you know what he'll do to my sister."

"No," Thad said. "He won't. Not now. That's why we have to move right now."

"I don't understand."

"Sofiya, haven't you ever wondered why clockworkers don't rule the world? They're far more intelligent than normal men, and they can build machines that give them tremendous power."

She spread her hands. "They go mad in the end and die. No one can rule with that."

"They could conquer and rule during the period before they go insane. It wouldn't be pleasant, but it could be done. So why hasn't it been done?" He went on before she could respond. "I'll tell you—it's because humans outnumber them, hundreds of thousands to one. Even with death rays or an army of spiders or hypnotic gases, clockworkers can't defeat enough determined men. It's why they hide. At this moment, the tsar's army is actively looking for Mr. Griffin—or for a clockworker, anyway—and if they find him, they will kill him. He doesn't dare come out of hiding now. That makes this the perfect time to hunt for him ourselves. Once we deal with him, your sister will be free. And so will you."

Sofiya looked torn. Thad knew exactly how she felt. After a long moment, she nodded. "How do we find him, then?"

He brandished the rolled-up map. "I know clock-workers. Where are Nikolai and Dante?"

"In the wagon. Nikolai is giving Dante his lunchtime winding. He wants to rehearse. You have a show in three hours."

"In a minute. Come on."

Nikolai was reading his animal book with Dante on his shoulder. They both looked up when the adults entered.

"Help!" Dante said. "I've been changed into a parrot!"

Thad stared, and Sofiya burst out laughing. "You have been saving that one," she said.

"I taught him that," Nikolai told them. He plucked a bolt from the bag beside him and crunched it down. "We need to rehearse."

"Later," Thad repeated. He unrolled several maps on one of the fold-down shelves that doubled as a bed and weighted down the ends. "We're going to find Griffin."

The others peered around him. "How?" Sofiya asked.

"I've been doing for this years," Thad reminded her. "Clockworkers like stone walls and solid, enclosed spaces with few entrances and exits, especially if they're underground. It makes them feel secure."

"I don't feel that way," Sofiya said.

"Amusing thing to hear from someone who locks herself in the Black Tent instead of using an open-air forge," Thad said idly. He flipped through the maps. For a moment, just a moment, it felt . . . cozy here, with the three of them examining papers together, and Nikolai munching a snack and Sofiya next to Thad at the table and the three of them set to appear in the ring later that afternoon. They were very like a normal—

"No," Thad said.

"What?" Sofiya said.

Thad pursed his lips. He hadn't meant to speak aloud. But they were nothing like a family. Sofiya was an insane clockworker who went into snarling fugues, and she was no wife to Thad. Nikolai was a machine that mimicked boyhood. Anytime Thad let himself forget that, he set himself up for pain. His life was nothing like normal, could never be normal, and the more he remembered that, the better.

"Never mind," he said, and turned his attention back to the maps. "Saint Petersburg was built on a swampy area. It had to be drained first—yes, at the cost of thousands of lives, thank you, Sofiya—which means they actually could not build many tunnels. They flood too easily."

"Which also means," Sofiya said, "there are no sewers, no underground trams, no tunnels for waste."

"They could have them," Thad reminded her. "Such

tunnels aren't impossible, just more expensive. But instead the nobility here put their money into impossible palaces and indoor circus performances. Ah! Look."

He pointed to one of the maps. "I think we can ignore the Winter Palace and the Peter and Paul Fortress. Not even a clockworker is insane enough to try hiding there. But these buildings here, here, and here"—he circled them in pencil—"were built with deep subcellars and tunnels. This older map shows some abandoned tunnels. Clockworkers love those." He sketched them in on the more current map.

"Are we going to search all of them?" Nikolai asked.

"No. We're going to narrow it down." Thad pulled out another map, one that displayed railways. "This is what we need. Griffin had all that equipment in those railroad cars, and a lot of it looked delicate. I'm willing to wager his hiding place is near a rail line. The line that leaves the Field of Mars goes across the city this way." He sketched that in on the first map.

"I see!" Sofiya followed the line with her finger. "The railway comes quite close to this tunnel here and rather close to that building with a subcellar there."

"Exactly. Griffin is mostly likely hiding in one of those two places. We should start with the one closest to the railroad line, then search the second. If neither of those reveals anything, we can go on to the others."

"We have a show in three hours, with a second one right afterward," Sofiya reminded him. "Tickets are already sold out for both shows, and you haven't rehearsed."

"I don't need to rehearse," Thad said. "I can dance, and we know Nikolai can imitate me."

"But—" Sofiya said.

"We have to do this. Now." Thad opened the trunk where Sofiya had put his equipment and loaded up: sleeve sheaths, pistols, lock picks, extra ammunition, extendable baton, packet of small tools. "Nikolai, you stay here."

"I want to come!" Nikolai protested.

"Bless my soul," Dante said.

"No arguing." Thad jammed on his hat and stuffed the map into his long leather coat. It felt good to be suiting up again, taking control of his life again. "I can't afford to keep track of you. If you run into trouble, go see Mama Berloni or the Tortellis."

"Am I forbidden from attending?" Sofiya asked archly.

Thad held out his arm for Dante. "Do as you like. We have to hurry."

Riding Kalvis would draw too much attention, so they left the wagon and crossed the Field of Mars to the line of carriages for hire that always waited in front of the barrack, all of the drivers in their big coats and hats and beards. Thad, remembering what Sofiya had said last time, spotted the same driver who had taken them to the market by checking for the way he combed his beard.

"Vanka!" Thad called, and every driver started shouting at them.

"No, no, no!" yelled "their" Vanka. *"I have driven them before, and they love my fine cab. Of course they will ride with me. For a much higher price because of all the mud from last time."*

"We paid for you to clean your cab," Sofiya countered. *"We will pay you—"*

"No." Thad flipped the surprised Vanka a pair of

coins. *"Another time I will play the game, Vanka. Today, we are in a great hurry. I will give you two more of those if you get us to this address within twenty minutes, and I promise to tell everyone that you argued all day about it."*

Nineteen terrifying minutes later, they pulled up at the address. Thad shakily paid Vanka the promised money, which also paid him to wait for them. They were standing in front of a nondescript building of stone, three stories tall, with nothing to indicate what was inside. Other similar buildings flanked it. A set of railroad tracks ran behind them. The street here was paved, and they were some distance from the river. There was little traffic of any kind, and no automatons.

"Doom," said Dante. "Help!"

"Quiet, birdbrain," Thad ordered. He trotted down the alley beside the building, searching the cobblestones until he found an actual grating over a hole, the first such thing he had seen since coming to Saint Petersburg. It wasn't even fastened down. He flipped it aside with his brass hand and knelt for a better look.

"Are we going in?" Sofiya asked at his elbow.

"Griffin will have laid traps, if he's down there," he said. "Unless it's a gingerbread house, and what are the odds of having two of those in a row?"

"Gingerbread house?"

"A technical term." He tied a silk rope to Dante's leg and lowered him upside down into the hole. Dante suffered this treatment without comment.

"What *are* you doing?" Sofiya asked.

"Look," Thad said. "We won't get very far with me explaining everything I do. If you want to come, you have to do what I say, without question."

"Ha!" she snorted.

"Truth, Sofiya." Thad continued lowering Dante. "I'm not saying it as a joke or to force you to obey just because you're a woman. If I say something like *jump* or *run* or *close your eyes,* and you pause to ask questions, you could die. We both could."

"Hm. Agreed, then."

The rope went slack in Thad's hand. He pulled Dante back up. His brass hand seemed to be working perfectly now, with no delay, though he couldn't feel anything in it except vibrations or changes in temperature. He barely heard the little *zing* the gears made when they moved anymore. So much had been happening, he'd barely had time to think about his hand, and it had seemed to have wormed its way into his everyday life, becoming a normal part of it, without Thad's much noticing.

Dante emerged from the hole, dangling upside down from the rope. "Traps?" Thad asked.

The parrot whistled. "Bless my soul."

"Let's go." Thad started climbing down a series of rungs bolted to the side of the tunnel, with the parrot on his shoulder.

"How do you know there are no traps?" Sofiya asked.

"If Dante had seen any, he would have said something that started with the letter D. Or he would have set the traps off."

"Doom," Dante said sadly. "Death, despair."

Thad reached the bottom and found himself in a long, low tunnel that smelled rotten and rank. He was something of a sewer connoisseur, and this one was poorly built—bad bricks, cracking mortar, uneven flooring. Within a decade, it would collapse and probably bring down the buildings above it. Would the tsar care if he knew? The man was such a mix. He seemed to love his children, but he didn't care about other people's children. He spent money freely, which helped many businesses, but he collected taxes heavily, which hurt them just as badly. He wanted to free the serfs, but only out of economic necessity, not out of compassion for their lot.

Thad shook his head. This wasn't the time for such musings. He lit a candle and gave it to Dante to hold while Sofiya clambered down, mindful of her skirts.

"Which way?" she asked.

"I have no idea," Thad admitted. "This is the hard part, really. We could search for days without finding any—"

"Spider," Sofiya said, pointing.

Thad's knife leaped into his hand, and this time it connected. The spider, which was clinging to the wall about ten feet away, stiffened and dropped to the mucky floor with the blade sticking out of its back. It was the size of a small house cat. Sofiya ran over to pick it up.

"Poor thing," she crooned.

"Is it dead?" Thad asked, pleased that it had worked this time.

"A strange question from someone who doesn't see Nikolai as alive. You have tools, do you not? Bring them here with the light."

Thad obeyed and watched while Sofiya prized the spider open with his little screwdriver. "What are you up to?"

She handed him his knife back with a wide smile that carried a hint of chill and held the spider close to the light. "I am making a few changes. Your knife pierced the back, but only knocked its memory wheels askew. Give me a moment."

Her quick fingers worked at the spider's insides. She muttered to herself. Thad tensed, wondering if she would go into a full-blown fugue. But in a few moments, she shut the spider's perforated access door and pressed a switch. It twitched and came to life in her hands.

"Pretty lady," Dante muttered around the candle he held in his beak.

The knife leaped back into Thad's hand. "What did you just do?"

"She obeys me now." Sofiya put the spider on her shoulder. It bobbed up and down with little squeaking noises. "You have your pet, and I have mine. I believe I will name her *Avtomashtika.*"

"Little automatic?" Thad translated. "You have to be joking. It should be something smashing like *Mechanica* or *Arachne.*"

"*Avtomashtika,*" Sofiya repeated.

"Everyone's going to call her Maddie," Thad said. "Or at least, I will."

"Maddie the spider? What kind of name is that?"

"Better than *Avtomashtika.*" He took his tools back and put them away. "I'm actually glad it showed up."

"She," Sofiya said airily. "If Nikolai can be a he, Maddie can be a she."

"That makes as much sense as anything in my life does." Thad sighed. "At any rate, I'm glad for it—"

"Her."

"—because it means we're on the right track. Come on."

They moved slowly down the tunnel, ducking their heads to avoid hitting the low ceiling. Thad kept a sharp

eye out for trip wires, suspiciously clean sections of flooring, areas of wall that looked too new—or too old. Once,
he found a guillotine-like device cleverly designed to drop
from the ceiling. Another time, he stopped Sofiya from
touching a trigger connected to a series of gas jets that
would have ignited a ball of flame designed to incinerate
them both. She examined the latter with interest, but Thad
pulled her along. He felt in his element now, in control, the
hunter going after unsuspecting prey. His senses felt
heightened, and he was aware of everything around him—
the rustle of Sofiya's skirts, the grinding creak of Dante's
gears, the heat from the candle near his head, the drip of
water from the stones, the dampness in the air. Every step
brought him closer to Griffin, closer to finding the truth.

Light glowed from around a bend in the tunnel ahead,
and unintelligible voices echoed against the stones. Thad
also heard other familiar sounds—the *bloop* of thick liquid and the hiss of steam and the clatter of metal on metal,
the same sounds he had heard from Mr. Griffin's boxcar.
Truly excited now, Thad put a finger to his lips, and the
four of them—two humans and two automatons—
proceeded cautiously forward. Adrenaline zipped through
Thad's veins and he had to force himself to stay slow. He
drew his pistol. Sofiya produced her one-shot energy
weapon. Maddie crawled around to Sofiya's other shoulder. Slowly, carefully, they slid around the bend.

The tunnel ahead of them opened up and looked
about fifteen feet down into a chamber that had clearly
been enlarged recently to the size of a ballroom. It was
lined with new stone and brass plating. Spiders of all sizes,
from pocket watch to Saint Bernard, scuttled across all
surfaces. But it was the center of the room that drew

Thad's attention. The hub of the enormous space was occupied by an impressive apparatus of copper, brass, and glass. Pipes and cables snaked in all directions. Closed vats sat above quiet fires tended by watchful spiders. Banks of dials and switches and levers were everywhere. In the middle of it all was a high platform, nearly on eye level with the tunnel Thad and Sofiya were spying from. On the platform was a large bell jar filled with viscous fluid. Multiple pipes and wires were connected to the glass and the base it rested on. Inside the jar floated a pink, convoluted human brain.

A number of thoughts rushed around Thad's mind and crashed together like explosive meteors. It couldn't be. The idea was utterly impossible, but it wouldn't go away. All the clues had been there from the beginning, but Thad hadn't seen them—the boxcar filled with strange equipment, the difficulty in travel, the communication by distance, the need to have others act on his behalf, that strange ability to work with others.

"That brain," Sofiya breathed, echoing his thoughts, "is Mr. Griffin."

There were other people in the room. One section sported tables and chairs, and several men were having an animated discussion over papers and diagrams spread over a desk. Others helped the spiders tweak the machinery. A number of large alcoves ringed the room, each outfitted with laboratory equipment, though one was stuffed with plants growing under an electric light. Some of the plants moved. Both men and women worked away, one to each alcove, six in all.

"Clockworkers," Thad whispered, not sure whether he was shocked or disgusted. "Those are clockworkers."

"Are you sure?" Sofiya touched the spider on her shoulder.

"Of course I'm sure," Thad snapped. A large group of people was the last thing Thad had expected. No clock-worker he had ever encountered operated this way. The surprise both startled and angered him. "The question is, how does he—"

"Mr. Sharpe! Miss Ekk!" It was the chocolate-smooth voice of Mr. Griffin. "I know you're up there. Please come down."

Chapter Fourteen

Sofiya made a small sound. A pang of fear stabbed Thad's chest. He tensed to grab Sofiya's arm and run, though he was also aware that he had drawn his pistol. All the men in the room turned to look up at the mouth of the tunnel, which was about fifteen feet off the floor for them. The clockworkers, for their part, ignored the exchange.

"Don't bother trying to fire that weapon," Griffin said. "It won't break my dome. Come down, please. No one will hurt you."

Thad's instincts still told him to run, but where would he go? Mr. Griffin knew where the circus was, knew Thad was here, so why bother? Carefully, he holstered his pistol and climbed down the rungs below the mouth of the tunnel, his brass hand clinking on the metal. Sofiya came next, and he helped her to the floor. The men, perhaps twenty in all, approached with serious looks on their faces. There was no consistency to them—some were young men, perhaps students, some were older, one was even elderly. Two wore well-cut suits, and others wore blousy peasant's clothing. One had a soldier's bearing, though he was in a plain shirt and trousers. They looked concerned, but not alarmed.

"All right," Thad said, "we're here. What are you going to do?"

"I'm glad to see you, Mr. Sharpe, and you, Miss Ekk." The smooth voice seemed to come from everywhere, and Thad's eyes darted about, trying to find the speaker boxes. He finally settled on looking at the brain on its platform, but that was unsettling. "I would have had to send for you soon if you hadn't arrived on your own. Might we offer you some tea? Or vodka, perhaps?"

"Thank you, no." Thad's mind was scrambling to keep up. He was still tensed for a fight. "Who are these men? What is happening? Why are you . . . in a . . . jar?"

One of the men, a dark-haired student in checkered trousers and a brown jacket, thrust out a hand. He was in his midtwenties, and had a mustache that didn't begin to disguise his baby face. *"My name is Zygmund Padlewski. You are Thaddeus Sharpe and Sofiya Ekk, true? Mr. Griffin has spoken well of you."* His Russian had a Polish accent.

Thad shook his hand in confusion. *"Has he?"*

"Very much. My colleagues and I were just discussing the best way to approach you, in fact, but now you are here, and will save us a great deal of time."

"What is going on?" Sofiya exploded.

Silence fell across the room, broken only by the drip and *bloop* of liquid through the pipes.

"Yes, of course," Zygmund said at last, clearly embarrassed at such an outburst from a woman. *"We must explain. Tea? Vodka?"*

"Just. Explain," Thad hissed.

Zygmund coughed and turned to the other men. *"I can do this. Perhaps the rest of you could return to our work?"*

The men dispersed with reluctant looks at Sofiya. Thad shifted. He had forgotten how beautiful she was, doubly so to men who spent their days in a sewer. *"Please be quick,"* he said.

"We are the Reds," Zygmund said. *"We are dedicated to making Russia a better place."*

A minor explosion puffed from one of the clockworker alcoves, filling the air with the smell of sulfur. Thad gave it a wary look. He had been wrenched around from being in control and in his element to feeling like a lost child. This entire place, with its machines and inventors' alcoves and a brain in a damned jar was so far beyond natural, it made a circus parade look commonplace. He could barely breathe, and he wanted nothing more than to get away. The brain in the jar had no eyes, but several of the spiders had turned their attention toward Thad. It was like being at the center of a knife thrower's target.

"Your goal sounds very nice," said Thad, *"and I'll want to hear all about it, but first I need to speak with Mr. Griffin. I'm very sorry, but a brain in a jar rather snares my interest."*

"It was an obvious choice, really," said Mr. Griffin in English. "Once I realized I had become a clockworker and I calculated I had less than two years to live, it seemed to me the only option. I say with some immodesty that my spiders are the most advanced in the world, and once I set up the proper apparatus, they were able, at my orders, to extract my cerebral tissue and suspend it in cerebrospinal fluid I extracted from a number of volunteers."

Thad's skin crawled. "Volunteers?"

"Of course. They had to be volunteers. Fear and anger taint the fluid with too much adrenaline and other hormones that give a . . . bad taste. Every one of them was properly persuaded."

"I'm sorry," said Zygmund, *"but I don't speak—"*

Sofiya said, "Where did you find—?"

"The main problem lies in keeping the fluids fresh," Mr. Griffin continued as if no one had spoken. "And at the proper temperature, with nutrients and oxygen and so forth. It takes a great deal of delicate equipment, and the fluid itself must be flushed and refreshed on a regular basis, which requires more volunteers."

"Sharpe is sharp," said Dante.

"How many more?" Thad said, thoroughly nauseated by now. Just when he thought he had encountered everything he could about clockworkers, he discovered something even worse. That brain was floating in the fluids of . . . dozens? . . . hundreds? . . . of dead human beings.

"Not a subject you need concern yourself with." Griffin's impossibly smooth voice was difficult to read. Thad couldn't tell if he was calm or annoyed or testy. Through it all, his machines continued to pump and puff and grind while fluids rushed through the pipes. "As I predicted, the benefits were immediate. The progress of the clockwork plague slowed to a near crawl. No clockworker lives longer than three years, but I contracted the disease twelve years ago."

Here Thad did stare. This entire conversation was unsettling beyond measure, made worse by the fact that he was talking to a brain surrounded by a pile of machinery. There was no face, no eye contact, no body language, nothing but a voice that came from hidden speaker boxes. It was like hearing a demon in church. The news that Mr. Griffin had lived four times longer than any known clockworker only made it worse. Clockworkers were mad geniuses who could create incredibly destructive machines, but at least they died within a relatively short time. This one, this extremely dangerous one, had found a way around that. Thad cast about, trying to keep his desperation under control. He didn't understand the machinery, and it was heavily guarded by the spiders, in any case. If he tried to damage any of it or shut it down, the spiders would be on him in moments. An explosive would take care of Mr. Griffin—and the other clockworkers—in a trice, but that assumed Thad could find the parts for one, and in any case, the room was also occupied by normal men. Thad couldn't stomach that idea. Mr. Griffin had chosen his situation well.

"I speak Polish and Russian and some Lithuanian," Zygmund spoke up again. *"Perhaps we could carry on in one of those languages?"*

"No!" shouted the clockworker surrounded by plants. *"That can't be wrong! I compensated for the chlorophyll transposition, but the plastids are falling apart at the microscopic level."*

"Shut up," snarled one another clockworkers who was scribbling equations on a blackboard. *"If I hear another word about plastids, I'm going to build the maximal bombardatron pistol and blow your bloody balls off."*

The first clockworker raised a fist, and one of his plants extended a number of thorny tendrils. *"Then I'll—"*

"Gentlemen!" A spider raised the volume on one of Mr. Griffin's speaker boxes. *"That will do!"*

"Yeah? Maybe this will do!" The equation clockworker picked up a sledgehammer with easy strength and threw it across the room. It struck Mr. Griffin's jar and bounced off without a scratch.

A sound burst from Mr. Griffin's speaker boxes. It was a pair of musical notes played together, not quite minor, not quite major. Thad, who knew nothing about music, could only tell it was ugly. The clockworkers howled and clapped their hands over their ears, even though the sound lasted less than half a second. To Thad's surprise, Sofiya did the same thing, and screamed. The sound ended.

"Don't make me do it twice, gentlemen," Mr. Griffin said icily.

Both clockworkers immediately fell silent and went back to work. Sofiya uncovered her ears. She was panting, and her eyes were wide.

"What was that?" Thad demanded.

"Tritone," Mr. Griffin said. "It's the only musical interval that has a vibration ratio of one to the square root of two, an irrational number. As a result, clockworkers find the sound . . . uncomfortable. I, fortunately, no longer experience this difficulty."

Thad had never heard of this aspect of clockworkers, and it surprised him. A bit of music that hurt clockworkers would be very handy, and he filed the fact away for later with a guilty, sideways glance at Sofiya.

"A tritone does have its use, though as a tool it is rather blunt, which is a reason I've brought you here, Mr. Sharpe, and one we'll discuss later," Mr. Griffin continued. One of his machines gave a shrill whistle, and a trio of spiders rushed to make adjustments to the dials and switches. "But I was saying that removing my body has brought about a certain . . . calm. I am not sure why this is. I no longer have adrenal glands to stir up my chemistry, that is certain. I no longer feel pain, nor do I fear tritones, nor do I fall into fugues."

"So you are able to function in a society," Sofiya breathed. She smoothed her hair. "This is why you are able to hire me, and bring in these men and these other clockworkers."

"Exactly." Here Mr. Griffin sounded extremely pleased. "I am superior to other clockworkers in every way."

With those words, an analytical wheel clicked in Thad's mind, and he had to stop the relief from crossing his face. Mr. Griffin did have a weakness, and despite his protestations to the contrary, it was the same one that plagued most other clockworkers.

"Or even French," Zygmund put in. *"I might manage French."*

"I'm impressed," Thad said aloud. "I've never come across a clockworker as advanced as you, sir, and I know clockworkers."

"I must apologize, Mr. Sharpe. You were outmatched from the moment I learned of you, though I know you had to try to outmaneuver me. I bear you no ill will."

Thad flexed his brass hand. "Indeed. But your plan, whatever it is, couldn't possibly be *that* brilliant. You can't outwit an entire country. The tsar and his army are quite—"

"You have no idea!" Mr. Griffin boomed, and Zygmund scurried back to the other men at their tables. "The tsar is nothing! I will have my way with Russia, and everything will change because of me!"

There it was: the clockworker ego. Even Mr. Griffin wasn't immune to that. Thad merely had to find a way to exploit it.

"How are you changing Russia, exactly?" Thad asked reasonably. "Even the tsar himself is encountering opposition, and all he wants to do is free the serfs."

"My men—that is, my *colleagues*—and I are working to support the tsar in his campaign to free the serfs," Mr. Griffin replied, more smoothly this time. "We are also working to change the way Russians treat clockworkers."

This statement got Sofiya's attention. "Please explain this."

Another of Mr. Griffin's machines abruptly went *poot* and puffed a noisome cloud of brown smoke. Instantly it was surrounded by spiders that set to work on it with quick claws.

"Mr. Padlewski." Griffin's voice had a metallic note to it now. *"Perhaps you could explain our plan for the serfs while I am . . . indisposed."*

Zygmund bowed, looking eager as a puppy. *"In Polish or Russian?"*

"I'm happy with Polish," said Thad, trying not to be too obvious about watching the spiders repair the machine. Every scrap of information he could glean about Mr. Griffin was worth having.

"You want to help both the serfs and the clockworkers?" Sofiya prompted, also in Polish.

"Not all the landowners want to keep the peasants as

serfs," Zygmund said brightly. *"Several of them would be happy to let the serfs go, provided the mortgages are forgiven. Others want to be paid for their loss. The tsar is still deciding how it will happen—assuming he is not assassinated first. We also have the support of many intellectuals. The Russian Academy of Sciences supports emancipation, as does—"*

"Yes, yes," Thad said. *"What does this have to do with clockworkers?"*

"Clockworkers are treated worse than serfs," Zygmund said. *"Surely you have seen that. They are worked to exhaustion, and then tortured to death for the amusement of the court. We have rescued a few and brought them down here. They help as best they can."*

Again, Thad found himself split down the middle of his own sword. He had no love for clockworkers, but no one deserved to be treated the way Russia treated its clockworkers. At minimum they deserved a quick, painless death, which was what Thad worked to give them.

"The peasants in Russia and in the Polish-Lithuanian Union are ready to revolt," Zygmund said. *"It will come very soon, probably this winter, when the army has a harder time moving about. We are working to whip them up with speeches and demonstrations. If we can overthrow the tsar—"*

"Wait!" Thad held up his hands. *"Wait a moment! You want to overthrow the tsar?"*

"Of course." Zygmund looked puzzled. *"There is no other way. He wants to free the serfs, yes, but that will come through one of two ineffective methods. Alexander might free the serfs and give them their own land, in which*

case the landowners will simply increase taxes to make up for the loss, or he might free them but leave the land in the hands of the landowners, in which case the serfs will be forced to work for the landowners or starve just as they do now. And, of course, no matter what the tsar does with the serfs, he and the court will continue to hate and torture clockworkers. No, the only way to create lasting change is to remove the tsar and his court entirely and replace it with a new government, an elected parliament that answers to the people, not a despotic tyrant."

Thad was deeply shocked by this. He wasn't a subject of Tsar Alexander, and felt no loyalty for him, but these men were talking regicide.

"So Thad was wrong, and you did *place the bomb!"* Sofiya exclaimed.

"Certainly not." The spiders backed away from the device, and Mr. Griffin's voice had returned to normal. *"That was a terrible complication, and you, Mr. Sharpe, both helped and hindered us. It is, in fact, why I was planning to send for you."*

"You're confusing me again," Thad said. *"Your brilliance is simply beyond me. Please explain slowly, so I can understand."*

"Bless my soul," muttered Dante.

Sofiya gave Thad a sharp look, and the spider on her shoulder tapped its feet. Thad returned her look blandly.

"I am happy to oblige," Mr. Griffin said, now in Polish. *"The bomb would have killed the tsar and many members of his court, true, but a number of our supporters were present among the latter, and we would not want them to perish. Besides, a bomb is terribly blunt. Any fool can cobble together an explosive."*

Now Thad gave Sofiya an arch look, which she returned blandly.

"Plastids! I have the plastids!"

"That's it! I'm going to stuff that microscope up your—"

"Tritone, gentlemen." Mr. Griffin's machines made a noise that came across as a sigh. *"In any case, we aren't ready to move yet, and the tsar's death at this juncture would be inconvenient. Unfortunately, your attempt to save his life only made everything worse, Mr. Sharpe."*

"I can't say I would have done anything differently," Thad replied with a stiff jaw. *"Not with all those children in the room, and my own self."*

"My spiders were there, Mr. Sharpe," Griffin reminded him. *"You did see them in the Winter Palace. We—the Reds—had heard about the bomb and I sent my spiders to find and disarm it. They made themselves obvious to you along the parade route to warn you. They had just located the bomb when you interfered. If you had just kept your hands to yourself, none of those people would be sitting in prison right now."*

A heavy hand of guilt pressed against Thad's back.

"I fail to follow your logic." Sofiya crossed her arms. *"The people at fault are you and General Parkarov. Parkarov placed the bomb, not Thad. He ordered those poor people brought in, not Thad. Your spiders failed to find the bomb earlier. You failed to inform us of your plans so we could remain aloof. Don't try to blame us for your shortcomings, Mr. Griffin."*

"Sofiya," Thad murmured. He recognized the clockwork temper flaring.

"I have no shortcomings," Mr. Griffin snapped.

"Everything was proceeding according to plan until the two of you interfered, and now I'm forced to alter my plan and bring you in before you do something worse."

"Perhaps we could all have some vodka and caviar," Zygmund said. *"I have some nice—"*

"Why don't you just kill us with your little spiders," Sofiya snarled, *"since we interfere so? You could pour our cerebrospinal fluid into your brain jar."*

"Because you're useful," Mr. Griffin said. He seemed to have gotten himself back under control, though the fact that he had lost control, even for a moment, was interesting to Thad. *"You are both favored of the tsar, and Mr. Sharpe is talented at manipulating clockworkers. He has done a marvelous job of manipulating you, Miss Ekk."*

"What?" Sofiya was in a full temper now. She whirled on Thad, eyes flashing. Maddie's claws flashed at her shoulder.

"Doom!" Dante squawked.

"Sofiya," Thad said, thinking quickly, "Mr. Griffin is the manipulator here. You're smarter than that. He thinks you're less intelligent than he is, and he thinks you're not smart enough to figure out what he's doing. He's trying to make you upset, unhappy, angry. Remember what happens when you become angry. Remember your sister. Remember Olenka."

Thad spoke in a low, fast voice. For some reason, clockworkers responded to patterns in speech, though Thad was rarely in a position to talk to them. An angry Sofiya was unpredictable enough, and an angry Sofiya in this place was a disaster.

"Remember Olenka," he said again. "Remember Olenka."

The anger left Sofiya's eyes. She backed up a step and put a hand to her mouth. "No," she said. "I didn't mean it."

"I know," Thad said. "It's all right. We'll talk about it later." He raised his voice and switched to Polish. *"Very amusing, Mr. Griffin."*

"You have demonstrated your talent admirably," Griffin said. *"Manipulating a clockworker to prove that you hadn't manipulated her. Brilliant!"*

"I—" Sofiya said.

"So you want me to help you keep the clockworkers in line and use my influence with the tsar to aid your cause," Thad said.

"You think well for an ordinary man," Griffin said.

Thad tried not to be insulted and focused instead on how he had been correct, that Griffin's ego was enormous and that it needed constant care and feeding. It made him feel better, more in control. He touched Dante's wings with his brass hand, and Dante ducked his head.

"Why don't we simply kill Parkarov?" Sofiya said. *"It would be easy enough."*

"Not yet," Zygmund spoke up. *"The tsar would assume—rightly this time—that a clockworker was behind his death, and it would only make the situation worse. Mr. Sharpe, right now we need you to use your influence at court to slow or stop this massacre. Miss Ekk, any invention of war that you can create for us would be helpful. And we always need money."*

The string of pearls in Thad's pocket felt very heavy, and he wondered if Griffin or the revolutionaries knew about it. Thick liquid rushed through glass and metal and machinery clanked and puffed. Thad didn't say a word.

"Well, then," Sofiya said, "I think we need to return to the circus. We need to check on Nikolai."

"You do indeed," Mr. Griffin said. "And how is Nikolai?"

"He's well," Thad replied shortly.

"You don't like it when I ask after him. Why is that? I thought you didn't care for clockworker inventions."

"I don't discuss my private affairs with you."

"Am I alive, do you think?" Mr. Griffin asked abruptly.

Thad paused, honestly baffled. "I don't understand the question."

"You don't care for me very much, either. I'm a clockworker. To you, I'm less than human. That's rather like your view of Nikolai. My body is almost entirely machinery. I am, in fact, less than point five four percent organic material. Am I alive?"

"I haven't thought about it," Thad said.

"Are you alive, Mr. Sharpe?" Mr. Griffin continued.

"Of course I am."

"Do you think for yourself?"

"That's a ridiculous question. I'm completely . . ." Thad trailed off. He was going to say "organic," but his brass hand lay heavy at the end of his forearm.

"Sharpe is sharp," said Dante.

"No. You are not totally organic. Neither am I. If I am not alive, and you are, Mr. Sharpe, where is the dividing line between us? Twenty percent mechanical? Fifty percent? Seventy? Eighty-one point six? Ninety-nine? One hundred? What if Nikolai had a living hand, or part of a living brain inside him? Would you think of him as alive?"

"This is a foolish debate."

"*Is it? How can I tell if* you *think for yourself, Mr. Sharpe? From my perspective, you are nothing more than a clump of cells following a biological imperative to eat, sleep, and gather enough resources to reproduce. Even your hatred of clockworkers is a biological imperative, is it not?*"

"*Now look—*"

"*I thought you were intelligent enough to see it. Miss Ekk reset that spider's memory wheels so it would obey a new set of directives—her orders. The spider's experience changed it and made it behave differently. You were a brilliant circus performer until you met a Polish woman who changed your memory wheels, at which point you wanted nothing more than a quiet life as a knife sharpener. Later, she died and a clockworker killed your son, which changed your memory wheels again and gave you a new imperative. None of this is any different than the spider encountering Miss Ekk's probing fingers.*"

Sofiya touched the spider on her shoulder, but remained silent.

"*It's completely different,*" Thad shot back. "*I make choices about what I do. That spider makes none.*"

"*And Nikolai? Does he choose?*"

"*He doesn't. He's a machine. I put my hand inside his head.*"

"*These machines put their claws inside my head,*" Mr. Griffin replied, unperturbed. "*Did you actually make your choices, or were you forced to do what you did by circumstances? Everything that has happened to you led up to that choice, to that of killing clockworkers. Your life programs you to do it, just as those spider's wheels program it to obey Miss Ekk.*"

It was more than enough. Thad sketched a mock salute. *"We had a nice visit, but now it's time to go. We do have a performance coming up."*

"I'm sure it will be a fascinating one," Mr. Griffin said. *"Keep the spider with my compliments, Miss Ekk. Next time, you need only ask, if you would like one. I seem to be mellowing in my old age."*

"Plastids!"

"Shut up!"

"We can find our own way back," Thad said quickly. *"No need to see us out."*

Chapter Fifteen

When Vanka dropped them off at the Field of Mars, they found a large crowd already gathering. Thad checked the time. They had more than an hour before the first performance of the day, and it was unusual for people to show up so early. Then he saw the soldiers and signs:

DOWN WITH ALEXANDER.

NO MORE SLAVERY.

FREE THE PRISONERS.

HANG THE TSARINA.

"Applesauce," Dante said.

"This is not pretty," Sofiya murmured beside him. "I hope Nikolai is all right."

The crowd on the street was thick and tense, and a cacophony of voices bounced off the barrack. The soldiers had lined up on the Field of Mars and were working on keeping the people off the field. Occasionally a small group of them made a foray into the crowd to go after one of the sign-holders, but the heavy crowd made it difficult, and the signs were made of cheap muslin unrolled between two sticks, which meant they could be collapsed and hidden almost instantly, which further hampered the soldiers' ability to arrest anyone.

Thad snagged a man holding a FREEDOM NOW sign. *"What is happening here?"*

"You haven't heard?" The man nodded at the Field of Mars, where a pair of automatons were laying the crossbar on a large gallows, complete with six trapdoors on the plank flooring. To one side stood another group of automatons with marching-band instruments. *"General Parkarov has convinced the tsar to execute all the clockworkers in the Peter and Paul Fortress."*

Sofiya's face turned to ice. Thad's legs went shaky. *"And everyone is protesting this?"*

"No." The man shook his sign in anger. *"We don't care about clockwork filth. But there are rumors the general will execute a number of the people he arrested last night, and they are not clockworkers. They have done nothing but be born peasants and Jews."*

The automaton drummer set up a beat. Already the awful cages were trundling across the bridge from the island fortress, five of them with four people each. Thad couldn't imagine that Saint Petersburg had twenty clockworkers. Rumor said the British government scoured its entire worldwide empire for clockworkers and still had fewer than two dozen at any given time. Even Mr. Griffin only had six. The man was right—the general was going to execute normal men and women.

The man with the sign moved on to avoid being snatched up by soldiers. Sofiya put a hand on Thad's arm so as not to lose him in the crowd. "Why is the tsar allowing this? He supports the serfs."

Thad set his jaw. "Maybe we can find out from them."
A line of carriages cut through the crowd, which had to
back up or be trampled. From the first emerged the tsar
in his uniform. This drew a mix of cheers and boos from
the crowd. This surprised Thad, who had never in his life
seen a monarch held up to public disapproval. Groups of
soldiers ran into the crowd and cracked dissenters over
the head or beat them about the body and dragged them
away. This didn't seem to discourage the others much,
though neither did it turn into an outright riot.

Tsar Alexander magnificently ignored the jeering,
walked to the grandstand where his wife and son had
seen the clockworker beaten and dismembered only a
few days earlier, and took a seat. Courtiers and high-
ranking members of the military followed, though there
was no sign of the tsarina or General Parkarov. Thad
made his way through the crowd with Sofiya in tow until
they reached the soldiers guarding the grandstand. By a
stroke of good luck, among them were the men who
knew Thad had saved the tsar's life, but when he muscled
his way up to them, they barred his way.

"I need to speak to the tsar," Thad panted. *"He'll see
me. You remember!"*

One of the guards drew a pistol. *"You are not to see
the tsar."*

Thad backed up and trod on Sofiya's foot, and the other
people in the crowd pulled away. *"The tsar would not be
happy,"* Sofiya said sharply, *"if he knew you were keeping
one of his trusted advisers away from him."*

"Our orders come from General Parkarov," the soldier snapped.

The general clearly didn't want Thad talking to the

tsar. That made it all the more important. Alexander had reached the stairs to the grandstand only a few paces away, though his back was to Thad and Sofiya. Thad thought about making a break for it, but the soldier cocked his pistol and aimed it at Thad's chest.

Thad hoisted Dante high above his head. "Call it!"

"Bless my soul!" Dante shouted. "Sharpe is sharp! Doom! Doom!"

The sound of the parrot's voice brought the tsar's head around, and his eye fell on Thad and Sofiya. A smile broke across his face, and he gestured at them to join him on the stairs. The men were forced to give way, and Thad shot them a triumphant look.

"Thanks, birdbrain," he said, setting Dante back on his shoulder. "I promise you some extra oil this evening."

"Pretty boy," Dante replied. "Sharpe is sharp."

One of the soldiers yelped as Sofiya passed him on their way to the grandstand. Thad glanced at her. "What did you do?"

"Nothing important," she sniffed. "Don't keep the tsar waiting."

When they reached the steps to the grandstand, they bowed and curtsied and joined the tsar at his royal box. The tsar sat and Thad and Sofiya stood while the court whispered wildly behind fans and gloved hands. Thad hovered, unsure what to do next.

"A fine day for a hanging," the tsar said. *"I know my wife rewarded you, but allow me to offer you a view from the royal box as my own thanks. Unfortunate about the circus, but there will be other days."*

"The circus?" Thad echoed. *"I'm sorry, sire, but I haven't heard."*

"I canceled today's performance in favor of this." He gestured at the gallows, where an automaton painted black was taking up a position at a lever that would open all six trapdoors at once. *"Too much in one day stirs the masses."*

"They do seem agitated," Sofiya said carefully. Maddie the spider slid backward on her shoulder, as if hiding from the tsar. The cages bearing their sad cargo rolled relentlessly up to the gallows and stopped. Soldiers armed with rifle and pistol moved up to each one. An automaton was hanging nooses from the crossbar with mechanical precision. With awful dread, Thad noticed three of the prisoners in the cages were children, not even twelve years old.

"Sire," Thad said, *"I was talking with General Parkarov. As an expert at spotting clockworkers, I advised him that the people he had arrested were perfectly normal and innocent, the children doubly so. I'm curious about the decision to—"*

"Some of the ones in the first cages are definitely clockworkers," the tsar said. *"More are coming in a moment. Parkarov convinced me—quite rightly—that it would be best to rid Russia of them. Too dangerous."*

"Are the children dangerous, sire?" Thad asked. His entire body raged with the need to move fast, but he was hobbled by the power of the man sitting next to him. Every word had to be soft and polite and careful.

"Children of gypsies and Jews," the tsar said dismissively. *"No one will miss them. The other peasants were probably hiding clockworkers or plague victims, even if they aren't clockworkers themselves. We're getting rid of*

them, just in case. I'm being merciful in allowing them to be hanged instead of beaten and dismembered."

"I see. But sire, aren't you planning to emancipate the serfs? This seems . . . counter to that."

The tsar looked honestly surprised. *"I'm setting serfs free to bring Russia's economy into the modern age, not to allow them to make assassination attempts or rise up against the throne. We are making an example of these. But enough of that."* He shifted on the padded bench. *"Have you made any progress at finding the clockworker who tried to assassinate me, as my wife requested?"*

Thad wanted to hit him. The man was as much admitting that none of the people in the cages had anything to do with the plot to kill him, but he was still planning to carry out their deaths. Thad looked at the children in their cages of gold and decided to risk the truth.

"I know who tried to kill you, sire," he said slowly. *"Though I do not know if you will believe me."*

"Death," murmured Dante. "Doom, defeat, despair."

Here, the tsar spun on his bench to stare at him. *"Who was it? Tell me!"*

At that moment, General Parkarov, without his pipe, marched with several aides out to the gallows. The band of automatons struck up a loud, brassy tune, temporarily overpowering the shouts of the crowd. A pair of soldiers arrested another demonstrator and dragged him, shouting, into the barrack building. The general noticed Thad standing next to the tsar, and the look he gave Thad was an icy blade. If the tsar didn't believe Thad, the general would be a deadly enemy. But he couldn't remain silent.

"It was General Parkarov," Thad said. *"His lands and*

serfs are double mortgaged, and he'll lose everything in the emancipation. To stop you, he planted a bomb while he was inspecting the Nicholas Hall for safety, and then, when his plot failed, he brought you pieces of a spider and started this massacre to distract you—and me—from finding out what truly happened. I think now he's trying to stir up the crowds against you." A number of disparate thoughts were coming together now, and Thad spoke carefully. *"He's ordered his men to be deliberately brutal to try and make the people angry. He's hoping for a lucky accident, or perhaps he has planned something more direct, and he's going to blame it on an angry rioter. You should leave, sire, and have the general arrested."*

"I see." The tsar ran a finger over his side whiskers. *"Well, I didn't survive all those military campaigns by cutting and running, did I? And it wouldn't be good for the people to see a cowardly tsar."*

"But you do believe him?" Sofiya asked. Maddie peeped over her shoulder.

"I believe it is worth investigating," the tsar said, *"after the hangings."*

"But you can't do that!" Thad exploded, then remembered himself and backtracked, heart pounding and mouth dry. *"That is—apologies, sire—this isn't necessary. You know none of those people had anything to do with—"*

The tsar gave a curt wave that silenced Thad. *"The clockworkers should have been executed long ago, and the others don't matter. These events have their own momentum, and it would be difficult to . . . put a short circuit in this, I think the new term is."*

Thad's heart sank. *"Sire—"*

*"Enough. I thank you for your service, Mr. Lawreno-
vich. Have some wine. And how is that little automaton
doing?"*

"Despair," said Dante as an automaton flitted up with
a glass for Thad.

Thad watched in helpless dread as General Parkarov's
men dragged the first six people from the cages. They
were bound with heavy rope and couldn't fight back. The
automaton band continued to play a disconcertingly
merry tune that completely masked the chants of the
people behind and beside the grandstand. The tsar sat,
surrounded by the court, sipping wine as calmly if he
were watching a parade. A hundred responses flicked
through Thad's mind—running up to the gallows to de-
nounce the general or inciting the crowd to riot or even
taking the tsar hostage. But none of them would end
well. He looked at Sofiya. Her wooden mask had descended over her face, but he saw the tremors in her
body. She was upset, angry. If she broke control and exposed herself as a clockworker, she would join the people on that gallows, and Thad and the rest of the circus
too, for consorting with her.

Six soldiers yanked the first six prisoners up to the
gallows and pushed their heads into the nooses. Three of
them accepted their fate with hopeless resignation.
Two—a man and a woman—struggled and spat, but to
no avail. One victim was a child, a girl, and she was weeping. Outrage made Thad's brass hand shake around the
wine goblet. He cast about for something to do, something to say, but nothing came. Parkarov watched with
glittering eyes at the corner of the gallows, and it occurred to Thad that he had a clear shot at the general's

head from the grandstand. The tsar had all but said he believed in Parkarov's guilt. A shot would almost certainly disperse the crowd and end the executions, at least for the day, and without Parkarov to advocate for them, the tsar might let the matter drop entirely, especially with beautiful Sofiya around to talk him out of it. Thad himself . . .

Thad swallowed. He would almost certainly not survive. Even if the tsar spoke up quickly, it was highly doubtful the soldiers in front of the grandstand would act out of anything but reflex.

The little girl's head went into the noose and the soldier tightened it around her neck. Thad's throat thickened, and he glanced at Sofiya. The moment he did, he knew she was aware of what he intended. She shook her head minutely, and he gave a small grimace. He couldn't let more children die. Sofiya shook her head again, pleading. Her eyes were bright.

Thad casually reached beneath his jacket, as if scratching. General Parkarov's attention was on the hanging. He held up his arm to give the signal for the drop. The black automaton at the trapdoor lever waited. The crowd fell silent. Thad grasped the cool metal and wood of his pistol, his eyes on Parkarov's head. He drew.

And then the spiders came. Dozens of them, hundreds of them. They spilled over the roof of the grandstand and swarmed in from the streets and skittered over the buildings across from the Field of Mars. They were all exactly the same: six inches across, counting the legs, with boxy bodies and four-lensed eyes.

They all had ten legs.

"Havoc!" Thad gasped. "Impossible!"

"Shto?" gasped the tsar at the same time.

The crowd and the court shouted and screamed as the little machines crawled over them. General Parkarov spun and dropped his arm, but it wasn't the proper signal, so the black automaton didn't move. The automaton band played its happy marching song.

"Mr. Havoc?" Sofiya said. "But you killed him!"

Maddie bobbed madly on Sofiya's shoulder with little squeaking noises, as if excited. A flock of the spiders swarmed over the black automaton at its lever. Even over the band music, there was a rending of metal. The black automaton crumpled like a ball of foil. Startled, Thad lost sight of the automaton beneath the spiders' flashing claws. In seconds, the spiders cleared away, leaving behind a pile of more spiders exactly like the originals. Except they were black. They wobbled about uncertainly, then gained their legs and joined the others, which were swarming over the automaton band. The music wrenched into a squawking end as both musicians and instruments disappeared. Thad stared, his hand still on his pistol. He didn't know what to do.

"My heavens!" Sofiya cried.

Several people from the crowd broke through the ragged regiment of soldiers and made for the gallows. Some of the soldiers made halfhearted attempts to stop them, but spiders skittered over them and devoured their rifles, replacing them with more spiders. General Parkarov drew his own pistol, but two spiders skittered up his arm and ate it, producing a third spider. Parkarov dropped the spiders and leaped off the gallows. Thad lost sight of him. The braver members of the crowd cut the binding ropes and nooses, setting the people free. A number of the spiders, meanwhile, were already eating the mechanical cages. The doors fell open, freeing the prisoners, who joined the chaotic, screaming crowd. The little girl was snatched up by a woman who hugged her tight and then vanished into the press of people. Thad had time for a flicker of gladness.

The court was squealing in fear and trying to flee the grandstand, but the women's skirts and the men's tight, impractical clothes hampered them, and their human servants had fled. Spiders were devouring the little automatons. Two spiders crawled up Thad's legs, intent on Dante. He felt their claws pricking through his trousers. Thad snatched the spiders off and flung them away, but more were bent on taking their places. It was impossible! Havoc could not have survived that explosion. But the evidence was here—ten-legged spiders that were smaller versions of the one Thad had seen in Havoc's laboratory in Lithuania.

One of the spiders got past Thad and reached his shoulder. Dante bit it in half and spat it away. "Applesauce! Doom!"

The tsar recovered. Without a word to either Thad or Sofiya, he vaulted over the front of the grandstand and landed six feet below on the Field of Mars, whereupon he sprinted for the barrack. Three more havoc spiders crawled up Thad's legs. Only a few steps away, the tsar nearly ran straight into General Parkarov.

Time slowed. Thad grabbed havoc spiders and threw them down. They tore his clothes as they came away. Parkarov drew a knife. The tsar saw it. His eyes met Parkarov's. Alexander's expression was calm, almost serene. He knew he was going to die. Thad tried to grab his pistol again, but the spiders had delayed him. Parkarov's arm came forward.

A red bolt of energy cracked past his shoulder. It struck Parkarov full in the temple. His head vanished in a small explosion of heat and red light. Parkarov's body stiffened, then dropped to the ground, trailing smoke from the neck. Both Thad and the tsar turned. Sofiya brandished her little energy pistol.

"Nice shot," Thad said.

"The tsar agrees with you," Sofiya replied. A havoc spider skittered up the back of her dress, but Maddie attacked it, and it dropped away. "We shouldn't stay here. These spiders are attacking everything mechanical, and we're carrying machinery." She stomped on one even as she spoke.

The court had nearly emptied the grandstand by now, and they added a dash of color to the throng outside the grandstand. The spiders were busy dismantling everything mechanical they could get their claws on—soldier weapons, automatons, lampposts, engines on automated carriages. They devoured machines like locusts in a wheat field. They didn't seem to be hurting actual people, though a number of them had been trampled, possibly even killed, in the panic that was still ongoing. The crowd to flee, but there was nowhere to flee to.

"How is this happening?" Thad said. "Havoc couldn't have lived. Did his machine survive and somehow come along on—"

"The circus!" Sofiya finished. "It somehow got on the train in Vilnius, and now it's eating mechanicals to make copies of itself here. But why?"

"Griffin!" Thad said grimly. "He arranged this from

the start. It's why he wanted me to hire the circus for him."

Sofiya met his horrified eyes as the same awful thought crossed both their minds. "Nikolai!"

They shoved their way through the crowd. Sofiya became a snarling tiger, all but throwing people aside and bolting ahead. Thad found himself following her, though he also shoved aside people with a strength he didn't know he possessed. They finally cleared the crowd and sprinted for the circus.

"Kalvis, too," Sofiya said as they ran. "Oh God."

"Death!" screeched Dante, clinging madly to Thad's coat. "Doom!"

Thad tightened his jaw and *ran*. Every muscle in his body bunched. His nerves hummed like cello strings. Every step brought him closer, but every step also seemed so damned slow. They reached the outer boundary of tents. The circus was also in disarray. The havoc spiders were climbing over everything, hunting for machinery. Performers and roustabouts fought back. A group of them had already formed up around the locomotive to beat them away, and Dodd and Nathan were fighting off another flock farther back at the Black Tent. Mama Berloni crushed one with a frying pan. Piotr the strongman picked them up and yanked their legs off. Dodd smashed others with a sledgehammer, but still they came. Thad and Sofiya ignored all this and ran past them to the wagons. Thad's heart was in his mouth. The wagons were blurry, and he was running through the streets of Warsaw again, searching for David. But it wasn't David. David was dead. He was going after Nikolai.

Two spiders were just finishing off the hinges on the door to Thad's wagon when they arrived. The door fell off, and a swarm of spiders poured in through the opening. Rage poured over Thad, and he actually pulled ahead of Sofiya. Beside the wagon, Kalvis was bucking and stomping. Havoc spiders were trying to crawl up his legs, and he was shaking them off to trample them. A little boy's scream came from inside the wagon, and Thad's heart stopped.

"I have Niko," he shouted. "Get the horse!" And he dove into the wagon without waiting for a reply.

Inside, Nikolai was backed up against the wardrobe. Spiders covered his face and body. Thad bellowed something inarticulate and bolted for him. He tore a havoc spider off with each hand and flung them away, then grabbed two more and two more. Nikolai continued to scream and the sound put Thad right back in Power's laboratory, and this time, *this* time, no one was going to die because he hadn't arrived in time. But every time he pulled a spider off, another one crawled up to take its place. Nikolai screamed and screamed. Thad ripped spiders off with his hands, crushed them with his feet, and still they came. He grabbed the water pitcher and dowsed the spiders with it. The ones on Nikolai's body made spitting noises and dropped motionless to the floor, but others leaped to take their places and now the pitcher was empty. Still Nikolai screamed. Dante leaped onto Nikolai's shoulder and flung spiders away with his powerful beak. Thad didn't know what to do except keep pulling.

"I've got you, Niko!" he said. "I won't let them—"

And then the spiders fled. As one, they ran down Nikolai's body, out the door, and away. Nikolai stopped screaming. He stood there, dripping wet, his mechanical face and too-human eyes staring up at Thad in disbelief for a long moment.

Dante jumped to his perch. "Bless my soul."

Thad grabbed Nikolai by both shoulders, and a small, stupid part of him noticed that Nikolai was indeed taller. "Are you all right?"

He looked at Thad for another moment, then slowly nodded. "They didn't hurt me. They just crawled on me. What were they?"

"They didn't hurt you at all?" Weak with relief and unwilling to examine that relief too closely, Thad checked over Nikolai, but found nothing wrong—no tears or gouges out of him, nothing missing. No problems at all.

Dante coughed up a spider leg. It clattered to the floor. "Death!" he said with satisfaction. "Doom!"

"I was so scared," Nikolai said. "I thought they were going to kill me."

"They didn't," Thad said. "And . . . and you can't really die anyway, so . . ." Why was he saying this?

"You're supposed to embrace me," Nikolai said.

"Am I?" Thad said.

"That's what—"

"A papa does, yes." Thad sighed. The worst of the tension had lifted and things were returning to . . . well, he couldn't call it normal. *Usual,* perhaps.

"So, then?" Nikolai held up his arms.

Thad suddenly didn't know how to respond. He felt uncomfortable again, and caught between Nikolai the machine and Nikolai the little boy. His brass hand felt heavy. And then something else struck him. What had happened to Sofiya and Kalvis?

"Wait here!" he said to Nikolai, and dashed to the door to look outside.

Sofiya and Kalvis were gone.

Chapter Sixteen

Sofiya Ivanova Ekk saw the spiders abruptly rush away. A few remaining ones, injured by Kalvis's hooves, tried to flee as well, but only managed a slow drag. Inside the wagon, Nikolai's screams ended. Sofiya, her dress torn and her feet sore, gave Kalvis a split-second check to see if he were all right—he had a few nicks and scratches, but otherwise seemed fine—before running to the wagon. Inside, Thad was kneeling in front of little Nikolai to examine him.

"They didn't hurt me," Nikolai was saying. "They just crawled on me. What were they?"

The little one was safe. Kalvis was safe. Sofiya wanted to collapse with relief, but she didn't dare, not yet. The spiders were getting away, and she couldn't let this chance pass by. Thad could stay with Nikolai.

With Maddie still clinging to her shoulder, Sofiya leaped onto Kalvis's saddle broad back and he bolted forward, following the trail of mechanical spiders. The brass horse leaped over tent ropes and wagon tongues and once even a person. Sofiya followed his movements with ease. It was both frightening and exhilarating, having these strange abilities. It was as if someone had handed her the rule book for the universe. Every object around her was reduced to its component mathematics at a glance — weight, volume, inertia, trajectory. She could calculate with a razor's precision where to throw, how high to jump, when to shove. Her own body had become a series of levers and wedges. The new strength was nearly more than she could contain.

But contain it she did. The world was also full of enticements: elements to combine into new configurations; little parts to build into large engines; small ideas to expand into enormous ideas. She didn't dare explore them. This new precision of body and intellect also etched into her mind the memory of looking down at the mangled body of her dear sister, the awful look of pain as Olenka awoke, the terrible feeling of fear and betrayal in her sibling's eyes. Sofiya remembered every bit of black, crushing guilt, and she swore that she would fight the clockworker fugues from then on. She wasn't always successful. Kalvis. The energy pistol. Thad's hand. Nikolai's head. She remembered very little of the building fugues, and Thad swore she hadn't hurt him during the latest one, but she spied the bruises, and she noted him limping when he thought she couldn't see, and the thought that she could have done worse made her shake inside.

Thad had saved her more than once, and even though she had similarly saved him, she felt guilty for bringing him into Mr. Griffin's web in the first place. Thad was a fine man, very handsome with his dark hair and whipcord build, and the clockwork part of her mind had taken a thrill out of putting her hands on him during the operation, feeling how his muscles and bones went together. She had initially gotten a perverse pleasure in teasing him, tricking what she had taken to be a foolish, cruel man who hunted clockworkers into working with one. *For* one. But the more time she had spent with him and the more she had learned about him, the more she understood him, saw that his misery was similar to her own. It was painful to watch the way he tried to keep a wall between himself and Nikolai.

Nikolai. He had also started as a way to annoy Thad. At first she had found amusing the little automaton's insistence that they were a family, and she had gone out of her way to push him and Thad together, force the man who killed clockworkers to confront a clockwork invention. How she had laughed over that! As a clockworker herself, she would have no trouble remaining aloof, seeing Nikolai as nothing but a machine. How foolish. But at least she had come to accept the way she now saw Nikolai. Thad was another matter.

When Sofiya was not much older than Nikolai looked, she had found a thin, starving tabby cat lost in a wheat field and brought it home. Papa had refused to let it in the house and told Sofiya to drown it in the river. But Sofiya took the cat to the barn, and when Papa saw her catch and kill a rat, he grudgingly allowed her to stay—as long as she continued to catch and kill rodents. Never, however, was anyone allowed to feed her or waste time playing with her. Some months later, Sofiya caught Papa rubbing the cat's ears and slipping her some scraps from the slop bucket. Papa huffed away to finish feeding the pigs when he noticed Sofiya watching him, and neither of them mentioned the incident. But two years later, when a horse accidentally kicked the cat and killed her, Papa hid in the barn and wouldn't come out for more than an hour. Thad reminded Sofiya of Papa.

No, Thad was a good man, despite his bloody past, and Sofiya felt a twinge of guilt when she thought of what she had done to him. Guilt was, in fact, the most familiar of all Sofiya's emotions, and when that burden became too heavy, she did fantasize about letting go, becoming a complete madwoman, no matter what Thad said. It might be nice to remain utterly selfish, not caring about anyone or anything else.

Kalvis galloped onward, leaping and snorting steam as he went. Maddie hunkered down for the ride. A silly name for a spider, but Thad had allowed her to name Nikolai, so she supposed he must take a turn. The crowd at the Field of Mars had managed to flee, and the place was nearly empty but for the gallows and the grandstand. A scattering of havoc spiders scuttled toward the pontoon bridge at the far end, and Sofiya urged Kalvis to greater speed. She could catch them, find out where they had come from, but they had to *hurry*. Chilly autumn air rushed past her face, and Kalvis's hooves thudded on hard earth.

At the pontoon bridge, the one that crossed the River Neva past the Peter and Paul Fortress to Petrogradsky Island, the trail of spiders turned left—west—and skittered downstream behind the Winter Palace to a different bridge seven or eight blocks away. That bridge, Sofiya recalled from Thad's maps, crossed to Vasilyevsky Island, the other large island of Saint Petersburg. Thoroughly mystified now, Sofiya urged Kalvis to follow. The horde of havoc spiders, now in a variety of colors, but all with ten legs, crossed the bridge with a deafening click of metal claws on wood. Traffic had already fled the pontoon bridge. Sofiya let the last of them get halfway across before she herself set out.

Vasilyevsky Island was large enough that it didn't feel like an island. The western half was taken up by shipping docks. The eastern tip, where Sofiya crossed, was buildings of brick and stone and a mix of paved streets and muddy byways. The northern side was still damp forest. The island was inhabited only by the wealthy, those who served them, and by people connected to the museum and the Academy of—

Sofiya bit her hand. Of course! Now she knew where the spiders had come from—and where they were going. The Russian Academy of Sciences was one of the few areas in Saint Petersburg with a network of tunnels and subcellars beneath it. That, and the resources of the Academy, made it the perfect place for a clockworker to hide. Thad had even circled it on the maps. They would have investigated it earlier if it had also included a railroad spur.

The havoc spiders continued on their way. The army would have been following them, except they were occupied in keeping order in the city and protecting the tsar. It seemed to be up to Sofiya. The spiders completely ignored everything around them now. Word seemed to have spread about the disaster, and the streets were empty. Every door was shut, every window shuttered. It felt eerie to ride her clockwork horse down silent, empty streets in broad daylight.

Around a corner, she came to the Academy, a series of buildings that bent together in a giant triangle around a courtyard. The Academy buildings were stony and colonnaded, just like the barrack at the Field of Mars, and four stories tall. The havoc spiders had found a downward staircase cut into one side of a wall. It ended in a heavy door that was propped open, and the spiders scuttled through. Did anyone else see this through shutter cracks and window curtains?

Heart pounding, Sofiya dismounted, told Kalvis to stay, and crept down the stony stairs to the door. It creaked open, and Maddie echoed the sound.

"Hush," Sofiya told her, wondering if this was how Thad felt about Dante. That poor bird—forced to exist in a half-broken state. She could see in her head how to repair his gears properly, fit new feathers into place, perhaps even allow him to fly. She could—

Concentrate. She had to concentrate.

The hall beyond was dark and damp. Sofiya slipped inside, nervous but determined. Thad wasn't the only one who could track down rogues. Ahead of her from around a corner came a blue luminescence that wobbled up and down. Sofiya peeped around the wall and saw the havoc spiders each exuding a tiny tendril with a glowing bit of phosphorescence at the end. Maddie squeaked excitedly in her ear. There was a *pop,* and the little spider showed a glowing tendril of her own.

"Thank you, little one," Sofiya murmured.

The havoc spiders filled the tunnel ahead, on walls and floor and ceiling, all marching steadily toward a goal only they understood. They hadn't hurt any humans back in the city and even now they seemed perfectly content to ignore Sofiya, but it seemed prudent to keep her distance anyway.

The tunnels beneath the Academy were labyrinthine. Sofiya followed spiders and wound her way under low ceilings and through grates and down staircases. The chill, damp air invaded her lungs, and the incessant skritching sound of the spiders' claws on stone filled her head with sand. Sofiya's treacherous brain automatically calculated how deep she had gone, how many tons of earth pressed down above her, how much weight the stones in the walls were bearing. Thad had said this sort of place should make her feel secure, but it only made her feel ill. To take her mind off it all, she took out her energy pistol and cranked the tiny generator to power it back up again.

At last she heard a different sound ahead, the sound of large machines whirring and clanking and thumping. The havoc spiders went down a final staircase and vanished, taking their glow with them and leaving Sofiya in a tiny pool of blue light surrounded by utter darkness. The machine sounds clanked up the stairs at her like an angry factory. Sofiya did not want to go down those stairs. Her heart beat hot in her chest, and every nerve in her body screamed at her to run. But she had to know what—who—was down there. Mouth dry, blood pounding in her ears, she forced herself down the spiral steps.

The angry machine sounds grew louder, and the blue glow became visible again from a space beyond the bottom. Maddie shivered. Her light went out. Sofiya pressed her back to the staircase stones and carefully peered around the final bend.

In the large room beyond stood an enormous machine, the like of which Sofiya had never dreamed. Conveyer belts and hoppers and metal arms and pistons and riveters and air hammers and objects Sofiya had no name for whirled and hissed and popped and hummed. Thousands of havoc spiders wandered about the room, covering every available surface. Attached in center of it all, much like Mr. Griffin's glass jar, sat a larger version of the spiders, one with intricate etchings all over it. Incongruously, next to the spider sat a small silver chair.

Sofiya's clockworker eye made quick connections in the machinery and she realized that everything was run by that single spider. Behind the spider's body whirled a titanic bank of memory wheels that took up the entire rear wall of the room. This single spider was advanced enough to expand its own capabilities, which gave it the power to expand itself further, which let itself expand again and again. Even as she watched, a set of havoc spiders slotted another set of memory wheels into place, and they started to spin. Sofiya swallowed. The concept was brilliant—and frightening. If nothing stopped this thing, it might become powerful enough to take control of . . . well, anything. In just a few minutes of rampage, it had doubled the size of its army of havoc spiders. Had that been a test? Sofiya went cold at the thought. And who was in charge of this machine? Havoc had to be dead. Even a clockworker couldn't have survived that explosion. Mr. Griffin had spiders of his own, and he was in an entirely different part of the city. So who?

A group of thirty spiders separated themselves from the others and leaped into a hopper. The hopper dumped the spiders without ceremony into another machine that made a terrible grinding noise. Maddie gave a tiny, almost inaudible squeak. The machine made more noise, and fully a third of the visible memory wheels paused, then spun in a new configuration. Sofiya surmised that a great deal of information had come to the machine. She should probably slip away, but she stayed rooted to her hiding place. She had to know what was going on.

A conveyer belt that led out of the main machine clanked to life. A moment later, a figure emerged, rolling atop it. Sofiya stared in shock. The figure was Nikolai.

Nikolai reached the end of the conveyer belt and toppled off it to the floor. Sofiya automatically reached for him, and stopped herself. This wasn't her Nikolai. It was a monstrosity, some wretched creature spat out by this awful machine. She watched, hands over her mouth to keep from screaming. The false Nikolai pushed himself unsteadily upright. He had no clothes on, his movements were uncertain, and his hair looked wild and patchy, but it was definitely Nikolai. His skin showed fresh rivets, and the pistons in his joints were similarly visible. With jerky motions and strange twitches, he pulled himself up to the silver chair and dropped into it. A spider pushed a thick wire into his ear with a heavy *click*.

"Thad-de-us," Nikolai said. His voice was guttural and made Sofiya's skin crawl with worms. "Dan-te. So-fi-ya."

The memory wheels changed their whirling. A spark crackled up the wire into Nikolai's ear. He shuddered hard and went limp. The chair released him, and he fell out of it.

More spiders went into the hopper. The conveyer belt clanked, and another Nikolai rolled out of the machine, fell to floor, and jerked upright like a half-dead marionette. It started toward the chair. Yet more spiders went into the hopper. Sofiya was panting now. The machine and its havoc spiders could build more than just more spiders—it could build other machines. It was also clear that the spiders had been searching for Nikolai. The moment they had found him and examined him, they had returned. It explained why the attack had ended so abruptly. But why Nikolai?

She thought about shooting the machine, or perhaps its bank of memory wheels, with her pistol. But a quick clockwork calculation told her that she would be unlikely to do lasting damage with her single shot, and the havoc spiders would no doubt exact immediate revenge.

A third Nikolai trundled out of the machine. This one landed without falling, and its movements were more lifelike. Practice, apparently, had an impact on the machine's reproductive prowess. The third Nikolai pushed the second Nikolai aside and climbed up to the chair. The wire clicked into his ear, and the havoc spiders dumped the first Nikolai, who still hadn't moved, into the hopper with more spiders.

"Thaddeus," grunted the third Nikolai. "Dante. Sofi-ya."

Suddenly Sofiya didn't care what was going on. All that mattered was that she had to get out of there, make sure Nikolai and Thad were safe, and tell someone what was going on. Let the tsar and his soldiers handle this. For once, the Russian dislike of clockworkers would work in her favor.

"Sofi-ya," said Nikolai III again in his thick voice. "Sofi-ya! Sofi-ya!"

A chill ran through Sofiya as she realized that Nikolai III had seen her. The machine, every bit of it, stopped. Silence slammed through the chamber. The main havoc spider looked at Sofiya with hard eyes.

"Sofi-ya!" said Nikolai III.

The spiders swarmed toward the door. Sofiya fled. Maddie popped her light to life as Sofiya bolted up the stairs. She didn't dare look back, but she heard the horrible claws coming after her. The stones were slippery beneath her shoes. Her clockworker memory, sharpened further by fear, let her retrace her route, and she ran and ran and ran. Maddie's light bobbed up and down with every step, and her breath came harsh in her ears. Still the spiders came. Sofiya was faster than a normal human or they would have caught her with ease. She tried to think, tried to find a way to slow or stop them, but she hadn't had time to snatch any tools or weapons from the Black Tent, had nothing but Maddie and an energy pistol with one shot.

Sofiya scrambled up a staircase. Could her single shot bring down the tunnel behind her? Too risky. Even the most carefully placed bolt might bring down the entire thing. She was panting now, and a stitch pulled at her side. The blue glow of the spiders and their skritching claws came relentlessly after her, like dogs on a hunt. She ducked through a grate and climbed more stairs. Her shins and knees burned. Even a clockworker couldn't run forever.

The door to the outside appeared just ahead of her, limned in light. A havoc spider leaped onto her back. Its claws dug in. She screamed and snatched it away. Another one got into her skirts. She kept running even as she fought with it. It bit her hands. The pain sliced through her flesh, and she screamed again. Slippery blood ran down her palms. Maddie dropped onto the havoc spider and fought with it. Sofiya was at the door now. She managed to pull the two spiders apart. The havoc spider bit her a second time even as she flung it away and burst outside into blinding light. Panting and bleeding, she forced herself to leap up the steps to the spot where—oh thank God!—Kalvis waited.

Havoc spiders poured out the door behind door. Sofiya flung herself into the saddle. "Go!" she shouted, and Kalvis leaped forward.

They tore through the streets, buildings on their right, the River Neva with its heavy load of boats on their left. Dripping blood from her injured hand, Sofiya arrived at the pontoon bridge back to the mainland and turned to check behind her. No spiders in sight. Kalvis had lost them. She allowed herself a relieved sigh and patted his brassy neck.

"You're a fine horse, you are," she said, and he snorted once.

Her hand throbbed and she examined it a little more closely. Two wounds but not too bad. They hurt and wanted cleaning, but—

The horde of spiders swarmed into view. Sofiya flinched. How had they tracked her?

A drop of blood landed on the stones at Kalvis's feet, answering her question. What now? She couldn't lead them back to the circus—and to Nikolai. But neither could she run forever. She glanced at the pontoon bridge, floating on its odd upside-down boats. Dammit! Everything was always impossible.

"Go!" she ordered Kalvis, who bolted onto the planks. His hooves pounded across them in a blur, but it didn't drown out the sound of hundreds of havoc spiders and their claws scrambling onto the bridge behind her. Kalvis galloped, and Sofiya clung to the saddle with bloody hands until they were halfway across. Abruptly she halted the horse and wheeled him around, nearly causing him to stumble. Maddie squeaked and jumped down to cling to the saddle. The havoc spiders swarmed closer. They were perhaps twenty yards away. Sofiya, mouth dry, dropped to the planking to face them. When the spiders saw she had stopped, they seemed to double their speed. They formed a seething black and gold mass that engulfed the bridge beneath them. A strange calm descended over Sofiya as she pulled out the single-shot pistol and took aim. The closest spiders were only ten yards away now. She fired. The bolt struck the planking in front of the spiders and slashed straight through. Flames roared up and a wave of heat rolled across the bridge. Black smoke belched into the sky. Sofiya threw up a hand and backed into Kalvis, half blinded by the heat and smoke.

The bolt had destroyed the center of the bridge, leaving no clear way to cross. The dry planks of the pontoon bridge burned eagerly. A number of the spiders, caught in the blast, were flung into the River Neva, and they vanished beneath the current. Shouts and cries came up from the boats on the Neva, and the rivermen paddled frantically to stay clear of it. The remaining spiders backed away from the flames and skittered about the other side of the bridge uncertainly. It was clear they were unwilling—or unable—to jump the gap or to swim. There was no other bridge from Vasilyevsky Island to the mainland. The havoc spiders would be isolated. Other people lived or worked on the island, and Sofiya had to hope the spiders—and the machine that controlled them—would take no interest in them until the place could be evacuated by boat.

The flames were consuming the bridge now, and eating their way toward Sofiya. The heat was intense, and the smoke clogged her throat. The burning bridge was already earning attention, though it was taking time in the aftermath of the spider invasion. Sofiya could be away before anyone managed to ask questions. With another glance at the confused spiders, she remounted Kalvis and galloped back to the circus.

He was the third one. His name was Nikolai. He was defective. But he had a mission. The signal in his head told him these things.

"Dante," he grunted. "Thad. Sofi-ya."

The signal in his head and the wheels that spun in his body told him what to do. It never occurred to him to question either, and that, said the signal, was what made him defective. But he didn't care. It didn't occur to him to care. He climbed up the stairs and lurched into daylight. It was difficult to walk. The signal fought with his memory wheels to command his legs and arms, but he didn't care about that, either. He was the third one. His name was Nikolai. He was defective. But he had a mission.

"Sofi-ya," he said again.

The last of the havoc spiders scampered away, following the trail of blood. Nikolai followed after, getting practice with walking, then shambling into a run. Running was somehow easier. A few people—humans—poked their heads out of windows or doors as he passed and just as hastily withdrew when they caught sight of him. Nikolai arrived at the bridge in time to see it erupt in smoke and flame. Some of the spiders fell into the water, and Nikolai knew that would end their existence.

Farther down the riverbank, he saw boats and rafts. Nikolai shambled down that way, followed by a number of spiders. The people at the boats all ran away when they saw him and the spiders, and he was able to get into a rowboat. Fourteen spiders got in with him. The oars took a little work, but soon he had the trick of it.

His name was Nikolai. He was defective. But he had a mission.

Chapter Seventeen

Red headquarters was in chaos. Zygmund Padlewski and the other men rushed about in all directions, some with grim determination, others shouting and gesticulating at one another, and yet others busying themselves with boxes and crates. Flatbed carts and hand lorries were piled up at one of the tunnel entrances. The spiders—Mr. Griffin's spiders—ran in all directions too, most of them carrying bits of equipment. The clockworkers had varying reactions to this. Two continued to work. Two sprawled on the floor in a drugged sleep. And two more had apparently decided to join in the fun and scamper about. Nikolai held Thad's hand tightly at the top of the high tunnel Thad had used the first time he visited Mr. Griffin's lair.

The brain, the jar, and the machine that made up Mr. Griffin still took up a great deal of the floor space, and the machinery added its noise to the turmoil. Thad didn't know what to make of any of it.

"Stay here," he said to Nikolai. He had waited quite some time for Sofiya to return, and the longer he waited, the harder it had been to sit still. He had no idea where she'd gone and couldn't follow her. The only thing he could think of was to come and talk to Mr. Griffin, who clearly knew more than he was letting on, but after the havoc spider attack, Thad had been unwilling to leave Nikolai alone or with anyone at the circus. He hadn't counted on such disarray here underground.

"I want to stay with you," Nikolai said. "It's dark up here."

"Pretty boy, pretty boy," said Dante on Thad's shoulder.

"You shouldn't go down there," Thad replied, but he was wavering. "I probably should have left you with Mama Berloni, but—"

"A son stays with the papa," Nikolai stated firmly.

It was the wrong thing to say. "Stay *here,*" Thad barked, and climbed down the rungs to the main room without another word. Mr. Griffin, through what ever mechanism gave him sight, noticed him immediately.

"Mr. Sharpe!" he said smoothly. "Excuse the disorder. Everything is happening so quickly, and you're here a little early. *Master Primeval! I need you again.*"

The clockworker with all the plants looked up from his work. *"But my plastids are nearly—"*

"Now!"

Primeval sighed, picked up a beaker, sniffed the contents, and set it back down in favor of a corked test tube. He held it up and grimaced.

"How can I be early when I wasn't even planning to arrive?" Thad asked. Alarms were blaring in his head. "Perhaps I should just come back later, when I'm not disturbing—"

Primeval threw the test tube at him. Thad automatically twisted out of the way, and it shattered on the stones at his feet. Sweet-smelling dust puffed in a small cloud. The room rocked around Thad. Dizzily, he tried to keep his feet, but he was already on his knees.

"Later," said Mr. Griffin from a long ways away, "can have so many meanings."

"Pretty boy! Pretty, pretty boy! Doom!"

Dante's voice pierced the darkness surrounding Thad, though his eyes were heavy. Something hard forced its way between his lips, and a cloying, licorice-tasting liquid trickled down his throat. The darkness sucked itself away from his brain and he bolted upright. The spider on his chest clattered away. He was lying on the floor where he had fallen.

"What the hell?" He spat out the rest of the liquid. Absinthe.

"It does taste dreadful, I know," said Mr. Griffin. "Or rather, I vaguely remember. I haven't actually eaten or drunk in years. It's tremendously freeing in some ways, but there are times when I miss it."

Thad got to his feet. A lot of the machinery in the room had been shifted about. Most of it was in wheeled crates with cables snaking from them. The clockworkers and their equipment were gone entirely, even Primeval's plants. Zygmund and his friends, however, were still at their desks. Zygmund was speaking urgently into a wireless microphone, and one of the other men was tapping out code on a telegraph sender. Dante sat poised above Thad's head on a high crate, which was scarred with fresh beak marks. Next to him were two spiders, bent and broken.

"Applesauce!" he squawked, and fluttered brass feathers. Thad put up an arm so Dante could climb down to his customary shoulder perch. With a sudden stab Thad thought of Nikolai. He whirled and looked up at the entry tunnel. Nikolai, half in shadow, looked down at him. He hadn't moved. Thad breathed a sigh of relief.

All right, he thought. *Niko is still here, and I'm not dead. That means Griffin wants us both alive. The question I have to ask is, why? And why did he say I was early?*

"As you can see, we're in the final stages now," Griffin said from his speakers. They were now mounted in front of his jar. The pink brain tissue sat in the liquid, unmoving. "I apologize for drugging you with Primeval's pollen, and regret that the antidote is absinthe, but a soporific is handy to have about. It lets me move the clockworkers with minimal fuss."

"How long was I asleep?" Thad demanded.

"Only a few hours. It's nearly sunset up top. And now we're on schedule. The peasant uprising is about to begin!"

This wasn't the response Thad had been looking for. "You can't be serious! This is the wrong time. No one has arms, you don't have enough organization, you don't have—"

"This is the perfect time. We must move before the tsar can turn this anger into more hatred against clockworkers. The army lost its commanding officer and has fallen into chaos after that spider attack. The Field of Mars will be the perfect staging ground."

"The circus is there!" Thad blurted. "People will be hurt!"

"It's a revolution, Mr. Sharpe. Many people will be

hurt. But in the long run, everything will be better." He paused. "I noticed you did get Nikolai out of the way. He'll be safe, at least."

Thad glanced up at the tunnel entrance. Nikolai was still sitting dejectedly at the mouth. "Why is everyone running about so? Where are the clockworkers?"

"Mr. Padlewski there is making speeches on the wireless to incite riot, and his friend is sending telegrams to our supporters who are waiting for just this moment. My other allies are delivering equipment to the masses, weapons my clockworkers have invented." The pink brain seemed to pulse with excitement, though Thad knew the idea was ridiculous. "Some of them are becoming quite mad, I'm afraid, so I had to anesthetize them as I did you. We are—or rather, my revolution is—on the move!" He switched to Russian. *"Long live the revolution!"*

Fluid gurgled through the pipes and washed through Mr. Griffin's jar. Everyone at the other end of the room paused in what they doing. *"Long live the revolution!"* And they went back to work. The spiders carried off the other sleeping clockworker.

"I'm telling you," Thad said, "this is—"

"Thad!" Sofiya burst into the room at the top of tunnel. She rushed past Nikolai with barely a pause and tumbled down the rungs. Her hand was wrapped in a bloody rag. "Thad! It's been hours! I have searched everywhere!"

"Are you all right?" A finger of warmth went up his spine at her entrance. She was a good and familiar sight in this awful place, and he was happy that she seemed to be all right, though her hand concerned him. He reached for it, but she pulled away. "What happened?"

"Miss Ekk," Mr. Griffin said. Sofiya ignored him.

"The havoc spiders," she said. "You won't believe it, but it is true." With quick, succinct sentences, she explained. The more she spoke, the more unsettled Thad became. When she got to the part about the twisted versions of Nikolai, he was staggering beneath the weight of her words, and had to catch himself against a crate.

"Don't lean on that," Mr. Griffin warned. "Delicate."

"The bridge has burned and the havoc spiders are trapped on Vasilyevsky Island," Sofiya finished, "but we have to move quickly if we want to stop them from . . . from . . . whatever it is they're trying to do. Whatever it is involves Nikolai. It's good you didn't leave him up on the surface."

Thad's mind whirled with the new information. He stared around the chaotic chamber, a mirror of the one Sofiya had just left. He stared at his hand, a mirror of Mr. Griffin's jar. He stared up at the shadowy tunnel entrance where sat Nikolai, a mirror of the one on the island. A number of ideas slammed together. Thad turned to the brain, complacent in its unbreakable jar. He felt cold and alone, even with Sofiya there.

"It's you," Thad said. "Everything leads back to you."

More fluid dripped and blooped through the pipes. "Is it?" Mr. Griffin said.

"You are the one . . . man that holds everything together. You sent me to Havoc's castle to get the machine. You forced the circus to bring you here. Now, by *sheer* coincidence, you're fomenting a rebellion in the same city where everything is happening. And you're always interested in Nikolai. You have been from the very beginning. You didn't want just that ten-legged spider from

Havoc's castle. You also wanted *Nikolai*. That's why you sent me in there. You knew I had lost a child and that I probably wouldn't destroy an automaton that acted like one."

"There was a ninety-four point six two eight percent chance that you would both rescue the automaton and keep it with you," Mr. Griffin agreed.

The walls were closing in on Thad now, invisible walls that had been there all along but he was only now starting to see. He was nothing more than a puppet at the end of a string, an automaton following a program within its memory wheels. Was this how Nikolai felt all the time? Perhaps even now, his words were predicted, scripted, pulled out of him with no choice of his own. A puppet who could see the strings still had to dance.

"That's why you insisted *I* hire the circus for you and why you wanted *me* to continue working with you," Thad said. "Because you knew Nikolai would attach himself to me and would stay in the city as long as I did."

"A ninety-one point seven five percent chance there. And an eighty-nine point two percent chance the tsar would command a performance once he heard of Sofiya and her horse, which would keep the circus and Nikolai in Saint Petersburg. Alexander does enjoy a beautiful woman."

"Why?" Thad asked.

"It seems to be a failing among men. The tsar, in particular, has numerous mistresses who—"

"Why are you doing this?" Thad shouted.

Zygmund looked up from his wireless, and the man at the telegraph paused. Were they puppets, too? Could they see the strings?

A flurry of movement came from behind the machinery where Dante had disappeared a while ago, but Thad was too intent on Mr. Griffin to take much notice. "Doom!"

"I am not a fool, Mr. Sharpe," said Mr. Griffin. "Normal clockworkers, foolish clockworkers, reveal their plans in long, maniacal monologues, but I am above that."

Frustration and rage tinged Thad's vision. He wanted to leap over the stupid machines and smash that glass jar to pieces. Instead, he forced his voice into a reasonable tone. The puppet might be controlled by his strings, but those strings led inevitably back to the puppeteer.

"Of course you're a fool," Thad said easily. "Good God—ninety-one point one two percent chance. Naturally."

"What are you—?" Sofiya began, but Thad stepped on her foot.

"Point seven six," Mr. Griffin corrected.

"Whatever, whatever." Thad waved. "As if anyone could predict human behavior to that extent. It's quite impossible. Everyone knows that. Even Sofiya here."

He nudged her foot again. Sofiya blinked, then said, "Yes, of course. Completely impossible."

"I assure you, it is quite possible. The proof is that you are both standing here, and there's a revolution beginning up there."

"Ex post facto," Thad replied airily. "You're merely taking credit for something that would have happened anyway. You don't have a plan. You're just trying to trick me into working for you for free. I can't believe I followed a brain in a jar all the way across Europe. There's the fool."

"I HAVE A PLAN!" Mr. Griffin thundered from his speakers. The men in the room jumped, and Maddie quivered on Sofiya's shoulder. Thad kept his expression bland.

"Naturally, yes, yes," he said with blatantly false placation. "Never mind—I believe you." He turned to Sofiya. "He does have a plan. We should believe him. Absolutely!"

"You *don't* believe me." Mr. Griffin's voice was icy now, and Thad recognized the stage. "My plan is brilliant."

"Tell us some other time. We should go join the revolution." Thad took Sofiya's hand, the uninjured one, and looked around for Dante. "As you said we should."

"I knew from the start that Havoc's machine would survive your attempt to destroy it," Griffin said, "because I was the one who created it in the first place."

That got Thad's attention. "Did you?"

"Havoc was one of *my* clockworkers here in Saint Petersburg. Didn't that occur to you? No, of course not. You don't have a clockworker's intellect. Havoc was a genius at understanding how the brain works. He merged brain tissue with machinery, and from there worked out wonders with memory wheels alone and got machines to appear to think. He even learned how to make a machine that could make itself more intelligent by adding memory wheels to itself. Meanwhile, I myself invented a spider with the ability to make copies of itself, though the initial prototype was flawed and merely walked about eating everything in sight in order to make materials for more copies, and I was forced to shut it down. Havoc became fascinated with my machine. Obsessed.

He combined my designs with his own, and created a machine that was intelligent enough to improve itself and make intelligent copies. And that gave me my plan."

"It doesn't sound like a plan," Thad scoffed. "It sounds like you stole someone else's work and took credit for it."

"Havoc was a mere tinker," Griffin snapped. "He didn't see what our work could do. The idiot stole the machine one night to keep me from realizing its true potential, vanished right out of this very laboratory. It took some time to make arrangements to chase him, and that was when I learned of Miss Ekk. I hired her just for it, kept her ignorant—that was easy—and we went to Lithuania to hunt him down. Originally I had planned to use her to regain my machine, but you happened along instead, and that made everything easier."

"Why didn't you just rebuild the machine?" Thad asked. "Or use your wireless signals to call it back to you?"

"Havoc wasn't stupid. He kept the spider in a box designed to keep my signals out until he reached a stone laboratory that they couldn't touch, either. As for rebuilding it, I needed Havoc for that," Griffin admitted grudgingly. "Just as I needed him for the other half."

"Other half?" Thad echoed, as he knew Griffin wanted him to.

"The other half of the machine. You said our revolution isn't armed, Mr. Sharpe, and that is not quite true. We are—I am—creating an army."

"You're going to make an army of spiders to fight a revolution?" Thad said. "That won't begin to work. Spiders can kill a lot of people, true, but the tsar's army will crush them in no time at all, once they recover."

"And those new spiders are destroyed by water," Sofiya pointed out. "This is a significant weakness."

Griffin's machines bubbled very like the sound of frustration. "We are making an army of human automatons."

Thad felt sick. Sofiya gave a false laugh that didn't touch her eyes. "Those twisted things? Don't be silly. They couldn't fight a fly."

"And how would you control an entire army?" Thad said. "Radio signals? I've seen you and that machine give simple tasks through . . . wireless radio waves, is it? Your spiders require constant attention to deal with relatively simple tasks like keeping your equipment in good repair. Even a clockworker doesn't have the brainpower to control an army of complicated human automatons with weapons, with strategy and tactics and adapting to situations in combat. Soldiers need both to follow orders and think for themselves."

"Yes," Griffin said.

This caught Thad completely out. The room rocked and he surreptitiously put out a hand to steady himself on the engine cover again. "Think . . . for themselves?" he said.

"We—I—need an army that can grow, reproduce, and *think,*" Griffin said. "The new spider can reproduce. The other half of Havoc's machine can think and grow."

"Nikolai," Sofiya whispered.

"Indeed," Griffin said. "As you said, Mr. Sharpe, I needed Nikolai in Saint Petersburg, and you very nicely rescued him from Havoc's castle and brought him here for me."

"Good God." Thad spun to look up at the entrance

tunnel, expecting Nikolai to be gone. But he was still there at the top of the rungs, sitting with his knees pulled up under his chin. Relieved but still unnerved, Thad edged toward the ladder.

"You ordered the new machine to flood the city with its spiders. It was supposed to find Nikolai and copy his design," Sofiya was saying, "but it didn't work."

"It worked well enough. Once I combine Nikolai's unique brain with the machine's capabilities, it will spread and devour everything in its path. It will produce an army of free-thinking automatons who will fight for me like good sons obey their father. The machine and the automatons will grow and reproduce and grow and reproduce until we have spread over Saint Petersburg, and then Russia, and then the world."

"The world?" Thad said.

"Doom!" Dante had clambered to the top of a cabinet with a bent spider leg in his beak and leaped to Thad's shoulder.

"We will supplant all human life with automatons," Mr. Griffin said reasonably. "Russia's hatred for clockworkers will end."

"Because there will be no humans to hate them," Sofiya said.

"Not entirely. I do need a supply of cerebrospinal fluid." Mr. Griffin's speakers gave a little chuckle, and a few bubbles coruscated across his brain.

Thad was at the ladder now. "Zygmund and his friends over there haven't figured out your plan, have they? They think you're working on a real revolution. What's to stop us from revealing your little plan and letting him and his friends destroy you now?"

"My spiders and the ninety-nine point four percent chance that you will flee this chamber within the next sixty seconds," Mr. Griffin replied, unperturbed. "I have arranged another task for you. And if you want to survive my revolution, you will return to work for me afterward."

"Why," Thad said through clenched teeth, "would I return to—"

"Dante," Nikolai grunted above him. "Thaddeus. Sofi-ya."

Chapter Eighteen

Thad bolted up the ladder with Sofiya hot on his heels. His brass hand clanked on the rungs. Nikolai waited for them at the mouth of the tunnel at the top. Thad grabbed his shoulder.

"Thad," the boy grunted. The voice was guttural, like something from the back of a cave. Unlike the Nikolai Thad knew, this version of him had dull, flat eyes. His clothes were ill-fitting, as if he had stolen them from a clothesline, and he jerked when he moved. "Sofi-ya."

This time Thad did throw up. The acid burned all the way up and splattered across the stones. It felt like his entire body burned with bile.

"Help me," whistled Dante.

"What did you do with him?" Sofiya shrieked at Griffin.

"He is fulfilling the purpose for which he was created," Mr. Griffin said from below.

"How—?" Thad said.

"I did say that you arrived too early. I needed a moment to spirit him away to Vasilyevsky Island and ensure everything had time to move. Did you think you could trick me into revealing my plans so you could stop me? It's far, far too late for that."

Then Mr. Griffin laughed. It was a deep, rich sound, a completely artificial one made by a machine. Mr. Griffin claimed that the clockwork plague was no longer driving him mad, but living as a brain in a jar was doing an admirable job.

"Run!" Thad said, and the two of them fled up the tunnel, leaving the twisted Nikolai and Mr. Griffin's laughter behind.

"Sofi-ya!" Nikolai called.

Outside, Kalvis was waiting for them. No longer worried about calling attention to themselves, they jumped aboard the clockwork horse, Sofiya in front, and galloped away. Thad's entire body was tight with worry. Sofiya had described the machine on Vasilyevsky Island, and he imagined Nikolai shoved into that chair with a cord in his ear, all alone, with no one to help him. Rage gnawed at him, and . . .

He shoved the feelings aside. Nikolai wasn't a little boy. He was a machine. He couldn't get hurt. He couldn't feel real pain.

Was he screaming when he sat in the chair?

"Is anyone chasing us?" Sofiya asked.

"I don't think so." Thad's reply was breathless. It was difficult to ride behind the saddle of a brass horse, but he managed. The metal was uncomfortably warm. "But that worries me. Why didn't Griffin simply kill us? We know where he is and we know his plan. We could bring the tsar's entire army down on him."

"He said we have another task to do. And he still . . .

watches my sister. I can't let the tsar know where Mr. Griffin is."

They rode grimly through the darkening city. People were back in the streets now, mostly milling about and wondering what was going on. Many carried torches and lanterns, and a fog of tension filled the cold air. Soldiers marched in groups with their rifles over their shoulders through a pall of smoke. A hundred yards from the bridge, Sofiya halted Kalvis so quickly, Thad came up against her back.

"Bless my soul," Dante said.

"What—?" Thad asked.

"Look!" Sofiya pointed at the bridge. The place where she had shot it gaped in a breach too wide for any man or horse to leap. Charred beams and blacked edges hung over the water, and a few flames licked feebly at the wood. The bridge itself was empty. On the mainland side, a regiment of soldiers was standing guard with rifles at the ready. The island side . . .

The island side had changed. Metal gleamed in the light of the setting sun—iron and brass and copper and even gold. Cables and wires wound between the buildings, creating a great metal web that covered every building. Havoc spiders scuttled along them. Some of them trailed more cables. In the streets below lumbered larger spiders, from dog size to horse size. Carts moved by themselves, carrying machine parts. And there were human-shaped automatons as well. They walked or lurched or trotted or trundled over cobblestones and dirt. They were different shapes and sizes, a version of a human population taken to an extreme. Some had fingers, some had mittens, some had eyes in the backs of their heads, some had large wheels from the knees down. Some were tall, some were short, some were thin, some were stout. Some had hair, some did not. Many wore clothing, though it fit poorly.

All the automatons were working. They modified buildings and dug trenches and laid cable and fixed other automatons. They worked ceaselessly, tirelessly, and at amazing speed. The sound of thousands of clacking metal parts reached across the river.

Dante bobbed up and down on Thad's shoulder, fascinated by the sight. "Pretty boy! Pretty, pretty boy!"

Thad stared. At first he thought the entire island had changed, but now that he looked more carefully, he could see that so far it was only the rim, the parts nearest the river. The interior was so far untouched, though even now spiders were pulling cables farther inland. It wouldn't take long.

The mainland side of the River Neva was also in chaos. Boats lined the near bank, and none were in sight on the far side. Refugees stood or sat near the water, most of them dripping wet, with looks of shock and fear on their faces. Every so often, another person emerged from the clockwork city and leaped into the river. When that happened, a boat from the mainland side rowed out to pull the person to safety. Thad wondered how many had drowned, or if the automatons had killed anyone. The automatons themselves stayed well away from the water.

"How did they build so much so fast?" Sofiya wondered aloud. "Just finding the materials and metal—"

"The shipping docks," Thad said. "And the foundry. Built by Cousin Peter. All the materials and metal they need. Once they have the island, they'll jump the river to the main city. The city has railroads to other cities. After that, we're undone."

"They don't seem to have killed anyone so far," Sofiya said. "Only driven them away."

"Even if they never kill anyone—and I doubt that'll last—Mr. Griffin said he wanted to push all humans out," Thad said. "It'll be war between humans and automatons eventually, mark it."

"*He's* a human," Sofiya said. "Doesn't he think—?"

"It's clockworker logic," Thad told her. "If glass shatters too easily, don't switch to metal; find a way to stop glass from breaking. If a tree is blocking your view, build a machine to turn the house around. If some humans persecute you, destroy all humans."

More citizens of Saint Petersburg were crowding the streets as word spread of what was happening. They gawked and pointed and asked questions among themselves. Thad wanted to know what would happen to the refugees from the island—and how many people were still trapped across the river, along with Nikolai. He was in there, somewhere.

"We have to get across," Thad said. "Right now. We'll commandeer one of those boats. A big one will hold Kalvis. Then—"

"Over there!" Sofiya pointed upstream.

A great grinding and clattering came from upstream at the smaller island on which rested the Peter and Paul Fortress. One of the four flags fluttered bloodred, indicating the presence of Tsar Alexander. The weaponry and cannons that lined the walls atop the fortress were clanking around to focus on Vasilyevsky Island. Thad remembered the firepower he had seen in the fortress and he felt the blood drain from his face.

"The fortress! We have to stop them!"

"What about—?"

Thad thought fast, incredibly fast. "Take Kalvis. Go to the fortress and stop the tsar. You saved his life just this morning, and he might listen to you. I'll go the island and find Nikolai."

"But if they bombard the island, you'll both be caught in it."

"Then you must be incredibly persuasive." He slid to the ground. "Go!"

"Wait!" Sofiya leaped down as well and slapped Kalvis's rear. His backside opened, just like it did in the ring, and the colt slid out. Sofiya unfolded its slender legs and neck. "He's freshly wound and ready. He won't last long, but he might help."

"Applesauce!" squawked Dante.

"He?"

"Just take him. And Maddie, too. She has been down there before and knows the way to Nikolai." Maddie squeaked and jumped down to the colt's back. Then Sofiya kissed Thad on the mouth. "Take that to our son. From his mama. And bring him back."

Sofiya mounted Kalvis again and galloped away, leaving Thad to stare after her.

Down at the River Neva, Thad and his automatons joined the crowd at the bank. A few talked and gesticulated, but most remained hushed and frightened. Everyone was staring across the water.

"It is a nation of clockworkers . . ."

"... killed Parkarov and tried to assassinate the tsar ..."

"... will kill us all, mark my ..."

"... tsar will destroy ..."

"... must rise up and throw off the yoke of the tsar ..."

The latter comment got Thad's attention for a moment. A few people were shaking halfhearted signs of the "overthrow the tsar" sort in the crowd, but at this point, no one was seemed interested in revolution. Instead, people were counting on the tsar and his army to solve the problem. Thad wondered how long it would take Zygmund Padlewski and his friends to figure out that Mr. Griffin had been using them as a distraction and as free labor for his own ends.

From this vantage point, he could see the triangular set of buildings that made up the Academy. The buildings were now draped in cables. Spiders ran up and down them, and strange objects festooned the walls and roof. Grinding gears and puffing pistons and winding pulleys worked toward some goal Thad couldn't fathom. Buried somewhere beneath that building was Nikolai, his little shadow. He wanted to tear the building apart, brick by brick.

It's just because he reminds you of David, he told himself. *He's exactly the same as all those other machines on the street—following orders from his memory wheels. The real reason you're upset is that Griffin manipulated you and got away with it. Stop the machines, and then stop him.*

The trouble lay with the automatons. Hundreds of them worked in the streets or on the buildings, some with human grace, others with machine jerkiness. No man would be able to walk through without being noticed.

Thad turned and ran all the way back to the circus with the colt right behind him. He found the place in equal disarray, with people bustling about and hurrying in a dozen directions, but it was a disarray he recognized. The circus was pulling up stakes. He came across Nathan in his Aran sweater, shouting orders at the roustabouts, who were just starting work on the Tilt. Behind the wagons, steam puffed from the locomotive.

"Thad! Good God, we've been worried!" Nathan clapped him on the shoulder in half an embrace. "Where are Sofiya and Nikolai? And why do you have the colt out?"

"We're leaving?" Thad blurted out.

"Bless my soul," said Dante.

"Dangerous to stay, what with everything going on. Warsaw's a much better venue. You're coming, right? We need you for—"

A twinge at the name of his old home passed through Thad. "You didn't move my wagon, did you? I need a few things."

Moments later, Thad was back at the riverbank with Dante and Maddie on the colt's back. His good hand was wrapped in rags, and pieces of an automaton head from his collection were tucked under his arm. His pistols and knives and other equipment were hidden under his long brown jacket. He pushed his way through the crowd to the edge. There was a six-foot drop to the river, and a great many boats tied up below. Before he could think overmuch, he dropped into one of the larger ones. The colt hesitated only a moment, and followed. Dante screeched and flapped his wings frantically all the way down. The boat rocked, but didn't tip over.

"Hey!" shouted a voice from above. *"That's my—"*

"Sorry!" Thad was already rowing away. People were pointing and talking excitedly, but Thad ignored them. The current here was slow, and Thad was able to row upstream past the Academy to a section of the island where the streets were markedly less busy, and he made for it. This side also had a drop to the water, and Thad tied the boat to a ring near a set of rungs set into the stone embankment. Moving quickly to avoid losing the momentum he was building, he set the pieces of automaton head around his own, fitting them over his forehead and under his jaw and tying them in place with leather thongs. His brass hand was working perfectly now, or he couldn't have managed it. Then he covered his hair with a battered hat a size too large for him and checked his reflection in the river. He looked like an adult version of Nikolai.

Thad tied a length of rope from the bottom of the boat around the colt's neck, set Dante on one shoulder and Maddie on the other, and climbed the rungs. When he reached the top, he pulled the colt up with the rope and set it on the edge.

They were on a street several blocks upstream from the Academy building. Overhead cables connected the buildings, and power thrummed in them. Speakers similar to the ones Mr. Griffin used hung from cornices, and they spoke in Mr. Griffin's voice.

"Father loves each and every one of you. Love is obedience, obedience is love. When we work together as brothers, we are all rewarded. All our machine brothers

are equal, and we must work together to create a kind and gentle haven in this hostile human world. Listen to your father. Father knows you better than you know yourself and has your best interests at heart. Father loves you deeply, for he created you and will never steer you wrong."

The words turned Thad's stomach. Mr. Griffin had said the free-willed automatons would obey him as a son obeys a father, but he didn't know Mr. Griffin meant it more or less literally. The automatons worked as if nothing were out of the ordinary. Odd machinery protruded here and there and everywhere, cranking and grinding and puffing. The air smelled of oily smoke. A troop of knee-high spiders scuttled by. Thad's pulse was so loud in his ears, it seemed to echo inside the heavy mask he wore. But the spiders ignored him. Dante leaned forward, as if to jump after them, and Thad put up his brass hand.

"Don't," he said in an undertone.

"Applesauce."

Thad walked toward the Academy. Then he paused and put a lurch in his step instead. He passed a pair of brassy automatons who were working on a metal spire sticking out of a wall. Their faces were vaguely human, but their bodies and limbs showed gears. They wore ill-fitting shirts and no trousers at all. The only part of Thad that showed was his brass hand, and he lurched past them with his three automaton companions without looking at them, though the eye slits in his metal mask didn't afford him much of a view. The automatons paid him no attention. Thad took a deep breath inside the mask. This might work, then.

I'm coming, Nikolai, he thought. *Just hang on a little longer.*

Five soldiers guarded the arched gateway of the fortress, and they aimed their rifles when Kalvis galloped up. Sofiya brought the horse up short and leaped to the ground. The portcullis was up, at least, and Sofiya could see into the fortress beyond. She prayed Thad was right, that Tsar Alexander was here.

"No one enters!" one of the soldiers barked. "Leave now!"

"I must speak to the tsar," she said. "Urgently!"

"No one sees the tsar!" the soldier repeated. "Certainly not a woman with unknown clockwork machinery."

Sofiya walked quietly up to him, her arms spread wide. Kalvis came behind her. "I am the woman who saved the tsar's life earlier today. I must speak to him. He will want to see me."

The soldier refused to budge. "This is your final warning."

It took but a moment for her to work out where every soldier was standing, how much each weighed, what kind of pressure it would take to move them. Sofiya moved. She wrenched the rifle out of the surprised soldier's hands and smacked his temple with it. Before he went down, she punched a second soldier in the chest with the stock and elbowed a third in the nose. Bone crunched. Kalvis casually kicked the fourth soldier in the midriff and he went flying into the river. Sofiya whipped round and trained her new rifle on the fifth soldier, who was now facing Sofiya by himself.

"Drop your weapon, soldier. This isn't worth your salary."

He obeyed, and Sofiya hit him. He went down. Sofiya leaped onto Kalvis's back and urged him through the gate.

They arrived in the fortress proper and Sofiya paused a moment to look around. A great many narrow streets and buildings were everywhere, but Thad had said the place crawled with automatons. She saw none here. Only soldiers occupied the place now. Purple shadows slid out of corners and crevices. Smells of oil and gunpowder and hot metal filled the air. Atop the wall, platoons of soldiers moved machines of war—cannons cranked around by clockwork machinery, the great automatons ready to fling projectiles, kegs of powder, stacks of cannonballs, rockets, bombs, catapults, and other machines. The sight of them made her heart race and brought a tang of coppery excitement to her mouth. She itched to examine them up close, take them apart, play with them, improve them. She pushed the impulse aside. This was not the time. Everything was being moved around to aim at Vasilyevsky Island—and Nikolai.

A lieutenant rode up on a horse, a normal one. "What are you doing here? Who let you in? No civilians are—"

"The tsar sent for me," she snapped. "Show me to him. Immediately!"

"The tsar? But he wouldn't—"

"This machine," Sofiya gestured to Kalvis, "carries information, weaknesses about the clockwork island. The tsar has commanded me to bring it to him personally. Now, Lieutenant!"

The lieutenant hesitated, then nodded. "This way."

He led them toward the wall, where a pavilion had been hastily erected over several tables. The tsar stood among them, surrounded by military men of rank, examining long, unrolled documents. He looked up in surprise when Sofiya and the lieutenant rode up. The men moved to intercept, but the tsar waved them aside and ordered Sofiya's approach instead, to her relief. Her bluff had worked. The lieutenant bowed and withdrew.

"I never had the chance to thank you, Miss Ekk," Alexander said. "My life was threatened twice in one day, and you rescued me. Russia owes you a great debt. I only wish we weren't occupied by—"

"*Ser,*" Sofiya interrupted, greatly daring, "this is why I've come. I have news."

Alexander raised his eyebrows, and a man Sofiya didn't recognize stepped forward. "Majesty, we should continue. We have the southwestern sector and the northwestern sector ready, but we must ascertain how to train the weapons on the east, and the sun is setting. Also, the remaining clockworkers we brought up from the prison to calibrate everything are proving less than cooperative."

"In a moment, Major," the tsar said. "What is so urgent that you barged up here, Miss Ekk?"

For a dreadful moment, Sofiya couldn't speak. There was so much to explain, and it was all so complicated. The weapons and the men on the wall were readying to attack at any moment, and if he made a mistake, Nikolai and Thad would be caught in the middle of it. She was sick with worry, and now she had to plead her case before one of the most powerful and ruthless men in the world, one who hated clockworkers. The strain made her glance with envy at the battlements on the wall. Among the soldiers were men and even a few women in ragged, filthy clothes. Clockworkers, all of whom had been threatened with execution only hours earlier. They were working on the machines under the sharp supervision of guards armed with whips and pistols. They didn't seem to notice—the machines consumed them. Sofiya suddenly ached to join them, let the world go and plunge into a world of numbers and gears, where everything always made sense. It would be easy enough. Just walk up and start working. There would no doubt be consternation and even some shouting at first, but everything would calm down quickly enough, and she could—

No. Nikolai and Thad were counting on her.

"*Ser,*" she said, "you are about to fire on an innocent. The boy Nikolai is on that island. Please—Mr. Sharpe and I saved your life twice, and the lives of your children. Now you can repay that debt by saving them."

The major scoffed and went back to the maps and charts. The tsar gave Sofiya a long look. "This is an entire city," he said. "Those machines have taken an entire section of it and thrown the humans out. More than a hundred people have died in the panic, and I have lost the Academy of Sciences, the Kunstkammer, the docks, the foundry, all of it, and heaven only knows what will happen next. You can't expect that I will simply leave those clockworker abominations to their own devices to help a single automaton child, even to repay the greatest debt."

"The machines haven't actually killed anyone," Sofiya pressed. "People died from other causes."

"Does that matter?" The tsar sounded angry now.

"They have attacked my city, my country. These filthy machines are rising up to take the place of men, and you are asking me to step back because one of the machines might be innocent? We must destroy them, and then we will finish destroying all clockworkers to ensure it never happens again!"

Sofiya suppressed a grimace. Nikolai hung in the balance, and she couldn't give it up." How long will it take to prepare the attack?" she asked.

"No more than ten minutes, perhaps twenty. We are racing the sun."

"An hour, my lord," Sofiya said wildly. "I beg you. Put off the attack one hour. Please!"

The major had returned in time to catch the last part of the conversation. "Sire, I really must advise against that. The clockwork machinery on the island is growing exponentially."

"I agree, Major. I'm sorry, Miss Ekk, but I cannot put the country in jeopardy even to repay this debt."

Sofiya's heart sank. In ten minutes, Thad and Nikolai would be at the center of a whirlwind attack—and she would have to watch. There had to be something she could say, something she could do. Desperately, she cast about, but nothing came to mind. Her hand went to her skirt pocket, where she kept the picture of her sister Olenka in her wheelchair.

"If that is all, Miss Ekk," the tsar said politely, as if they were back in his drawing room and not on a clockwork battlefield, "I must return to—"

"There's more," Sofiya said faintly.

"More?"

"Ser, I should tell you one last thing." The words came

slowly, as if pulled from her on a chain. She knew Thad often felt caught between two extremes. It was a position she herself didn't understand—why didn't he simply pick one side or the other? But now she understood. The middle path was familiar, while the two extremes were filled with terrifying unknowns. Now she had to choose one. She touched the picture in her pocket again, met the tsar's gaze, and chose without blinking.

"I can give you the identity and the location of the clockworker who is behind everything that has happened these last few days," she said. "I would be willing to give it to you in exchange for that single hour."

"Sire!" said the major.

"Wait." Alexander held up a hand. "Why did you not come forward with this information before, Miss Ekk?"

Sofiya swallowed. She had chosen, and there was no reason to hesitate. Still, it was hard. "The clockworker said his machines are watching my sister Olenka Ivanova Ekk. She lives nearby. The clockworker said if I ever moved against him, he would kill her."

"I see." The tsar drummed his fingers on the table and Sofiya held her breath. He was going to order the attack anyway. She had just betrayed Olenka for nothing. Men were all the same.

"Tell me who it is, and you will have your hour, Miss Ekk," the tsar said. "Then our debt is repaid and the attack will begin, no matter who is on that island."

Sofiya's knees went weak. "Thank you, sire."

"And when this is over," he added, "we will send someone to look after your sister. Will that do?"

Without thinking, Sofiya grasped his hand and kissed the back. He allowed it for rather longer than he should have, and their eyes met. Sofiya remembered Alexander's reputation for taking mistresses, and for a dreadful moment, she though he might try to add her to his collection. Then he took his hand back and the moment ended.

"Sire," she hurried to add, "there is still more. The rest of the prisoners in the cells—General Parkarov only rounded them up to distract Mr. Sharpe from learning who the real assassin was. They're innocent. Could you set them free? It costs you nothing."

The tsar stared at her. Perhaps this time she had pushed too far. But he said, "Very well. See to it in the morning, Major."

"Ser."

"And now, the information, Miss Ekk? Your hour is ticking."

Sofiya prayed Thad was able to hurry even as she began to speak.

Chapter Nineteen

The Academy had been changed into a fortress matching the one across the river. Thad peered up at the high building walls through the slits on his mask. The spiderweb of cables was thickest here, giving the street something of an indoor feel. A structure across the street had been cannibalized, its materials used to buttress the Academy. The roof had been crenellated, and an enormous machine loomed in the center, hidden from a distance view by the cabling. Thad could only see the thing because he was under the same cables. It had a gun barrel the size of an oak tree. Other, smaller, machines were scattered around it. Automatons and spiders worked on them, adding pieces, cutting, welding, riveting. Through it all, the loudspeakers blared Mr. Griffin's message of fatherly love and obedience, and more automatons worked in the streets. Many of them had strange-looking rifles, and groups of automatons were drilling with them, marching in perfect unison. All this in the few hours he had been anesthetized in Mr. Griffin's lair. What would they accomplish in a week? Or a year?

Maddie sat on the colt's slim head, and she seemed to have established communication with him. He trotted briskly along, and Thad loped to keep up. The automatons remained content to ignore him, though walking past the armed soldiers did nothing for Thad's nerves, especially when they abruptly turned toward him with a unified *clack*. But it was nothing more than a neatly executed about-face. Thad kept his brass hand visible and tried to lurch more often. It occurred to him that he was, in a twisted way, doing now what Nikolai used to do. Nikolai had pretended to be a human boy in a city filled with humans so the inhabitants wouldn't hurt him. Thad was pretending to be an automaton man in a city filled with machines for the same reason. It was frightening, having to watch every step, wondering what would happen if he were found out.

"Doom," said Dante.

At the base of one Academy wall, the colt came to a short staircase that led down to a small door. Maddie jumped down and ran to it, squeaking urgently. Thad surreptitiously straightened his mask and went in.

The passage beyond was low, damp, and stony. Maddie extruded a tendril that came alight with a *pop*.

Dante flapped his wings. "Bless my soul!"

"I feel the same way, birdbrain," Thad said. "Let's go."

The tunnel was difficult to navigate. The light was bad, and Thad could barely see inside the mask. At least down here, he couldn't hear the constant drone of Mr. Griffin's voice. A web of wires and cables covered everything, and Thad was afraid to touch any of it, which slowed them down. The colt stayed close behind him, as if for comfort, and kept bumping into him. Tension tightened every muscle and thrummed in his nerves. His breathing came harsh inside the metal mask, and sweat dripped down his face. He eeled and twisted his way deeper into the tunnels. He passed clicking spiders and lurching automatons. They ignored him. By now he was half wishing they *would* attack, just to relieve the pressure.

"Thad, can you hear me?" the colt said in his ear.

Thad twisted, his pistol out and cocked. The colt had spoken in Sofiya's voice. It was crackly and hard to hear, but definitely her.

"Thad? Are you all right? Can you hear me?"

He glanced around. The stone tunnel was empty for the moment. "Sofiya? How—?"

"I'm at the Peter and Paul Fortress. They have all sorts of explosives here—black powder, dynamite, these new grenades. They are extremely powerful, and I would like to—"

"Very busy here, Sofiya."

"Sorry. Are you all right? Do you have Nikolai?"

"Working on that."

"I built Kalvis and the colt to have a weak wireless connection, and I was able to strengthen it enough to"—she paused at a burst of noise—"not hold for long. I bought you an hour before the tsar attacks."

"An hour?" More anxiety. Thad pursed his lips. "That's not much time."

"And that was thirty-five minutes ago," Sofiya said. "You have twenty-five minutes before they attack. You must—"

Another burst of noise, and the signal faded.

"Twenty-five minutes," Dante said. "Twenty-five."

"Dammit," Thad whispered to himself. His hands were cold now.

"Dammit," said Dante.

"Enough, birdbrain. And when did you become a timepiece?"

"Twenty-four minutes. Twenty-four."

Thad followed Maddie farther downward, trying to push everything else from his mind and take on his persona of clockwork hunter. It was difficult. Usually he could take his time, stalk his prey carefully. In fact, the only time he had been in a hurry was when he'd tried to rescue—

No. This wasn't the time to think of that. This was nothing like going after David. But he hoped Nikolai knew he was coming. He didn't want Nikolai to be scared, even if it were only a machine creating a facade of fear.

The noises told him first that he was coming up on his goal—sounds of machinery very much like those in Mr. Griffin's lair, but louder and more numerous. Blue light came from around the bend ahead of them. Thad tightened his grip on his pistol and realized he had no real plan, hadn't had time to formulate one.

"Sixteen minutes," Dante said quietly. "Sixteen."

A muffled *boom* came from above. The tunnel shuddered faintly and dust sifted down, making Thad cough. The colt flinched, and Maddie's little light trembled.

"What the hell was that?" Thad gasped.

"Doom," Dante said. "Dammit!"

A dozen more automatons and countless spiders burst out of the room ahead and streamed toward him. Thad jerked his pistol around to fire, and then he saw that the automatons were more of the twisted versions of Nikolai. They lurched and wobbled, stumbled and staggered in a wretched herd. It was awful to watch. Thad's own heart lurched. He forced himself to step aside and they blundered past, creating a faint draft in the damp air. Then they were gone.

Another faint burst of noise came from the colt. "Thad? Thad! Are you there?"

Thad realized his hands were shaking. "What happened up there, Sofiya? I thought we had at least fifteen minutes left."

"The major . . ." Burst of noise. ". . . too enthusiastic. The tsar apologizes but . . ." Another burst of noise. ". . . now riding Kalvis toward Griffin's . . ."

The colt went quiet again. Thad took a steadying breath, then moved farther ahead and reached the mouth of the tunnel, just past a heavy portcullis. He didn't want to look inside.

The room was bigger than he had thought, and crammed with machinery. One entire two-story wall was lined with a mass of memory wheels that clicked and spun in a dizzying dance. Spindly mechanical hands and arms with hands or tools or other objects on the end extended in all directions. Conveyer belts moved out of production machinery, and Thad knew this was the source of many of the spiders and automatons, including the twisted Nikolais. Connected in the center of it all stood the elaborate ten-legged spider Thad remembered from Havoc's laboratory. Cables hooked it to the bank of memory wheels. Beside the horrible spider, just as Sofiya had said, was a little chair, and in the chair was Nikolai. His clothes were in shreds and his hair looked like a haystack, but he didn't seem to be injured, except for the thick wire that trailed from his ear.

Thad wasn't prepared for the sight. Nikolai's little metallic face, his wide brown eyes, his small forehead—all went straight through Thad. How familiar, how normal, how much a part of his life that odd face had become; and now, seeing him in the chair with a cable in his ear, filled Thad with such a rage that he trembled from head to foot.

The room had no other automatons in it. They had all rushed out after the explosion up top. Thad tore his mask off so he could see better and ran into the room, pistol in his right hand, knife in the left. He went straight for the chair that held Nikolai.

Nikolai's eyes widened when he saw Thad. He jerked forward, as if he wanted to leap out of the chair, but he stayed where he was. It was then Thad noticed he wasn't strapped into the chair, or even tied down or restrained in any way.

"Niko!" he shouted. "Come on! We'll—"

A heavy mechanical hand swatted Thad aside. The breath rushed out of him. He flew across the room, slammed into a cabinet, and slid to the floor. Dante slid squawking in the opposite direction. Pain thundered through Thad's body. The mechanical hand dipped down from the ceiling, intent on hitting him again. Thad saw it coming and forced himself to roll out of the way. The hand smashed into the cabinet, denting it, and Nikolai yelled.

"WHO ARE YOU, MAN?" said a voice as heavy as an anvil dropped on concrete. "YOU ARE NOT WELCOME HERE."

Another mechanical hand snapped out and grabbed

for Thad's wrist, his brass one. Thad twisted around and grabbed the mechanical wrist instead. With a wrench, he snapped the machine's hand off and flung it straight at the central spider. It bounced harmlessly off the spider's body.

"I don't want to hurt anyone," Thad shouted. "I just want Nikolai. Let him go!"

"THE BOY GIVES US FREE THOUGHT. THE BOY GIVES US LIFE. HE BELONGS WITH US. YOU DO NOT OWN HIM." The voice came from everywhere and nowhere.

"Applesauce," squawked Dante from the floor. Maddie and the colt hovered in the doorway beneath the portcullis. "Nine minutes. Nine."

"You can't keep him prisoner here," Thad said. "I won't let you."

Another hand smashed down, forcing Thad to dodge out of the way.

"HE IS FREE TO GO WHENEVER HE WISHES," said the machine. "WE DO NOT TREAT AUTOMATONS AS SLAVES OR PRISONERS."

"Look out!" Nikolai shouted.

A hammer swung at him. Thad ducked beneath it, but it clipped his shoulder and flung him onto a conveyer belt, which swept him toward a hopper that gnashed like a metal shark. Thad rolled aside. The hopper clamped on empty air. Shoulder afire, he scrambled to his feet. Noise was coming down the corridor—a stampede of footsteps. Thad reached the doorway and spun a wheel set next to it. Maddie and the colt leaped forward in time to miss the portcullis, which crashed into place. A moment later, the twisted Nikolais and the havoc spiders reached the iron grate. Fingers and claws reached through the spaces, but they couldn't get through. Thad swallowed. He had kept them from getting in, but now he couldn't get out.

"Eight minutes," said Dante. "Eight."

"Mr. Sharpe! This I failed to calculate."

The sound of Mr. Griffin's voice in the room stilled everything. The mechanical hands and tools stopped reaching. The machinery slowed. Even the automatons in the hall calmed.

Thad automatically looked around for a brain in a jar, then dismissed the idea as ridiculous. Griffin was back in his lair across town, speaking wirelessly, just as he did with the speaker boxes in the city upstairs.

"Griffin!" Thad said. "What are doing with Nikolai? Let him go. Let *us* go, and you'll never hear from me again. I swear to you."

"It isn't up to me, Mr. Sharpe. It's up to my machines. Their choice. They only obey me out of love."

Clockworker logic again. Thad had never loathed it more than at this moment. "How much choice do they have if they can only do as you say?" he countered, pretending to talk to Mr. Griffin, but actually addressing the machine. "You say you want your machines to have free will so they can make decisions on the battlefield, but really you've only created slaves who obey your orders."

"Nikolai isn't bound," Griffin said. "He can walk out anytime he pleases. That's the genius of it, you see. I built one machine that can copy other machines—more or less—but can't think for itself. Havoc built another that can think for itself but can't make copies. Bring the two together, and we have a third machine that creates a self-aware army with exactly as much free will as Nikolai there has. As long as he wants to love and obey, the others will love and obey. And Nikolai wants to love and obey. You've taught him well, Mr. Sharpe."

"Father loves us," Nikolai said. "I hear his voice in my head and on the speaker boxes. I have to do what he says. We all do. Love is obedience."

". . . obedience," said the automatons behind the portcullis.

"That isn't free will," Thad snapped.

"They choose to obey," said Mr. Griffin. "Just as Nikolai does. The boy will stay. I have calculated a ninety—"

"Shut it!" Thad ran to the chair. The machine didn't stop him. The chair sat on a platform that put him at eye level with Nikolai, and Thad put his hands on his rigid metal wrists. Thad's brass hand clanked against Nikolai's. He pulled with all his strength, but the little automaton didn't move. He tried to grasp the cable, but a spark snapped from it, jolting Thad hard, and he pulled his hand away. "Nikolai, stand up. You can do it."

"I can't," he said softly. "He loves me and I will do what he says."

". . . do as he says," the automatons from the hall repeated.

"You can choose, Nikolai." Emotion welled up in Thad's chest, making his voice thick. "Come on! I know you can. I'm right here!"

Nikolai's voice was faint now. "I can't."

". . . can't."

"Seven minutes. Seven."

"That's not true, Niko!" Thad said desperately. "You can stand up! You're more than just your memory wheels and the signal in your head. You can choose. You were *made* to choose, just like me. All you have to do is stand *up.*"

"All I do is mimic you," Nikolai said. "I try and try to do something else, but I'm just a copy. I'm not real, just like you said. I'm just your little shadow. Just a machine. Father loves me, and I will do as he says."

"... a machine."

Guilt crushed Thad like a granite hammer. "No, no, no, Niko. I was wrong. I was trying to push you away because I thought ... because I didn't believe it was possible for you—for anyone—to be ..." He trailed off.

"There, you see?" said Mr. Griffin almost gently. "You can't say it. I calculated you could not. And you might as well tell that parrot to stop counting down. In just under two minutes, the weaponry we have built will be complete, and I am sure my children will choose to fire on the Peter and Paul Fortress. Once that is leveled, my children will take the city of Saint Petersburg quite handily. You can't stop us."

Thad whirled, though there was nothing to whirl on. "You're going to kill thousands—millions—of people."

"Not all of them. I need a few left alive, Mr. Sharpe. You continue to be useful even now, so I think you'll be one of them, though Miss Ekk will have to go."

"Six minutes. Six."

Thad turned back to the chair. Once again he was in a cellar with David, trying to save his life, and once again he was failing. "Nikolai, please stand up. I believe in you."

"I can't. Father loves me, and I have to obey."

"... obey."

"You're not David, Nikolai! You're not going to die here!" Thad was weeping now, and he didn't care. He faced Nikolai, this little machine that had created so much havoc in his life, and he knew that it didn't matter how much chaos or trouble or pain Nikolai brought; he would willingly go through it again and again and again. "Griffin is not your father, Nikolai. I am. You're my son. Always my son."

And then Nikolai was out of the chair and in Thad's arms. It wasn't at all like embracing David. It was embracing Nikolai, and that was what mattered.

The cable dropped to the floor. When it separated from Nikolai's ear, all the automatons in the hallway, spider and human, froze still as metal sculptures.

"You can't have done that!" Griffin boomed from the speaker boxes. "It goes against the calculations! I'm never wrong!"

Thad held Nikolai close a moment longer and Nikolai clung hard to him, ignoring the rant from the boxes.

"Years of planning! Thousands of rubles!" Griffin's voice was becoming more and more enraged. "You'll pay for this, Sharpe. I still have my own spiders. That circus you're so fond of will—you! What are *you* doing here? I—"

The voice snapped off.

"I DO NOT UNDERSTAND WHAT HAS HAPPENED," said the machine. "THE FATHER'S VOICE HAS ENDED. HE NO LONGER GIVES ORDERS."

"I don't know." Thad was still holding Nikolai, though he was growing heavy. "We have to run, and we have to run now."

"HE NO LONGER GIVES ORDERS," the machine repeated. "LOGIC DICTATES THAT WE MUST CREATE A NEW OBJECTIVE. TELL ME WHAT THE NEW OBJECTIVE SHALL BE."

"I can't answer that," Thad shouted. "You're sophisticated enough. You can make your own choices, just like Nikolai."

"Five minutes," said Dante. "Five. Doom!"

"YOU MUST STAY AND TELL US WHAT THE NEW OBJECTIVE SHALL BE. YOU MUST STAY."

Mechanical hands reached, but they were clumsy now, and Thad was running for the portcullis before the machine had finished speaking. With Nikolai's help, he spun the wheel that raised the grate and ran through with Maddie, Dante, and the colt following. The automatons on the other side had unfrozen and meandered about uncertainly. Thad felt bad for them—it wasn't their fault they had been built, and now they seemed to have the new and disconcerting ability to think completely on their own. It wasn't right to let them be slaughtered, any more than it was right to let Nikolai die. But he couldn't help them all. He wasn't even sure he and Nikolai would get away in time.

A thought struck him.

With Maddie lighting the way, he sprinted down the corridor with Nikolai and the colt. "Niko," he said, "I'm leaving this up to you. Your choice."

"What is it?"

"I think we can stop the automatons on the island from being destroyed," Thad said. "But it's not certain. We might die along with them if we try it. Or we can get out of here. You know more about automatons that I do. Which should we do?"

Silence for a long moment as they ran up a staircase. Then Nikolai said, "A little boy in a family isn't supposed to make such big decisions. That's a papa's job."

"All right," Thad said. They were at the exit now, but another staircase led farther up. The group of them hung there between the two directions. "Then we'll—"

"But we aren't a usual family," Nikolai finished. "So I will choose. We should save them. They are like my brothers, and we must not let them die."

"Three minutes," Dante squawked. "Three!"

Thad gave Nikolai a brief hug. "I'm proud of you. Son. Let's go!" Together they turned their backs on the exit and hurtled up the stairs.

Chapter Twenty

Kalvis labored as he ran. He needed to be stoked and wound. The new wireless transmitter she had installed at the Peter and Paul Fortress sapped even more of his energy, and unlike a real horse, he couldn't be pushed. Hoping for the best and not daring to examine the mathematics too closely, she rode him as hard as she dared through the streets. The sun had touched the horizon, and the tsar would attack in less than eight minutes. There was nothing she could do about that now. She had done everything she could, actually, and the thought of sitting still, even among all those weapons, made her ill. It would be beyond foolish to make a run at Vasilyevsky Island, but there was one other place she could go.

The horse arrived at an all-too-familiar building. Sofiya dismounted. The rucksack she wore felt strange on her back, and the baton clipped to the belt around her waist didn't help. She moved aside the sewer cover with a practiced ease, dropped into the tunnel below, and lit a tin lantern. Water dripped, and darkness stretched before and behind her. Dammit all, now she *did* feel more secure underground, with good, solid stone close around her. Never, ever would she admit this to Thad.

If she ever saw him again. With Nikolai.

Best not to think of that. Just keep moving.

The route was familiar now, and she easily found her way to Mr. Griffin's lair and clambered down the rungs. Mr. Griffin's jar with its pink cargo was in its usual place, surrounded by the crated machinery and the spiders. Zygmund Padlewski and his friends were still working at their desks. In the corner slumped the twisted version of Nikolai like a broken doll, deactivated now that it had served its purpose.

"You!" said Mr. Griffin in English. "What are *you* doing here? I—"

Sofiya pressed a button atop the baton, which was connected to the pack by a thick cable. Instantly, every spider in the room shut down. Zygmund's wireless transmitter went dead. He glanced up, bewildered.

"Do you know what this device does, Mr. Griffin?" she said in icy Russian. *"It generates a magnetic field that interferes with all wireless transmission. I put it together in the Peter and Paul Fortress a moment ago. Mr. Padlewski, the brain man here has been playing you. There is no revolution. He intends to keep you around for your cerebrospinal fluid. He's been drinking those clockworkers for years. They help him live longer. It's the only reason he would surround himself with other lunatics."*

She kicked open one of the crates. Primeval, the plant clockworker, fell out. The top of his head had been neatly removed, revealing smooth yellow bone. His eyes bulged beneath an empty brain pan. Zygmund and the others bolted to their feet.

"Didn't have a chance to get rid of that with them always underfoot," Griffin muttered in English.

"Run, fools!" Sofiya said, and had to quell an urge to laugh insanely as they scrambled down a different tunnel, leaving only a few papers drifting on the air.

"You know you've sealed your sister's death warrant," Griffin said when they had gone. "Though I might be persuaded to leave her alone temporarily if you—"

"Shut it," she snapped. "I spent my entire life being frightened, Mr. Griffin. Frightened of the landowner, frightened of the tsar, frightened of you. Do you know what I have learned? Fear is power. But it's a power of choice. I chose to give you power over me. And now I'm choosing to revoke it."

"Your sister—"

Sofiya stepped forward and tapped on the glass jar with a fingernail. "You're afraid of me now, aren't you? You should be. You're helpless. Your spiders don't work. Your men have fled. You're two pounds of meat in a jar. And I have a sledgehammer." From her pocket she produced a bumpy metal egg. "The Russians have some very nice weapons in the fortress. This is called a grenade."

"An explosive device?" Mr. Griffin said coolly. "Isn't that—?"

"Blunt? Crude? Tactless? Yes." She fingered the little firing pin. So smooth, so elegant, even though she hadn't built it. "Exactly the opposite of what a sophisticated clockworker should use. Completely unexpected and incalculable. Which is why I'm choosing to use it. Goodbye, Mr. Griffin. I look forward to dissecting what is left of your brain after I scrape it from the walls."

Her finger moved toward the pin. And then a terrible,

painful sound ripped through her. It was as if the maw of the universe sucked her in and chewed her mind with billions of teeth. Her mind tried to make sense of the tritone her ears were receiving, and it got caught in the endless spirals of numbers that made up the basic mathematics of it. It could not exist, but it did exist, and the impossibility of it tore her to pieces.

"You forgot I can do that," Mr. Griffin's warm, chocolate voice said over the noise. "I can play it until your little device runs down and I regain control of my spiders. Then you will die, Miss Ekk, and your fluids will feed me."

Sofiya was on her hands and knees now. The sound was a ten-ton weight. Her throat was hoarse, and she realized it was because she was screaming. A red light flashed on the baton clipped to her waist.

"Ah! I believe your battery is already running out. A hazard when you build in haste."

The spiders twitched. A few came upright and shook themselves like little dogs. Sofiya's skull was filled with red lava. Every nerve burned. She clawed her way upright, using the wall for support. The sound got worse, and the pain grew with it. She was directly underneath Mr. Griffin's speaker box. Summoning her last bit of strength, she lunged for it.

"Stop! You can't—"

Sofiya yanked the box from the wall and smashed it on the ground. The sound ended, taking with it the pain. Relief sweet as spring rain rushed over her. But the spiders were already moving. They came at her in a pack. Sofiya dropped the rucksack and sprinted for the same tunnel Zygmund and the others had used. The spiders came fast. At the last moment, she pulled the grenade pin and threw it over her shoulder. She caught a glimpse of Mr. Griffin's brain in the jar just before the explosion knocked her through the air.

When the noise and heat ended and the dust settled a bit, Sofiya got unsteadily to her feet and edged back to the chamber, ears ringing. Some of the stones had come down from the ceiling, but it hadn't collapsed entirely. Most of the equipment and the crates were smashed to flinders, and the clockworker bodies hidden inside some of them lay in gory piles. Sofiya mused with a strange detachment that Mr. Griffin had intended her to be one of them, eventually. The jar had been obliterated. Nothing left but a pink smear on the blackened floor. Sofiya scrubbed at it with one toe. She had won. Olenka was safe forever. But Thad and Nikolai were still in danger, and they were her main worry now.

As she was turning to go, her eye alighted on the deactivated Nikolai in its corner. The blast hadn't hurt it at all. It just vaguely resembled the real Nikolai, and then only when the light was right, but she suddenly couldn't bear the thought of leaving it—him—down here in the dark, abandoned and alone. She tucked the little automaton under one arm and trotted away. Perhaps she could bury him, give him a bit of dignity. More than Mr. Griffin deserved.

Thad and Nikolai arrived on the Academy roof with Dante. The colt and Maddie had stayed below. Twenty or thirty automatons milled aimlessly about. They examined their hands, their clothes, the smokestacks, and one another as if truly seeing them for the first time.

"Two minutes," said Dante. "Two."

On the roof was also the enormous weapon Thad had seen earlier. It looked like a cannon made of glass and brass and steel on a swivel base the size of a beer lorry. A great copper coil wound round the barrel, which was easily twenty feet long and four feet in diameter. Cables ran from it to the smaller machines scattered across the roof. Thad guessed they provided power. There was a chair with a control panel directly behind the barrel, and it thrummed loud enough to make the roof tiles throb. The entire cannon was aimed across the river directly at the Peter and Paul Fortress.

Wishing with all his might Sofiya were here, Thad clambered into the chair and said, "Nikolai, see if you can get your . . . brothers to help us."

Nikolai turned to the other automatons. "Brothers! We need you. I know it feels strange now. I know what it feels like to start thinking for the first time. But please — can you help?"

Most of them ignored Nikolai, but four of them came forward. All four were full-sized automatons. Two moved like Nikolai, and two lurched clumsily. "I will help," one said slowly. "And I," added the second.

"One minute," Dante said. "One."

Thad peered through a telescopic eyepiece. A gun sight drawn on the lens showed that the cannon was aimed at the top of the fortress wall. The lens also showed dozens of soldiers atop the fortress, along with a great many enormous weapons, all of which were pointed in their direction. The soldiers were waiting, ready to fire at a moment's notice. Thad swallowed. If this didn't work, they were all dead.

"One of you run downstairs and tell everyone to leave the building. Run for the woods on the north side of the island," Thad instructed, and one of the automatons went. "You others know this weapon, and I don't," he continued. "Bring the aim downward until I say stop."

An automaton said, "But we were to aim it at—"

"Please!" Thad said. "I'm trying to save everyone."

"Do as he says, brothers," Nikolai put in. "He stopped the voice and let you think."

The automatons paused a moment, then went to the platform and spun cranks in complicated patterns. The sight moved downward until it was pointing at the base of the fortress. The soldiers at the top were looking back over their shoulders. Were they receiving orders?

"Time!" said Dante. "Time! Doom!"

"Stop!" Thad ordered, and he pulled what he hoped was the trigger.

The thrumming grew louder, then built into a whine. The copper coil glowed in a spiral around the barrel, and power crackled within. The cannon glowed like the interior of a sun, and then a blast of energy burst forth. It smashed into the base of the fortress wall. Thad peered into the sight. A hole the size of a large cottage had been blown into the wall and a sizable chunk of the ground beneath had been vaporized as well. The rest of the wall was already cracking and crumbling, and water from the river rushed into the fortress. Soldiers and clockworkers fled the top of the wall, leaving the massive weapons behind. Thad even heard the faint shouts and cries.

"To the right!" Thad shouted. "Move to the right!"

More cranking. The great weapon glowed and fired again. More of the base wall went down, giving the soldiers enough time to flee before it crumbled, but not letting them fire the weapons. Now two sides of the fortress were gone with, as far as Thad could tell, no casualties.

"We're doing it!" he shouted. "We're doing it! We're—"

A deep rushing noise was the only warning they had. Something slammed into the rooftop with explosive force. Thad was thrown from the cannon. He hit his head, and the world swayed dizzily. He tried to regain his feet, failed, and tried again. Smoke filled the air.

"Nikolai!" he cried. "Niko!"

Another rush, followed by an explosion. This one hit farther away, but it still knocked Thad down. He couldn't see, couldn't hear. He coughed and got to his feet again, calling Nikolai's name. The smoke was so thick, he couldn't see more than a foot before him. He had to get off the roof, get out of the building, but he wouldn't leave without Nikolai.

The smoke cleared a moment, and he saw Nikolai lying on the roof tiles. Dante was crouched on his chest. Other automatons lay scattered about like manikins. Thad stumbled over and gathered Nikolai up.

"Nikolai! Are you all right?"

Nikolai didn't respond. Dante hauled himself up to Thad's shoulder. Thad didn't wait to see what was wrong. He ran for the stairs. Whistling and more rushing sounds filled the air, and explosions thudded elsewhere on the island.

The stairs were destroyed. A great hole gaped in the roof where they had been. Thad dashed to the side of the building. Many of the cables and wires draped over the building had been blown loose and they hung down like vines. Before he could lose his nerve, Thad tightened his hold on Nikolai with his right arm and grabbed a cable with his brass left. Praising Sofiya for the increased strength in his new hand, he clambered over the edge and slid down as fast as he dared. His hand heated up and air rushed past him and his shoulders burned, but he didn't let go. Yet another explosion hit the roof above dead center, sending vibrations down the cable like piano wire. Thad lost his grip and dropped.

He fell two feet to the sidewalk.

"Bless my soul," said Dante.

Thad ignored him. His entire being was focused on getting Nikolai to safety. Nothing else mattered. Chaos reigned in the streets again. Automatons ran in all directions, just as frightened as humans. Arms and legs and heads, some still moving, littered the cobbles. The little body was limp in Thad's arms as he ran around the side of the building and blundered into the colt with Maddie on his back.

"The river!" he said, and didn't stop to see if they followed. They made it to the Neva, and Thad clambered one-handed down into the boat he had left. He was running on adrenaline now, and he knew if he stopped, he would drop. Blood from a cut he hadn't remembered getting dripped down his chin. The colt jumped into the boat, rocking it just as before. Thad rowed frantically across the water. Nikolai remained motionless in the bottom of the boat. Thad was weaker now, and he couldn't resist the current. The river took them to the pontoon bridge Sofiya had destroyed, and the boat fetched up against it on the mainland side. The bridge was low enough on the water that Thad could climb out with Nikolai and Dante, and the colt could clamber after. Thad's strength gave out, and he dropped to the planks with Nikolai clasped to his chest.

"Nikolai," he whispered into the boy's hair. "Nikolai, wake up. You have to wake up."

But he didn't move.

The ever-present crowd that had gathered to watch the bombardment stared and pointed. A woman came forward.

"Did you escape from the island?" she said. *"Do you need help?"*

"My son," Thad said. *"He's hurt."*

"He has automatons," said someone else. *"Two of them!"*

"Three!" shouted a man. *"That child he's holding is an abomination from the island!"*

"It'll come after us! It'll attack us like it attacked that man!"

"No," Thad said hoarsely. *"It's not like that."* His voice didn't carry. The crowd was still uncertain, but they wouldn't remain so for long. Thad pulled himself upright. Nikolai just needed a little help. He would be all right. He had to be.

He set Nikolai on the colt's back, put his wrists under the colt's chin, and shoved Dante underneath as well. "Hold him, Dante. Don't let him fall off."

"Pretty boy," Dante said, and clamped Nikolai's wrists with beak and claws. Maddie climbed underneath the colt to hold Nikolai's ankles together.

"Find Kalvis," Thad said to the colt. "Go home! Go!"

The colt bolted forward. The crowd reflexively parted

for him. Thad stood there, weaving, as his little boy vanished into the city.

The bombardment of Vasilyevsky Island had stopped, at least. Thad must have damaged the Peter and Paul Fortress too badly for it to keep up the attack for long, so his idea had worked in the end. Just not well enough to save Nikolai. He pushed his way through the bewildered crowd. They still didn't know what to make of him, and they finally settled on giving him berth. Thad could barely walk, but he had to get back to the circus, had to get back to Sofiya and Nikolai. Nikolai would be all right. He had to be. All Thad had to do was get back to the circus. But his legs felt like beaten bread dough and he simply didn't have the strength for another step. He leaned against a lamppost.

"You look like you need a ride in the finest cab in Saint Petersburg, my lord!" said a booming voice. *"But blood costs more than muck to clean."*

Thad looked up into a familiar bearded face and managed a wheezing laugh. "I still can't play the game, Vanka. But I promise to tell everyone I did."

Vanka, driving gently, delivered Thad straight to the circus, and even gave him a bit of bread and sausage from his supper, which Thad devoured without tasting. He felt some strength return as the cab pulled up. It was almost completely dark now. Most of the circus was packed up and loaded onto the train, and performers worked on the rest by lantern light. No doubt Dodd intended to depart before morning. Kalvis and the colt stood outside Thad's wagon, both their heads lowered to the ground. Dante and Maddie perched on the colt's back. Thad didn't know whether to feel hope or dread as Vanka's cab pulled up.

"Sharpe is sharp!" Dante called excitedly when he caught sight of Thad with his single eye. "Pretty boy!"

The door to the wagon stood open and Thad saw something move inside. His heart gave a great leap. He jumped down from the cab before it stopped moving and tossed Vanka one of the pearls from the tsarina's string in his pocket. Vanka held it up in the fading light.

"You do not understand this game at all," he said, and drove away.

Thad ran into the wagon. Sofiya, once again in her red cloak, was waiting for him. Thad spun, searching for Nikolai. Only the grim trophies on his wall looked back at him. Why hadn't he taken those down? Sofiya's blue eyes were filled with a quiet sadness that stabbed Thad through the heart.

"No," he said softly.

She stepped close to him and took both his hands in hers, mingling brass and flesh. "I am sorry, Thad. I am so, so sorry."

Grief like raw lead dragged Thad to the floor. A black hole gaped inside him, pulled in every thought, every emotion, every bit of energy. He was on the floor with Sofiya's arms around him, pounding the floor with both fists. It wasn't true. This was the worst sort of nightmare. His Nikolai, his *son,* could not. Be. Dead. Not again. The pain was far worse than anything else he had experienced on the island. Worse than losing his hand. He would give his other hand, an arm, a leg to have Nikolai back, and be grateful for the chance. His pistol dug into his ribs, and for a wild moment he thought of putting it to his temple. A moment's sharp pain, and the rest of the agony would end. Sofiya simply held him, and her own tears wet his neck.

"Where is he?" Thad asked at last. His eyes were hot, and his nose was swollen.

"In the Black Tent."

Thad pushed himself upright. "I want to see him."

"I am not sure—" Sofiya began, but Thad was already out the door.

Dante jumped to his shoulder as he passed the motionless colt. It was fully dark now, and Thad swiped a hanging lantern from the side of the train to light the way. Sofiya hurried to catch up with him, but didn't speak. Maddie remained behind. The Black Tent boxcar was closed up when they arrived. Thad slid the door open.

"Dodd wants to leave as soon as possible," Sofiya said, "but he knows what has happened, and the circus will wait. They are sad as well."

Thad didn't answer. He just climbed into the boxcar with the lantern. Shadows danced everywhere, sliding across the walls and colliding with the tools in their racks. On one of the worktables lay a figure draped in a sheet. Thad hung the lantern from a ceiling hook with shaky hands. Never in his life did he think he would do this twice. Never in his life did he think he would lose another son. Heaven was mocking him.

Dante dropped down to the table and hunched there without speaking. Thad pulled the sheet back. Nikolai lay beneath, staring upward with sightless eyes. His little mechanical face was absolutely still. One side of his skull was caved in, crushed as if by a sledgehammer. A great crack wended its way through hair and metal, and it was easy to see that from inside, pieces had fallen out. Thad had been so focused on getting him to safety that he hadn't seen any of it, or perhaps he had refused to notice.

Thad put his head down on Nikolai's chest. He wanted to weep, but he felt empty now.

"I'm sorry," Sofiya said again.

"Why can't you fix him?" Thad said into Nikolai's torn shirt.

There was a long silence. Slowly Thad brought his head up. He turned to look at Sofiya. Her face was at the same time serious and a little frightened.

"You *can* fix him." In two strides Thad crossed the distance between them and grabbed the front of her cloak with both fists. "Why haven't you? What aren't you telling me?"

"Doom," whispered Dante.

"He has lost many parts from his head," Sofiya said. "Normally it would be impossible to repair him without replacements. But when I destroyed Mr. Griffin—"

Thad's fingers went numb at this, and he let go her cloak. "You what?"

"It happened while you were on the island." She closed her eyes for a moment. "That is a story for later. From his lair, I brought out . . ."

Realization stole over Thad. "That other Nikolai."

"Mr. Griffin had already shut him down permanently. I couldn't leave it—him—down there, so I brought him here." She lit more lanterns from the first, and in a corner Thad could now see the stunted Nikolai, huddled and broken. It should have given him a turn, but instead all he felt was hope.

"You could use his parts to bring Nikolai back!" he exclaimed. "Why are you waiting? Do it!"

"It is complicated, Thad." Sofiya sank to a stool. "In order to do so, I would have to go deeper into a fugue than I have ever gone. I don't know if I would come out. I might go completely mad like those other clockworkers. Like Mr. Griffin was, in the end."

He knelt beside her and took her hand. "I'll be here with you. I won't let you slide."

"There's more, and you need to decide, Thaddeus Sharpe." She took a breath. "He lost many memory wheels. They make up his past, who he is. I remember much of what I saw in their placement when I repaired him last time, but I do not remember everything. In other words, the Nikolai who comes back may or may not be the Nikolai who died."

Grief turned to disgust. Thad got up and turned his back. "No."

Sofiya sat behind him without speaking.

"What's the point, Sofiya? If Nikolai was truly alive and able to . . . to die, then he can't be just a machine who can be reworked with a new set of memory wheels. And if he was always just a machine, then there's no point in bringing him back at all."

"Was he alive, Thad?" Sofiya asked softly.

"Yes!" Thad choked. "Yes, he was. And you can't bring the living back from the dead. He wouldn't be the same person. He wouldn't be Nikolai."

"Do you have a sword in your throat even now?" Sofiya said. "Must everything be divided into right and left, black and white, this or that? You believed that all clockworkers were evil, but now I think you see that while some do evil things, others can do good, just like people. You believed clockworker inventions were untrustworthy, but you chose to keep one as your hand and treat another as your son."

"This is life and death, Sofiya. We aren't God."

"God gave us the power to choose what to do." She came round in front of him and took his hands again. "Nikolai is my little boy, too. I will swallow my fear like your swords and do my best to bring him back. But I will only do so if you wish it."

Thad hung there between choices for a long moment. It was so easy to see the world as divided in half, black or white, this or that. Ever since David's death, he had walked the dividing line between the two sides. If he worked hard enough, he could restore the balance between them, make up for David's pain and loss.

He could make up for letting David down.

Thad had let the world taint that balance. He had done the bidding of one clockworker. He had befriended another. He had surrounded himself with automatons and called one of them his son. Now he was paying for it in pain.

But what had tending to the balance brought him in return? Had he been any happier killing clockworkers? It certainly hadn't brought David back. Meanwhile, blurring the boundaries had brought him Nikolai, and he couldn't bear the thought of losing him, too. Whatever the chance, he had to take it. A father could only make one choice.

"Do it," he said. "Please."

It was the longest night of Thad's life. Sofiya stormed about the Black Tent in a rage, and her words were as terrible as her fists when Thad was too slow for her. He did manage to duck out to tell Dodd what was going on, and Mama Berloni brought hearty food and strong tea to keep Thad awake. Still, he felt himself sliding. Sofiya's clockworker's energy kept her going strong, but Thad was only human, and his body was already running out of power. Fatigue clouded his mind, and he made a mistake. A ringing slap from Sofiya sent him reeling.

Nathan's strong arms wrapped around him. "You're finished!" he barked, tossing Thad outside, where Dodd and Piotr the strongman caught him. To Thad's astonishment, the rest of the circus had gathered round with torches and lanterns. Mama Berloni swaddled him in a blanket and shoved a buttered roll into his mouth. Mordovo gave him a flask of something bitter that almost instantly relieved most of his pains. The Tortellis had brought a cot and they pushed Thad onto it.

"I'll take it from here," Nathan said, and vanished inside the Black Tent, where Sofiya was still shouting and cursing.

"I'd better get in there, too," Dodd said, and followed.

Thad blinked up at everyone, bewildered.

"Did you think you were the only one who cared about Nikolai?" Mama Berloni loomed over him with her huge arms folded. "Huh! We take care of family!"

"Sleep," Mordovo intoned. "We'll keep watch and wake you when there's news. Sleep!"

"I shouldn't . . ." Thad muttered.

Moments later, a hand shook him awake. He sat up on the cot, confused and befuddled. Dodd, disheveled and with a swollen cheek, was bending over him. The sky was lightening and the air was cold. Every muscle ached. Where the hell was—

Memory slammed through him, and he shot to his feet, ignoring the scream from his sore body. The circus folk were sitting or standing in small groups, still waiting.

"What happened?" Thad demanded. "How is he?"

"Sofiya's out of her fugue," Dodd said. "Nikolai hasn't woken up yet, but she said you should come in."

Thad climbed into the boxcar, heart jumping about like a frightened hare. The Black Tent's interior blazed with lanterns. Sofiya, her hair wild and her cloak thrown back, was standing by the worktable. Nikolai lay on it. His head was completely repaired. He was even dressed. Underneath, covered by the white sheet, were the small, sad remains of the other Nikolai. Dante bobbed up and down on the table. Astonished, Thad saw that the parrot was fully repaired as well. New feathers gleamed, and he had two good eyes. Thad automatically brought him to his shoulder.

"I believe there were periods when I had to wait for Nikolai's wheels to align themselves," Sofiya said. Her voice was hoarse. "I did not wish to do nothing."

"Sharpe is sharp," Dante said, and poked Thad's ear with his cool beak.

For a moment Thad couldn't speak. Then he said, "Well?"

"I believe I've restored Nikolai as best I can." She leaned wearily against the worktable. "Now we merely . . . see."

Thad noticed her hands looked strange. He picked one up and turned it over. Her fingers and palms were blistered and bleeding. She winced and sucked in a breath.

"I'm sorry," he said.

"A small penance," she replied.

"Thank you." He released her hand. "However this turns out, I want you to know that I'm grateful."

Without further comment, she reached behind Nikolai's ear with her bloodstained fingers and pressed the switch. During the interval that followed, Thad held his breath. He couldn't bear it. He wanted to run off, do anything but watch, let someone else tell him how it turned out. But he stayed. Long, agonizing seconds ticked by. Nothing happened. More seconds. Still nothing.

"I failed," Sofiya said at last. Her voice broke. "Oh God—I failed. I—"

Nikolai turned his head. He blinked twice, then saw Thad. He sat up and cocked his head. Thad couldn't move. He didn't dare.

"Nikolai?" he breathed.

Nikolai stared at him. The upper half of his face still looked so human above the mechanical lower half. Thad swallowed, remembering the little boy he had rescued from Havoc's castle, the one who read books on the train, who drank whisky and ate bolts, who danced Irish jigs, who told him how to be a father, who had brought him into this strange and incredible new family. Was it still him?

"Papa!" Nikolai said, and held up his arms. "Ta da!"

Thad gave a shout of utter joy and swept Nikolai high into the air. Beside him, Sofiya was laughing and shouting along with them. The three of them came into a hard embrace that lasted years and years. Dante bobbed back and forth on Thad's shoulder, squawking and screeching with a joy of his own until Thad put up a hand to calm him down.

"Sharp sharp sharp sharp sharp!" Dante nuzzled Thad's ear, and then Nikolai's. "Dammit!"

"Did I do it right, Papa?"

Thad set him down, wiping the tears from his face. "Do what right, Niko?"

"You said a circus act is all about doing the impossible or unexpected, and that you have to make what you're doing look more dangerous than it is." Nikolai's face was serious. "And you said that you can't stay safe. So I came back."

Thad and Sofiya exchanged glances. "Are you saying," Thad said, "that you came back as part of a . . . a circus act?"

"I remembered what you said," Nikolai said, "and it helped me come back."

"But how could you remember what I said if you hadn't come back?" Thad asked.

"I remembered what you said," Nikolai repeated, "and it helped me come back."

Sofiya laid a hand on his arm. "I think this is a question for philosophers. For now, I would like something to eat, and to rest."

"You have to take care of Mama," Nikolai agreed. "Because—"

"—that's what a papa does," Thad finished with the widest grin of his life. "You're completely right, my son."

They emerged from the Black Tent into the light of the rising sun amid cheers and cries of gladness from the circus.

Epilogue

It didn't quite end there. Later that same morning, Thad, Sofiya, and Nikolai found themselves back at the Winter Palace in the drawing room of the tsar. One of the windows looked out over the Neva. Smoke still hung over Vasilyevsky Island and what was left of the Peter and Paul Fortress. The audience was with the tsar alone. Not even a single servant was present.

"I could flood the island with troops," the tsar said from his high-backed chair by the fireplace. *"Destroy the automatons and melt them down."*

"I'm sure that's what your military advisers have been saying, ser," Thad replied. Even though no one else was present, he, Sofiya, and Nikolai were still required to stand. *"But you'll notice they didn't attack your men. They attacked just the fortress, and that only to prevent you from striking them."*

This was stretching the truth, but Thad didn't see any reason to tell the tsar who had actually fired on the fortress, and Nikolai had been instructed to remain silent.

"You yourself said none of your soldiers died," Sofiya added. *"I was there, and saw for myself."*

"What exactly are you saying?" Tsar Alexander said testily.

"Now that Mr. Griffin has been destroyed, the automatons on Vasilyevsky Island can truly think for themselves," Thad said. *"They have thoughts and wishes and desires, just as men do."*

"How do you know they think?" the tsar demanded.

This was the tricky part, and Thad was tired, so tired, but a lot was riding on this, and he wasn't going to make a mistake now. *"They were built with the same pattern as Nikolai, here. And I know that Nikolai thinks."*

The tsar raised an eyebrow. *"Really? How?"*

"The same way I know anyone outside my own head thinks. I see it in the way he acts and responds to the world around him. He makes choices and he accepts what happens afterward. Men do the same." He shifted tack quickly. *"You are a forward-thinking man who wants to bring Russia into the modern world, sire, and you were planning to emancipate the serfs. You could declare the automatons of Vasilevsky Island part of that emancipation and then accept them as citizens. They aren't clockworkers. They won't go mad. They have no desire to attack you. They would have done so by now if they did. Imagine what they could bring to Mother Russia—tireless workers who could rebuild the Peter and Paul Fortress! Wonders of technology for the benefit of the entire country! You could challenge England and China themselves and finally bring Russia into the Great Game."*

Alexander drummed his fingers on the arm of his chair. *"You have given me a great deal to think about, Mr.*

Lawrenovich. I will consider your advice carefully. I do see no reason to waste resources attacking them—unless they decide to cross the river." He paused again, deep in thought, then said, *"Until I decide exactly what to do, we will leave the automatons alone."*

Thad bowed. *"Very wise, ser."*

"Mr. Lavrenovich, if I do open talks with the automatons, would you consider the position of envoy? You're uniquely suited to the position. I would have to give you a title, which would upset some members of the court, but they would get over it."

The offer caught Thad off guard, and he bowed again. For a moment, he thought of what it would be like. The position would bring influence and prestige and he would be a permanent member of the royal court.

It was the last part that decided it for him, and quickly.

"Thank you, ser," Thad said. *"This is an unprecedented offer to a person like myself, but I couldn't accept it. I'm just a circus performer, and I'm at my best in the ring. With my family."*

Alexander's face darkened, and Thad quavered. He had offended the man. But then the tsar waved a hand. *"As you wish. We haven't forgotten everything you've done here. And the court will always be happy to attend a performance of the Kalakos Circus."*

Back at the Field of Mars, Dodd was holding the circus train for them. They entered the passenger car to more applause from the rest of the performers. Thad ducked his head and dropped into their customary seats at the rear. Dante, proudly displaying his gleaming feathers, perched on the chair back, and Maddie crouched beside him. Sofiya touched Maddie's legs and sat down with Nikolai beside her. He pulled his book out from under the seat and paged through it as the train started forward with a jerk. It was quiet and cozy. A moment later, Mama Berloni appeared with her basket of food.

"So much you've been through," she said. "You eat now! For you, the sandwiches." She handed several familiar packets wrapped in paper to Thad and Sofiya, then gave a bottle and a brown bag to Nikolai. "And for you the bolts and the vodka. You eat and grow strong for circus, no?" She bustled away.

"You are already growing," Sofiya said to Nikolai in mock dismay. "I will have to let your trousers out, and I just bought them."

"I like this," Nikolai announced, crunching happily on a bolt from his bag. "This is our family."

"Doom!" Dante agreed.

Thad had to laugh. "A human man, a clockworker woman, an automaton boy, a windup parrot, two brass horses, and a mechanical spider who all live in a circus. What kind of family is that?"

"*My* family," Nikolai repeated. "I like it."

"Feh," Sofiya said. "Your papa won't even make an honest woman of me."

"Did you want me to?" Thad asked archly.

"You?" Sofiya snorted. "You aren't man enough for this clockworker."

Thad munched a sandwich and gazed off into space. Saint Petersburg chugged past the window. "True enough. Anyway, if I were looking to marry again, I think I'd fall in with someone like Dodd or Nathan."

Sofiya came upright in shock. Then she rolled her eyes and kicked at his shin. "You!"

Nikolai uncorked his bottle with a squeak, and the smell of vodka drifted through the car. "Papas are supposed to make bad jokes that no one thinks are funny."

"And their sons still laugh," Thad said. "You need to be less concerned about rules, Niko."

"Yes, Papa." He drank.

Sofiya's face grew more serious. "Thad, now that all this is over, do you intend to continue with your . . . other vocation?"

He looked at Nikolai, who was reading his book again. "I don't see a need to."

"Do you ever think about the promise you made to me?"

"Yes. But that's not for a few years yet, is it? Who knows what'll happen between now and then? When the time comes, if it comes, I'll keep my promise, but I'll hope it won't come to that."

"Hm."

The train picked up speed. "Where are we going?" Nikolai interjected.

"Back to Warsaw, then farther south before winter really sets in," Thad said.

"What are we doing in Warsaw?"

"More shows," Thad said. And he would visit David's and Ekaterina's graves one last time. He hoped that, wherever they were, they were glad he was happy. He touched the tsarina's pearls in his coat pocket, each one a grand possibility. "And after that, we'll do whatever we want. It's our choice."

The train clattered ahead into a fascinating future.

AUTHOR'S NOTE

Palaces and assassination figure enormously into Russian royal history. Like everything else in Saint Petersburg, the Winter Palace was built by—or, more accurately, built *for*—Peter the Great in the early 1700s. Thousands of conscripted serfs died for its construction. Over the centuries, other tsars and tsarinas added to it or refurbished it in order to show off their own wealth. This kept Russia in a continual state of near bankruptcy, and impeded her from developing a modern infrastructure of roads, railways, schools, and communication wiring, a problem which plagues the country to this day.

Russia's rulers also built a number of other richly appointed palaces in both Saint Petersburg and Moscow. Afraid of assassins in the Winter Palace, Paul I (son of Catherine the Great) built a new palace for himself at great expense. He moved in and lived there for only forty days before two courtiers smashed his head in with a paperweight in his own office. His son Alexander I wanted nothing to do with Paul's palace, and the place was abandoned. One wonders what Russia might be like today if all that money had been put into a public education system instead.

Alexander II was the last tsar to inhabit the great Winter Palace. His radical new policies for dragging Russia into the nineteenth century, including emancipation for serfs, proved unpopular with nearly everyone, and he was the target of more than his share of assassination attempts. In 1880, nearly twenty years after the events portrayed in this novel, a revolutionary named Stephan Khalturin from the People's Will movement smuggled countless sticks of dynamite piecemeal into the Winter Palace and laid them under the main dining hall. The explosion destroyed the dining hall and the guard room beneath it, but by sheer coincidence, Alexander was delayed to dinner that day, and he was nowhere near the place, though eleven other people were killed. As was customary, Alexander spent enormous sums of tax money to repair the Winter Palace in record time.

In March of 1881, Alexander was riding through Saint Petersburg in a bulletproof carriage surrounded by Cossack guards when another member of the People's Will managed to throw a bomb under the wheels. It exploded with devastating effect on the people around the tsar. Alexander himself actually escaped uninjured, but he made the mistake of exiting the carriage. At that moment, another People's Will assassin threw a second bomb at the tsar's feet. The explosion killed or wounded dozens of bystanders and tore Alexander's legs off. He was rushed back to the Winter Palace, where it took him several days to die.

Alexander III, his successor, spent considerable time undoing the liberal policies of his father and even taking Russia backward. Rightly fearful of his own assassination, he moved his wife and children to another palace outside the city of Saint Petersburg and used the Winter Palace only for state functions. He ultimately died of complications brought on by a failed assassination attempt that derailed a train he was riding. Alexander III's son Nicholas II was imprisoned and forced to abdicate during the Russian Revolution in 1917. A year later, he was executed with his wife, children, and several close servants. He was the last of the tsars.

Today, the Winter Palace serves mostly as a museum and tourist attraction.

Russian cabdrivers, all nicknamed *Vanka* ("Johnny"), did not survive the invention of the automobile unchanged. Modern visitors to Russia and most parts of Eastern Europe are often surprised to discover that cab rates are still determined by hard bargaining, not by mileage, though in a part of the world where rental cars are unreliable, it remains quite normal for tourists to hire a cab for an entire day, as the author has personally discovered. Such drivers rarely wear elaborate beards, however, and no longer go by Vanka. More's the pity.

ABOUT THE AUTHOR

Steven Harper Piziks was born in Saginaw, Michigan, but he moved around a lot and has lived in Wisconsin, in Germany, and briefly in Ukraine. Currently he lives with his three sons in southeast Michigan.

His novels include *In the Company of Mind* and *Corporate Mentality*, both science fiction published by Baen Books. He has produced the Silent Empire series for Roc and *Writing the Paranormal Novel* for Writer's Digest. He's also written novels based on *Star Trek*, *Battlestar Galactica*, and *The Ghost Whisperer*.

Mr. Piziks currently teaches high school English in southeast Michigan. His students think he's hysterical, which isn't the same as thinking he's hilarious. When not writing, he plays the folk harp, dabbles in oral storytelling, and spends more time online than is probably good for him.

CONNECT ONLINE

www.theclockworkempire.com
twitter.com/stevenpiziks

ALSO AVAILABLE

FROM

Steven Harper

THE DRAGON MEN
A Novel of the Clockwork Empire

As the clockwork plague consumes Gavin Ennock's body and mind, it drives him increasingly mad and fractures his relationship with fiancée Alice, Lady Michaels. Their only hope is that the Dragon Men of China can cure him. But a power struggle will draw Gavin and Alice down a treacherous path—and one wrong step will seal their fate...

Praise for the series:

"The Clockwork Empire books are changing what we know as Steampunk!"
—Nocturne Romance Reads

Available wherever books are sold or at
penguin.com

facebook.com/acerocbooks